Praise for

THE SHARK
"This romantic thriller is tense, sexy, and pleasingly complex."
—*Publishers Weekly*

"Precise storytelling complete with strong conflict and heightened tension are the highlights of Burton's latest. With a tough, vulnerable heroine in Riley at the story's center, Burton's novel is a well-crafted, suspenseful mystery with a ruthless villain who would put any reader on edge. A thrilling read."
—*RT Book Reviews*, four stars

BEFORE SHE DIES
"Will keep readers sleeping with the lights on."
—*Publishers Weekly* (starred review)

MERCILESS
"Burton keeps getting better!"
—*RT Book Reviews*

YOU'RE NOT SAFE
"Burton once again demonstrates her romantic suspense chops with this taut novel. Burton plays cat and mouse with the reader through a tight plot, credible suspects, and romantic spice keeping it real."
—*Publishers Weekly*

BE AFRAID
"Mary Burton [is] the modern-day Queen of Romantic Suspense."
—Bookreporter.com

HER
LAST
WORD

MARY BURTON

HER LAST WORD

Montlake
Romance

Published by Montlake Romance, Seattle

www.apub.com

Amazon, the Amazon logo, and Montlake Romance are trademarks of Amazon.com, Inc., or its affiliates.

ISBN-13: 9781503950061
ISBN-10: 1503950069

Cover design by Caroline T. Johnson

Printed in the United States of America

HER LAST WORD

THE DISAPPEARANCE OF GINA MASON INTERVIEW FILE #1

Kaitlin Roe

Monday, January 1, 2018; 1:00 a.m.

My name is Kaitlin Roe. I am the lone witness to the abduction of my eighteen-year-old cousin, Gina Mason. Not a day has passed in the last fourteen years that I haven't remembered those last moments with Gina and the masked stranger on that dark road. For years, my inability to save Gina has tortured me. To dull my guilt and regret, I've made too many unwise choices. Drinking. Drug use. Sex. Mine has been a life not well lived.

But that has all changed.

Now, I've put on the brakes, sobered up, and returned to Richmond, Virginia. I'm willing to face the people who see me as a drunk and a liar. My goal is to interview and record anyone and everyone attached to Gina's case and then edit all those interviews into a podcast that, I hope, will shine a light on my cousin's case. Maybe I will finally find a way to bring her home.

PROLOGUE

Thursday, March 15, 2018; 6:00 p.m.

"Hi, I'm Gina Mason, Saint Mathew's class of 2004! Welcome to the Rebels' soccer team—district finalists three years in a row!"

Remembering the videotape of Gina made the cramped, hot space under Jennifer Ralston's bed bearable. He'd been here for almost three hours impatiently waiting for her. The tulips arranged into a heart shape beside him gave him comfort and strengthened his resolve.

For fourteen years no one had known Gina's fate, and not knowing was torture. Gina had been everyone's friend, especially Jennifer's, and this woman along with others had abandoned his angel on that dark road. Gina's loss had fueled a kaleidoscope of blackening thoughts that had finally driven him here.

He lightly fingered the ivory handle of his eight-inch hunting knife. Just a few more minutes. She was coming.

"Today, I want each teammate to say a little about herself. Tell me what you love most, your favorite color, your secret crush, and if you could have a superpower, what would it be?"

A key slid into the front door, and a trio of locks gave way. A familiar chime of the home security system announced her arrival. The keypad chirped with each digit entered into it, and then three dead bolts clicked back into place. The sequence never varied.

He took solace knowing he wasn't the only one who'd been tormented by Gina's disappearance. Jennifer pretended she was fine, but he knew she wasn't. She rightly blamed herself for what had happened to Gina.

He curled his fingers around the knife handle. Heels tapped on polished wood floors, a purse dropped to the small foyer table, and keys clanked into the blue ceramic dish. One shoe hit the floor and then the other.

A light snapped on, illuminating the staircase to the second floor as bare feet padded through the house toward the kitchen. Drinkware clinked as Jennifer poured the evening's first glass of wine. He'd been watching her long enough to know she drank to forget. Seconds passed, and then another clank of the bottle against glass. Round two. She was right on schedule.

The wooden staircase creaked. He stilled his breath and hushed the voices in his head. The lights in the bedroom switched on and revealed her pretty manicured toes as she walked by.

"My favorite color is blue. I love the color so much I named by dog Bluebell. And my secret crush is Angel on Buffy.*"*

Fourteen years was a long time without a trace of Gina. He might not ever be able to bring Gina home, but he could finally serve up justice.

Jennifer would be his first. Her sentence: death by a thousand cuts.

Her phone rang, shattering the silence and sending fresh ripples of tension through him.

She answered on the third ring. "Hey, sis," she said, a little breathless. "Yeah, I'll be ready in a half hour. What? No, you have to come. Ashley, we promised Kaitlin we'd both be there."

Taking several sips, Jennifer listened to her sister's prattle.

"Kaitlin is now a communications professor at the university." Silence. "Why are we going? It's more a question of why we wouldn't go. Besides, Kaitlin's podcast may help reopen Gina's case and give us all some goddamned closure."

Gina. The name scraped and jabbed. Jennifer didn't have the right to speak her name. Honoring Gina now rang hollow.

More silence and then, "Yeah, Kaitlin interviewed me for her podcast. She's changed since high school. Calmer. More serious. Figures, right? Okay. Meet me here in a half hour."

Jennifer moved into the bathroom and turned on the shower. Soon steam wafted out of the room as she flipped on her music playlist, the light rock dating back to her high school days.

Her unbuttoned blouse slid off next, and then she wiggled out of her skirt. She hung both neatly in the closet before unfastening her bra and slipping off her panties. She stepped into the shower.

Getting out from under the four-poster bed was only a little awkward. He had done a trial run last week with no issue. He rose up without a sound, leaving the white tulips undisturbed.

The glass shower door was heavily fogged, but he could see the silhouette of Jennifer's sculpted body. Her slim hips moved seductively to the rhythm of the music. She leaned back, dipping her head under the hot spray, and arched her full breasts as the water glided over her nipples. As she lathered shampoo in her hair, a drummer's downbeat thumped against the tiled walls.

"If I could have a superpower, it would be flying. The idea of soaring high above is thrilling."

Straightening his shoulders, he took a step forward. The floor creaked between the thump, thump of the music.

Her fingers, immersed in soapy bubbles, stilled. He imagined her brain, the most primal part of any human, rightly whispering of danger. *You're not alone.* She hesitated, slowly turned, and wiped away the fog with her hand. She opened her left eye, their gazes locked, and then the next moments played out in slow motion.

Faced with this unexpected threat, her mind seemed to momentarily short-circuit with disbelief and confusion, before realization took hold.

She gasped and stumbled. Soap dripped into her eyes and forced her lids closed. With trembling, frantic hands she quickly wiped the suds from her face and braced.

The music's downbeat pulsed.

She drew in a breath to scream.

The music swallowed the first cry as she backed up, slipped, and slammed onto the shower floor. She groped for the shampoo bottle, hurled it at him. He easily deflected it.

His hands trembled with excitement. He had waited so long for this moment. He silenced her scream with the first rapid thrust of his knife. Blood spattered his goggles. The hot spray of water and blood made his grip slippery. He adjusted the knife in his hand and lunged again. Blood and water swirled around the drain.

She swayed forward and clenched the arm of his suit. Her nails dug in but couldn't penetrate the material. He never imagined there could be so much blood as he watched it trail away.

The third thrust sent more blood running down her flat belly and then her long legs. His white laminate suit was covered in soap, water, and blood.

He hesitated before his next strike, giving her a moment to raise her right arm and block his attack. The blade cut neatly through the flesh in her forearm.

She stared up, her eyes wide and searching.

He turned the knob to shut off the water. The soft music drifted around them. "There are so many terrible ways to die, Jennifer," he said.

"Why?" The word was barely a whisper.

It was a stupid question, and he sidestepped it. "Did you ever wonder what happened to Gina?"

"What?"

"Do you ever think about where she is now? I do. Every night. So many terrible things could have happened to her."

"I know you." Her voice trailed off.

Her pain focused her attention completely on him. He knelt beside her so she could get a good look at his eyes. "Accept your punishment, and you will feel peace."

"No."

"It's the only way now." He slowly wrapped her fingers around the knife handle and gently placed his hand over hers. He felt a strong bond with her now.

He raised the knife to her neck. "Jennifer, do you want to do it, or should I?"

Tears filled her eyes. "I don't want to die."

"Punishment is never easy, but once you accept it, you will feel better."

She shook her head. "No. Please."

"We'll do it together." He drew the sharp tip across her throat, slicing her milk-white flesh. Blood sprayed on him, the walls, and the door as her eyes rolled back in her head and her fingers slackened.

"And if I could fly with that Angel . . . my life would be perfect."

"Jennifer, when you see God, put a good word in for me."

INTERVIEW FILE #2

THE 911 CALL

Sunday, August 15, 2004; 11:42 p.m.

It was a hot, muggy night when I stumbled up to the front door of
the Riverside Drive house. I was fairly new to the area and still easily
turned around. It was nearly midnight, and the residents of this affluent
neighborhood weren't accustomed to drunken late-night visitors. I'd lost
track of time and to this day don't know how I made it up the hill from
the river to the Hudson residence.

Dispatcher: *"911. What's your emergency?"*

Caller: *"My name is Jack Hudson. I live on Riverside Drive.
There's a young woman on my front porch. She's banging on
the door and begging for help."*

Dispatcher: *"Have you spoken to her?"*

Caller: *"Just for a second. She appears drunk. She's incoherent.
Hysterical . . . Oh, shit! She just threw up in the flower bed."*

Dispatcher: *"Do you know why she's upset?"*

Caller: *"She claims she and her friend were attacked on Riverside Drive. Her friend was then kidnapped."*

Dispatcher: *"Did you ask the woman her name?"*

Caller: *"Her name is Kaitlin. I didn't catch her last name. She lives down the street with the Mason family. They have a daughter, Gina."*

Dispatcher: *"I've dispatched officers. What is the woman doing?"*

Caller: *"She's pacing in my driveway."*

Dispatcher: *"Is she bleeding or hurt in any way?"*

Caller: *"I can't tell. Let me flip on the porch lights."* Feet shuffle. A switch clicks. *"She has blood on her arms. Jesus, she looks insane."*

CHAPTER ONE

Richmond, Virginia
Thursday, March 15, 2018; 9:00 p.m.

Homicide detective John Adler held up his badge for the uniformed cop and caught the young officer's surprised expression. There'd been lots of rumors circling around about Adler during his prolonged leave of absence. He had kept up enough to hear his new nicknames, including Firewalker, Burning Man, and his favorite, Hot Pants. He didn't begrudge the dark sense of humor cops developed to stay sane.

Three months ago, Adler and his rookie partner, Greg Logan, had been investigating an arsonist who'd set seven fires in the Richmond area and killed three people. Working off an informant's tip, they'd approached what they thought was one of the arsonist's former residences.

Adler had entered first. Logan had been ten feet behind him when Adler flipped on a kitchen light switch, which instantly triggered an incendiary device. The blast blew behind Adler and seared the skin on his back as its force threw him forward. His ears ringing and fire roaring around him, he'd pushed up on his hands and knees and staggered toward his partner, who had been near the explosion. Logan had been thrown across the room and was lying in a heap.

He'd pulled his partner from the burning house and called for help. They'd both survived, but Adler had spent a couple of weeks in the burn unit. Logan had lost his left leg.

The uniform shifted and, lifting the tape, grinned. "Detective Adler. Good to have you back, sir."

"Thanks."

"You're a hero."

Though he didn't mind the humorous nicknames, Adler hated the designation of hero, a title he didn't want or deserve. "Is Detective Quinn inside?"

"Yes, sir."

The crime scene tape was looped over the wrought iron railing of the townhome in the historic Church Hill district. Spring was teasing the city with a warm spell and had lulled them into thinking winter had passed. But he knew Mother Nature wasn't ready to dismiss winter.

This section of town was picturesque and loaded with charm. Finished with the buzz of nightlife and the lure of laughing crowds, he'd opted to move out of the city to the country two months ago. He liked the idea of not locking his doors, but he had been a homicide cop too long not to.

He climbed the steep stone steps and strode across the porch past an oval brass plaque that read RICHMOND, VIRGINIA, 1903. This house, like the city, had deep roots. Church Hill was the original location of the city, and then like most urban areas suffered when the population fled to the suburbs. Now the tide had changed, and after decades of neglect and decay, Church Hill was enjoying a renaissance. Young professionals seeking a trendy address were willing to ignore poverty and crime. They snapped up these forgotten homes and undertook major renovations while keeping the architectural charm of the period. The drug dealers, pimps, and prostitutes would have to live somewhere else.

Adler fished out black latex gloves from his coat pocket as he paused in the entryway. This house had the typical floor plan of its era. It was built long and narrow with high ceilings. To the right, a parlor connected to a dining room via huge wooden pocket doors. The occupant had done what many did and flipped the parlor and dining rooms. When the pocket doors were closed, expensive home-entertainment and computer equipment were hidden from view and hopefully safe from theft.

The center hallway shot straight to a kitchen, and he caught a glimpse of the standard white marble countertops and stainless steel appliances, the favorite of current remodelers. To his left was a long staircase with an ornate hand railing rising to the second floor. The flash of a camera above told him he'd find his latest case upstairs.

The 911 call had come from the victim's sister. They'd planned a night out, which included a lecture and then drinks. When the sister couldn't get the victim to answer the door, she'd used her key. She found her sister stabbed in the shower.

Adler threaded his fingers together, working the gloves deeper onto his hands as he paused by the stairs and looked toward a side table where a woman's oversize black purse sat. Next to it were keys attached to a brass key ring shaped like the letter *C*. Several steps from the table were black pumps. One stood upright, and the other tilted gently against it like an old friend. It didn't appear she had been hurried or forcibly rushed when she came in the door.

He walked toward the kitchen, where an open bottle of wine sat on the marble counter. He moved to the back door in the kitchen. The dead bolt was unlocked. He twisted the knob, and as he pulled the heavy door open, he heard a chime. The security system appeared to be in working order.

A brick patio covered most of the backyard. There was a strip of grass and then a garage. An alley was just over the fence. It would've been easy enough to walk up the alley after dark and slip into the yard without being noticed.

He stepped back into the house, then moved toward the stairs leading to the second floor. More flashes and the buzz of conversation drew him to the front bedroom overlooking part of the side alley between this house and the neighboring one, as well as East Broad Street.

He saw a skirted four-poster bed, and beside it, discarded undergarments as well as a forensic technician's yellow evidence marker. The undergarments weren't ripped or torn. It appeared as if the victim had removed them while undressing. Slip off shoes downstairs, pour wine, strip.

His attention shifted to the bathroom, where a forensic technician snapped pictures of a nude female's body sitting upright in the shower. Her legs were spread, and her hands lay on the inside of each thigh. She appeared to have been posed.

He pushed aside the disgust he felt in the face of such sadistic violence and focused on what this evidence told him about the killer. It had not been enough to murder her. She had to be humiliated. Whoever had done this had been angry.

She'd been stabbed multiple times in the abdomen, arm, and neck. One of the cuts had hit her jugular and left arterial spray on the glass door and tile walls. She had soap in her hair. Shampoo bottles lined a niche, but one lay outside the shower.

"Victim's name was Jennifer Ralston, aged thirty-two," Detective Monica Quinn said as she came up behind him.

Adler faced his newest partner. Quinn, generally efficient and composed, looked stricken. Her lips were pressed tightly together, and her posture was rigid. Her five-foot-ten, chiseled frame was the by-product of daily weight training and running. No matter how long the job kept her each day, she worked out. Breaking a sweat and drinking single malt whiskey kept her sane. Judging by her expression, she'd be logging more miles on the road and extra shots before bed.

He understood doing whatever it took to process this job. His sanity these days came in the form of bathroom demolition and remodeling.

Quinn smiled. "Glad to have you back."

"Hell of a first day back on the job."

"I'm surprised you didn't pack it in after the explosion."

His father had wanted him to do just that, reminding Adler that his private-school education and University of Virginia law school degree were wasted as long as he carried a cop's badge. Time to run for state senate. Adler had disagreed.

"I like my job."

Her gaze lingered an extra beat. "How's Logan doing?"

"Mending. Still has a lot of rehab in front of him."

A brow arched. "I offered to visit, but he said no."

"Don't ask the next time. Otherwise he'll never say yes."

"Duly noted." She flipped open her notebook.

"I saw the victim's purse in the entryway," Adler said. "Was anything taken?"

"Doesn't appear so. Her wallet was there with cash and credit cards intact. Her phone is on her nightstand. Nothing appears disturbed in the house. I'd bet money, judging by how clean everything is, that she puts the purse and keys in the same place every day."

"The back door was unlocked."

"And there are footprints in the backyard by the alley fence. I think our guy left through the back door."

"How did he get in without tripping the alarm?"

"Good question. Her sister used her key to get in the front door and said the alarm was set. Said the victim is always mindful of security and always had the alarm on."

The killer knew the security code and had a key. "Is there a lock on the side and alley gates?"

"Yes. They're combination, both brand-new, identical, and locked."

"Why would the victim not have heard the security chime?"

"I think he was in the house before she arrived home," Quinn said.

"He was waiting for her?"

She walked toward the yellow evidence marker by the bed and lifted the beige bed skirt. "Have a look."

He pulled a small flashlight from his pocket and shone it underneath. The beam skimmed over wood floors, and there were white tulips arranged into the shape of a heart. "Jesus. He was waiting for her under the bed."

Quinn's lips curled in contempt. "Yes, he was."

"Did he leave any other mementos behind?"

"No. But the forensic team is also going to sweep under the bed. Keep your fingers crossed for hair samples, a fingerprint, saliva, or semen. The team estimates they have at least twelve hours of evidence collection in front of them."

"Why isn't there a trail of blood leading from the bathroom?" Adler asked. "The killer should have been drenched in it."

"Our boy must be watching *CSI* and worried he'd leave DNA behind," Quinn said. "If I had to hazard a guess, I'd say he wore a personal protection suit. He figured it would keep the blood off him and contain the DNA."

There'd been no signs of blood on the stairs or in the kitchen. "So the killer strips off the suit in here and bags it along with whatever he used to clean himself up."

"That's my guess."

He straightened. "Signs of sexual assault?"

"Impossible to tell. That's the medical examiner's call, but there's no bruising on her arms, legs, breasts, or groin area, and there appears to have been no struggle in the bedroom. I think he waited for her, and when she stepped into the shower, he made his move."

"Did you shut off the water?"

"No. It was off when I arrived here. Ms. Ralston's sister, Ashley, thinks the water was turned off when she arrived. She was pretty hysterical when I spoke to her."

"Where's she now?"

"In one of the cruisers out front."

Another look into the bathroom allowed him a better view of the body. The victim was young, pretty, and fit. As he searched her still-stricken features, his gaze rose to the spot above her head. Drawn in blood on the wall of the shower was a heart. "Another heart?"

Quinn's expression was grim. "Sick bastard."

"The killer turned off the water because he wanted us to see his message. Why the hearts?" Adler asked.

"I don't know, but I bet there's nothing random about this."

Quinn was right. It would have taken time.

The detective work would soon shift to knocking on doors and searching for any surveillance cameras that may have captured images of the intruder.

He returned his focus to the victim's home environment. He noted, as Quinn had said, that Jennifer Ralston kept her home immaculate. Her matching gray towels were monogrammed with the letters *JR* and were clean and neatly folded. Her razor had a fresh blade, and a collection of perfumes lined a sparkling mirrored tray. In her medicine chest was an old prescription bottle for an antibiotic and a much more recent one for anxiety. The same physician's assistant practicing at the nearby hospital had prescribed both.

"Lady keeps her house neat," Adler said.

"Too neat."

Her straight-backed posture and the crisp lines of her blouse and jeans had him commenting, "You always struck me as the orderly type."

She closed her notebook. "My gym bag is organized, and my house is acceptable. Ms. Ralston took organization to a higher level."

"Maybe."

"Speaking of homes, I hear you're ripping apart a shack in Ashland."

"I am."

"You needed a project?"

"I did."

Two and a half weeks after the explosion, the day the doctors ampu-
tated Logan's left leg below the knee, he'd bought the seventy-year-old
three-thousand-square-foot house in Ashland, an old railroad town
twenty miles north of Richmond. The historic home was located in the
city center, and he'd paid over asking price to close the deal. In less than
a week, he'd had a contractor lined up to help him demo and gut the
downstairs. While on leave, he'd filled his time meeting with architects,
designers, and landscape architects and visiting Logan.

The reno was a couple of weeks from completion, and the break-
neck pace had cost him a small fortune. But he was in the house and
finding a new routine. These days he rose before five a.m. thanks to
the Amtrak train that lumbered along the track through the center of
Ashland. The beast rattled every plate and window, and at first, it had
startled him awake. Now the rumble, grind, and squeak of the engine's
wheels were comforting reminders that life moved on. You had to keep
moving, or you were going to be left behind or run over.

Downstairs the uniformed officer posted at the front door greeted a
new arrival. Seconds later the clatter of a stretcher on the first floor signaled the entrance of the medical examiner's two technicians. The pair
carried up the gurney, but the woman trailing behind them approached
the detectives. She was tall, slim, and in her midthirties. Long dark hair
was coiled into a bun at the base of her neck.

"I'm Jessica Everett. I'm a death investigator with the medical examiner's office. Are we clear to remove the body?"

Adler and Quinn nodded to each other and stepped back.

Everett moved to the bathroom threshold, and her expression softened briefly with sadness before she crossed to the body. She laid her
hand on the victim's shoulder as if offering comfort. She and her assis-
tants then laid out the body bag and gently lifted Jennifer's naked body
into it.

As she zipped up the pouch, the room's heavy silence was shattered
by footsteps and heated voices echoing from downstairs and then a very

loud, "I want to see the police! If I have to sit any longer in that damned car, I'm going to go insane!"

Peering down the stairs, Adler spotted a young woman dressed in jeans, a gray silk top, and a tailored black jacket. She wore her brown hair in a tight ponytail that accentuated dark-framed glasses.

Her gaze locked on Adler. "I need a cop who can give me answers."

Adler glanced back and motioned to Jessica to halt. "Let me get her out of the house first."

"Of course," Jessica said.

He descended the stairs and escorted the woman outside, away from her sister's body and the ME's technicians. "I'm Detective John Adler."

"Is Jennifer really dead? I saw all the blood, but I was afraid to touch her."

"Yes, ma'am. She's gone."

She ran a shaking hand over her head. "I can't believe I was too terrified to touch my own sister."

"I know it was tough for you." Adler led her down the sidewalk several paces and angled her so she couldn't see the front steps of her sister's home. "No one would blame you for being afraid and upset. I'm sorry, I don't know your name."

"I'm Ashley Ralston. I live in Rocketts Landing. We were supposed to go to a lecture tonight. Jesus, I told her to be careful. I told her to call the cops again, but she said she had it handled." Her tone reflected frustration, grief, and shock.

"Why did you want your sister to call the cops again?"

Confusion and annoyance knotted her brows. "Because she had a vibe someone was watching her. She was certain it was a stalker."

"What made your sister believe she was being watched?" Adler kept his voice calm, almost monotone, hoping she'd hear his steadiness. His life might be a chaotic cluster with his return to work, the renovation of a new home, and keeping up with Logan's recovery, but he could still be her momentary life raft.

She drew in a deep breath. "No specific issues she could put her finger on except the cat."

"Cat?"

"Jennifer came home a couple of weeks ago and Morris was missing."

"Maybe she accidently let him out."

"That's what she thought at first, but the more she thought about it, the more convinced she was that the last time she saw Morris he was sunning himself on the sofa in the front room. He did that every morning. Jennifer searched for hours and put up flyers all over the neighborhood, but no one ever contacted her."

"Was there anything else bothering your sister?"

"The feeling you get when someone has been in your house, but you can't prove it." Ashley shoved out a breath. "She said the other day she hadn't had the feeling in a few days. She thought maybe it was work stress. Too much caffeine." Tears filled her eyes, and she pressed her fingertips against closed lids. When she looked up, the tears fell down her cheeks. "How did Jennifer die?"

"We're still collecting evidence," Adler deflected. "Did she receive any letters or communication giving her reason to worry?"

"She said no, but I'm not sure. It was like she was always trying to convince herself this problem couldn't be real in the face of everything else she had going on."

"What else was happening in her life?"

"She had trouble at work, and this house was way too expensive for her to maintain." She brushed away a tear. "And she kept telling me she was over the breakup but, again, I wasn't convinced."

"A breakup. Who had she been dating?" Quinn asked as she joined them on the sidewalk.

Ashley dragged the back of her hand over her nose. "She saw a guy from work for a while. He ended it months ago, but she still missed him."

"How did it end?" Quinn pressed.

"As far as breakups go, it was benign. Jennifer said it was smarter to keep the sex out of the office."

"What's the guy's name?" Adler asked.

"Jeremy Keller. He's one of the partners at her company, Keller and Mayberry."

Adler pulled out a black leather notebook. "What's your address and phone number?"

She recited the information.

From a pocket in the notebook cover, he pulled out a business card. "What type of cat was Morris?"

"A purebred Siamese. He has a chip."

"Okay. I want you to call me directly if you recall anything else. I'll likely have more questions for you later."

She took the card and absently flicked the edge with her finger. "Sure. Thank you."

"You said you live in Rocketts Landing?"

"Yeah."

"Did you drive?"

"No, I Ubered over."

"I'll have an officer take you home."

As she turned to leave, Adler asked almost as an afterthought, "What was the lecture you were planning to attend tonight?"

"A local communications professor was speaking. We went to high school with her. She's making some kind of documentary or podcast about a classmate of Jennifer's who went missing fourteen years ago. I'm not really sure about the particulars of this lecture. It could be anything, knowing Kaitlin. She always did march to her own drum."

"What's Kaitlin's last name?"

"Roe." She pulled out her phone. "I have the address. Jennifer texted it to me."

Adler scribbled the name *Roe*.

"It's a warehouse studio just across the river in the Manchester district." She rattled off the address and time. "She's probably still there. There was a reception after her talk. Until ten, I think. What does Kaitlin have to do with Jennifer?"

"Maybe nothing. Trying to piece together her last day."

"Jesus, it's her *last* day." She tipped back her head, but the tears rolled along her cheeks. "I can't believe this is happening."

He motioned to the patrolman who'd approached. "This officer will take you home."

She looked up at the house. "I can't leave my sister."

"We'll look after her," Adler said. "I promise."

She wiped away another tear and allowed the officer to escort her to the waiting patrol car. She didn't take her eyes off Adler as the car drove away.

Quinn handed him a printed postcard encased in a plastic evidence bag as the medical technicians carried the stretcher onto the porch and down the steps toward the waiting van. "It's a handmade invitation to a lecture scheduled for tonight," she said.

Adler studied the postcard. The time was underlined with three red lines.

He flipped the card over to see a black-and-white image of huge boulders in the rapids of the James River. The picture captured the rising sun illuminating a thick mist hovering above the river's waters. He knew the location of the picture. It was Pony Pasture, a popular spot where people gathered on warm days to sun, swim, and drink.

"Kaitlin Roe." Saying the name drew the memory closer to the surface. And then he remembered.

INTERVIEW FILE #3

Motive for Murder

.

Talk to a homicide detective about motive, and they'll tell you there are three primary driving forces: sex, revenge, and money. Gina was a girl everyone liked. She lived a clean life. After she vanished, the police dug into her past expecting to find signs of risky behavior that had lured the killer to her. Revenge: Whom had she wronged? Money: Whom did she owe? Sex: Whose heart had she broken?

The police search turned up nothing in Gina's behavior that signaled trouble. So they shifted their focus to the people who knew her. Cops understand that most murder victims know their killers, and the chance a random stranger is involved is almost nonexistent.

The spotlight landed on me. My past substance-abuse problem meant I was the likely troublemaker. The provocateur. For weeks, that spotlight didn't move. The cops examined every aspect of my life, grilling me about my brother's death, my troubles in Texas, and my poor academic performance at Saint Mathew's. As much as they pushed and dug, they didn't initially find any motive or evidence linking me to the crime. That connection would come six weeks later when a pawnshop owner called in a tip about an unrelated crime.

CHAPTER TWO

Thursday, March 15, 2018; 10:15 p.m.

The event hadn't attracted the crush of interest Kaitlin had hoped for. Only seven people had shown up to hear her lecture. A few were her students angling for extra credit, and there was a retired couple interested in making their own podcast. One attendee confessed she had come for the free wine, crackers, and a night out away from the kids. No sign of Jennifer or her sister. That stung.

Still, she welcomed the chance to talk about her project. Saying it out loud made it feel real. Her podcast had yet to be realized beyond a handful of interviews, but announcing it publicly, if even to only a few people, meant she had to follow through with it.

Kaitlin walked her last guest, a student, to the front door. Remembering the flowers, she turned and picked them up and handed her the extravagant arrangement. "Enjoy."

"Are you sure?" Amy's short dark hair framed a round, serious face.

"Yes. And thank you for opening up the space. I can't believe today of all days, I was running late."

"Oh, no worries. Don't you want to keep the flowers?"

Kaitlin glanced at the vase of white tulips that had been delivered to this room right before the start of her lecture. "Not my color."

"Who sent them to you?"

"An anonymous admirer." She had no card and no idea who would send them. It was unsettling. If she'd been alone when they'd arrived, she'd have pitched them. But she hadn't been by herself, so the delicate flowers had stood front and center as she lectured.

"See you in the study session on Saturday," Kaitlin said.

"I'll be there." Amy glanced toward the podium and an enlarged picture of Gina. "You never said why you're digging into the Gina Mason case."

Black shoulder-length hair swept over Gina's smooth shoulders, and a V-neck drape set off a strand of white pearls likely handed down through generations. Dark eyes ignited with laughter, soon to be extinguished by a horrific future.

"She needs to be remembered, to be found and brought home."

"Yeah, but why her? Why you?"

This was the piece of the documentary she'd not shared tonight. It was one thing to dictate into a recorder at home, but another to talk about it here. So she'd skirted her involvement in the case, telling herself it was better to appear objective. Soon, however, the story would demand more honesty and more vulnerability from her. "It's a compelling story."

Amy hesitated as more questions clearly bubbled below the surface. But Kaitlin checked her watch; the kid got the hint and let them go. "Right. Well, terrific story. I can't wait to find out how it ends."

"Me, too."

Kaitlin opened the door, wished the girl a good night, and watched as she crossed the street to her small car. She waited until the little red vehicle's lights popped on and the tires were rolling before she closed the door. She pulled down the shades over the big display windows and locked the dead bolt. She paused, then clicked it open and closed again. A habit she'd picked up after Gina's disappearance.

She unpinned her hair and ran her fingers through thick blond strands accentuated with long dark roots. After kicking off her clogs, she knuckled her toes against the hard floor and massaged out the tension.

The room's ceiling rose fifteen feet to accommodate the building's pipes, and the HVAC ducts crossed overhead with industrial fixtures that cast a harsh light onto the concrete floor and unfinished brick walls. Outside, the rumble of a broken muffler mixed with the beat of an unrecognizable rap song as a car drifted past.

This location probably hadn't been the best place to hold the event. Its semi-industrial address all but guaranteed most genteel people would not venture here after dark. However, Kaitlin was saving her money for the podcast, and free space was welcome.

She faced the enlarged high school senior picture of Gina mounted on a portable easel.

"I'll find you," Kaitlin whispered.

Outside, the shouts of young men reverberated on the other side of the door. She tensed and waited for them to pass. When it was silent again, she released the breath captured in her chest.

Maybe once she finished the podcast, the university would cut her a deal and have her lecture on their dime. Or better, she'd pick up a corporate sponsor. Maybe one day, she'd make other podcasts. Find other missing girls like Gina.

She grabbed the trash bag from a metal can and began collecting the discarded plastic cups of wine and crumpled napkins. She had the space until midnight, enough time to clean and close up. Rolling her shoulders, she worked the tension from the muscles knotting her back. When she'd gathered the trash and tied off the bag, she started stacking the chairs and placing them on the cart.

Kaitlin thought again about Jennifer, who had assured her she would attend tonight. She pulled her phone from her pocket and switched the ringer on as she checked for any texts or voicemail. Nothing from Jennifer.

Kaitlin had already interviewed Jennifer once, but had wanted to set up a second session with her tonight. She texted Jennifer: Missed you tonight. Hope all is well.

A knock on the window startled her. She gripped the phone in her hand and took an instinctive step back. Her heart in her throat, she quickly slipped her shoes back on.

A fist pounded on the front door. "Ms. Roe? This is Detective John Adler."

Detective John Adler? She recognized the name and the deep, gravelly voice. She'd visited the city's homicide department several months ago, expecting to talk to someone about Gina. Adler and his partner had been on their way out. The detective had been tall and smartly dressed in a dark suit that fit his trim body well. He'd also been brusque. He'd had no time to talk to her.

"I know you're in there. I see the light and the movement. Open the door, I'd like to talk to you."

Her grip on her phone tightened as she walked toward the door. Long fingers hovered over the dead bolt. "How do I know you're Detective Adler?"

"I'll hold my badge up to the window," he said.

The statement carried a tone of finality as if his proposed solution answered all her questions. When metal clinked against glass, she reached for the shade and peeked. The gold shield read *Detective* in bold letters. On the other side of the fold was the name *John T. Adler*.

"Why are you here?" she persisted. "It's been months since I came by your office." She'd heard about the fire and knew he'd been on leave. Given the pictures she'd seen of the burned-out house, she was amazed he'd survived, let alone returned to the job.

"Jennifer Ralston."

That answer caught her a little bit by surprise. "Did Jennifer send you?"

"I'm not having this conversation through a door." An edge sharpened each word.

Jennifer hadn't shown for the lecture, but a cop had. Not good.

She unlocked the door and cracked it slightly. Detective Adler wore a well-cut dark suit, white shirt, and a red tie, just as he had that first time she'd seen him at the station. Black hair was peppered with gray and brushed away from chiseled features. The fire had driven the lines around his eyes and mouth deeper, adding more interest to a face already hard to forget.

"What about Jennifer?" she asked.

"May I come in, Kaitlin?"

She opened the door and stepped back. "What's going on?" she asked.

"I understand you were giving a lecture on the Gina Mason disappearance." He held up the invitation for tonight's event between two fingers, waving it like a challenge.

This was the second time he hadn't answered her question about Jennifer. Cops were good at dodging answers. She'd tried to interview him as well as several law enforcement officers who'd worked Gina's case, but so far, only silence from the blue wall.

"Did Jennifer mention my name to the police? Is my research upsetting you or someone who worked the original investigation?"

"Can we sit?" Another question to answer a question.

She stepped aside but kept the door ajar. As he walked into the space, she noted the faint scent of an expensive aftershave with a woodsy citrus base. His gaze swept every corner and exit.

"Do you have a personal stake in the Gina Mason case?" he asked.

"If you'd bothered to return my call, I could have explained it to you months ago."

"I'm asking now. What's your connection to Gina Mason?"

He didn't apologize or explain why he'd blown her off. She automatically bristled. She wasn't crazy about cops or their questions. But making an issue out of this inquiry would only lead to more questions. "I was with her the night she vanished."

"You were a witness?"

"Yes. I tried to tell you that, but you were in a rush to leave the station."

He studied Gina's poster. "This is Gina?"

She was losing patience. Cops didn't ask questions unless they had a good idea of the answer. But for some reason, he wanted to play dumb. "Don't tell me you decided to finally follow up on my visit and have a lead in the Gina Mason case?"

"As I mentioned when you cornered me several months ago, I was working in the robbery division when she went missing. Our division arrested a guy who later became a suspect in the case. Refresh my memory about the night she vanished."

"We were walking along Riverside Drive near her parents' house. A man came out of the woods. He took Gina and told me to run. You arrested Randy Hayward a few months later for stealing from his mother. He got seven years in prison for that and another drug-related charge."

Memories appeared to click in Adler. "Hayward was caught fencing his mother's stolen silver a few weeks after Gina disappeared. But Mrs. Hayward reported the robbery the night Gina vanished, placing Randy near Gina and you that night," he said. "Though he was within walking distance of the crime scene, the cops were never able to make a case against him. There was no physical evidence linking him to Gina."

She nodded. "His mother hired a good attorney. Cops never got a confession. But most of the cops believed he was involved in the crime."

His rigid jaw pulsed at the joint. "Why did you invite Jennifer to this lecture?"

"Jennifer was one of the last girls to see Gina alive. There were four of us hanging out by the river the night Gina vanished. Jennifer was one of them. I interviewed her for my podcast." His grim expression didn't fit with a man looking into a cold case. "Detective, I'm still not sure why you're here. Are you here about Gina's case?"

Some of his edginess softened. "I've come from the scene of a homicide. Jennifer Ralston was murdered."

The blood rushed from her head, leaving her lightheaded and nauseated. Her throat constricted with the rush of emotion. She fought the urge to throw up. "Jennifer? Are you sure it's Jennifer? I spoke to her five or six hours ago."

"Yes, I'm sure." His deep, steady voice left no doubt. "She was found in her home. How did you know her?"

Did. Past tense. Shit, this couldn't be real. Kaitlin ran a trembling hand through her hair, and he pulled up one of the chairs. She sat and crossed her arms, trying to hold her grief and shock at bay until she got her bearings. "I've known her since high school," she whispered.

"I am sorry. This can't be easy for you."

"No." The swirl of disbelief, anger, and sadness mirrored what she'd experienced after Gina was taken.

"Why are you asking about Gina now?" His tone was softer, kinder, as he pulled up a second chair and sat across from her.

She moistened her lips. This was one of those times she wished she still drank. "Gina was never found. She needs closure."

"But why you? Is this some kind of artist's way of pointing out how the cops failed to close this case?"

"They did fail," she said, cutting her eyes toward Adler.

Less than a foot separated them as he studied her like a puzzle with too many missing pieces. "That's the reason you decided to open this fourteen-year-old cold case?"

"You need more, Detective Adler?"

"I've been a homicide detective too long not to know when there's more, Kaitlin."

She blew out a breath, wrestling with her temper and the guilt she'd carried since the night Gina vanished. Lying or avoiding the question might stall him, but it wouldn't erase what she'd done. "Gina's kidnapper told me to run. I could have stayed and fought him. I could have tried to save my cousin, but I didn't. And she's gone."

Absently he rubbed the scar on his right hand as he studied her. There might have been a slight softening of the gaze. "Why were you living with your aunt and uncle in high school?"

"My brother killed himself a few years before that. I got into drugs to numb the pain. I started to spiral down fast. My mother thought rehab and a fresh start in Virginia would save me."

He didn't speak, letting the silence push her to finish her explanation.

"After I returned to Texas, I thought I was getting on with my life. I was doing well for myself. None of my new friends knew about what had happened here. And then I went to a costume party." She felt ridiculous articulating the answer.

He looked at her with genuine interest and no hints of judgment. "What does a party have to do with this?"

Despite herself, she could almost imagine he was here to help and they were on the same team. "This time two years ago, I ran the film division of an ad agency. The firm was having a Halloween party." Telling him what happened was awkward. "It was a costume party, and one of the guys in accounting showed up wearing a clown mask. It had a big grin, a round red nose, arching eyebrows, and orange hair." She blew out a breath. "The instant I saw it, my chest tightened and I freaked out."

He was listening very closely.

"The man who took Gina was wearing a clown mask just like that one. There are probably thousands like it in the world. But this one triggered a panic attack." The episode couldn't be backpedaled or whitewashed. The skeletons in her closet wouldn't be ignored any longer.

"And you decided to make a podcast."

He made it sound so simple. "First, I started by going back to AA. Without the booze to dull my feelings, I started really thinking about

Gina again. I realized what happened fourteen years ago hadn't left me. I quit my job and moved back to Richmond."

He removed a notebook and Montblanc from his breast pocket. "Where did you work?"

"Hayes Morgan Advertising Agency." She hesitated to add information but knew honesty now might help her gain his trust. "When I worked there I went by the name Lyn Tyler."

He wrote down the name in heavy, bold block letters. "Why change your name?"

"After Gina vanished, I came under media scrutiny. There were a lot of unwanted calls that didn't let up until I moved back to Texas. I finally started using a different name."

"So you have what amounts to a panic attack and decide to return to Virginia. You said you spoke to Jennifer. Have you interviewed anyone else?"

"Other than Jennifer—Erika Crowley, anyone who knew Gina, and the now-retired detective assigned to her case. I'm still trying to get an interview with Randy Hayward, but he's in your city jail facing murder charges and won't see me."

He made notes as she spoke and then lifted his gaze to hers. "I need copies of all your interviews, starting with Jennifer's."

"The audio files are raw and unedited. I'm not ready to share them yet."

"I'm investigating a murder. Are you saying you're refusing to cooperate?" In an instant, challenge stripped away any gentleness in his tone.

Renewed anger crushed whatever connection she'd imagined between them. "So far I've gotten no help from you or any other cops. I left a dozen messages with the missing person and homicide departments. And you're accusing me of not cooperating?"

"You have information, Kaitlin, and I need to see it."

She stood and slid her palms over her jeans. "I don't trust cops."

He stood and towered over her as he shoved the notebook and pen in his breast pocket. "I picked up on that. But that isn't an excuse to hold back information in a murder investigation."

"I can't believe my project has any bearing on your case. Gina vanished fourteen years ago."

"How can you be certain they aren't linked?"

Kaitlin was sure. At least nearly. But she knew the doubt would eat away at her. Better to take her chances with this cop than carry more regret.

He leaned in a fraction. "Can I take that silence as a yes? Or do I get a warrant?"

Guys like him held all the cards. She could play hardball and stall, but she didn't have the legal firepower or money to fight it. "I can drop off a disc at your office."

He fished a card from his breast pocket and handed it to her. "I'd like it tomorrow."

She flicked the edge of the card, studying his name and *Homicide Division*. Cops were chameleons. They changed personas instantly. Savior. Tormenter. Two sides of the same coin. "Sure."

He looked around the studio, surveying windows, exits, and locks. "Have you noticed anyone following you?"

"No." The skin on her neck tightened. "Why, should I?"

"You're here by yourself?"

Tension rippled over her body. "Yeah. The last guest left a few minutes before you arrived. I've a few chairs left to stack, and I'll be done."

"I'll walk you to your car, okay?" The question mark didn't soften the directive.

Her knee-jerk response was to refuse. The farther she stayed away from him, the better. But Jennifer's death had rattled her. Already she replayed their interview and wondered what she'd missed. Jesus. Jennifer was dead. "Thank you."

Adler loaded the last chairs onto the stack as she collected her backpack, folded up the picture of Gina, and slid it into a portfolio case. She fished her mace and keys out of her bag. "I need to dump the trash."

He picked up the trash bag. "Let's go."

"Right."

At the door, she shut off the lights and stared into a darkness ripe with an eerie weight now pressing on her chest. Anxious to leave, she snapped the door wider. A rush of cool air greeted her. She raised an unsteady hand, shoved the key in the heavy dead bolt, and locked it. She started toward the dumpster in the alley, but he stayed slightly in front while keeping her near the wall.

He followed her across the street to the lot where her SUV was parked beside a dark cruiser.

"Thanks for the escort."

"Where do you work?"

"I teach film at the university."

"You've a degree in film?"

"A bachelor of arts and a master's."

"How long have you taught?"

Given another set of circumstances, he'd have sounded conversational. "About six months. Not a full professor. I'm an adjunct."

"And before that you said you worked for an ad agency in Texas?"

"Yes. A sizable pay cut."

"Who's financing this project?"

"My savings. The university job. Frugality. I make it work."

He nodded, sizing her up. Light from a streetlamp cut across his angled face. "I expect Jennifer Ralston's interview tape tomorrow."

"I said I'd drop it off."

She slid behind the wheel, and as she raised her key toward the ignition, her hand still shook. She sat for a moment and drew in a breath, willing her muscles to unwind.

"You all right?" he asked.

She gripped the wheel. *Breathe in. Breathe out.* "Jennifer really is dead?"

"I'm sorry."

"It would be cruel to lie." Adler didn't look like the type that played games, but another cop had lied to her after Gina went missing, so she was wise to be cautious.

"I would never do that," he said.

Gray eyes scrutinized her so closely it was hard not to look away.

"You'll keep me updated on Jennifer's case?"

"We will talk again."

She closed her door and turned the ignition. He patted the top of the car, and she pulled away. A glance in the rearview mirror captured him standing on the deserted street, staring at her like a hunter. And she was in his crosshairs.

INTERVIEW FILE #4

The Night Gina Vanished

Sunday, August 15, 2004

We had gathered on the large rocks on the James River at Pony Pasture Rapids. I was witnessing a celebration. Gina, Erika, and Jennifer were heading off to college in less than a week, and this gathering was their private send-off. I felt privileged to be included because I was only a rising junior. This evening would never have been open to me if I'd not been Gina's cousin.

Pony Pasture is part of the James River Park System, with the Huguenot Bridge just upriver. Called by some the Redneck Riviera, it attracts thousands of sunbathers, swimmers, and kayakers daily during the summer. We'd arrived after sunset, officially trespassing and violating park rules when we hopscotched over the trail of massive boulders onto the river.

The sultry evening began simply with a few laughs, and then Jennifer had produced a plastic quart bottle of lemonade spiked with vodka. I knew when the nectar came to me I should have passed. I hadn't had a drink in almost eleven months. I had promised my mother I'd get my life together. But I was naive enough to think I could stop at one drink. So I took a sip. The cool, sweet liquid slid over my tongue, quenching one thirst and igniting another. Shortly after, the bottle was half-full and we were drunk. My head spun. I'd never had so much fun in my life.

Then Jennifer wobbled to her feet. She had to go because her grand-parents were coming into town early the next day. She called her sister, Ashley, for a ride. Soon, at least I think it was soon, a blue sedan pulled up and headlights flashed. Jennifer and then Erika got in the car and left. Gina and I were alone.

We inspected the jug, now nearly empty. Time to call it a night; we began to walk toward my aunt's home a half mile down the road. We'd not gone more than a few hundred yards when I had the first suspicion someone was watching us. It was the creepy sensation you get at the base of your skull that sends shivers down your spine. When I looked up, Gina was ten yards ahead of me. Not a big deal, but there was no moon that night. I ignored the fear, attributing it to the booze. I barked at Gina to wait. She told me to hurry. My flip-flop snagged on the gravel road. I stumbled and called out to her. I heard nothing in the pitch blackness. In only a few seconds, I caught up. She was bracing, her face white, and her lips drawn tight with fear. Standing beside her was a man in dark clothing wearing a clown mask. He was holding a large knife to her neck.

No one spoke for a moment. He told me to run.

My mind was blurred by the booze. I remember staggering and trying to stand straight. I wanted to run. I was so afraid. And then Gina began to scream. I focused and saw the large jagged blade press-ing against her cheek and blood running down her neck and chest. I stumbled forward and saw Gina's ear on the ground, her silver earring still looped through the pierced lobe. He'd sliced off her ear.

"Run or I'll kill her." The clown raised the severed ear as if it were a trophy. "One, two . . ."

I don't remember what I did next or how much more time passed before I turned and ran.

CHAPTER THREE

Thursday, March 15, 2018; 11:15 p.m.

Adler watched Kaitlin Roe drive away. He couldn't get a full read on her. She was nervous and edgy, but he sensed a resolve. Her blond strands blended into long dark roots, drawing attention to her angled face and sharp brown eyes. Her green V-necked sweater was full and loose, but when she'd moved, the fabric had clung to a tight body and full breasts. She'd filled out the worn jeans nicely.

When she'd first tried to meet him months ago, he and Logan had been responding to a call. The explosion happened a day later, and his promise to call Kaitlin Roe back was forgotten.

There was no forgetting her now. In fact, getting her out of his head wouldn't be easy. As he drove back to the homicide scene, he ran a search on Kaitlin Roe. There were no charges pending against her in Virginia. There'd been a speeding ticket in Montgomery County last year, which she'd paid.

An Internet search of Lyn Tyler pulled up references to her advertising job in Dallas. She wasn't listed on the staff page, but when he clicked on prior events, he found a variety of pictures featuring her at corporate functions. If he hadn't been looking for her, he might have missed her. Her hair was fully blond, and the makeup she wore made her look too perfect. In one cocktail setting, a blue sequined dress skimmed her trim body, and tall heels made her already-long legs look, well, pretty damn stunning. In another image her dress was black and fitted, and she was holding a crystal award while surrounded closely by several older men. Kaitlin was grinning at the camera while the others were enraptured by her.

This version of Kaitlin would have turned his head when he was a younger man. But he preferred the woman who'd demanded a meeting with him and whom he'd found tonight in the deserted meeting space stacking chairs. *She* was interesting. She had dropped whatever mask the Texas Kaitlin had been wearing, and didn't seem to care what he or anyone thought.

Next he called the police records division and asked for the Gina Mason investigation book. Maybe there was a connection between Jennifer's and Gina's deaths.

At the murder scene, he found Quinn sitting in her car. The forensic team was still inside the townhome processing evidence.

He tapped on Quinn's window, and she reluctantly set aside a thermos of coffee and climbed out of the car. "Ready to knock on a few doors?" he asked.

She rolled her shoulders. "Ready to wake up the good citizens."

He checked his watch. Eleven thirty. Yeah, they were going to disturb a few people, but the earliest hours in a murder investigation were the most critical. Now was the time to talk to anyone and everyone.

"So how did it go with Kaitlin Roe?" Quinn asked.

He outlined the details of her project. "She says she did an interview with Jennifer Ralston. I've requested it from her and the Gina Mason files from records."

"How did Ms. Roe react to the news of Ms. Ralston's death?"

"She was upset, but held it together. I suspect she's had some practice hiding her emotions."

"I suppose cops make her nervous."

He thought back to when he'd first seen her. She'd appeared tense, but he'd been too focused on another case to find out why. "She came by the police station in December. She caught Logan and me outside the station as we were headed to a call. She wanted to talk about a cold case. It was a day before the explosion, and I forgot about her until tonight."

"In your defense, you did get blown up."

"Yeah." Thinking about Kaitlin now, he couldn't believe he'd forgotten her.

Quinn burrowed her hands in her pockets. "Let's get this party started."

They started with the row house standing five feet from Jennifer Ralston's home. Adler rang the bell, paused, then banged hard on the black lacquered door for nearly thirty seconds before lights clicked on in an upstairs room. Curtains fluttered, and then the door opened to a guy in his midtwenties. He was wearing sweats and an inside-out sweatshirt. His expression was annoyed until he glanced at Adler's face next to the badges he and Quinn held up.

"Jennifer Ralston was murdered tonight in her home," Adler said. "Mind if we ask you a few questions?"

His eyes widened as the words sunk in. "Shit. I mean, sure, ask me anything."

"What's your name?"

He rubbed the sleep from his eyes. "Ah, my name is Mike Noonan."

Footsteps sounded on the stairs, and another young man came down. He was dressed in athletic shorts and a torn Brew Thru shirt and carried a bat.

Adler held up his badge, his other hand sliding to his weapon, watching until the second man lowered the bat and leaned it against the wall.

"Hey, sorry," the second man said. "What gives? I have to be up at five."

Adler explained the situation. "What's your name?"

"Thompson," he said. "Chuck Thompson."

Adler scribbled the name. "How did Jennifer appear to you lately?"

Chuck glanced at Mike. "I rarely saw her."

Mike's brows knotted. "She's been kind of skittish lately. I said hello to her the other day, and she flinched. Dropped her groceries. Her apples rolled down the sidewalk, and I chased after a couple. I apologized. She tried to laugh it off, but her hands were shaking."

"Did you ask her what was wrong?" Adler asked.

"I did. But she looked embarrassed. Said it was no big deal."

Chuck rubbed the dark stubble on his cheek. "She was always a fanatic about closing her curtains and locking her doors. I figured city living was scaring her. Some people love it, while others just can't get comfortable with it."

Quinn looked confused. "How so?"

"You know, they can't tune out all the street sounds. Someone drags a trash can along the alleyway, and it sounds like they're in the next room. There's only about an arm's length between the houses. Like I said, it's not for everyone."

"And you don't think Jennifer liked it?" Quinn asked.

"She was raised in the burbs. Took her months to learn to parallel park," Chuck said.

"But she stayed," Adler countered.

"She planned to sell. She's been fixing up the place for weeks. Jennifer said she wanted out."

"When did she plan to put the house on the market?" he asked.

"In April, I think," Mike offered. "She signed a realtor about a month ago. They were waiting for warmer weather. The neighborhood looks its best in the spring."

"Ever see anyone watching her house?" Quinn asked.

"Anyone linger?" Adler added.

"I work twelve hours a day," Mike said. "I'm barely home myself."

Chuck shook his head. "I mean, there are a few houses on the street getting renovated, so we see all kinds of new faces around here these days. It would be easy for a stranger to blend in right now."

Mike shook his head. "Her cat went missing two weeks ago. She was crying when she knocked on my door."

"Did she find it?" Adler asked. Ashley Ralston had told him all this earlier in the evening, but he always confirmed witness statements.

"If she did, she didn't tell me," Mike said.

"Did she date anyone in particular?" Quinn asked.

"There was Jeremy," Chuck said. "He was around for a few months, and then he stopped coming by."

"Does Jeremy have a last name?" Adler asked, again double-checking Ashley's answers.

"Keller," Chuck said. "He's an engineer in her firm. I did see him around a few weeks ago. He was ringing her doorbell, but she didn't answer. It was late. I figured it was a dry booty call."

They'd confirmed Ashley's information and tossed in an extra tidbit about Jeremy. "Okay. Thanks." He handed the two men his card. "If you think of anything else, give me a call?"

"Yeah, sure," Mike said.

Chuck nodded. "Absolutely."

The detectives left the two standing in their doorway as they moved to the next row house. By four, they'd spoken to six neighbors. Most had seen the flashing lights but hadn't been alarmed. Another burglary, most assumed. All were taken aback by the news of her death. A few noted she'd grown jumpy recently, and a couple emphasized she'd appeared to improve in the last couple of days. One woman swore she saw a man lurking in the bushes across the street in the park and said she had called the police. A patrol car arrived, but the officer found no one.

Of the six homes they'd visited in the last few hours, four reported having cameras and promised footage. In the minutes before sunrise, they walked down the uneven brick sidewalk back toward the Ralston crime scene. It was still lit up, and technicians continued to process the scene. They'd only be getting in the way if they entered now.

"I want to have a look at the alley." Adler moved to the wooden gate that led to the side alley. The lock on the gate had been cut.

Quinn rubbed her hands together. "A uniform cut it for me so I could search the backyard."

As he pushed through the wooden gate, several bells on the other side clanged and clattered. "They look new. Early warning system?"

"She was fortifying her house."

The backyard was narrow and long. At the opposite end was the small garage he'd seen earlier. He found the garage door locked but the side window unlocked. Adler opened the window. He shone his flashlight into a space that was barely large enough for one car. Hanging from the sidewalls were lawn chairs, Christmas lights, autumn wreaths, and Halloween decorations. The kind of crap that was cool a handful of days but was useless the rest of the year.

"Where's her car?" All signs suggested Jennifer had entered her front door.

"It's a blue Honda parked several spaces down. I searched it and found nothing out of the ordinary. I suspect she found a spot out front and took it."

To the right of the garage was a gate leading into the alley that ran between Twenty-First and Twenty-Second Streets. There were two dumpsters in the alley. "What day is trash pickup?"

"Thursday. The forensic team already checked the dumpsters. They were recently emptied, and the few bags present didn't contain any evidence."

"We need to expand the radius. The guy might have parked a couple of blocks away."

"I've already asked the uniforms to canvas the area dumpsters tonight."

"Good deal." He strode back toward the large brick patio bordering the back door. There were several planters filled with fresh dirt and winter pansies.

Two orange flags marked areas where two fresh footprints had been noted by the first responder. The forensic investigator had photographed the impressions and then taken plaster castings of each. The casts had already been transported to the lab, but it would be another seventy-two hours before they fully hardened. Preliminary accounts described it as a man's tennis shoe, size ten or eleven.

The back door's lock and the area around it were coated in dark graphite fingerprint powder. The forensic technician had also dusted the glass panes directly to the right and left. Adler studied the doorjamb, the frame, and the threshold. Nothing appeared out of order.

"If her house was going on the market in a few weeks, then the realtor would have a key," Adler said.

"Good point," Quinn said. She flipped through her notes. "According to the neighbor, Larry Jenkins was her realtor, and he owns Dogwood Homes. Since we don't have a forced entry, it would be worth it to pay him a visit today."

"What about cleaning crews?"

"She did have a crew come in a week ago to deep-clean for the upcoming open house. I don't have the name."

"Given the evidence, I believe our intruder had a key and knew the passcode."

"There's basement access," Quinn said. She pointed to a small window at ground level secured on the inside with a lock. It had also been dusted for fingerprints. "The window is located above the washer and dryer. No footprints on either appliance, but maybe they've been cleaned. There's also a security sensor on the window."

As Adler straightened, he thought about the flowers under Jennifer's bed. "How long had the killer been in the house hiding before Jennifer arrived home?" he asked, more to himself.

"Hard to say. He'd have needed time to get inside, put on the suit, and climb under the bed," she said.

"Were there any signs of the victim's blood anywhere in the house other than the bathroom?"

"No. Not a drop."

"Not an easy trick considering how she died."

"Takes planning. He came prepared."

"Whoever did this has been thinking about it for a while." The ex-boyfriend came to mind. Murders by strangers were really uncommon. "Let's talk to Jeremy Keller." He checked his watch. "Doubtful his office will open for a couple of hours."

"I have his home address."

"Let's pay him a visit."

Adler offered to drive, and soon the two detectives were on the road. In the predawn hours, the traffic was nonexistent. The drive to the ultramodern home on the river took twenty minutes. The house and its surroundings were dark.

Out of the car, the detectives walked up to front steps made of a sleek gray stone leading to a very expensive teak front door. The roofline rose into a sharp peak, the top section sporting a bank of full-length windows.

Adler stood to the left of the door and Quinn to the right. He rang the bell. He waited fifteen seconds, and when there was no sign of life in the house, he rang the bell again while Quinn banged on it. Nothing.

"He's not here, or he doesn't want to talk to us," Adler said. "Let's look in the garage window."

They moved to a garage lined with clean modern windows. He shone his light inside and saw enough to confirm there was no car.

Keller's absence wasn't suspicious in and of itself. Not uncommon for a young adult male to spend the night somewhere else.

Adler checked his watch. "It's after six. Do you have his phone number?"

"I do." She read it off.

Adler dialed the number. The call went to voicemail. He opted not to leave a message. He wanted to deliver the news face-to-face so he could observe Keller's reaction.

Adler and Quinn drove to a fast-food restaurant and went through the drive-through. Quinn ordered a bacon-and-egg biscuit and black coffee. He went for the same.

"This stuff is going to kill us," she said.

"No one gets out of here alive." But no crappy meal was going to do him in.

"When's the last time you saw Logan?" she asked.

"A few days ago. He has his new prosthetic, and he's learning to walk."

"He and Suzanne were a little rocky. They okay?"

"We didn't talk about his wife." He hoped the marriage was solid enough to sustain through Logan's injury.

They ate the rest of the meal in silence and then made their way to Keller and Mayberry Engineering thirty minutes away. When they arrived it was seven a.m., but the building was lit up.

A large sign embossed with a **K&M** logo resembling towering mountain peaks hung behind a smooth pine receptionist desk, where a young blond woman in a crisp red dress already sat. She smiled. "May I help you?"

Adler showed his badge, and she immediately rose to her feet.

"I'm looking for Jeremy Keller."

She looked a little startled. "I'll get him right away." She disappeared into a maze of gray cubicles.

Minutes later a tall, lean man with thinning red hair and sporting tortoiseshell glasses shrugged on his suit jacket and adjusted his tie as he quickly walked toward the detectives.

"I'm Jeremy Keller," the man said while extending his hand.

"I'm Detective Adler, and this is my partner, Detective Quinn. Is there someplace we can talk privately?"

Jeremy reached for his monogrammed cuff and tugged it with a jerk. "Sure. The conference room." He led them into a corner room dominated by a mahogany table surrounded by twelve leather-bound chairs. He quietly closed the door and invited them to sit. "What's this about?"

"Does your company always open this early?" Adler asked.

"We have a big deadline. I was here all night."

"Never left?"

"Correct. It's not unusual in this line of work."

"That explains it. We stopped by your house an hour ago," Adler said.

"As I said, I was here. We have a big presentation in two days. May I ask why you would go by my home?"

"You also didn't answer your phone," Adler countered.

Keller's frown deepened. "I don't when I'm working. What is this about, Detectives?"

"One of your employees, Jennifer Ralston, was murdered in her home last night." Adler enunciated the words slowly, watching Jeremy's face. Some murderers were good at feigning shock. Most, however, did it poorly. Adler couldn't always articulate why someone's reaction was off, but he knew it when he saw it.

Jeremy's face paled, and he flinched as if struck. "Jesus, are you sure? I saw her yesterday. We were in a meeting, and she was excited about heading up a new project."

"We're sure. You said you saw her yesterday? When was that exactly?"

He stared absently for a moment and then shook his head. "About five." He slumped farther into the leather chair. "We were sitting right here. I wanted Jennifer to stay late, but she was adamant she had to leave."

Adler angled the chair slightly toward Jeremy, knowing his body position suggested they were on the same team.

Quinn sat across from them. He and Quinn hadn't interviewed as a team yet. Normally partners fell into a rhythm. Call it good cop/bad cop roles or whatever, but having a balance of adversarial versus supportive interview skills worked. Most people had seen enough TV cop shows to spot the technique, but real-life situations brought a ton of adrenaline and stress. It was only natural to gravitate to the guy throwing you a lifeline, which in this case would be Adler.

"Do you have any idea who might have done this?" Quinn asked.

"Kill Jennifer? Shit. I can't believe I'm even having this conversation. No. I don't know anyone like that. She was well liked by all her colleagues. A good person."

"Someone didn't see it that way," Quinn said.

"How was Ms. Ralston's performance on the job?" Adler asked.

"She was great. She was one of our most productive managers. Her attention to detail was annoyingly amazing."

"Did you notice a difference in the last couple of months?" Adler asked.

"I could tell she was a little distracted. In late February, she was not quite on her game and missed a few details. I called her into my office. She swore she was fine, but I could see something was bothering her."

"Did she tell you what it was?" Quinn asked as she studied an architectural drawing on the wall behind Keller.

"No."

"Did her distraction have to do with the personal relationship she shared with you?" Quinn asked.

"What?" Jeremy's face reddened. "Jennifer and I weren't really in a relationship."

"What would you call it?" Adler asked.

"Friends." He paused. "With benefits."

Quinn nodded. "I see. Was she more into you than you were into her?"

Jeremy stammered. "You're making it sound like I might have hurt her."

"Not at all," Adler offered. "We're trying to figure out who killed her." He leaned forward a fraction. "When did you two end your relationship?"

"About six months ago. There were no bad feelings on either side," Jeremy insisted. "I'm dating again, and I know she dated other men. She told me about a guy last week."

"How'd you feel about that?" Quinn said. "Did it bother you a little?"

"No." He shoved his hands into his pockets.

"Did she mention his name?" Adler asked.

"No."

"Why were you at her house a few weeks ago?" Adler asked.

"I was dropping off papers she'd left at the office. She didn't answer the door, so I left."

"Did she ever mention having a stalker?" Adler asked.

"A stalker? No. A couple of times Jennifer was late to work. Once she said her tire had been slashed. I thought it sounded like an excuse. She got so mad she slammed the receipts from the tire repair shop on my desk."

"How long did she act stressed?"

"A few weeks. I asked her about the troubles, and she said they'd stopped. I almost made a quip about her imaginary friend but thought better. She was wound pretty tight."

"Wise move," Adler commented. "Did you or her coworkers ever see anyone lingering around?"

"No. No one ever brought anything to my attention."

"Have you ever heard the name Gina Mason?" Adler asked.

"No."

"What about Kaitlin Roe?"

Jeremy nodded sheepishly. "Jennifer wrote the name on her blotter and circled it several times."

"You notice doodles and scribbles for all your employees?" Quinn asked.

"Jennifer had suddenly canceled a business meeting with me back in late February. It wasn't like her, and it made me curious."

"So you searched her office?" Quinn pressed.

"You've got it wrong. I looked around," Jeremy said.

"You didn't want her, but didn't want anyone else to have her?" Quinn was deliberately provoking him to gauge his reaction.

He held up his hand. "You're twisting my words."

Adler dialed back the dialogue. "We're trying to fit all the pieces together, Mr. Keller, so we can leave here and find her killer."

"I feel like I should have an attorney."

"Again, we're simply gathering information. Can you tell me a little more about what you do here?"

"We're civil engineers. Site work. Environmental assessments."

"Environmental work," Adler said. "What does that entail?"

Keller shook his head. "I'm not sure why it matters."

"It may."

"Gas and oil spills. Wetlands."

"Sounds like messy work. Does it require a protective suit?" Quinn asked.

"Sometimes. Why?"

Quinn deflected the question. "Did Jennifer do any environmental work?"

"Sure. She was solid in the field."

"So she'd have worn one of those suits?" Adler asked.

"Sure. Why do you care about the suits?" Jeremy asked.

"Sorry. It was a tangent." Adler repeated several of Quinn's questions, again to see if Jeremy's responses remained consistent. Finally, after fifteen minutes of questions and answers, the detectives stood. Adler handed Jeremy his card.

Jeremy took the card but didn't meet his gaze. He absently rubbed his forearm. "Thank you for telling me about Jennifer."

"Your arm okay?" Adler asked. "I noticed earlier it seemed to bother you."

"Racquetball injury."

"Sucks getting older," Adler said.

"Can we see your arm?" Quinn asked.

"Why?" Jeremy asked.

"I want to strike you off the list," Adler said.

"What list?"

"Suspect," Quinn said.

"I didn't hurt Jennifer."

"The sooner we can exclude you, the sooner we can find the person who killed your friend."

Jeremy hesitated and then unfastened his cuff and rolled up his sleeve. A deep-red scratch snaked up over his forearm to his elbow.

Quinn pulled out her phone and snapped a picture.

When it came to questioning a suspect, the most critical hours were the earliest in an investigation. The longer people had to think, the more pat their answers became. Right now, Jeremy was a little off guard, and the detectives knew it.

Quinn snapped several more photos. "Thanks for your cooperation."

"Sure, I guess," Jeremy said.

As Jeremy rolled down his sleeve, he furrowed his brow. "I didn't take her seriously. I thought Jennifer was jerking me around after we stopped seeing each other."

"May I take a quick cheek swab?" Quinn asked as she pulled out a Q-tip encased in a vial.

Adler offered a warm grin. "DNA. I want to clear you of this investigation as soon as possible."

Jeremy looked relieved. "Sure, I guess."

Quinn quickly snapped open the seal on the vial and removed the Q-tip. "Open." She swabbed the insides of his mouth before replacing the Q-tip in the vial without saying a word.

Jeremy rubbed his hands through his hair. "Jesus, I can't believe this is happening."

"Can you point to anything else that was bothering Jennifer?" Adler asked.

"Someone sent her flowers. They came with no notes. At first she thought they were from me. I assured her they weren't, but I don't know if she believed me."

"Do you know which florist delivered them?" Quinn asked.

"No."

"Where were they delivered?" Adler asked.

"To her home, I suppose," Keller said.

"When you dated, what was she like?" Quinn asked.

"Driven. Quiet and moody at times. Other times fun."

"Was she safety conscious?" Adler asked, remembering the three dead bolts on her front door.

"Yes. She said you could never be too careful."

"Any reason why?"

"Once I showed up late. She'd started drinking without me and was a little tipsy. She was looking at old pictures and pointed to one taken when she was about sixteen. She was grinning from ear to ear in the picture. Jennifer said it was the picture of 'the girl she'd been.' She spoke about herself as if that girl had died."

"Did she explain the comment?" Adler asked.

"No. We ended up in bed and distracted. It was an amazing night."

"Can we see her cubicle?" Quinn asked.

"Sure." Jeremy led them through the cubicles overlooking the woods behind the building.

There were three stacks of papers on her desk. Three pencils were lined up to the right, as if standing at attention and waiting for orders. On her wall were her diplomas and professional designations.

Adler sat at her desk and opened the middle and side drawers but found nothing that caught his attention. Behind the desk on the credenza were a potted cactus and a picture of a smiling Jennifer standing arm in arm with her sister, Ashley.

"Call us if you think of anything else, no matter how inconsequential," Adler said.

"Absolutely."

Jeremy escorted them to the reception area. Instead of leaving right away, Adler turned to the receptionist. "Did Jennifer ever receive any mail or deliveries that may have upset her?"

The receptionist glanced toward her boss, and when he nodded, she said, "She did receive a letter. She opened it in front of me and slammed it in the trash without saying a word."

"Remember what was on the envelope and letter?" Adler asked.

"There was no return address. Plain white envelope. Handwritten. Block letters. I thought the sender had been a draftsman."

"Postmark?"

"Richmond."

"Good memory," Adler said.

She shrugged. "Hand-addressed letters are out of the ordinary and stick out."

Adler leaned toward her a fraction. "Did you look at the letter after she threw it in the trash?"

She looked sheepishly toward Jeremy.

"Tell them," Jeremy said. "It's all right."

"Yes, I looked at it. I never look at personal information, but her reaction made me worry for her. It was just a hand-drawn heart."

"In pen, pencil, ink?"

"Red ink," she said.

"Any similar letters?" Adler asked.

"No."

"See anyone suspicious hanging around?" Quinn asked.

"No."

"Was she dating anyone else?" Adler asked.

"Not that I know of."

"Thanks," Adler said. "Mr. Keller, we'll be in touch."

Outside, Quinn slid on her glasses with such deliberate slowness it was clear she was pissed. "Our victim has an ex-boyfriend, and a killer who had access to her house and lingered in her house for several hours before he killed her."

"You think Keller killed Jennifer?"

"Stalkers generally have had some interaction with their victims before their behavior turns dangerous."

"Fair point, but before we start chasing after Keller, I want to hear Jennifer's interview with Kaitlin," Adler said.

INTERVIEW FILE #5

The First Few Hours

Everyone who came in contact with Gina on her final day second-guessed their last words. Would it have made a difference? Should I have told her to stay home? Was it smart to drink by the river at night? What if I'd called a cab for us all? Was there someone lurking around I should have seen?

There were a few who for a long time maintained hope she was alive. Maybe she was being held somewhere. Maybe she had escaped, was suffering from amnesia, and didn't remember. One reporter wrote an entire article about women who'd survived years of captivity, even suggesting Gina might be her abductor's sex slave.

The survival rates for girls like Gina drop substantially after twenty-four hours. And if the victim is a child, the window of rescue narrows to the first three hours.

As I tape this on March 1, Gina has been missing for 4,946 days. Her critical hours have long passed. And still I hold out hope she is alive.

"I'd like to see my baby brought home," Audrey Mason said. "I want her eternal resting place to be beside me and her father. She deserves better than what life gave her."

There were a lot of variables coming into play that night. Remove any one, and circumstances might have been different. Gina might still be with us today. But wishful thinking doesn't do anybody any good.

CHAPTER FOUR

Friday, March 16, 2018; 9:45 a.m.

Kaitlin had called Erika Travis Crowley, the fourth girl with Gina the night she vanished, several times for another interview. Erika had not returned any of her calls, so Kaitlin had gotten the hint and left her alone. But now that Jennifer was dead, she felt compelled to see her and tell her what had happened to a woman they both knew. Erika might have blown off Kaitlin, but surely she'd want to know about Jennifer.

It was raining when she parked in front of the large colonial in the upscale Far West End neighborhood. The yard was neatly manicured and the garden beds freshly mulched. She dashed up the long driveway to the front door, painted a shiny black lacquer, and pressed the bell.

Seconds passed, but there was no sound or movement in the house. Then she heard footsteps, and the door opened. Erika was dressed in a sleek black yoga outfit. Her hair was pulled back into a smooth ponytail, and her makeup looked immaculate.

Erika's brows knotted as she focused her attention on Kaitlin's face. "I told you I'm not talking to you again."

"I'm not even here about that. I came to tell you Jennifer Ralston is dead."

Erika nervously twisted the large diamond engagement ring nestled against a wedding band with her thumb. "What are you talking about? She's fine."

Rain dripped on her. "No, she was murdered in her home last night."

Erika folded her arms, shaking her head. "Jennifer. Dead. I don't believe it."

"Yes." Even though she'd been up half the night trying to process the news, she still couldn't fully accept it. "The cops visited me last night and told me."

Erika shook her head, but still didn't invite her inside. "How did she die?"

"I don't know."

"Do they have suspects?"

"Not that I know of." Kaitlin stepped forward slightly. She hadn't intended to use Jennifer's death to push her own agenda, but like it or not, she and Erika were the remaining survivors from the night Gina was taken. "Erika, we're the last two girls alive who were with Gina that night. Don't you think we should sit down and talk more? It can be off the record."

"What's there to talk about? What's done is done. I can't save Gina or Jennifer." She shook her head. "I said too much already."

"Don't you think about that night?"

"No, I don't. It was tragic, but there's nothing I could have done then or now."

"Do you ever wonder if we could have helped her that night?"

"Like I said, I hadn't thought about it until I made the mistake of talking to you." She reached for the door handle. "Thank you for the news. Please leave my property."

The door closed in Kaitlin's face, and locks on the other side slid into place. For a moment she simply stood staring. Erika had Kaitlin's number. When and if Erika was willing to talk, Kaitlin would be there.

Back in the car, she drove across town to the Richmond City Justice Center. She'd been there three times since Randy Hayward's recent incarceration, but he'd refused to see her. This morning, however, she'd received a call from the jail.

"Will you accept a call from Randy Hayward?"

She shoved her hair out of her eyes and sat up in bed. "Yes."

A click and then, "Kaitlin, this is Randy. Come by the jail. I've something for you."

"What is it?" she asked.

"I'll tell you in person." The line went dead.

Now, as Kaitlin moved through the front doors of the jail into the modern, clean lobby, she shook off the raindrops. The lights were oddly bright, a nice break from the dreariness outside.

Her stomach tightened at the thought of seeing Randy. They'd dated when she'd been a know-it-all sixteen-year-old and he'd been a twenty-one-year-old college dropout who lived down the street from Gina. She'd been a lost soul, abandoned by a mother who sent her to an aunt in Virginia to get sober. She'd missed home so much and was still grieving for the brother who'd committed suicide. Despite her tough demeanor, she'd been vulnerable, and Randy had been happy to take advantage. Their relationship had run hot for a couple of months until a Fourth of July party when he'd hit her after she'd refused a beer. She'd known in that moment if she stayed with him, she wouldn't make it.

The last time she'd seen Randy in the flesh had been in a police lineup. Once the cops placed Randy in the area the night Gina vanished, they'd quickly determined Kaitlin's connection to him.

The day of the lineup her nerves had been scraped raw after weeks of police questioning, media scrutiny, and sleepless nights. She could barely breathe, but she'd stood in the small stifling room with her mother and aunt at her side. Through a two-way mirror, she'd watched the six men file past her. She'd recognized Randy of course, but she couldn't say with certainty he'd taken Gina. She'd never seen the abductor's face and only heard his voice. She'd asked the cops to get each man to speak. *"Run or I'll kill her."*

All the men in the lineup had repeated the phrase, and none of the voices had resonated. The cops had been frustrated, and her aunt had been furious. They'd all pressured her to listen to the voices again. She had. But she couldn't identify the abductor.

Now she approached the front guard station and showed her ID, which she was required to leave with the guard. Her purse and phone weren't permitted in the building and remained locked in her car.

She'd done her homework on Randy since she'd begun work on this project. He'd had a string of crimes in the interim since Gina died, and his last three-year stint in prison had ended in early January. Less than six weeks later, he'd obtained a knife and went into a convenience store to steal cash to fuel his meth habit. Instead, the female clerk confronted him, screaming for him to leave. Without hesitation, he'd stabbed the blade into her belly twice, severing an artery. The hemorrhaging put the clerk in a coma, and though the ER docs had stabilized her, she died a week later. Randy was facing capital murder charges, and the Commonwealth of Virginia still had the death penalty.

"Who're you here to see?" the guard asked.

"Randy Hayward," she said.

"Does he know you're coming?"

"Yes. He called me this morning."

Dark eyebrows rose. "You his public defender?"

"No. I'm here to talk to him about an old case."

The guard shook his head. "I'll let 'em know you're here. Can't make promises he'll see you. What's the name?"

"Kaitlin Roe." She wondered what had changed since she'd first started calling him. Had he heard about Jennifer?

To the left was a room where the families met with the bail bondsman. Three women, one with a baby, waited their turn to post bail.

"Ms. Roe," the guard said. "Follow the signs to the visitor's room."

"Thank you." She crossed the carpeted floor to double doors. Following the signs, she made her way to the room.

The air smelled stale and the walls seemed to close in. The doors on the other side of the thick glass opened. A muscular man was escorted to the seat on the other side, and he made no attempt to hide his curiosity as he sat. Her memories of Randy Hayward were of a wiry younger man of twenty-one. His neck was thick with muscles and his skin covered in tattoos.

If at twenty-one his eyes projected juvenile insolence, at thirty-five his gaze telegraphed the cold calculation of a man who'd spent much of his adult life in prison.

She searched his eyes, expecting some flicker of recognition, and when she didn't see any, she was relieved.

Then he winked and picked up his phone. She lifted the receiver to her ear.

"Well, look what the cat dragged in."

"Randy, it's been a long time."

He leaned back, his gaze drinking her in. "I got to say, girl, you're a sight for sore eyes."

Girl. His pet name for her. Charming until he confessed he couldn't remember names too well and called all females *girl.*

He lowered his gaze to her breasts. He grunted. "You sure know how to break up the daily routine."

Revulsion slithered over her. "I came to talk to you about Gina Mason."

"Who?" He held her gaze.

"Gina Mason. You remember. She vanished fourteen years ago." And then she caught herself. The con was conning her.

He ran his tongue over his lips. "Right. Gina. The cops were sure I'd killed her. Boy, did they ever want to find her. They had a posse full of cops on the hunt, but they couldn't prove anything. You know better than anyone. You had your chance to identify me, and you didn't." He made a sucking sound. "What ol' Randy gave you was pretty special, wasn't it? Popped your sweet cherry and made you his woman."

She separated further from her rage and self-recriminations. Stupid choices could not be taken back. What mattered was now. "I'm making a podcast about her. I'm hoping she can finally be found."

He narrowed his eyes, assessing her. "I'd forgotten all about her. I'd have thought they'd have found her by now."

"She's still missing. But you know all this, otherwise why call me?"

"Why do you want to find her? I always thought you were a little jealous of her. What was it you called her?"

Goody-Two-Shoes. "I don't remember."

His eyes never left her. "I hear Mrs. Mason died."

Kaitlin and her aunt had talked about the podcast in her final days. She'd been worried about her aunt's reaction and had been pleased when she'd given her approval. "Eight weeks ago."

"Mrs. Mason was my mom's friend. They played tennis together. I truly liked her. She was always nice to me. Maybe I should have met with her before I got locked up again. I could have shared a few secrets."

"What kind of secrets?" Kaitlin asked, even knowing he would lie.

He shook his head. "I don't know. What kind of secrets do you think I have?"

"You tell me."

"I know where she is," he said, grinning.

Everyone assumed Gina had died long ago, but no one really knew. However, the surety humming under his statement took her aback. "Randy, no one knows what happened to her. You said so yourself."

"That's right. That's what I said."

"What're you saying now?"

He cracked his knuckles, and she noticed the letter tattoos on his fingers. D-E-A-D on the right hand. K-I-L-L on the left.

He was center stage in her life again, and the glint in his eyes told her he liked it. "It's important to you that she's found, isn't it, girl?"

"It is, Randy. And maybe it's important to you, too."

"Do the cops still care?"

"I have no idea. I care, and I know you care. You grew up down the street from Gina. You grew up with her. You told me once about your crush on her. We both still have a connection to her."

"So, if I did have information about Gina, what would you do for me?"

"Randy, what do you want?"

He slowly ran his tongue over his teeth. "Girl, I've missed you. Just seeing you is bringing back some fine memories."

"Do you want money?"

"A few extra dollars in my canteen account would be appreciated for now, but I'm looking for more. I'm facing the death penalty this time."

Ah, the real reason he called. He'd received word from the attorney on his case. "You killed a woman in a convenience store."

"I didn't mean to. I jabbed the knife at her thinking I'd scare her. But the dumb bitch moved, and the blade went right into her gut. Severed an artery. Not my fault."

"What do you want?"

"Mom isn't taking my calls anymore, and that means no more money. I've got an attorney, but he keeps telling me to sit tight. I'm tired of waiting and wondering how I'll get out of this mess." Anger deepened the lines on his face. "If this situation is getting fixed, I'm going to have to pull a rabbit out of my ass."

"What does this have to do with Gina?"

He pointed both his index fingers at her as if he were a dueling cowboy. "Everything, sugar."

"The cops placed you on Riverside Drive the night Gina vanished. Did you see what happened?"

He leaned forward, his gaze burning into her. "And if I did?"

"Did you *see*?"

"Maybe."

He had no soul. His single priority was saving his own ass. And if he could play her in the process, all the better.

"What do you want?" she asked again.

He grinned.

It was a smile that was too familiar. The one he had always produced when they were dating and wanted to string her along.

This trip had felt necessary an hour ago. And maybe it was. You couldn't pick and choose the demons you face. "You weren't around when Gina vanished. My bet is you were in your parents' garage smoking meth. You talk a big game, but you can't deliver. Like always."

As she moved to rise, he held up a hand. "Hold on there, Kait-*lin*. Don't be in such a rush to leave. We were getting reacquainted. And I've missed seeing you so much."

"Unless you can help me find Gina, you won't see me again."

A smile twitched at the corners of his mouth. "You're cute when you talk tough."

She gripped the receiver and looked toward the door, anxious to be out of here and free of him.

"You were there on the road," he said.

"Already reported in the media, Randy."

"You were so drunk you could barely stand."

She slowly looked back at him. "Again, the entire city knew I was a lush before I left town. You're boring me now."

He shrugged, his grin widening. "I know where she is."

The hair on the back of her neck rose. She sensed Randy wasn't playing around anymore. She sat back down and stared at him, waiting for him to show his cards.

He steepled his index fingers and pointed to her. "Your blond hair threw me off. I like it better dark. Gina had dark hair."

She remained silent because she didn't trust her voice.

"He told you to run."

"I asked you and everyone in the lineup to say *run*."

He tapped a finger against his chin as if trying to remember. "He cut Gina's ear." He drew his finger across his right ear. "Sliced it right off. And that ear had an earring in it. I remember because I gave the silver dangles to you. You must have lent them to Gina."

The blood drained from her face, leaving her lightheaded. It was a detail the media had never learned. As she sat in her chair, she remembered all the blood that had soaked her T-shirt. Gina's blood. She'd never been able to explain how her blood came to be on her, but it was there. "Where's Gina?"

Randy shook his head as he winked. "I don't have many cards left to play, so I gotta be smart with this one. I want a lot more than your baby browns batting at me before I spill what I know."

The bait was too tempting not to bite. "I'm listening."

"Get me someone who can make me a real good deal. I'm not sure who you need to talk to, but you'll figure it out. You're smart. Smarter than Gina."

INTERVIEW FILE #6

Mrs. Audrey Mason

Monday, January 15, 2018; 4:00 p.m.

It's not easy facing Gina's mother again. She's in hospice care. It's cold, almost always a given during January in Virginia, and the hint of snow lingers in the air. The light is dim, but the walls in Aunt Audrey's room are painted a cheerful blue, and paper snowflakes made by a group of first graders hang from the tiled ceiling. And there is a bright arrangement of white tulips by her bed. It cheers me to know someone else is also thinking about her.

Despite how it all ended between us fourteen years ago, I had loved her. She'd opened her home to me and loved me like a daughter.

She's in what looks like a regular bed hooked up to a morphine drip. A bright-yellow kerchief covers her balding head. She smiles, but is too weak to sit up. We talk about my podcast, and she wants to be on tape. The idea of going to her grave without knowing what happened to her daughter frightens her.

I kiss her on the cheek, and then we begin.

Our family was always small. It was Aunt Audrey and my mother. Gina was an only child. As I've said, I had a brother who committed suicide when I was fourteen. In the days after Gina vanished, Aunt Audrey and I were united in our terror and grief for Gina. And then as the weeks passed and the cops eventually turned their questions against me, Audrey began to doubt me. Why did I have Gina's blood on my shirt? My inability to remember frustrated her, but the breaking point came at the police lineup with Randy Hayward. When I couldn't identify him as the attacker, she'd broken down and asked me to leave her home.

Fourteen years later, I heard she was dying. I came immediately and for weeks visited her daily. In an odd way, we are united again. When I tell her about the podcast, she smiles. She wants people to remember Gina.

"Aunt Audrey, what do you remember about that night? You said once you had a bad feeling about that day."

"I really didn't want you two girls to go, but it seemed silly to keep you home that night." She traces the thin blue veins on her pale-white hand as she glances toward the tulips.

"Why?"

"Gina and I had had a terrible fight that day. You weren't there to hear, but we had never shouted at each other like that."

"What was the fight about?"

"I caught her talking to Randy Hayward. He was trouble, and I told her so. She laughed and said she wasn't you and she'd be fine."

We sit in silence for a minute.

"I woke up at midnight out of a sound sleep. I dreamed Gina had drowned. It left a sick feeling in the pit of my stomach, so I got up. I called her phone, but she didn't answer. She always answers. I called again. Nothing. I knew something had gone terribly wrong."

Audrey's last day was a gray winter morning. I was at her side listening to her breathing growing shallower with each inhale. Another fresh arrangement of white tulips arrived for her. There still was no card or note. And she never opened her eyes again so that I could show them to her. As her life slipped away, I was more determined than ever to find Gina.

CHAPTER FIVE

Friday, March 16, 2018; 11:00 a.m.

The rain had stopped, but the air remained wet and raw. Adler parked in front of the two-story frame house at the corner of Libby and Grove Avenues. The tony area was just east of the University of Richmond, and it was home to several trendy restaurants, expensive clothing boutiques, and an exclusive school for girls.

Adler saw the discreet **DOGWOOD HOMES** sign, climbed the front steps, and pushed through the door to find a young man sitting behind a desk. Slicked-back hair accentuated a sharp jawline. He wore a crisp white shirt but no tie. His smile clicked on. "Can I help you?"

Adler removed his badge from his breast pocket. "I'm Detective John Adler. I'm looking for Mr. Larry Jenkins."

"That's me. I own the company." His brow furrowed.

"I have a question about a property you're representing."

"Which one are you talking about?"

He rattled off Jennifer Ralston's address. "In Church Hill."

"I know the address well. Ms. Ralston signed the sales agreement a few days ago. The house is supposed to go on the market in a couple of weeks. What happened?"

"Right now I want to know who has access to the property." If Adler explained there'd been a homicide, the whole dynamic of the conversation would change. Every word would be measured and weighted. Calculated.

"I do."

"Anyone else?"

"I know Jennifer hired a stager a couple of weeks ago. There was also a painter to touch up the kitchen and a plumber to fix the downstairs sink in the bathroom. The gardeners aren't scheduled to come until next week. Properties like hers go quickly, and the ones that are pristine will get multiple offers above asking price."

"She's not been in the house long. Why sell?"

"Why not ask her?"

"I'm asking you."

He shoved his hands in his pockets. "Why do you care what I think?"

Adler raised a brow and leaned into his personal space, waiting for an answer. He could play this cat-and-mouse game in his sleep.

Jenkins relented and released a breath. "She said she didn't like the city. She wanted to move to the suburbs. What's really going on here?"

Adler let the silence linger between them, reminding Jenkins he ran this show. "She was murdered last night."

Jenkins blinked for a moment as he processed the news. He slowly stood up but kept his hands on the desk to steady himself. "This is awful. Her sister must be devastated."

"You know Ashley Ralston?"

He rubbed his temple. "I went to high school with Ashley. We graduated the same year." His eyes narrowed. "You look familiar. Did you go to Saint Mathew's?"

"I did, but a few years ahead of you." Mention of Saint Mathew's redirected his thoughts back to the Mason case. "So you would also have heard about Gina Mason."

"Everyone at Saint Mathew's knew about Gina. It's a small school. There were just over sixty kids in the graduating class. The news hit everyone hard. At the ten-year reunion the class president had a moment of silence for her."

"Were Jennifer and Gina good friends?"

Larry took his hands off the desk and stood more erect. "How does Gina relate to Jennifer's death?"

"You just said everyone knew each other, and both these girls are dead. Just making sure I have all the pieces."

"Sure, they were great friends."

"Did you know a student named Kaitlin Roe?"

"Kaitlin? Sure. She was Gina's cousin and a couple of years younger. Everyone at Saint M. knew about Kaitlin's circumstances. It was a small community." He fiddled with his watch. "Funny you should mention Kaitlin. She came by here last week."

"Why?"

"She's making a podcast about Gina. She's on this mission to find the truth about her."

"Why was she talking to you?"

"She's talking to everyone in Gina's class. She can't guarantee what she'll use."

"How did you feel about the podcast?"

"I don't know. Doesn't seem like it will do much in the long run. But I guess it makes Kaitlin feel a little less guilty for leaving her cousin. I didn't have any new information to tell her. Most likely my interview will end up on the cutting-room floor."

"Were you there the night Gina vanished?"

"I was on vacation with my parents. I didn't know what had happened for several days. It was a surreal time. Soon after, all the kids went to college. I guess life just kept moving forward." He slowly came around the desk. "How did Jennifer die?"

"I can't say right now."

"And this happened last night?"

"It did."

He twisted a gold cuff link. "I don't know what else to say."

"How many employees do you have?"

"It's just me."

"And you had a key to her house?"

"As did the housecleaning service."

"Where is the key?"

"In a locked box."

"Can I see it?"

"Sure." Jenkins moved to a metal cabinet mounted to the wall in a back office. He punched a number into an electronic keyless lock, and the door opened. There were several dozen sets hanging in the cabinet. He handed Jennifer's key to Adler.

The key was labeled with the number twelve and a four-digit code. "What are these numbers?"

"The small number corresponds to her address logged in a separate location, and the four-digit number is her security passcode."

"Who else has access to this cabinet?"

"Just me. I planned to go out there today to put a lockbox on the front door with a key inside it. Should I still go?"

"No. It's an active crime scene now." Adler pocketed the key and handed him his business card. "Please call me if you think of anything else."

Jenkins studied the card as if it held a clue about what just happened. "I should call Ashley. She must be so upset."

"I'm sure she could use a friend now."

Adler left, and fifteen minutes later when he pulled onto Jennifer Ralston's street, it was quiet. The forensic van and cop cars had cleared away. No watchful neighbors or reporters lingering for now. He parked in front of her house, climbed the stairs, and broke the yellow crime scene tape seal.

As he entered the foyer, the security system chimed in the eerie stillness of the house. When he'd been here last night, the small space had been buzzing. There'd barely been enough space to move around.

He commonly returned to murder scenes after the chaos had cleared. It gave him the chance to process the observations made earlier and begin to imagine the scene from both the killer's and victim's perspectives.

Inside, he paused to tug on black latex gloves while he studied the high heels still undisturbed at the front entryway table. He examined the purse and keys as the foyer mirror tossed back his reflection. He looked ten years older since the bombing. He felt even older.

He imagined Jennifer would have looked in that mirror every day. Women tended to use mirrors, sometimes to admire but more often to critique. He looked away, seeing little point in either.

He moved to the kitchen and tested the back door. It was locked. He flipped the dead bolt, and as he opened the door, the alarm again chimed a warning. Why hadn't the killer tripped the alarm? He closed and locked the door.

He opened several cabinets to find dishes perfectly stacked. In a utensil drawer, the forks, spoons, and knives were polished and arranged in neat stacks. On the counter was an arrangement of apples. All the stems were facing up. Complete order.

Opposite the counter was a nook area serving as a home office. There were several pictures pinned to a bulletin board above the desk. All featured a smiling Jennifer with her cat, a dark Siamese with a bent right ear.

A small laptop rested in the center, papers stacked uniformly on the left, unopened mail on the right. He flipped through the unopened mail to find several bills and a couple of pieces of junk mail. He sat and opened the small drawer. Pens, pencils, paper clips, and stamps. He wondered how she found the time to be so meticulous.

He pulled the drawer out a little farther and ran his hand along the back edge inside. The wood was smooth, empty, and then his fingertips brushed what felt like paper.

He removed a stack of five folded notecards bound by a rubber band. The author had used block lettering and bold black ink.

He read each note.

My Girl, you're still a beautiful woman.

My Girl, would you like a ride to work?

My Girl, I think about you all the time.

My Girl, remember that last summer by the river?

My Girl, what is your biggest regret?

The contents of each note were benign enough. However, if the author were a stalker, the repeated anonymous messages signed only with a heart would have been menacing. The heart written in blood in the shower or the flowers under her bed proved it.

Adler checked, and Jennifer had not filed any police reports. If she had been worried about a stalker, she'd not reached out to the police.

He pulled a plastic evidence bag from his pocket and bagged the notes. He checked the remaining drawer, but it contained more office supplies. He opened the computer and discovered it was password protected by a six-character code.

He tried the year of Jennifer's birth plus her initials. That didn't work. He tried her address. Nope. Didn't work. He typed in *Morris.* No success. Resigned, he decided he'd have to leave the encryption to the geeks in the tech department.

Next he inspected the refrigerator. Fully stocked with fresh vegetables and several bottles of sparkling wine. There was also a takeout container from a pub just around the corner. In the freezer, chocolate ice cream and a bottle of top-shelf vodka stared back at him.

In the living room, an old fireplace painted in black lacquer looked as if its flue had been sealed and was no longer functional. She had arranged candles in the base of the fireplace in a circular pattern, which he supposed was to create a mood. All staged. He moved to a small closet packed with winter coats and several styles of boots. On the top shelf was a box. He lifted the lid and inside found a scrapbook. He sat in the overstuffed chair by the fireplace and opened it. The pictures dated back several years.

He turned the pages slowly until he came to a collection taken on the boulders at the James River. He spotted Jennifer immediately and noticed all these pictures featured not only her, but also three other girls. He flipped over one of the pictures. The inscription read: *Me, Erika, Kaitlin, and Gina.* He focused on Kaitlin's face. The rich sweep of mahogany hair warmed her face and mirrored the color and texture of Gina's. They could have been sisters.

Both Kaitlin and Gina wore wide grins. However, Kaitlin's eyes were tired, whereas Gina's were bright. In another image the girls were standing on the boulders at Pony Pasture. Behind them, the river was low, leaving exposed large granite slabs for kids to sun themselves on warm days. Had these pictures been taken right before Gina vanished?

He replaced the photo and turned the page. After the river pictures the book was blank. The memories ended.

Using his phone he took snapshots of the images. What were the chances Jennifer had narrowly avoided a kidnapping and then fourteen years later ended up murdered?

His phone rang. It was Kaitlin.

"I have that recording." Her voice had a rusty edge that sounded seductive.

"I'm at Jennifer Ralston's home now."

"Okay. I'll meet you. Wait for me."

He found himself looking forward to seeing her. Given another set of circumstances, he'd have welcomed the prospect of pursuing her. "See you soon."

***

Kaitlin grabbed her jacket and descended the stairs to her car parked in the lot. She drove up into Church Hill and found a spot a half block beyond Jennifer's townhome.

She shoved her hands in her pockets and moved up the brick sidewalk toward the row house encircled by the yellow crime scene tape. As she stared up at it, Detective Adler strode out the front door. His expression was grim as he stripped off black latex gloves and came down the sidewalk toward her. She wasn't the only one having a bad day.

"I went to see Randy Hayward," she said.

"So he agreed to see you."

"He called me out of the blue and asked to meet."

"You gave him your number?"

Using a tactic from his playbook, she deflected his question. "He's an important piece of the puzzle."

"And?"

"And he said he knows how to find Gina." She held up her hand before he could voice the rebuttal glistening in his narrowed eyes. "I know, he's a thief, liar, and con man. But he said Gina's attacker had cut her ear off. That detail was never mentioned in the press. The cops told me not to tell anyone, and I didn't. Hayward also knew the earrings she wore were borrowed from me. He gave them to me as a gift."

Adler's glare was unnerving. "How long has he been in jail?"

"One month. He couldn't have killed Jennifer."

He didn't respond.

"I know Gina wasn't your case. But Hayward wants me to find someone whom he can deal with. I thought about you."

He stared at her. "What does he want?"

"He wants to trade what he knows."

"For a reduced sentence?"

"I suppose. He's been in and out of the system for over a decade," she said. "He knows how it works."

"I'm not in a position to make a deal with him," Adler said.

She wasn't going to let Adler off that easy. "But you know who can?"

"Yes." He tightened the fingers around the latex gloves. "It's a hell of a long shot."

"Isn't it worth pursuing? Gina vanished in your jurisdiction, and there's no statute of limitations on murder."

"Assuming Gina is dead," he said.

She cocked her head. "You think she's alive?"

His jaw pulsed. "No."

The flap of yellow crime scene tape caught her attention, and a glance past him reminded her how brutal Gina's death had probably been.

Saying nothing, he opened his phone and held it up to her. It was a picture of her with Gina, Jennifer, and Erika. Her chest tightened, making it hard to breathe.

"When was this taken?" he asked.

"The last night."

"How do you know?"

"Gina is wearing the green dress, and I have on that white top. It's what we both wore that night. Where did you get this? I've never seen it before."

"It was in Jennifer's photo album."

"Ashley snapped several pictures of us when she dropped Jennifer off." Feeling suddenly unsteady, she handed back his phone and fished in her backpack for the disc of Jennifer's interview. She wasn't planning on giving him every interview she'd done just yet because she didn't fully trust him, but she needed his help with Randy. Give a little to get a little. "This is the interview I did with Jennifer."

He tapped the disc against his hand. "Let me make some calls about Hayward. I won't jump too quickly, because I don't want him thinking he's in control. He's not."

Urgency churned in her belly. "He really might know something about Gina, and maybe Jennifer."

"He might. Might not. But he does know what you want, and he's using it."

Adler was right. Wanting led to vulnerability. "Detective, it's our best option right now."

"Okay, I'll make some calls. He's kept his secret fourteen years. He can keep it a little longer."

"Any idea who killed Jennifer?"

"A few." He made no attempt to share.

She nodded toward the security camera mounted on the house across the street. "There are cameras everywhere here. One of them must have captured something."

The crooked smile again tugged the edge of his mouth. "I've done this before."

"Right, sure." She tightened the grip on the strap of her backpack. "Jennifer's mother died about five years ago. And her father died when she was a kid. It was just Ashley and Jennifer."

"You keep up, don't you?"

"When it comes to the girls by the river I do." She shook her head. "Have you requested Gina's missing person file?"

"I have."

She chose her next words carefully. "Be warned, it paints me in a bad light. I'm a different person than I was then. I made terrible mistakes. I can't make them right, but I can help bring Gina home."

75

Mary Burton

"Your name does have a tendency to come up."

"With whom?"

"Larry Jenkins."

"Yeah, I talked to him last week. He wasn't helpful. He remembered me and was more interested in making cracks about my high school days. I was as infamous at Saint Mathew's as Gina was famous."

He ran his hand down his red silk tie. "Why did Jennifer leave the river early that night?"

"She was hammered. She could barely stand up."

"Where did she live?"

"About a half mile from Pony Pasture, not far from Gina. Knew the area like the back of her hand."

"Did she see anything? Did she have any new information for you?"

"No."

"How did she get home?"

"Ashley, her sister, picked her up."

"So Ashley was also there?"

"Ashley dropped her sister off and then later returned to get her. I remember the Ralston family car pulling up. Jennifer said she didn't remember anything after getting in the car."

"And you saw Ashley?"

"I assumed it was Ashley." She frowned. "I can't say for sure, but Jennifer confirmed it was her sister when I interviewed her."

"Have you spoken to Ashley since you returned? Did you interview her?"

"No. I haven't gotten to her yet."

He studied her. "Does this tape include all your interviews?"

"No."

"Why not?"

Honesty was her new policy thanks to AA. She didn't like it. Old habits died hard. "Because you're a cop. And I don't trust cops."

"Why not?"

76

"Go back and read the case files. Watch my interviews with Detective North. He pretended to be on my side. And then he leaked my name to the press and denied it because I was a minor. My life turned to shit after that."

"He leaned on you."

"He was certain I knew more than I did. He thought the media would tear the truth out of me."

"And?"

"Can't get blood out of a turnip."

Adler seemed to weigh and measure all her answers. He didn't trust her either. Smart man. "I would have done the same thing."

"When you work out something with Hayward, let me know."

"*When?* You speak as if it's a done deal."

"Detective Adler, you strike me as the kind of guy who moves fast."

Not rising to the bait, he asked, "Hayward will get a visit from me before any deal is proposed. Where are you parked?"

"Up there."

"I'll walk you to your car, again."

The words were polite, but his tone made it clear he wasn't asking but telling. Though she bristled, she fought the urge to argue. He'd said he'd look into it. And, despite her better judgment, she believed him. Acceptance allowed her to ease her white-knuckle grip on control.

He slowed his pace as he walked her to her car. The afternoon air was soft, and a delicate breeze from the river rustled the budding branches. It could have been a moment easily enjoyed if only they weren't a half block from a murder scene, he weren't a cop, and she weren't paranoid.

He waited as she opened the door to her car and slid into the seat. She closed the door and quickly turned on the engine while rolling her window down.

"Whoever did this to Jennifer could be watching," he said, leaning close to her so only she could hear.

"Why would anyone be watching? She's dead."

"He was keeping tabs on her."

"She had a stalker?"

"Maybe. This kind of guy gets his rocks off not only following his victim, but also monitoring the cops during an investigation. I suggest you be careful."

She'd spent the last fourteen years being careful because she feared the unseen. And she was damn tired of hiding. "I'll keep it in mind. But I'm making my podcast. I need to make it, now more than ever."

"Why?"

She didn't answer right away. "You really want to know?"

"Do I look like I'm being polite?"

"No."

"I'm not."

"Whatever happened to Gina sent ripples through so many families. None of us—Jennifer, Erika, or me, our families and friends—were ever the same after she vanished. Time doesn't heal all wounds."

"That's your only motivation?"

"You think I'm holding back?"

"I don't see the other interview tapes."

"When you get Gina's case file, can I read it?"

He shook his head, no hints of apology in his expression. "You're on the wrong side of the blue line."

"I'm aware."

He patted the top of her car. "In the meantime, suspend your podcast interviews until I can figure out what or if anything links Jennifer's murder to Gina's disappearance."

Smiling, she shook her head. She wasn't stopping, and if anything she was more motivated than ever to find Gina. "I'll take it under consideration, Detective."

INTERVIEW FILE #7

ONCE A LAWMAN, ALWAYS A LAWMAN

Thursday, February 15, 2018; 11:00 a.m.

ONCE A LAWMAN, ALWAYS A LAWMAN. The saying is burned into driftwood and hangs over retired missing-persons detective Joshua North's bed at the Oak Croft Retirement Center. The room is bathed in beige except for a lone bouquet of wilting red, white, and blue balloons in a corner. A piece of untouched chocolate cake, sporting a tilting, unlit candle, sits on the small table beside Detective North's recliner. It's his seventy-eighth birthday.

As he does every day, he insists on shaving and donning his khakis and pressed white shirt that is now his unofficial "uniform." It's important he proves to himself he's the same man who retired from the department thirteen years ago. A year after Gina Mason vanished.

Time has mellowed some of my anger toward this man. But in full disclosure, I will never forgive what he did. I balance my own slice of cake, trying not to notice his hollowed cheeks and sunken eyes. It's easier to hold on to anger when I picture him taller and stronger. Like the cake, this man had seen better days.

"Thank you for seeing me." I steady the dessert plate on my knees.

I first met North in the emergency room fourteen years ago. I was still intoxicated and so agitated by the trauma of seeing Gina taken, I could barely sit still. When he pushed open the curtain of my examination cubicle, I felt protected. I needed help, and I thought it was him. He found people. He could end this nightmare.

I could easily underestimate him now, until I look behind the thick silver-rimmed glasses and see sharp blue eyes staring back.

"I haven't seen you in a long time. Kaitlin Roe, right?"

"You remember me."

"Your hair is different. A little older, but I remember you and Gina Mason. Her kind of case haunts cops." His eyes never leave me. "What have you been up to?"

"College. Film degree. Thought I'd move to LA and make films but was hired by a Dallas PR firm to make commercials. Life got comfortable. Time passed."

All true. What I don't mention are the panic attacks, the drinking, and finally a desperate outreach to AA.

"Why are you doing this interview?"

"I want to find Gina. Maybe if someone hears my podcast, they'll remember something and speak up."

"Don't be so sure everyone's going to be happy about this project. Politicians, cops, the people who became obsessed with her—none of 'em want you digging up the past."

"I couldn't care less. It's time."

Police searches went on for months after Gina vanished. There were hundreds of tips that led nowhere. Some were cruel hoaxes, others were cases of mistaken identity, and even a few psychics called. Gina's mother was still visiting psychics and tarot-card readers until her death. The media produced first-, fifth-, and tenth-anniversary stories. But all the leads and exposure took the case nowhere.

"I lost track of the man-hours I invested. We all busted our butts trying to find her. Have you recently talked to the cops?"

"The case is technically still open, so no one will speak to me. I've *lost track* of how many messages I left."

He doesn't look bothered by my frustration. "I'm surprised you came to see me. You hated me."

"I'm still not fond of you. But I want to find Gina."

He presses against the pillows supporting his back. "Did you ever remember anything more about that night?"

I hear the challenge behind his words. "Not more than I did fourteen years ago. I've tried, but I can't fill in all the pieces."

Detective North brushes imaginary lint from his creased sleeve. "Don't beat yourself up. I know I was rough on you."

"Why didn't you believe me?"

"Too many holes in your story. Her blood was on your shirt. Your failed memory. Your relationship with Randy."

"Randy's back in jail on murder charges."

"I know. I keep up." He sighs. "I leaned hard on him. I wanted to keep pressing, but finally had to settle. The guy never wavered from his story, and his parents were connected and had money. He was arrested for burglarizing a home in his parents' neighborhood a few nights before Gina vanished. He got seven years for that conviction. To this day, I believe I got my man when I arrested him. Sometimes you lose and take what you can get. No way he'll skate this time."

CHAPTER SIX

Friday, March 16, 2018; 3:00 p.m.

Kaitlin had never been good at taking instruction, especially from cops. She'd learned firsthand no one was really safe no matter how carefully they played it. She parked at the end of the gravel driveway and studied the brick home covered in ivy and surrounded by boxwoods. It looked as she had remembered. A little digging had told her Randy's mother, Ruth, still lived here.

Out of the car, pad and recorder in her purse, Kaitlin knocked on the door. Through its glass panes, she saw the flicker of movement before footsteps sounded in the hallway. The door opened to an older woman with sweeping white hair who was dressed in a flowing cream-colored shirt, black slacks, and flats. Her makeup was immaculate, and she wore a strand of pearls with a diamond clasp.

"Yes?"

"Mrs. Hayward?"

"That's right."

"I went to school with your son, Randy. My name is Kaitlin Roe."

The smile vanished. "What are you doing here?"

Good to be remembered. "I went to see Randy earlier today."

"Why?"

Kaitlin adjusted the backpack on her shoulder. "I'm making a podcast. I'm trying to draw attention to the Gina Mason disappearance."

A neatly painted brow rose. "I'd think you'd want to forget what happened to your cousin."

"I tried. I can't."

Mrs. Hayward shook her head. "I've worked hard to put that time behind me, and I'm not interested in opening old wounds again." She moved to close the door.

Kaitlin blocked it with her hand. "I'm not here with a grievance. I have a couple of questions about Randy. Honestly, I just want to find Gina."

Mrs. Hayward didn't try to shove her. "You're not the first reporter to contact me."

"I'm not really a reporter. I'm looking for Gina. I might not ever find her, but at least she won't be forgotten."

"People don't want to remember."

"It's not a matter of what they want."

Her eyes narrowed. "You dated Randy for a couple of months. How old were you? Sixteen?"

"Yes."

"A girl that age had no business dating a twenty-one-year-old man." She shook her head. "I remember seeing you with him. You looked at him with adoration."

"I was young and foolish."

"Yes, you were."

"I remember you told me to stay clear of him. I wouldn't listen."

"No, you didn't. And I should have told your aunt about what was going on, but I didn't want the trouble." Her head cocked a fraction. "Do you still have a soft spot for Randy?"

"No. This has nothing to do with him."

"Good. Because I don't have any more love left for him. He isn't worth it."

Kaitlin sensed a small opening. "But you didn't believe that then. You thought you could save him. I know you fought hard to keep Randy out of prison fourteen years ago. I know you loved him."

She fiddled with a silver bracelet banding her slim wrist. "I'm his mother. It's natural for me to try and save my child."

"It must hurt to know he's back in jail now and facing the death penalty."

"I gave up on Randy a long time ago. He's called me several times since his last mishap, but I've not taken his calls."

Randy's mother had always brushed off her son's violent tendencies as misfortunes or bits of trouble. Kaitlin fought back bitterness. "I only care about Gina."

A large diamond ring dwarfed her arthritic finger. "Do you think this podcast will make the police take a second look at Randy? Are they going to try to prove he hurt that girl?"

As handy as a lie would be, Kaitlin reached for the truth when she could. "I want the police to take another look at her case. And if that means looking at Randy again, then so be it."

Mrs. Hayward drew in a breath and stepped aside, creating more space in the doorway. "Come inside. I only have a few minutes."

"Great. Thank you."

Kaitlin followed Mrs. Hayward into a living room designed with a large bank of windows that were decorated in floral silk drapes. The lot was wooded and sloped straight to Riverside Drive. A few buds clung to the branches, but none had blossomed. The river and road were visible now, but shortly all the foliage would bloom, making it nearly impossible to see the road. By her calculation, Mrs. Hayward's house was a quarter mile from the spot where Gina was taken.

Mrs. Hayward lowered herself into a wingback chair. "You were with that poor girl when she vanished."

Kaitlin sat in a chair beside the older woman and angled her body toward her. "Yes, when she was abducted."

"You didn't identify Randy in the lineup."

"The man who took Gina was wearing a mask. And as you may have heard, I was drunk."

"I heard." She drew in a breath and slowly let it out. "I heard you were the one who spiked the bottle of lemonade the girls were passing around."

That wasn't true. Yet everyone believed the former drug addict had not only provided the booze but also loaded it with Ecstasy. She'd done worse before in Texas, but not to Gina. "Would you believe me if I denied it?"

"I'm not sure anymore." Mrs. Hayward pursed her lips. "Why were you so sure it wasn't Randy?"

"I wasn't. I just couldn't say it *was* Randy. I couldn't send him to prison for life unless I was certain he'd done it."

The older woman rubbed a twisted arthritic thumb against her smooth palm. "I wish you had identified him. I wish to God you had. Even if you had lied, I'd have understood."

Kaitlin allowed the silence to hang between them.

"Randy was difficult as a baby. Maybe his father and I spoiled him because we wanted him to be happy, but no matter what we gave him, it was never enough."

Randy was good at using people and making them feel guilty when they didn't give him everything he wanted. Kaitlin had gotten free of him, and it appeared his mother was doing the same. "He made me feel the same."

"I suppose we have that in common." The older woman stared at Kaitlin for a long moment. "I'm not taking his calls this time. I'm not helping him again."

Kaitlin didn't respond, sensing the woman had more to say.

"Randy dated every girl at Saint Mathew's at one point. He liked them pretty and young." She plucked at an imaginary thread on her pants. "But Gina always said no to him. That girl won points in my book. At first he took her rejection in stride, but as he got older, it bothered him more and more."

"Why? Do you think it was his drug problem?"

"The meth and heroin made him paranoid. He started to take everything harder and had terrible mood swings." She shook her head. "Listen to me talking about such drugs so casually. When I first heard about them, I had to go to the library and look them up."

"They're insidious."

"I thought Randy would grow up. He had barely finished his second year of college and was on academic probation. His father and I wanted him to get serious about school. But he liked to play. He liked his drugs. He liked the girls." She absently stared at a painting of herself and Randy as a young mother and son. "The cops asked me if Randy knew Gina well."

"You told them he didn't know her that well."

Her brows knotted, and she slowly expelled a breath. "I thought I could save him. I thought if I gave him one more chance, he'd straighten out his life. So I told the police he didn't know her."

"But he did know her. Several of her friends knew he wanted to go out with her and she rejected him."

She shrugged. "Hearsay from a bunch of teenagers looking for some fame and attention. I knew my boy better than anyone, and I made that clear to the police."

"If you knew him so well, then you knew he didn't like hearing no."

She was silent for a moment. The habit of guarding old secrets was hard to break. "With Gina, he had met his match. It made him mad when she ignored him. I never told anyone, not even his father, but her rebuffs made him want her even more." Mrs. Hayward suddenly looked vulnerable. "What did he say when you went to see him?"

Kaitlin slowly folded a sheet of notebook paper, buying time before saying, "He says he knows where Gina is."

Mrs. Hayward's serene face crumpled, revealing raw pain. She raised a trembling hand and pressed it against closed eyes, until finally she opened them. Watery blue eyes reflected a blend of sadness and unchecked anger. "Randy is a liar. You know that."

"I do. I've reminded myself a dozen times in the last few hours. But he knew details no one else did."

"What details?"

"I don't think I can say," Kaitlin said.

"Why not?"

"The police are looking into it."

Mrs. Hayward tipped her head, holding back tears desperate to spill. Her lips trembled before she steadied herself and met Kaitlin's gaze. "Don't let him use Gina to get out of this latest charge. He used me more times than I can remember. I had hoped time in prison would make him a better man, but it's made him even more evil."

"Do you know about the current charges against him?"

"I keep track. If I hadn't helped him after Gina vanished, there would have been less suffering in the world for all of us, you included."

"What was he like around the time Gina vanished? Did he act more jumpy than usual?"

"He rarely slept then. I would hear him come in at all hours, and when he was here he was either watching television or pacing. I soon learned that meth could keep him up for a week or more. He spent a lot of time in the garden shed."

"Did you ever look in the shed?"

"Yes. One day he left the house in such a rage. Randy was in one of his moods, and it scared me. I went to the shed, thinking I'd find his drugs. I was going to destroy them."

"What did you find?"

"Nothing. I remember feeling so relieved." She twisted a pearl earring.

"Is the shed still there?"

"I had it demolished ten years ago."

If Gina had been in the shed, the evidence was long gone. "I remember Randy was close to Derek Blackstone and Brad Crowley."

Mrs. Hayward rose and moved to a Queen Anne desk, opened a bottom drawer, and removed a framed picture. She smoothed her hand over the image. "It was easy to love Randy then. He was so funny. So charming." She looked up. "That little boy died a long time ago." She handed the picture to Kaitlin. "Here he is with Brad and Derek. By the time Gina went missing, those two had moved on with their lives, whereas Randy was stealing my silver for drugs."

Kaitlin studied the image of the three boys who were standing in front of a fifth-grade graduation banner. "They all went to Saint Mathew's, didn't they?"

"Yes. Graduated with Randy. Did you hear Brad became a plastic surgeon?"

"Yes. He married Erika Travis."

"Does Erika seem . . . happy with Brad?"

"Hard to say. We only spoke briefly."

"Derek is a very successful lawyer. He called me after Randy's latest arrest. I didn't answer the phone, but he left a message. He wanted me to know he would protect Randy."

"How?"

"I supposed he'd act as his lawyer." Instead of explaining more, she shifted the topic, saying, "I heard about Jennifer on the news. Terrible."

"Yes."

"Randy couldn't have killed Jennifer." The mother still couldn't resist defending her son.

"No." Kaitlin scribbled down the names of Randy's friends. "Do you mind if I snap a picture of this?" she asked.

"Sure."

Kaitlin took several pictures of the smiling boys with her phone. "Thank you, Mrs. Hayward. Do you want me to call if I find out anything?"

Her lips thinned. "No, child. I don't want to know. Goodbye."

***

Kaitlin had not revisited the spot by the river since she left Richmond fourteen years ago. Returning now was harder than she'd imagined. Her chest tightened and her hands trembled as she stood on the narrow road hugging the river just under Mrs. Hayward's house.

The afternoon sun cast a warm glow on the rippling water lazily drifting past large rocks. The warmth of the sun took the edge off the cold and blustery air as she walked toward the outcropping of boulders that would be packed with sunbathers in only a few months. It looked so peaceful. So innocent.

She closed her eyes. The soothing sounds of nature grew silent in the wake of Gina's screams. Her cries. And when she opened her eyes, for a brief second, she saw the menacing clown mask.

Every fiber in her demanded she run now.

Run, Kaitlin. Run.

Her fingers curled into fists.

Breathless, she retraced the same path she had walked with Gina. She hugged the shoulder of the narrow road, remembering as an occasional car came flying by full of kids not paying attention. With each step, she felt the pull of the past.

"You're such a bitch, Gina. Can't you wait up?"

"Hurry up."

"God, I hate you."

Kaitlin was now a half mile from Pony Pasture and standing at the spot. Her heart pounded as fragmented memories rushed her from all sides.

The knife to Gina's throat and then her ear. Gina's screams. The blood. The seconds when she didn't remember but must have stood in shock and utter denial that this could be happening. A memory of those missing moments reached out and teased her, but it quickly drifted away. Why couldn't she remember?

A car drove by, and she sidestepped into a line of trees separating the river from the road. To steady herself on the sloping bank, she placed her hand on one of the trees. Its broken branch scratched her palm, and in an instant a memory emerged.

It was Gina's abductor. *"I told you I'd come for you, Gina."*

She closed her eyes and replayed the words that until now had remained locked in her subconscious. Was she remembering Randy's voice? She focused, trying to trigger more memories. She waited. Listened. But instead, the sounds of the river and wind in the trees came back.

Frustrated, she headed back to her car. "I'll make this right, Gina."

***

Adler was still processing Kaitlin's comments from their meeting as he dialed his phone. In the light of day, she had looked softer, not quite as tough as he'd first thought the night before. She had opened up to him a little, but still kept him at arm's length.

Trey Ricker with the Commonwealth Attorney's office didn't pick up. Adler wasn't surprised when it rolled to voicemail. "Trey, this is Adler. Got an idea to run past you about an inmate named Randy Hayward. Call me. Thanks."

He checked his watch. The Gina Mason case file should be on his desk by morning. In the meantime, he had the grim task of attending Jennifer Ralston's autopsy.

The drive along Broad Street from Church Hill into the heart of the city took less than ten minutes. He parked in front of the state medical examiner's building on East Jackson Street and made his way into the gray granite office. The state offices usually were closing by now, but given the nature of this crime, the medical examiner assigned to the case had agreed to expedite the examination of Jennifer Ralston. He rode the elevator to the basement.

A weight had settled on his shoulders as he pictured Jennifer lying lifeless in her shower. It never got easier. He knew the day it did, he needed to pack it in.

Adler stripped off his jacket and pulled on a set of scrubs. He found Quinn already gowned up at the foot of a gurney holding a sheet-clad figure. At the head of the table was Dr. Tessa McGowan, one of the pathologists who worked for the state medical examiner's office. Dr. McGowan was the newest to the team, but she'd quickly established herself as a top-notch professional. She stood a few inches over five foot and had a trim build kept fit by hiking and running. Black hair peeked out from her surgical cap, framing large expressive eyes. In her early thirties, she was also married to an agent with the state police.

"Detective Adler. We were just getting started," Dr. McGowan said as she pulled on latex gloves.

"Sorry for the delay. I went by the murder scene again to revisit a few observations."

Without looking at Quinn, he could tell she was expecting him to comment further. She would have to wait.

Dr. McGowan slid on protective eye gear and nodded to her assistant, a tall, slim man also gowned up. He pulled back the sheet to reveal Jennifer Ralston's pale nude body.

Adler mentally distanced himself. He couldn't think of her as a person. Her body was evidence now and demanded his full attention. The remains would tell the story of her death and possibly her killer's identity.

The victim's head rested in a cradle, her chin slightly tipped up to expose her neck. This position showcased the wound slicing deep across the neck and traveling over the jugular. Her blond hair, brushed back, accentuated the pallid face sprinkled with a dozen freckles over the bridge of the nose. The jaw was slack, the lips a faint blue.

Dr. McGowan tugged the overhead microphone a couple of inches toward her and began the autopsy with an external examination. She noted the injuries to the neck and abdomen and inventoried specific details. The first were the tattoos, including a peace sign on the underside of her wrist, and on her left hip the letters *GM* encircled by a heart. GM had to mean Gina Mason, and the heart resembled the one he'd found on the notes and her shower wall. On the right knee was a faint two-inch scar.

Dr. McGowan then reviewed a series of X-rays with the detectives. "She does have an old spiral fracture on her right wrist. It healed years ago but is likely attributable to someone or something twisting her arm so badly it broke."

"Any estimate on how long ago?" Adler asked.

"A dozen years perhaps." Dr. McGowan noted Jennifer Ralston by all appearances had been a healthy thirty-two-year-old woman.

Quinn shifted her stance but gave no other signal that the autopsy might have been bothering her.

Dr. McGowan peered up at the detective but said nothing. "Victim was stabbed five times. Three to her abdomen, once on her left forearm, which appears to be a defensive wound, and finally the strike that killed her, a slice through the jugular."

"The arterial blood spray on her shower walls supports the theory her heart was pumping when he inflicted the neck wound," Adler said.

"If you note the angles of the cuts, they all appear to slice downward." She curled her fingers into a fist and made a downward motion, simulating a knife strike. "Her killer was likely taller, or she may have fallen to the floor before the wounds were inflicted."

"She's what, five foot seven?" Adler asked.

"And a half," Dr. McGowan noted.

"She could have been sitting in the shower to shave her legs," Quinn said.

Adler arched a brow but didn't comment.

Quinn shrugged. "You try standing in a shower stall and shaving your legs. I dare you."

Dr. McGowan smiled. "Walk away, Detective Adler."

"Not touching it," he surrendered.

For anyone not in law enforcement, this gallows humor sounded callous. But humor helped cops blow off steam and mentally process the violence.

"No indication of drug use." Dr. McGowan grew serious again as she held up one of the victim's pale arms. "However, if you notice, there's faint scarring on the inside of her left bicep. As I go over the body I'll look for more scars like this."

"She's a cutter?" Quinn asked.

Dr. McGowan pointed out several more identical cuts on the inside of the left thigh. "I'd say she was at one time. These folks typically injure areas that won't impede their daily activities too much. They also choose areas easily covered by clothing so they can hide their habit. She must have decided the arms were too obvious. She also chose her left side exclusively. I assume she was right-handed."

"Cutting is supposed to relieve stress," Adler said.

"I spoke to the physician's assistant who prescribed the meds we found in her medicine cabinet," Quinn said. "The NP said Jennifer was visibly upset when they met in January."

"Did she say why Jennifer was upset?" Adler asked.

"Jennifer said she had bad taste in men. Had just gone through a breakup."

"Wasn't that Jeremy Keller last year?"

"I asked her, but I sensed this was a new guy," Quinn said. "The new guy didn't have a name."

Dr. McGowan positioned the body for a vaginal swab and examination. Adler didn't avert his gaze but found anger bubbling as he thought about the methodical stripping away of her dignity.

After the exam was complete, Dr. McGowan said, "There are no signs of pregnancy. There're also no traces of vaginal bruising or semen. She hasn't had intercourse recently."

That confirmed what Adler had hoped was true. "She hadn't been raped."

"Still believe this was sexually motivated?" Quinn asked Adler.

"The excitement for stalkers comes from watching," he said. "As far as they're concerned, they already share an intimate connection with their victim. And now only he shares her last moments alive."

"But most stalkers don't take it this far," Quinn said. "What was the trigger that ramped up the violence?"

It could be an imagined slight, job loss, or even something as simple as a wrong order in a restaurant. "Your guess is as good as mine, Detective. What about DNA?" Adler asked.

"The lab is testing the tulips left under the bed," Quinn said. "The chances are slim, but he might have arranged them before he put on his gloves and suit."

Dr. McGowan rolled the body to its side. "Swirl tattoo at the base of the spine, and more razor-thin scars on the underside of the left thigh. These cuts are still red and look fresh. I'd say these were done in the last six months."

He thought about the picture of the smiling girl with her friends by the river and how the album ended abruptly. He recalled Kaitlin saying so many people weren't the same after Gina.

"Several of the fingernails on her right hand are broken," the doctor said, inspecting French manicured nails. "These appear to be defensive wounds."

"Perhaps there will be DNA under the nails," Quinn said.

"There was a scratch on Jeremy's arm," Adler noted.

"And we didn't see his entire body," Quinn said.

Dr. McGowan inspected the remaining fingernails closely, scraped out samples from under two of them, and handed both off to her assistant. "You might have DNA to test."

She selected a scalpel from the instrument tray and pressed the tip against the pale skin at the base of the breastbone. With practiced skill, she slid the knife tip between and then under the breasts. She then sliced straight down to the abdomen, creating a Y-incision. Carefully the flesh was pulled away, exposing the ribs. She reached for bolt cutters and snapped each rib until the cage released and then set the cutters aside.

"The heart, lungs, liver, and kidneys all appear to be in excellent shape," she said. "All the stab wounds missed vital organs. All these injuries were survivable."

She removed the organs and set each on the scale for weight and measurement. Once they were catalogued, she dissected the stomach and examined the contents. "The victim ate within hours of dying so the food isn't completely digested. Victim's last meal appears to be chicken and salad, which are partially digested, so I estimate lunch was her last meal. She also ingested wine."

"There was an open bottle in the kitchen. It was half-full," Adler said.

"She had about ten ounces," Dr. McGowan said.

"She pours a glass in the kitchen, consumes most of it, and then refills."

"The cork was not in the bottle," Quinn said. "She was planning to drink more."

"Liquid courage to listen to Kaitlin's presentation?" Adler said, almost to himself.

Dr. McGowan repacked the organs in the body and sutured the chest cavity. She then made incisions on the side of her victim's neck to expose the jugular. A clean cut had severed it. "As I suspected, this was the lethal wound. Once the killer severed this artery, she would have bled out in a matter of minutes. It explains the massive amount of blood loss as well as the arterial spray on the shower walls."

No one spoke for a moment, before Adler asked, "Anything else you can tell us about her or her killer?"

"I'll run toxicology screens, which will take a few weeks. The nail samples will be sent to the state forensic lab."

"Thanks, Dr. McGowan," Quinn said.

Adler nodded his thanks, turned from the body, and left the room. As he stripped off his gown, a primal urge rose up in him. He looked forward to hunting down this son of a bitch.

Quinn pushed through the double doors. "You look as pissed as I feel."

He pulled out his phone and showed her the picture of the four girls by the river. "Found this in an album hidden in her house."

Quinn frowned as she studied the image. "I barely remember this case. I was working as a summer lifeguard, and my mother heard about it. It freaked her out so badly she called me at work. Told me the world was full of wackos." She shook her head. "Always listen to Mother."

"Didn't you say once your mom was part of the reason you became a cop?"

They'd known each other almost a year, but Quinn never discussed her mother. "Partly."

Adler picked up on the awkward reply and pivoted. "There were notes that appear to be communication from a stalker."

"But Ashley said there were no notes," Quinn said.

"They were hidden in a drawer."

"What do they say?"

"Nothing threatening. All beginning with 'My Girl' and each signed with a heart. I should have the Gina Mason files first thing in the morning. I'll check through them and see if there's anything that ties back to the Ralston case."

"Do you really think the two cases are connected?" Quinn asked.

"I don't have any evidence, but it's just too damn odd that a young girl is taken and likely murdered, and then one of the three girls to see her last is brutally stabbed."

"Someone doubled back to kill her after fourteen years?" She shook her head. "That is one heck of a long shot."

"I know." Adler then updated his partner on Kaitlin's visit to Hayward. "He says he can tell us where Gina is. He may have proof."

"He's manipulating Kaitlin, and she's too naive or emotionally attached to know otherwise."

"I hear you. It's likely a rabbit hole, but I'll check it out anyway."

She shook her head. "You've got a better chance of playing the lottery."

"But you still scratch the ticket, don't you?"

She muttered a curse. "The first lie out of that con's mouth, you need to walk away, John."

"Great minds think alike."

INTERVIEW FILE #8

Eyewitness Testimony

The worst evidence is eyewitness testimony. Many people believe the human brain functions like a recorder. However, psychologists have proven it's simply not true. We humans, in fact, recreate rather than play back recollections. We piece together the puzzle of the past with fragmented facts, stresses, biases, hopes, and emotions. The Innocence Project researchers reported that of the convictions overturned through DNA testing, over 70 percent had been based on eyewitness testimony. We want to remember, but most of us suck at it.

CHAPTER SEVEN

Friday, March 16, 2018; 7:45 p.m.

When Adler reached his desk, he discovered a large dusty binder. A quick look at the spine and he saw the label: **MASON, GINA, AUGUST 15, 2004**.

His office was in a small cubicle, offering him the illusion of privacy. Fluorescent lights hummed above his head and mingled with the buzz of conversations. There were a half-dozen detectives busy chasing leads. Others were on their computers tackling the everyday paperwork that cops had to slug through. How many nights had he wished to hell he could get away from this place when a homicide investigation ground on for days at a stretch?

Now after the bombing, he was so damn glad to be back.

He shrugged off his coat and draped it over his seat. Slowly he rolled up his sleeves and sat at his computer. He unwrapped a cold vending machine sandwich and took his first bite as he flipped the book open to Gina's high school portrait, the same one Kaitlin had used for her presentation. Dark hair swept over a round face glowing with a summer tan. White pearls circled her neck. She was beaming with youth and excitement. Alive.

"Jesus," he muttered. "I feel old."

He flipped through more pages and came upon a DVD. It read **Detective Joshua North interviewing Kaitlin Roe, October 4, 2004**. He popped it in his computer and took another bite of his meal.

Kaitlin appeared, leaning back in a metal chair, her elbow resting on its arm. Her chin was raised, giving her a stoic expression. Detective North entered the room and dropped a file on the metal table. She flinched slightly, but recovered her composure.

"You know what I think, Kaitlin," he said. *"I think you're a liar. A really good one at that."*

Adler checked the date. October 4, 2004. A little over two months into the investigation.

Kaitlin folded her arms over her chest. *"Aren't I supposed to have a lawyer?"*

"You aren't detained. You can leave anytime."

"Really?" She rose. *"Then I'll leave."*

"I thought we were having a friendly conversation here."

She faced him. *"You released my name to the press. I can't go into a McDonald's without someone asking what I did to Gina."*

"We've tried to play nice with you, but you've not been cooperative."

"He was wearing a mask!"

Despite her bravado, she was young and dealing with a seasoned homicide detective. North knew exactly how to push her buttons.

"Tell me what you do remember," North said.

"I already have."

"One more time. I'm getting old, and I don't remember so well."

Her eyes narrowed. *"We were by the river."*

"You, Gina, Erika, and Jennifer."

"That's right."

"Why were you there?"

"It was a celebration. The other girls were leaving for college soon." Her fists clenched.

"And you girls were drinking."

"Yes."

"We never found the bottle."

She didn't answer.

"Kaitlin, at this stage underage drinking is the least of your worries."

"I threw it in the river. It floated away."

"Did you spike it with Ecstasy?"

"No."

"Are you sure? I have your arrest records from Texas. You got yourself into some trouble, little lady. You strike me as someone who can get ahold of almost any substance."

"I didn't spike the bottle."

North opened his file and seemed to read something. *"You said you and Gina were walking to her house. That the other girls had left you."*

"Yes."

"What happened next?"

She pressed her fingers to her forehead. *"I was having trouble walking. I was drunk and kept tripping on my flip-flops. Gina got too far ahead of me, and I lost sight of her in the dark. That's when I thought I sensed something wrong. I ran ahead and was right. I saw him standing next to Gina."*

"Who?"

"The man with the clown mask holding a knife to Gina's neck."

"What did he say to you?"

She closed her eyes. *"He cut off her ear, and then he told me to run."*

"And you ran?"

Her answer wasn't audible, and North asked her to repeat it.

"I must have turned and run."

"How did her blood get on your T-shirt?"

"I don't remember."

If Adler had not been watching closely, he'd have missed Kaitlin's hesitation. Was it guilt? Pain? Anger? A lie?

"I know you're lying, Kaitlin. I think you spiked the drink with narcotics. Maybe you wanted everyone to have a real good time. Maybe you

wanted to mess with them. And you did. But the fun and games ended when something happened to Gina. Did she overdose?"

She folded her arms over her chest. *"It wasn't like that!"*

"Okay, Gina didn't overdose. But someone found you girls, and that cocktail is the reason all of you were so incapacitated and could barely walk, let alone defend yourselves. I'm amazed you all didn't drown in the river."

She didn't speak.

North was silent for a moment. *"You know what I think?"*

"I can't wait."

North smiled. *"I think you and Hayward were working together. I think he told you to spike the lemonade so Gina and the other girls would be too messed up to resist anything he wanted to try. Hell, you're twisted."*

"No!"

"He broke up with you, but you still loved him. I bet you'd have done anything to get with him."

Kaitlin shook her head. *"I didn't hurt Gina."*

"Sweetie, you drugged her. Made her defenseless. Hell of a friend you are."

Kaitlin's expression crumpled as if she'd been slapped across the face. *"I didn't do it."*

"You're complicit. Now all I have to do is prove it. And I will. Why don't you save us both a lot of time and tell me. If you had a conscience, you'd feel better, too."

Kaitlin rose. *"I'm leaving."*

"I'm just clowning around," he smirked.

"Go fuck yourself."

Adler rewound the DVD and froze it on the last expression the camera caught of her face. Raw pain was carved in the lines around her eyes and mouth. But he'd seen murderers feel deep remorse. It was possible to love someone, kill them in a moment of rage, and then mourn their loss.

And now Kaitlin was back in Richmond hooking up with her old boyfriend. It had come full circle, and Hayward was right in the middle of it.

INTERVIEW FILE #9

THE GIRLS OF SUMMER—JENNIFER RALSTON

Thursday, February 22, 2018; 7:00 p.m.

Jennifer Ralston sits perched on the loft apartment stool, her booted heels locked behind the stool's footrest. She looks around the city apartment, studying the exposed brick, unfinished dusty rafters, and tall framed windows overlooking the James River and the city's north side. In her hands, she cradles an RVA mug filled with hot green tea. Though Gina paid the ultimate price, we each lost a piece of ourselves that night.

"Is the microphone rolling?" Jennifer looks at my recorder.

"Yes."

"Is it cold in here, or is it me?"

"I know this room can be drafty. Can I get you a blanket?" I start to get up.

"I'm fine. I'm always chilled. A quirk, I guess."

"Why are you always cold?"

"I don't know. I haven't felt warm or safe since Gina's disappearance. I probably should have gotten counseling, but my mother thought seeing a shrink was a sign of weakness. I'm an adult now and know what Mom said is BS. And I'm not weak."

"No, you're not." I smile in what I hope is a reassuring way.

"Did you get help?"

"I did. But only last year."

"Why did you wait so long?"

"I wish I knew. I packed my life with activity to dull the pain. To forget. I finally realized if I didn't drop the baggage, it would consume me."

"So you decided to undertake your own investigation as a catharsis?"

"That's right." Pages flip in my notebook. "Jennifer, what do you remember about Gina?"

Jennifer's laugh is lighter. "The usual. Nicest girl. So popular. Always a kind word. I used to joke if you looked *perfect* up in the dictionary, you'd see her face."

"What were we talking about that night?"

"You should know. You didn't drink at first."

The point of me coming to Virginia was to get sober. I was just trying to keep it together. Not drink. But the temptation was too great. And in all honesty, I didn't like sobriety and all the memories it didn't suppress.

"Teenage girls. We must have been talking about boys."

"I suppose. That night is still a blur for me. Whatever we were drinking was loaded."

I hesitate. "You and Erika told the cops I brought the spiked lemonade."

I see her visibly stiffen, and she doesn't respond.

"I'm not trying to get anyone into trouble. I just want to find Gina."

A long silence. Finally she answers.

"Yeah, I brought it."

"It made sense to blame me. I was the most likely to, right?"

"Something like that."

"Did you spike it with Ecstasy?"

"No! I didn't. And I don't know who did."

I believe Jennifer on this one, happy at least one lie about me has been dispelled. But I don't dwell. This isn't about me. "You called your sister to come pick you up, right?"

"That's right. I could barely walk. So Ashley drove down to the river and picked me up. Erika hopped in the back with me at the last second."

"Do you remember anything else?"

"Lying in the backseat of the car. My sister was pissed."

"At you?"

"Someone else." Jennifer looks confident about this. "I think she was arguing with someone on the phone."

"Who?"

"I don't know. I assumed it was her boyfriend, because they fought a lot. But I passed out and didn't wake up until the next morning. I was in my own bed and wearing the clothes I had on from the night before, but I have no memory of arriving home. The cops were at our house, and all hell was about to break loose."

CHAPTER EIGHT

Saturday, March 17, 2018; 5:45 a.m.

Near-freezing rain dripped on the windshield as he parked across from Erika Travis Crowley's big white house. This upscale neighborhood didn't really stir until about six thirty, and a rain-delayed Saturday slowed them all the more.

However, Erika kept to a rigid, eerily predictable schedule. She didn't leave her house very often, but on Saturdays she exited her front door at exactly the same time and made the three-mile drive to the small yoga studio. She found comfort in keeping her world contained. Her house was her fortress from the truth. She'd betrayed Gina.

A check of his watch showed it was almost showtime.

Killing Jennifer had been exhilarating, and his body still buzzed with adrenaline. He readily accepted it was his job to dish out her punishment, but he'd not expected to enjoy it so much.

It was smarter to wait before he dealt with Erika and Kaitlin, but the morning rain was too perfect to pass up. Rain washed away so many sins. Better to deal with them now. He'd punish Erika accordingly, and for Kaitlin he had a special windowless room.

The front door snapped open. Black yoga pants and a fitted blue top covered by a snug gray jacket silhouetted a body kept ruthlessly in shape. Socks and clogs warmed her feet. Blond hair was tied into a sleek ponytail reminiscent of her times as part of the Glittering Trio at Saint Mathew's. Gina, Jennifer, and Erika had been at the peak of the school's social pecking order, and they knew it.

As he inched lower, the torn vinyl on the seat rubbed against his T-shirt. The magnetic sign on the side of the truck read TURNER PLUMBING. The letters were in red, a color easily remembered if anyone were watching. He'd stolen the truck and would soon ditch it.

Erika's Mercedes pulled out of the driveway, and he followed. He watched her race through a yellow light and then turn abruptly at the corner ahead.

He stayed several car lengths behind, careful to keep her in his sights. He knew where she was going, but today it was important he be there when she arrived.

He watched her pull into a parking spot near the back entrance of the yoga studio. Repeated observation revealed she preferred this spot because she could slip inside through the back door. That was Erika. She didn't like to interact with people much anymore.

He slid into the space beside Erika, parking within inches of the passenger side of her car. He opened his door and smacked it hard into the sleek, polished navy-blue finish, leaving an angry white scratch.

She glanced up, alarmed. For a second, she just sat there staring at him. And then she ducked her head against the rain and hurried around the car. Keys clutched in her hand, she studied the jagged white mark in the side door of her car as the rain dripped on her hair and shoulders.

"What have you done?" Her voice was high pitched and rippling with stress. "My husband is going to have a fit when he sees this."

Tugging a ball cap forward, he slid out of the car and made a show of studying the scratch. "Wow, did I make that?"

"Yes, you did. What the hell, why weren't you thinking?" She folded her arms over her chest, her teeth already chattering a little. As she looked toward the studio door, her shoulders tensed. The clock was ticking, and she was going to be late for class.

"I've a rag and some rubbing compound. I bet once I'm done with it, you'll never know there was a scratch." He moved to the back of the truck and opened the camper top.

Her jaw clenched as she shook her head and ran her finger over the jagged surface before following him. "You can't buff a deep mark out. It'll have to go to a body shop."

"Naw, I can fix it right up." He grinned as he rummaged for a tool in a dented red toolbox.

"You can't just rub it out!"

A car pulled into the parking lot, but the female driver barely tossed them a glance as she rushed through the rain into the building, a green yoga mat tucked under her arm.

She was inches away now. Mad. Spouting frustration. Closer. Closer. And then she ducked her head under the raised camper top. They were nose to nose.

Erika's demeanor changed. "Is this some kind of a joke? I told you we'd meet later."

He slid his hand into his pocket, removed a syringe, and plunged it into her arm. "No joke, baby."

She flinched and recoiled, dropping her keys onto the wet parking lot. "What the hell?" Already her words were slurring.

"I'm changing the plan. You're going to help me get Kaitlin." He picked up her keys and hit the trunk release on her car.

Her knees buckled as she tried to steady herself against the truck.

He wrapped his arm around her and shuffled her toward the open trunk of her car. Her response was an incoherent mess, but it didn't matter. Not now.

He drove twenty minutes north to the deserted parking lot of a closed gas station on Route 1. Weeds sprouted from the cracks in the asphalt, and the windows of the garage were covered in brown paper.

He drove around back and parked next to his truck. Moving quickly, he opened the car trunk and truck's camper top.

Erika lay on her side in the trunk, her body curled into a fetal position. It would be hours before the drugs were out of her system. He quickly lifted and placed her body in the back of the truck, then taped her wrists and ankles before he covered her with a tarp.

The drive to his house took a half hour. He was careful to watch his speed and put his blinker on each time he switched lanes.

When he pulled up to his home, he pressed the garage door button, and when it opened he carefully drove into the clean, neatly organized space. The door closed behind him.

Out of the cab, he walked to the back and opened the camper top. Now that they were alone, he had the time to admire her. He pushed back a lock of her blond hair. Her soft perfume wafted around her. She was beautiful. She'd kept her body fit and trim, and she was always dressed to perfection.

Now he was going to strip that perfection away. Like Jennifer, it was time to be punished. He lifted her into his arms and carried her into the house and downstairs to a darkened basement room. He'd been in this room so many times getting it ready for her, he didn't need light to know where to step or where to lay her. He knelt and settled her body on the cold floor.

He kissed her on the cheek, wishing he had time to linger. "It's time to pay for your crimes."

She appeared to frown, but she didn't open her eyes. He left her unconscious, locking the door behind him.

***

Normally Saint Mathew's wouldn't be open on a Saturday. But today was Saint Patrick's Day and also one of the school's biggest fund-raisers, which was scheduled for this afternoon. When Kaitlin had called the principal, Dr. Williams had agreed to meet her at the school before the hectic day began.

Kaitlin parked at the front entrance on the street. Saint M.'s, as the student's called it, had classes K through twelve, and many of the students had known each other since before kindergarten. That's how it had been with Gina, Erika, and Jennifer. Whereas the others shared a lifetime of school years together and affluent backgrounds, Kaitlin had been the outsider and dirt poor. Kaitlin's aunt had picked up the tab for her tuition.

The school's brick facade had a worn patina hinting to its nearly one hundred years in service. The planters out front were still filled with yellow winter pansies, as they had been when she'd been a student here. Come mid-May the groundskeeper would change out the pansies with yellow marigolds. The world kept convulsing forward, but Saint Mathew's stayed a steady course.

The signs on the school's front door advertised the afternoon garden fund-raiser as well as the upcoming song competition held between the four high school classes. This spring contest, which had seemed so important when she'd been a student, now was a pleasant triviality. Gina had been the leader of her senior class, and they'd won, of course. Whatever that girl had touched turned golden, and if Kaitlin were honest with herself, that Midas touch had made it hard to love her cousin.

Kaitlin pressed the intercom button by the front door, which she knew was always locked.

"Yes?"

"Kaitlin Roe to see Dr. Margaret Williams. I've an appointment."

"She's expecting you." The front door latch clicked open, and she entered the school. Smells transported memories better than sight or sound, and as she closed her eyes and drew in a deep breath, she could almost imagine the last fourteen years had melted away and nothing but happiness and hope lay before her.

Without glancing at directional signs she walked the hallway and ducked into the second door on the right that was still the office. Once inside, she introduced herself to the principal's secretary, who escorted her to the end of the hallway.

Dr. Margaret Williams rose from behind an old desk to greet Kaitlin. Kaitlin remembered Dr. Williams, who hadn't changed much in the last fourteen years. For such a large title, Williams was a tiny woman with dark hair, wire-rimmed glasses, and a warm but slightly wary smile. She ran a tight ship and was loved by both the students and the alumni.

"Thank you for seeing me, Dr. Williams," Kaitlin said, extending her hand.

"I'm always glad to visit with alumni. You said on the phone you're making a documentary about Gina Mason."

"A podcast. Gina and I were both students here at the same time. She was a senior. I was a sophomore."

Her smile sobered. "Of course, I remember you both. Tragic case." Dr. Williams motioned to the seat in front of her desk. "Please, sit. What can I help you with?"

Kaitlin lowered into the seat. "I need to know what happened to Gina."

"That's noble. How will a podcast help?"

"My hope is the piece will refocus the spotlight on her. Someone knows something. Maybe enough time has passed and the truth isn't so guarded."

Knitting her fingers together, Dr. Williams leaned forward. "Well, I'll do whatever I can to help."

Kaitlin flipped to a clean page in her notebook and turned on the recorder. "I don't have access to any police files, but I've read every article ever written about the case. You were interviewed by the police and media, correct?"

"I was. I joined the staff in January 2004, so I was here for the spring semester and onward. I got to know her quickly because she always stood out. To refresh my memory, I did pull the 2004 yearbook. Gina was very accomplished. I was a chaperone at prom when she was crowned queen. Her prom date was another senior, Tom Davenport. They were such a handsome couple."

Kaitlin scrawled down Tom's name as a reminder to call him next. "They broke up right after graduation. I lost track of him when I moved back to Texas. What's he doing these days?"

"He returned for the ten-year reunion a few years ago. He's a money manager. Doing well. Has an office here in Richmond on Main Street."

Gina had downplayed her breakup with Tom, saying it was mutual. *"Time for us both to go to college with a fresh start."* Like Kaitlin, the police had ridden Tom hard. "Was there anyone who didn't like Gina?"

"Not that I knew of. She was a lovely, sweet girl."

"When was the last time you saw Jennifer?"

Dr. Williams frowned. "That poor girl. Last year's Saint Patrick's Day fund-raiser. That class was always good about reunions, I think because of Gina. We all had a moment of silence for her."

"Did Jennifer have a date?"

"She did. An engineer, I believe. But I don't remember his name. I do remember she looked nervous. I think coming back here was never easy for her after what happened."

"What about Erika?"

"She was very reserved. The girl I had remembered was outgoing, but sadly she's not anymore."

"And her husband, Brad?" Kaitlin asked. "Did he come to the event?"

Some of the smile faded. "I did see him, but they left early. I didn't get a chance to visit with them."

"Why?"

"She said she wasn't feeling well."

"Do you know anything about a student named Randy Hayward? I know he was before your time. He'd have graduated with Brad Crowley and Derek Blackstone."

"I know of him, but we never met. I can tell you Derek has been a real friend to Saint Mathew's."

"Really?"

"He's a lovely man. He's an attorney and done quite a bit of pro bono work for the school. If you go into the meditation garden, there's a memorial bench in Gina's honor. He paid for it. In fact, he's receiving a service award this afternoon. He should be arriving at the school soon."

She remembered Blackstone. He was a tall, moody man who'd dated Ashley. "Good to have such a strong alumni network."

"We'd love to see you at your next class reunion. You're welcome to attend this afternoon's fund-raiser."

"I was only here my sophomore year. I never graduated."

"That doesn't matter to us. Once you're a Saint Mathew's student, you're always one."

"Thanks. I might try to come by this afternoon."

Dr. Williams removed a VHS tape from a drawer. "I did find this when I was looking in the archives for the old yearbook. VCRs were state of the art when the tape was made, but there are still a few machines around to play it."

"What is it?"

"A video of Gina. We have a VHS player in the teacher's lounge, so I watched it. She made it right at the beginning of senior year. It made me smile and cry. We can go up there now and see it, if you've time."

Kaitlin accepted the tape. It had been fourteen years since she'd heard Gina's voice. And she wasn't sure how she'd react. "I can get a video player at the university. Thank you. Is there anyone else here at the school who might have known Gina?"

"We do have a teacher on staff who graduated about the same year as Gina. Angela Baxter. She's here early like me to set up for the fund-raiser. We can ask her if she'd be willing to talk to you."

"That would be great. Mind if we do it now?"

"Sure. I'll walk you to her classroom."

Dr. Williams led Kaitlin up a flight of stairs and along a hallway decorated with glittering paper shamrocks. She paused at a door and knocked. "Ms. Baxter, I've a visitor who'd like to speak to you."

Angela Baxter capped a red pen and rose up from behind a wooden desk covered with stacks of papers. Bright images of rainbows painted by the students splashed the walls of the room, and large windows overlooked a student vegetable garden. In the rear of the room was a display of ten science projects, all contenders for first place in the school competition.

Angela came around her desk, and her smile froze when she looked at Kaitlin, who still didn't fit the Saint Mathew's mold as an alumna or parent of a prospective student. Still, she extended her hand and introduced herself. "Angela Baxter. I remember you."

Kaitlin accepted her hand, remembering the girl had been a gossip in high school and was always in everyone's business. "Angela. You look just like you did in high school."

Angela grinned. "You don't look like you've aged a day. Are you here for the alumni event?"

Dr. Williams explained why Kaitlin was there, and Angela's bright smile sobered. "Sure, I'd be glad to talk about Gina. I've a few minutes now."

"That would be great," Kaitlin said.

"I'll leave you to it," Dr. Williams said. "Kaitlin, I'll be in my office if you need anything."

"Thank you."

The principal laid her hand on Kaitlin's forearm. "You and Gina are in my prayers."

When Dr. Williams left, Kaitlin and Angela sat at two front-row student desks. Kaitlin pulled out her notebook and recorder and explained her project again. "What do you remember about Gina?"

Angela smiled. "I first met her in the third grade when I transferred to Saint Mathew's. We weren't friends right away, but even then she was the one everyone gravitated to."

"I remember you were friends also in high school, right?"

"We ate lunch together sometimes and shared a few classes. I wouldn't call us close friends, but in a small school like Saint Mathew's, we all knew each other."

"I remember you telling me that you'd heard rumors about Gina. Can you talk about those rumors?"

"There were some who thought Gina had staged the whole thing and that she'd run away. She fought with her mother the morning she vanished. And everyone knew she'd been under a lot of pressure to stay perfect."

Kaitlin caught herself before she rebutted the idea. Part of the podcast's purpose was to play devil's advocate and explore all the angles and theories.

"Do you believe that?"

"God, no. Gina loved the school, and she had the golden ticket to the Ivy League schools. She had it all. I mean, yes, she was under a lot of pressure, but she looked like she could handle it. Though when you arrived she seemed a little more stressed."

Kaitlin had upended her aunt and uncle's family. She'd not been easy or grateful for the chance. "How did things change?"

"You didn't fit in." Angela fiddled with a pencil resting in a groove on the desk. "But you hadn't grown up with us. I came to the school in third grade, and *I* was the *new* girl for years. No way as a sophomore you would've fit in."

"It was more than that, wasn't it?"

Angela nodded and shrugged. "You didn't want to be here. You weren't crazy about wearing a uniform. You definitely weren't happy about Friday-morning prayer. And then you decided if you couldn't be perfect like Gina, you'd be bad. That's when you started dating Randy Hayward. You know he ended up in jail."

"Yes, I heard. What do you remember about Randy?"

"He had come home for college spring break and announced he wasn't going back. He showed up at senior prom for God's sake."

"I didn't know that."

"He snuck in the back. Security caught him. Said he was an alumnus and was just visiting. They made him leave."

He'd had a rawboned look when Kaitlin had first seen him in late spring of '04. The collar of his worn leather jacket was popped, and she'd immediately seen he didn't belong at the school. His bad-boy reputation had been honey.

"Do you remember him with Gina?"

"He tried to talk to her at prom. She called him a loser, and it pissed him off. That's when security saw him and tossed him off the property."

"A few months later she vanished," Kaitlin remarked.

Angela cocked her head. "He was arrested that fall, right?"

"For burglary."

"He stole from his mother. He was a real piece of work. I don't know what you saw in him, Kaitlin."

"Neither do I. Do you think he knows what happened to Gina?"

Angela hesitated and then nodded. "Yes, I do. When I heard the cops had released him, I was shocked. I was sure we'd finally know what happened. Why did they let him go?"

"They didn't have enough proof."

"That's right. You couldn't identify him."

"Yep." Kaitlin imagined an accusation under the statement. She checked her watch, remembering why she had avoided Angela in high school. "I've a Saturday study session with my own students. I'm going to have to leave."

"Oh, yeah, sure. I hope I was some help."

"You were," she lied.

"You'll keep us posted on your project?" Angela's practiced look of concern hadn't changed since high school.

"I will."

"I'd like to hear it when you're finished. Maybe Saint Mathew's can sponsor a venue."

"Maybe."

Angela hesitated as if undecided about giving her a handshake or a hug. She smoothed her hands over her jeans, opting to do neither. "Good to see you."

"Yes." Kaitlin left Angela's room and made her way down to the main hallway.

On the way out of the school, she heard, "Kaitlin Roe."

She turned toward the deep masculine voice. It had been fourteen years since she'd seen Derek Blackstone, but he looked much the same as she remembered. His hair was a little gray at the temples, but he remained fit. He strode toward her, the folds of his jacket hugging a trim waist and broad shoulders.

Kaitlin moved toward him, closing the gap. She extended her hand, doing her best to look relaxed and confident. She took his hand, smiling as strong fingers clamped around hers. "Derek. You look great."

He allowed his gaze to roam over her before he released her hand. "I could say the same about you. What are you doing here? Investigating Gina still?"

"That's exactly what I am doing."

"Randy told me about your visit."

She hid her disgust for Derek, harnessing all the lessons she'd learned in public relations. "I assume he'll have news to share soon about Gina."

He chuckled softly. "You know I can't say anything about that."

"Anything you say is strictly off the record." He was too smooth and practiced to give a comment, but it didn't hurt to ask.

A dark brow arched. "No such thing, Kaitlin."

She couldn't resist the urge to press. "You dated Ashley in the summer of '04. You were only a mile from the river when Gina vanished."

His smile remained fixed. "I'm assuming you have a point to make."

"You were best friends with Hayward, and you knew him better than anyone. You would have been the guy he called if he'd done something stupid like kill Gina."

Blackstone's body appeared relaxed, and anyone looking at them would never suspect he was tense unless they could see how his eyes had now hardened. "You're wrong."

Dr. Williams appeared in the hallway and moved toward them. Blackstone leaned in and in a voice loud enough for only her to hear said, "Be careful. When you poke around in the dark, it's easy to find something that bites back." He winked, then turned toward Dr. Williams.

There was no missing Blackstone's threat, and Kaitlin wasn't foolish enough to dismiss it. As dangerous as Randy was, Derek was more so. But she was glad she'd seen him and had a chance to face him—and maybe rattle his cage a little.

She hurried to her car and drove along Grove Avenue toward the university. She parked and dashed to the audiovisual offices, where the department chair was tinkering with a microfilm machine.

"Stephanie," Kaitlin said.

The brunette swiveled in her chair and smiled. "What brings you here? More questions about audio equipment?"

She held up the VHS. "This time it's more basic. Can I use your equipment later today and transfer this to a DVD or a thumb drive?"

Stephanie took the tape. "I'll do it."

"Are you sure?"

"Yeah. I've got the time. Give me a day. This for the Gina project?"

"It is. It's supposed to be a tape of Gina."

"How's that going?"

"I'm no closer to finding Gina. I've also been reminded several times what a screwup I was in high school."

Stephanie shrugged. "Cut yourself a break. Most of us were screw-ups in high school. What's important now is that you're trying to find Gina. That counts."

"Sometimes it feels like it's too little and too late."

"It's not."

Kaitlin smiled. "Thanks. I've got to go. My study session is starting, and I'm on borrowed time."

Stephanie nodded. "I'll email you when it's ready."

"I owe you."

"I'd like to see Gina found, too."

INTERVIEW FILE #10

MEET GINA MASON

Wednesday, September 3, 2003; 8:00 a.m.

"Hi, I'm Gina Mason, Saint Mathew's class of 2004! Welcome to the Rebels' soccer team—district finalists three years in a row!"

The DVD captures the seventeen-year-old with violet eyes and a one-hundred-watt smile as she tucks a dark strand of hair behind her ear and throws a devilish grin. A high swipe of cheekbones and full lips give her a sexy look hard to miss. The camera likes her, and she likes the spotlight.

She claps her hands as her grin somehow gets three shades brighter. *"Today, I want each teammate to say a little about herself."*

Eleven months later Gina would be gone.

Viewing the DVD is heartbreaking, but I watch it to the end and hit "Play" to start it again. As much as I want to sink back into grief, I don't. I am here to give her a voice and bear witness to her fate. And until her full story is told, I will not rest.

"Hi, I'm Gina Mason, Saint Mathew's class of 2004!"

CHAPTER NINE

Saturday, March 17, 2018; 11:00 a.m.

Flames roared around Adler, licking up the walls and skimming along the ceiling. The flesh on his back burned as he gripped his partner's coat collar and pulled. With each jerk, Logan screamed, begging him to stop.

Adler's phone buzzed, startling him awake. He ran a trembling hand through his hair. He'd hoped to rest his eyes for just a moment but must have drifted off for the last hour. He didn't recognize the number, but clearing his throat, accepted the call. "Detective Adler."

"John Adler?" The woman's crisp voice cut through the haze.

He pressed his fingers against his closed eyes, hoping he could chase the sleep away. "That's right."

"Janet Yates at the rehab center. I have you as the emergency contact for Greg Logan."

He sat up and swung his legs over the side of the bed. "Yes, that's right. Is he okay?"

"Not really. Since he and his wife split, he's been unmotivated. A visit from you might help."

"He and Suzanne split?"

"From what I understand, it wasn't pretty."

Mary Burton

He shoved out a breath as he moved past paint cans and drop cloths to the coffee maker. "He's getting physical therapy now?"

"Yes. We're making adjustments to his prosthetic leg, and he's frustrated."

"I'll be there in fifteen minutes."

"Perfect."

Adler ran his fingers over the scars on his hand and reached for a mug and an espresso K-Cup on the makeshift counter. Five minutes later he had changed and, coffee in hand, headed out the door. Ten minutes later he pushed through the doors of the rehab center, showed his ID, and made his way to the ward. In the large room, multiple PT stations had a patient working out either alone or with a physical therapist. He spotted Logan standing between two parallel bars, balancing poorly on his prosthetic leg.

His military haircut had grown out and skimmed his ears, and his faded **ARMY** T-shirt was drenched in sweat. His muscled arms had grown in size while his face was leaner.

Adler understood a few things about feeling useless. After the explosion, he'd felt desperately inadequate when all he could hear were Logan's repeated pleas for painkillers.

He watched as Logan struggled to draw his right foot forward. Sweat was dripping down his arms. His face twisted into a grimace. The physical therapist before him was in her late twenties, not much taller than five foot, and had tied her red hair into a thick ponytail. Her name tag read **JANET**.

When Logan stumbled and then cursed, Adler came around so he was standing in clear view. Logan caught a glimpse of his partner's polished shoes and raised his gaze.

Gritting his teeth, Logan lifted his left leg and moved it forward a few inches. "Is that what you came to see?"

"If you're looking for someone to hold your hand or tell you that you're still pretty, I'm not your guy," Adler said.

Logan tightened his grip around the parallel bars. "So you're Suzanne's stand-in now?"

The anger was expected, and Adler didn't take it personally. No sane man went through this kind of shit without getting really pissed. "We're all pulling for you."

"Why are you here? I'm off the force. I'm just an ex-cop on full disability unless I want to ride a desk."

Logan loved being a cop, and a future assigned to a desk job was almost unthinkable. Adler had barely been able to look at Logan when he'd told his former partner he was returning to homicide. "Do you want me to leave?"

Silence. Logan looked to Janet. "Did you call him?"

Adler shook his head. "Why don't you worry about your job?"

"Job? Last I checked, I lost it."

"Your job is to walk. And last I checked your detective's skills are still intact." Adler shifted his gaze to Janet. "Mind giving us a moment?"

"Sure," she said. "I could use a coffee."

Adler walked behind Logan and pushed his wheelchair up behind him. When Logan kept standing, Adler nudged the back of his legs. "Sit."

Logan shoved out a breath and lowered himself. When he was seated, Adler pulled the wheelchair away from the bars and grabbed Logan's jacket hanging nearby.

"Where are we going?"

"I need fresh air." He pushed the wheelchair into the main lobby through the double automatic doors, and kept moving along the sidewalk still damp from the morning rain. They arrived at a secluded bench under a small tree. He sat while Logan locked the brake and tugged on his jacket.

"So is this a pep talk?" Logan asked as he shrugged on his jacket.

"God, no."

"A welfare call?"

Adler shoved out a breath. "What happened in that house was shitty." His throat tightened with anger. Up until now, he'd not been able to talk about the explosion. Now they had no choice. "I'll never pretend otherwise."

Logan drew in a slow, ragged breath. "Easy for you to say. You came out with hardly a scratch."

Adler took the jab. He wanted Logan to vent. "You're one hell of a cop, and you'll return to the job."

Logan stared toward the redbrick facade of the old section of the hospital. "Someone tell you this bullshit to motivate me?"

"No." His former partner wasn't making this easy, but then again Logan hadn't deserved what happened to him. "I always said you were destined for great things."

He glanced at his prosthetic as if it were an unwelcome visitor. "Right."

Adler caught Logan's eye and leaned forward. Several cars came and went. "Your wife left you?"

"Yep. Couldn't handle all this. I'm not the pretty face I was before the explosion."

"You never had a pretty face," Adler said, grinning.

Logan shot him a look of annoyance, not sure how to take the remark.

"Come up to Ashland. Move in with me. I'm renovating the place, and you're welcome."

"I don't want your pity."

"Good, because I'm fresh out. I do have a first-floor room, and after you install the handicap bars in the bathroom shower, you should be good to go."

Logan arched a brow. "Me install the bars?"

"You're good with carpentry work."

"Do I have to buy them as well?"

"I'll order them today."

A crooked smile rushed past the anger. "You make it sound so tempting."

"Telling it like it is. The first-floor bedroom, bathroom, and shower are set up so you can roll right in. The kitchen is a work in progress. New cabinets come next week and then countertops, but there's a temporary sink, stove, and refrigerator. Also, I have a nice yard looking onto the train tracks."

"I'm kind of fond of trains." Logan grinned slightly.

"You'll see a lot of them in Ashland."

"And then what?" Logan asked, turning serious again.

"You keep coming here. You keep working."

"And then?"

"And then you get back to being a cop," Adler said.

"I don't have two legs, remember?"

Adler tapped his index finger against his own temple. "Does this still work, or are you unable to think any more?"

"I think too much."

"Join the club." Adler focused on the metal leg feeding into the Nike tennis shoe. "You'll make it work." He scratched under his chin. "Besides, you know the old saying. Chicks dig scars."

Logan laughed. "Bullshit."

Adler was silent for a moment, then when he trusted his voice, said, "This kind of shit weeds out the pussies."

Logan sighed. "Fuck me. I'll do it."

"Good."

Logan rubbed the calluses on his palm. "So what're you working on these days?"

"Homicide. Stabbing. Hell of a case." Seeing Logan's interest pique, he steered the conversation toward the Ralston murder, which he recapped in detail.

Logan shifted in his chair. "A shitload of planning."

A thought occurred to him. "You're taking classes at the university while on disability?"

"Yeah."

"Ever heard of a teacher named Kaitlin Roe?"

"No." Logan dug his phone from his pocket and pulled up a site dedicated to rating professors. He typed in Kaitlin's name and pulled up her profile.

Adler studied the image. Her blond hair was swept in front of her face, effectively hiding half her features. White teeth flashed as if the camera had caught her laughing. A collection of bracelets hung from a slim wrist as she appeared to brush a wisp of hair from her face.

"She's hot," Logan said.

Adler rubbed his neck. He'd noticed. "What's it say about her?"

Logan scrolled through the comments. "Hates it when people are late to her class. Grades hard. Fair. Will organize extra Saturday study sessions if the class needs it. You have a hard-on for her?" A slight grin teased the edges of his mouth.

He'd thought about her a lot. She wasn't anything like his ex-wife or the women he'd dated since. Intense with a fierce drive, she wasn't afraid to shake up the status quo to get what she wanted. She also had a tight ass he thought about too damn much. "Her name came up in this murder investigation."

"I remember her now. And Gina Mason. How do the Mason case and the Ralston case relate?"

"I'm not sure yet. My priority has been Thursday night's stabbing. I spent the better part of the night going through the victim's financials and background. Bottom line is, Quinn and I don't have time to read the full Gina Mason case file."

"Keep talking."

"I need someone to go through it. How about you?"

"Me?" He laughed, but his eyes sharpened with interest.

"You were a good cop, Detective, and you still are."

"I don't know."

"Is that a no? Are you saying you're too busy chasing university skirt and doing homework to help?"

"Screw you."

"Detective Logan, I could use the help."

"What's the rush?"

"That stabbing I mentioned. She was one of Kaitlin's interview subjects. And a former witness in the Gina Mason case. There is also a prisoner, Randy Hayward, in the city jail who says he'll trade what he knows about Gina for a reduced sentence on a murder charge he's facing."

Logan's shoulders relaxed. "I can do this."

Adler reached in his pocket and pulled out his keys. He removed a second house key and handed it to Logan. "Pack your stuff and move in. The case file is at our house."

Logan reached for the key and fisted his fingers around it. "You sure about this?"

"The room on the first floor is yours. And if you ever thank me, I'll punch you."

"Take your best shot."

Adler clamped his hand on Logan's shoulder. "Get your ass in gear."

Logan grinned like a schoolboy. "I'm not going to cramp your style when you make a move on Kaitlin Roe, am I?"

"Doubt that'll happen." Adler laughed. "And no one gets in my way when I make a move."

***

As Kaitlin walked around the classroom and listened in on the student interviews, her phone vibrated.

She pulled it from her pocket and spotted Erika Crowley's name.

I'm ready to be interviewed, but it has to be today. Come to my house. Now before I lose my nerve.

Kaitlin was surprised to see the text from Erika. The way they'd left it, she hadn't thought she had a chance at another interview. If Erika knew something, Kaitlin needed to hear it. Given that Randy might tell his own version of what happened, it felt more important than ever to talk to Erika. The more facts she had, the easier it would be to sort Randy's facts from fiction.

Kaitlin glanced toward the clock on the wall and then to the students. She read Erika's text again.

With a sense of urgency, she moved to her desk and grabbed her knapsack, already calculating the time and distance between here and Erika's house. This time of day, she'd miss any traffic and make the trip in twenty minutes.

"Guys, I've had an emergency come up," she said. "We're going to have to end the session now."

"But we aren't finished," one student said.

"He was starting to crack," another joked.

"Sometimes a reporter or public relations professional has no control over the time." Which was true. Sometimes a reporter had time to warm up to the interviewee, and other times it all changed on a dime.

Groans rumbled over the class. "But I was getting to the good stuff," one young woman said.

"Send me your midterms by tomorrow at noon."

More grunts followed, but the students gathered their belongings and left the room. She locked up, hurried down the side stairs, and hustled across Main Street to her car.

As she wove in and out of traffic, the sense of urgency built inside her. The GPS on her phone noted her exit approaching, forcing her thoughts back to the moment. She decelerated off the exit ramp and headed toward the exclusive neighborhood. Her GPS guided her past manicured lawns until she arrived at the familiar white colonial. There were no cars in the driveway, but a light was on in the house.

Kaitlin texted Erika's number. I'm here.

A new text popped. Come inside.

The hairs on Kaitlin's neck rose as they had the night Gina was taken. She opened her glove box and fished out a personal alarm, which when pressed was loud enough to wake the dead. In a fight, a weapon could be turned against you, whereas an alarm disoriented an attacker with much less risk.

She slid the cylinder into her coat pocket and climbed out of the car. A woman a half block away walking a small dog was staring. Kaitlin waved, and the woman nodded.

Kaitlin hesitated at the base of the stairs and glanced at her phone before she climbed the stairs to the front door. She eyed the security camera mounted on the porch and then she pressed on the front door latch. She moved into the marbled hallway and looked up at the dark chandelier and then toward the light in the side room.

"Erika," she said.

She listened for a response but heard only the faint tick of a clock and her heart beating against her chest. None of this felt right.

"Erika. Where are you?"

A frustrating silence followed.

Her skin puckered with goose bumps, as it had fourteen years ago on the road by the river. She had just turned to leave when she heard the quick rush of steps inside the house with her. Her nerves jumped. Instinctively she fumbled for the button on her alarm and ran.

She caught the flash of a black hoodie and a clown mask microseconds before something hard cracked against her skull. Pain rocketed through her body, and her breath caught as she dropped to her knees in the hall. She dropped the alarm. Her vision blurred as her fingers scrambled for the device. A hand clamped on her shoulder as she pressed the button. "Get off me!"

She swung back blindly, and her fist connected with her attacker. He cursed, and seconds later a sharp pain sliced across her midsection and ricocheted through her body.

A shrill sound shattered her eardrums. The cutting pain in her gut made her nauseated as she struggled to sit up. A figure loomed over her and raised a knife but then paused. Cursing, he lowered the knife and ran toward the back of the house.

Blood soaked her blouse, and she pressed a trembling hand to the wound, thinking maybe she could stop the bleeding. The piercing siren wailing, she rolled onto her belly and crawled toward the front door. She was inches from the threshold when another wave of pain rammed through her body. She dropped to the floor. Footsteps sounded near her, but she wasn't sure if it was her attacker or savior.

She passed out.

INTERVIEW FILE #11

Loyalty Lost—Erika Travis Crowley

Saturday, January 6, 2018; 8:15 a.m.

It's a few minutes after eight in the morning. The coffee shop is buzzing with patrons anxious for their morning jolt of java. The aroma of nutmeg and cinnamon make the room feel warm and cozy and a haven against the cold January temperature. The barista wears a black, short-sleeved T-shirt that exposes his forearm, tattooed with a sea-horse in aqua waves.

I sit in the rear corner of the shop, my latte nearly finished. I have a ten a.m. class, and I'm not sure how much longer I can wait for Erika Travis Crowley, who promised to be here at eight sharp. In high school, I remember she'd always been late.

The bells jingle above the door, announcing a customer, and I look up again, hopeful to see Erika. A tall, broad-shouldered man with a thick beard lumbers toward the cashier as he types on his phone. He glances at me and moves on to get his coffee.

I'm about to check my phone for a possible message from Erika when the door pushes open with purpose. I look over to see a polished blonde wearing a brown coat, jeans, heels, and dark sunglasses that don't quite fit the time of day. It's been fourteen years, but I recognize Erika instantly.

I rise and wave my hand. The movement catches Erika's attention, and she studies me a beat, trying to reconcile her memories of me with the woman she sees now.

She glances from side to side, then hurries across to the small round table in the corner. She pulls off her glasses. "Kaitlin?"

"It's me." I sound cheerier than I feel.

We exchange a brief, if not awkward, handshake, and she sits. "I'm sorry I'm late. My husband was delayed leaving for work, and I wasn't interested in explaining where I was going, so I waited until he left." Her husband is Brad Crowley. He'd been a few years ahead of us at Saint Mathew's, and I still picture a serious, stern man with plans to be a surgeon.

"Thank you for seeing me. I ordered you a coffee, but I'm afraid it's cold."

"That's fine. I'm so wired. Just thinking about this interview has set my nerves on edge. I haven't been able to sleep for days. I worry now it was a mistake."

No one so far has been comfortable talking about Gina Mason. She still is sorely missed, and it still hurts.

"This doesn't have to be a formal interview or anything. Why don't we just talk?"

"Sure." She settles her small black purse in her lap and fiddles with the gold latch. "How did you find me?"

"It wasn't hard."

"Really? I don't like the idea of being so easy to locate."

"I understand." I've grown paranoid over the years about my address and online profile and taken steps to hide it all.

"Do you mind if I jump right in?" I flip a page in a thick worn spiral notebook. I've filled two of these in the last couple of weeks.

"I can't promise I'll answer any of your questions." She sounds unapologetic.

"Fair enough." I uncap my pen, always worried the recorder will fail or I'll miss a key detail. "As I said on the phone, I'm creating a podcast about Gina. What can you tell me about her?"

"I was jealous of her." She tries to smile and soften the confession, but it hangs between us. "We all wanted to be her, and all the guys we dated wished they were with her."

"How do you know what the boys were thinking?"

"My high school boyfriend confessed to it. Brad. He's my husband now."

"Brad liked Gina?"

"Yes. I know he loved me, but he was hot for her. He slipped and called me Gina once when we were doing it." She tucked a blond strand behind her ear.

"Did Brad ever talk to you about Gina?"

"Sure."

"What did he say?"

"Other than her being hot, he thought she was stuck up and that she believed she was better than everyone else."

"Did you tell this to the cops?"

"I never mentioned Brad's name to the cops."

"Why not?"

"Loyalty. I knew he didn't have anything to do with whatever happened. He was a horny teenager who could be insecure sometimes."

"So why are you telling me now?"

She shrugged. "I found out he's fucking his secretary. Loyalty is a two-way street."

Cold-case experts will admit spurned lovers are an excellent source for fresh case details. I don't speak, letting the silence prod her to say more.

"Want to know a secret?" Erika says.

"I love secrets."

She leaned in. "Brad gave me the Ecstasy the night Gina was taken. He told me it would loosen us all up."

Hearing her speak so easily about the drugs is jarring, but I stay focused. "You ever talk about Gina's case with Brad after she went missing?"

"I tried. He never wanted to talk about Gina."

"Why not?" I ask.

"I don't know."

She'd said Brad hadn't been involved in Gina's case, but something in me tells me to press again. *Nothing ventured, nothing gained,* I think. "I get the feeling that Brad had something to do with Gina's disappearance?"

She is silent, as if she realizes she might have said too much. "No, no, of course not," she adds quickly.

"You sound very sure."

"I am."

"When's the last time he saw Randy Hayward?"

She sits straighter. "He called from prison. Said he was about to get out and needed money. Brad, of course, obliged. They've been friends since kindergarten."

"The cops questioned Randy soon after Gina went missing. Do you think he knew something?"

"The cops dropped the charges because they couldn't prove anything."

"That's not what I asked. Do you think he knew more than he was saying?"

"I really don't know."

"Did Derek and Brad help him cover up something?"

Instead of answering she checks her watch. "God, look at the time. I have to go."

CHAPTER TEN

Saturday, March 17, 2018; 1:40 p.m.

Adler and Quinn showed their badges at the front desk of the Richmond city jail and made their way to a set of opening double doors as the guard on the other side saw them approach. They surrendered their phones and weapons into one of the secured lockers and waited for the next set of doors to open. Minutes later both were sitting in an interview room.

Hayward was brought in, and the instant he saw them he smiled. Cuffs rattled as he straddled the chair and sat. Adler introduced Quinn and himself.

"I've communicated with Trey Ricker in the Commonwealth Attorney's office. Your attorney has contacted him, and they're working on a deal as we speak. If you need confirmation, call Derek Blackstone," Adler said. "He'll give you the details. Once the deal is done we go directly to Gina."

Hayward's grin was sly. "I know where she is," Hayward said. "Sometimes I get my lefts and rights mixed up. But once I see where I'm going, I'll figure it out. It's only been a few months since I saw her."

Both said nothing.

"I visit whenever I can," Hayward said.

"Can you give me a general idea of the location?" Quinn asked.

"You mean like a teaser in a movie trailer?" Hayward asked.

"Yeah, a teaser," she said softly.

Hayward didn't speak right away, then said, "She's at least twenty miles from where she was taken."

A twenty-mile radius left a lot of territory.

"What do you remember about the night she was abducted?"

"Gina was wearing a green dress, and Kaitlin was wearing a tight, sexy white top."

Adler had been a cop long enough not to react to guys like Hayward, but there were some times when it took everything in him not to show his hand. "What else do you remember?"

"Kaitlin was scared, but she fought like a wildcat. Tried to save her precious cousin, but she didn't."

For a moment neither Adler nor Quinn spoke.

"Is Gina dead?" Adler asked.

Hayward wagged his finger. "I can't be telling you any more. Not until my buddy, Mr. Blackstone, seals the deal."

"We'll be back," Adler said.

"I'm counting on it. And bring Kaitlin, too," Hayward said.

"She's not a part of this," Adler snapped.

"She is now. If not for her, I'd never have gotten the idea to play my Gina card. No Kaitlin, no talk."

Adler now wanted Gina Mason found almost as much as Kaitlin. "I'll talk to Ricker and Kaitlin. It's not up to me."

"Give it the old college try, Detective. Hate for Gina to spend eternity lost to the world."

Outside, Adler removed his phone. He wasn't sure how Ricker would react to Hayward's newest condition.

"This sucks," Quinn said.

"I know."

"You think Ricker will allow Kaitlin to attend? He's a hard-ass."

"He will, if I press it."

Twenty minutes later, while Quinn followed up on a warrant, Adler pushed through the front doors of police headquarters and made his way to the captain's office. He knocked.

"Enter."

Adler found his new captain, Tobias Novak, standing behind his desk. He sported a clean-cut, Joe Friday kind of look, though the suit and strands of white hair didn't jibe with a much younger face. Standing beside the desk was Trey Ricker.

Ricker's dark tailored suit accentuated his tall, muscled frame kept trim by running. Light-blond hair was brushed off an angled face. "Adler. You're looking better than the last time I saw you."

"Thanks, Trey."

Adler and Ricker had grown up in the shadow of the Country Club of Virginia. They both came from old money, and both had attended Saint Mathew's from K through twelve as well as the University of Virginia undergrad and law schools. Adler's plan had always been to go into the law. And he had. He just took a different route.

Ricker's grip was strong, and his gaze didn't skirt away. "Hayward's attorney called me a few minutes ago and informed me he wants Kaitlin Roe there."

"What do you think?"

Ricker cracked the knuckle of his thumb. "I hate dealing with this piece of shit, but if it will seal the deal, fine."

Novak's eyes narrowed. "Why's an attorney like Blackstone bothering with Hayward?"

"They grew up together," Adler said.

Ricker nodded. "Both went to Saint Mathew's a few years behind Adler and me." Looking at Adler, he asked, "You know the school is having their big fund-raiser this afternoon?"

"I already sent my check in," Adler said.

"A little bird told me Blackstone is going to be there," Ricker said.

"Interesting. Sounds like an opportunity for me to get better acquainted."

"Small, small world," Ricker said.

Novak cleared his throat as he glanced at a file on his desk. "Adler, do you really think there is a connection between the Ralston murder and the Mason missing person's case?"

He still had no evidence other than the two victims ran in the same circles. Soon, he'd have to come up with more than a gut feeling. "I do."

"What do we know about Kaitlin Roe?" Novak asked.

"Cops interviewed her multiple times. She was no Girl Scout in high school, a fact she readily admits. She moved back to Dallas, finished school, and took a job in the corporate world."

"Until now." Novak shook his head. "Hayward is facing the death penalty, and Kaitlin shows up to plead his case?"

The urge to defend Kaitlin was quick and unexpected. "Kaitlin is sober now and wants to make this right. Regardless of her motives, this is the first break in this case in fourteen years. I'd like to take a run at this."

"Hayward couldn't have killed Jennifer Ralston," Ricker said.

"No."

Novak shut his file as his expression radiated frustration. "The media is going to love this one."

"He's right," Ricker said.

"Ricker, when did you worry about the press?" Adler asked.

Early in their careers, they'd had this conversation several times over a beer. What came first, the case or the career? Neither wanted to be the guy who put politics above a case.

Annoyed, Ricker shoved his hand in his pocket. "If Hayward can't hold up his end, I'm going to make it my personal mission to bury him."

"You'll have to get in line behind me," Adler said.

A muscle pulsed in Ricker's jaw. "And Kaitlin Roe can be present if she stays behind the yellow crime scene tape."

"Understood."

"I'll call Blackstone and work out the details," Ricker said.

***

Adler left Ricker and Novak, knowing this was a fragile victory. If Hayward were manipulating them, this was going to cost him political capital that he'd planned to use to help Logan. Not to mention, it would cost Ricker more, who'd stuck his neck out for him.

Quinn came up on his flank as he moved through the bullpen. When she read his expression she smiled. "So, it's still *Let's Make a Deal*?"

"It is."

"Good."

He checked his watch. "Saint Mathew's is having an alumni fundraiser starting right about now."

"And we care why?"

"Because Blackstone is supposed to be there."

"It won't look too good if we just show up."

"If an alumnus shows, it wouldn't raise a brow."

She cocked her head. "Well, my mama and daddy couldn't afford private school."

He shrugged. "Mine could."

"You're a Saint M.'s kid?"

"I am."

She laughed as she followed him to his car. "Jesus, Adler. You always gave off the rich-boy vibe, but I figured it was an act."

He slid behind the wheel. "Maybe you'll make some new friends."

She clicked her seat belt. "Not likely."

It took less than twenty minutes to drive to the school and find street parking a block away.

Out of the car, Quinn tugged up the collar of her shirt. "Do I look preppy enough?"

"You're a natural."

The parking lot was already full, and he could hear Irish music drifting from the sculpture garden. He dreaded events like this. His parents had dragged him to his fair share.

He adjusted his tie and buttoned his jacket, and they climbed the front steps and strode toward a table.

His grin froze when he recognized his ex-wife sitting at the table. Their divorce had been her idea, but he hadn't contested it. She'd thought she was marrying a future governor or senator, not a career cop. "Veronica."

Her smile instantly warmed and she rose, touching her now-pregnant belly with her left hand, which sported a diamond-studded wedding band. "John, how are you?"

He thought about all the times they'd talked about having children. When the time came to get pregnant, she'd asked him about leaving the police department and starting a "real" career. He'd found a reason not to quit, and she'd found a reason not to get pregnant. This went on for several years until a year ago, when she'd asked him for a divorce. "I'm great. How are you?"

She laughed. "I'm married."

"Congratulations. When's the baby due?"

Her smile turned extra bright. "Less than a month."

Their divorce had been final seven months ago. "I wish you the best."

Quinn stuck out her hand. "I'm Detective Quinn, his partner."

Veronica smiled. "Nice to meet you."

"Likewise."

"I wasn't sure you'd make it today," Veronica said to Adler.

"I thought I'd drop by."

Quinn filled out a name tag for herself and him. He peeled off the back of the tag and affixed it to his coat.

"Good seeing you, Veronica."

More people approached the table, providing them with a smooth exit.

"You look pretty cool about seeing your ex-wife," Quinn said.

"I am."

"Not that it's my business, but how long were you two married?"

"Ten years."

"Long time."

"Yes, it was." Seeing Veronica and this school reminded him of the life he didn't recognize anymore. They walked down the hall and stepped out the side door into the garden. At least thirty well-dressed people had gathered for the celebration. He scanned the crowd, easily spotting Blackstone.

"My high school reunions aren't this nice," Quinn said. "Best we got is a rented back room in a restaurant."

Seeing an opening, Adler motioned to Quinn, and they moved toward Blackstone, whose back was turned.

"Blackstone," Adler said.

The attorney turned, and the smile anchored in place didn't flinch. He extended his hand. "Detectives."

Adler matched Blackstone's firm grip. "I'm not wearing that hat now. I'm an alumnus."

"I'd heard something about that."

Adler hesitated a beat and released his hold. The attorney kept files on his opponents, and Adler imagined if he wasn't on Blackstone's list, he would be soon. "I hear Hayward came around the school often after he dropped out of college."

Blackstone adjusted a gold cuff link. "I thought this wasn't about work."

His smile widened. "I'm talking about a fellow alumnus visiting his old school."

Blackstone sipped his wine and grinned. "Right."

"What does Hayward have on you? A professional like you doesn't stick with a guy who's career poison."

Blackstone didn't blink. "I value friendship much like you do. I hear you're helping out a fellow cop injured in the line of duty."

Adler felt Quinn's gaze shift to him. "My guy's not a drug-addicted murderer."

Dark eyes hardened. "True friendship isn't always easy or convenient."

"Or maybe he has something on you." Adler studied his expression carefully. Blackstone was a master at hiding emotions, but a subtle tension tightening the edges of his smile tipped his hand. "Something that you just don't want the world to know about."

Blackstone looked relaxed, like the poker player holding all aces. "You're reading more into this than you should."

Adler smiled as Blackstone turned and walked toward the dais. He would figure out whatever else Hayward was hiding and nail him.

"I've seen enough," Quinn said.

Blackstone's deep voice followed them through the garden and through a side entrance. As Adler strode out of the school, his phone dinged with a text from Novak. He halted midstride when he read it. *Shit.*

Kaitlin Roe has been stabbed.

INTERVIEW FILE #12

A Reluctant Savior—Jack Hudson

Thursday, March 1, 2018; 1:00 p.m.

When I explain the purpose of my podcast to Jack Hudson, he's reluctant to talk to me, even though it's been fourteen years since I showed up on his doorstep drunk, terrified, and begging him to call 911. It's hard to blame him. My unexpected arrival propelled him into the spotlight and all the crap that comes with it.

Mr. Hudson is now in his late sixties, but he remains lean and fit. We sit at his kitchen table beside a large window that overlooks the bare trees and the river. "As soon as you said your name, I knew who you were. The media was camped out in front of my house for weeks. I hated that. I caught a few looking in my windows, and one went through the mail in my mailbox."

The blunt assessment feels like an accusation. But atonement isn't easy.

"I am sorry." Silence lingers. He doesn't accept my apology. "Can you tell me what you remember?"

He huffs out a breath. "It was a warm night. High humidity. I had gone to bed early. You woke me up out of a dead sleep. Startled the hell out of me."

"Did you hear anything before I showed up?"

"As I told the cops, I went to bed early. I didn't hear anything."

Looking out his window, I can hear the rapids. How did he not hear me scream? "Do you remember Gina?"

"Sure. She was a sweet kid. I'd watched her grow up. She shouldn't have died so young." His cat jumps up on the table, and he strokes her head before gently placing her on the floor. "She wouldn't have died if any one of the girls had shown any common sense."

He's right.

"Did the police talk to you about Randy Hayward?"

He taps his finger on the table. "Sure."

"Did you notice anything different about him or his mother's house the night Gina vanished?"

"Like what?"

"Sounds, a strange car in the driveway, shades closed when they were normally open?"

"The house was dark. No one appeared to be home. And as for Randy, he was always a weird kid. Sneaking around."

"Doing what?"

"He liked to look in windows."

"Whose window was he looking into?"

"Mine and a couple of my neighbors'. He didn't disturb anything or do any harm. His mother cleared it up, so no charges were filed."

"Did you tell the police?"

"No. I didn't want any more trouble."

CHAPTER ELEVEN

Sunday, March 18, 2018; 6:00 a.m.

Kaitlin Roe was accustomed to pain.

Guilt, sorrow, and remorse were dull, consistent pains she endured, but the physical agony now jerking her toward consciousness was something she'd never felt before. Liquid fire scorched every cell and sinew, trapping her breath as she expanded her ribs and attempted to draw in air. Her heart raced, and she swallowed as she waited for the vise grip on her midsection to ease before she tried to breathe again.

When the pain dulled to a throb, she lay still until the screaming in her body stopped. Had the monster from fourteen years ago returned? Panic made her heart beat faster. A deep-seated urge to survive goaded her to open her eyes so she could get her bearings.

Instantly the harsh glare of the fluorescent lights smacked her square in the face. Her head throbbed. She closed her eyes and regrouped before she slowly reopened them. Her head still throbbed, but she adjusted to the pain.

The beep, beep of a monitor had her slowly turning her head left toward the machine's green and red lights. An IV ran from a half-full bag to the thick blue vein in her arm.

Hospital. She was in a hospital? What had happened?

Her vision focused on the monitor, while she searched through the mental haze for her last concrete memory. She blinked while trying to scrape together the last images.

She had been at Erika's house. She'd stepped inside . . . and then whatever happened next danced out of reach. She had no idea what happened to her.

"Welcome back."

She turned her head toward the deep-baritone voice heavy with fatigue. Detective Adler sat in the chair by her bed. Dark stubble covered his chin, and his starched white dress shirt was wrinkled. Sleeves were rolled up, revealing hair covering muscled arms. His gun, as always, was holstered at his side along with cuffs and a phone.

He rose and leaned over the bed, staring at her with piercing gray eyes. Detective Adler. City of Richmond Homicide. But she wasn't dead.

She swallowed, her throat dry. "Aren't you early?"

"Early?"

"I'm not dead."

"No."

In the silence she felt the weight of worry, fear, and relief balled into a tightly coiled knot. He looked concerned.

She dug her fingers into the sheets, wanting to sit up and look him in the eye. She needed to prove to him, herself, and the doctors that she was fine. However, as soon as she engaged her core muscles, fire in her midsection flared, sending her collapsing into the sheets.

"You shouldn't be moving," Adler said.

She hissed in air between clenched teeth. "Just received that memo."

He reached for a cup and straw and held it to her lips. She took a tentative sip, afraid swallowing would hurt. But her mouth and lips were so dry. She sipped, and cool water brushed over her lips and soothed her parched throat. She couldn't remember when water had tasted so good.

"The nurse said only small sips."

"How long have I been here?"

"You've been out of surgery about eight hours. I received the call from dispatch because my number was one of your last phone calls."

She winced as she reached for a joke. "So people think we're an item?"

Frowning, he set the glass down with deliberate care. He laid the back of his hand to her forehead before sitting and scooting forward so they were eye to eye. "You're damn lucky to be alive."

She was almost afraid to ask. "What happened?"

"You were hit on the head and stabbed."

"Stabbed?" Her hand went to her belly, and fingertips gingerly felt gauze and adhesive. "I don't remember."

His eyebrows drew together, deepening his frown lines farther. "The doctor said you might have trouble with recollection," he said. "You have a mild concussion. What's the last thing you remember?"

She closed her eyes and drifted into the mist. "I was running a study session. The students were prepping for their exam project. Where was I found?"

The lines around his eyes deepened with a frown. "At Erika Crowley's house."

She met the gray eyes boring into her. "Why was I there?"

"She texted you."

"She did?"

"Her number and the text are in your phone. Do you remember the text?"

"Sorta." She ran her hand again over her stomach and felt the rough texture of the bandage. "I must have driven there."

"Your car was parked out front, and you were lying in the foyer facing the door as if you were leaving."

Erika. Puzzle pieces slid closer together. "I saw her on Friday. I went to tell her about Jennifer. She didn't want to be interviewed. And then she texted and said she would talk to me."

"That matches the text she sent you at 1:42 p.m. 'I'm ready to be interviewed, but it has to be today. Come to my house. Now before I lose my nerve.'"

That sounded familiar. "Who found me?"

"Erika's neighbor heard an alarm and called 911 at 2:17 p.m. The responding officer found you alone at the house bleeding out in the foyer. If not for the call, you would have bled to death."

Listening to him speak such startling facts with dispassion made it easy to believe he was talking about someone else. "Do you know who stabbed me?"

"No. I was hoping you could tell me."

It was hard to decipher his troubled, angry expression. Was it worry or suspicion? The last time she'd faced the cops they'd had a similar look. Her chest tightened with fear. She was innocent, but she didn't know if that mattered to him. "I don't know. I don't remember any of it." She gripped the sheets. "I want to remember." Sudden tears stung her eyes. "But I can't tell you anything."

"Take it easy. It'll come to you." His frown softened. "Have you received any threats or had the sense someone was watching you?"

"Like a stalker?"

"Jennifer may have had one." He expelled a breath. "My gut's been telling me Jennifer's and Gina's cases are linked. Your stabbing is the first solid connection."

She tried to focus, but her mind was too blurred. The pain was ratcheting up. Had there been someone watching? Was it the paranoia stalking her since she'd run away from her attacker fourteen years ago? "I don't know."

He laid his hand on her shoulder. "Okay. Let it go for now."

"How can I let it go?"

"I've got this, Kaitlin."

His definitive tone added weight to the promise and eased her nerves. To distract herself from the pain and the fear, she shifted to

smaller details more easily managed. "Where are my recorder and backpack? Were they taken?"

"No. Both were locked in the trunk of your car."

Embarrassment barely registered as she imagined this guy rooting through her backpack past tampons, crumpled receipts, and chocolate candy wrappers. She always locked her valuables in her trunk.

"Why didn't you bring your equipment?" he asked.

"I'm not sure. Where's my car now?"

"At your apartment. I had an officer drive it to your place. The recorder and your keys are in your backpack, which is in the nightstand by your bed here."

Not a big deal for someone to drive her car, but she'd grown so protective of her spaces that she didn't like the idea of anyone in her loft space, especially a cop.

"Is there someone I can call? Someone who can pick up a change of clothes for you?"

She'd let her friends drift away over the last few months. "My boss. Susan Saunders."

"I'll call her for you. What about family?"

"Mom's gone." She focused on the white tiled ceiling. "Am I going to be here that long?"

"A few days from what the doctor said."

"I don't have a few days." She struggled to sit again but immediately fell back in pain. "I don't want to be here."

"The surgeon stitched up your abdomen with over twenty stiches. No matter how antsy you feel, it's going to have to wait."

He was right. She'd been stabbed. Someone had tried to kill her.

As if he could read her thoughts, he said more softly, "I've been in your shoes. It sucks, but you've got to give your body time to heal before they'll release you."

She wanted to focus on anything other than herself. "You were hurt pretty bad recently."

"Blown up and burned." His blunt answer suggested he wasn't interested in sharing details.

The more she thought about being in an unfamiliar location exposed to all sorts of people, the more unsettled she felt. Anyone could come into her room while she was sleeping, and given the shape she was in now, there was nothing she could do about it. There were no locks on her door.

"What about Erika? Have you found her?" she asked. "She could tell you what happened."

"I spoke to the county police. There was no sign of Erika or her husband."

"I interviewed her for my podcast in January. She was late because she'd waited until her husband left for work. She didn't want him to know about the interview."

"Why?"

"I don't know."

"You get the vibe he might be abusive?"

"I don't know." She searched his face. "I saw her on Friday and told her about Jennifer. She didn't want to have anything to do with me."

"Her phone isn't transmitting a signal. Do you have any idea where she would go?"

"No." Again she rummaged through splintered recollections, but still found nothing that would help her figure out what had happened during the lost hours. Frustrated, she pushed her fists into the sheets and was determined again to sit up. Screw the pain. She wouldn't be sidelined, and she was going to remember. She tried to sit again. Immediately her body burned, and she hissed in a sharp breath as tears filled her eyes. "Damn it."

He took her hand in his, and automatically she squeezed his fingers until she sat up. His calloused fingers brushed her palm, offering comfort she did not want.

When the agony mellowed to an ache, she realized how tightly she'd been gripping his hand. Feeling foolish, she pulled her fingers free. She met his gaze. "And here I thought you were an asshole," she said.

"I get that a lot."

A smile quirked the edges of her lips. "If it's any consolation, so do I."

He shook his head. "A dead woman, a missing woman, an AWOL husband, and the person at the center of it all has a hefty slice in her gut. You attract trouble like this all the time?"

"Not in a long time." Fresh frustration quickly gained strength. "I need to remember who stabbed me. I don't think he's one and done. He's coming for me."

"You've been traumatized. Victims often don't remember their attack initially."

The label, *victim*, was another punch to the gut. After Gina, most saw her as a victim. People talked to her differently, some avoided her, and some believed she'd caused all her troubles. She'd have taken it better if Adler had called her a liar. "Fuck *victim*."

"The stitches say otherwise."

"Call me stupid. Foolish. Even naive. But don't call me a victim."

He studied her a long moment. He was a homicide detective who rooted among the lies for truths. Trained to unwind complicated evidence and piece them together into a coherent picture. "Like it or not, you're officially a case, Kaitlin. And you're probably right, he's going to make another run at you."

"You should be looking for Erika and Brad Crowley. I was at their place when this happened. They must have known something."

"Slow down. What do you remember?"

"I do remember her text now. And I remember parking my car and walking toward the front door. I think the door was open. I thought Erika would be there, but I didn't see her."

"All I know is you were just inside, unconscious and bleeding. The responding officer called for backup and the paramedics. The house was searched, but no one was found."

The image of her lying in her own blood added weight to what had happened. "I don't remember."

"Where else would Erika Crowley be?" Adler asked.

"I don't know much about her. I had the impression she lived a pretty isolated life."

"What do you know about her?" he asked.

"Only what she told me, which isn't much. I hadn't seen or heard from her in fourteen years. Hell, I didn't know her well then."

His silence, hefting too much weight, was a sure signal she wasn't going to like what she heard.

"We need to find Erika and Brad," she said.

"*We* aren't doing anything. I'll find them."

A sudden wave of fatigue hit, stealing some of her fire. "I'm in the middle of all this."

He rose, leaned over the bed, and braced his hand on the headboard and the side rail, careful not to jostle the IV in her arm. "I'm aware, and believe me, I'll not rest until I figure this out. We'll talk about it later. In the meantime, you're safe. I'll make it my mission to find this guy."

"No one could fourteen years ago."

He brushed a strand of hair from her eyes. "Now, I'm in the game. So the rules have changed."

Panic felt like weakness, but it was undeniable. "I can't defend myself now."

"You're in a lockdown unit. No one can get in or out, so rest. You're safe here."

Safe. What the hell did that mean? She hadn't felt safe in fourteen years. "And when I leave?"

"One step at a time."

"I've never been good at the patience thing."

"Rest," he said.

She shook her head. "What about Hayward?"

"He has his deal. But he won't lead us to Gina until you can be present."

"Randy never makes anything easy. He likes his games."

"He has a lot to lose; why play them now?"

"I have no idea." She tried to sit up. "When are we going?"

"Soon." He lifted his jacket off the back of the chair.

"Did he say where she is?"

"No. But nothing's going to happen in Gina's case until you're better."

He squeezed her hand before he left. When the door closed behind him, she forced herself to relax into the pillows. She stared at the white tiled ceiling a long moment before she closed her eyes, too exhausted and sore to fight.

INTERVIEW FILE #13

The Media Frenzy

Wednesday, August 18, 2004

"This is Steven Marcus with Channel Eleven news reporting from the Virginia State Police offices. Today, I'm here with Jennifer Connors, a public information officer, to discuss the case of Gina Mason. Eighteen-year-old Mason went missing three days ago.

"Ms. Connors, what can you tell us about the case?" Marcus asks.

The young reporter raises his microphone toward the petite blonde, who looks directly into the camera. "State and federal agents and officers have been working with the City of Richmond Police. They're currently running any and all leads and ask residents to call us if they have any information regarding Gina Mason."

"What should residents be looking for?" the reporter asks.

"Gina went missing from Riverside Drive near Pony Pasture. If you were in the area the night of August 15 and noticed anything out of the ordinary, please call us. Has a friend, family member, or neighbor exhibited a change in mood or appearance? Was there an unknown car parked in the wrong place? Is there anyone fascinated or frustrated with the media coverage of the case?"

"And who should they call?" Marcus asks.

As the phone numbers of several jurisdictions flash on the bottom of the screen, Marcus looks into the camera. His brow is furrowed and his lips draw into a grim line. When he speaks again, his voice cracks with emotion. "If you know anything, please call."

CHAPTER TWELVE

Sunday, March 18, 2018; 10:00 a.m.

Adler pulled up in front of the Crowleys' white colonial located at the end of a cul-de-sac. The lawn was neatly manicured, and freshly mulched beds were filled with azaleas ready to bloom. A yard flag hanging on the mailbox read SPRING. The house's wide front porch sported several rockers and yellow crime scene tape now tied between the posts.

He tried to imagine Kaitlin pulling up here. He'd bet she'd been anxious to interview Erika, given the fact that she'd left her class early and arrived here thirty minutes after she'd received Erika's text.

Technically Kaitlin's stabbing wasn't his case. Her case wasn't a homicide, and this county wasn't his jurisdiction. But he refused to stand on the sidelines, so he'd called his counterparts in the county and asked for and received the all clear to poke around the crime scene.

He crossed the street and strode up the driveway, noticing the bushes by the front of the house. They were tall and thick and a good place for someone to hide. Up the front stairs, he studied the brass lock. There were no signs of forced entry. The door had to have been unlocked or perhaps open when Kaitlin arrived.

He pulled on latex gloves. Breaking the tape, he used the key he'd gotten from the forensic investigator and opened the front door. A flip of a switch in the foyer turned on the lights of a chandelier and cast a warm glow over a collection of art hanging on the walls. The faint scent of pine cleaner clung to polished floors now littered with dozens of footprints left by the responding officers, EMTs, and the forensic team.

His gaze dropped to the dried pool of blood and a discarded gauze pad stained red. The blood was Kaitlin's.

Anger rolled through him as he thought about her lying here clinging to her life.

When Adler had received the text from Novak about her stabbing, he'd driven directly to the hospital. His badge had gotten him onto her floor and access to her doctor, who'd told him the assailant's knife had missed all the major organs but had nicked an artery. A few more minutes and she'd have bled out.

The doctor's assessment reminded him of conversations he'd had with Logan's doctors after the explosion. They'd said because Adler had used his belt as a tourniquet to bind his partner's left leg, he'd bought Logan the critical minutes that saved his life.

Kaitlin and Logan were fighters, tenacious and driven. And although neither thought of themselves as defenseless, that's what they were just now, and it was up to him to protect them both.

The sound of footsteps on the front porch sent his hand to his weapon as he turned to see Quinn. She wore jeans, a white blouse, a tailored black jacket, and midheeled boots.

He lowered his hand.

"Adler," Quinn said. "I heard you were headed this way. Thought you could use a second set of eyes."

"There's not much to see."

She tugged on latex gloves, stepped around the pool of blood, and moved past the two-story foyer into the living room and the bank of French doors that overlooked woods. "Pretty nice home."

"Brad Crowley does well for himself. He's a plastic surgeon who's made a name doing nip and tucks."

"Does Erika work?" she asked.

"She's a homemaker."

Quinn moved back toward him and studied the bloodstain. "I talked to a buddy of mine in county police. The security cameras across the street recorded Kaitlin visiting Erika on Friday morning."

"That's what she told me."

"So she's awake?"

"As of an hour ago. I just came from the hospital."

"Can she identify her attacker?"

"No. And she was wiped out when I left."

Quinn's jaw tightened as she shook her head. "So, what's the deal with her? Her name keeps coming up."

"She's at the center of all this. Her podcast project was likely a trigger for someone who doesn't want her digging up the past. If I had any doubts about Jennifer's death being connected to Gina's, I don't anymore."

"I thought Hayward said he could lead you to Gina?" Quinn asked.

"He says he will as soon as his attorney gets the plea agreement in writing. That should happen early next week."

"He couldn't have killed Jennifer."

"Agreed."

"Could he have collaborated with someone? Maybe an accomplice knew what happened to Gina and was willing to kill to protect it. Maybe Jennifer wasn't just an innocent victim?"

"I've asked myself all these questions," Adler said.

"How about this one. Ever stop to wonder if Hayward is working with Kaitlin? Maybe he used her to broker the deal with you and Ricker."

"That's possible."

Quinn rested her hands on her hips. "I hear a *but*."

"I think Hayward enjoys hurting Kaitlin, and when she contacted him at the jail, she gave him the perfect opening to do just that," Adler said.

"You think he's lying about Gina and this is all a sick joke to him?" Quinn asked.

"It's a real possibility, but I think he does know where Gina is, and he wants Kaitlin to have a front-row seat at the big reveal," Adler said.

"Kaitlin broke up with Hayward, correct?" Quinn asked.

"So she says."

"It's been fourteen years."

"Maybe he still feels possessive toward her."

"Possessive goes hand in hand with anger. If he can't have her, he'll go out of his way to hurt her."

Adler nodded. "He must know whatever information he has will hurt her."

"Or, playing devil's advocate, she still has a thing for him and she's using you to plead his case. What're the chances he'd have any kind of deal without her?"

As tempted as Adler was to reject Quinn's idea outright, he couldn't. "She didn't stab herself."

"Allegedly," Quinn responded.

Adler was silent. Quinn was asking all the right questions, but his gut told him Kaitlin was a victim. However, gut feelings weren't proof. "Any word on Erika or Brad Crowley's whereabouts?"

"According to my buddy in county police, nowhere to be found. No activity on their credit cards or cells. GPS on Erika Crowley's car led the county detective to a gas station parking lot on Route 1."

"That's not the burbs. What was she doing there?" Adler asked.

"Good question. Normally on Saturdays she takes a yoga class. But she didn't show up to class yesterday. Seems for a couple of months Erika has been parking at the yoga studio but skipping the Saturday-morning class and heading across the street for coffee."

"Is she meeting someone?" Adler asked.

"The studio owner didn't know."

"We need to look at that car. And visit that coffee shop."

"Agreed," Quinn said.

"The county detectives are digging into the Crowleys' financials?" he asked.

"They've requested a warrant."

"What kind of car does Brad Crowley drive?" Adler asked.

Pages in her notebook flipped. "Crowley drives a Lamborghini. And currently it's parked at a hotel in the city. He's registered there, but he isn't on the premises now."

"Why's he at a hotel?" Adler asked.

"Apparently he spent a lot of time there in the last year. I spoke to his office, and he's supposed to be attending a conference in northern Virginia for a few more days. He's not answering his phone."

"Just because the car is in Richmond doesn't mean he's not at the conference."

"My buddy is trying to confirm that," Quinn said.

Adler stepped around the bloodstain and moved into the center room. His gaze was drawn to the vaulted ceiling, the stone fireplace, and the sleek leather furniture. The Crowleys lived well and had spared no expense. Status mattered to them.

He moved to a grand piano sporting a collection of pictures featuring a beautiful blonde and a dark, muscled man. Most looked like they were taken at exotic locations.

"Which neighbor said they heard the alarm and called it in?" Adler asked.

Quinn nodded. "Across the street. Mrs. Nolan."

"Let's pay her a visit."

He locked the door behind them and looked toward the yellow colonial. A woman was coming out her front door with a heavy purse slung over her shoulder. They moved across the street and met her at her mailbox.

"Mrs. Nolan?" he asked.

The woman stood a little straighter and looked side to side as if she weren't sure about him.

Adler held up his badge. "I'm Detective John Adler, and this is my partner, Detective Quinn. Mind if we ask you a few questions?"

"Uh, sure. I already spoke to the police."

Adler smiled. "Just a few more questions, Mrs. Nolan."

"Okay."

He jabbed his thumb toward the Crowley house. "Mrs. Nolan, I understand you're the one who called 911."

"I am. I heard a loud alarm go off as I was walking past with my dog. Like I said, I already told all this to the detective."

"I'm with the city and working on a case that's possibly related to this one. I appreciate your patience."

"Sure." She shifted her stance.

"What did you see?"

"I saw that woman go inside. She had a rough edge about her and didn't belong here, so Buster, my miniature dachshund, and I lingered."

"How long was she inside the house before the alarm went off?"

"A minute tops. Like I said, I stayed outside the house and watched because I wasn't sure what she was up to. She came by the other day and visited with Erika, who did not look happy about it."

"And when you heard the alarm, you called the police?" Quinn asked.

"Yes. I always carry a phone. You never know even in the good neighborhoods."

"Did you see anyone else coming or going from the house?"

"I thought I saw a man run through the woods behind the house, but I didn't get a good look."

"Can you tell me anything about him?"

"Medium height and build. He had one of those hoodie things over his head. How is the woman doing? I understand she was stabbed."

"She's going to be fine."

"Were they robbing the house? I mean, the neighbors have all been trying to guess what happened. The consensus is that it was robbers turning on each other."

"Nothing like that," Adler said. "As soon as I can share something, we'll let you know. Thanks again, Mrs. Nolan."

Adler waved to the woman as she drove off. "She saw a man headed into the woods."

"She thinks. My buddy in the county police walked through the woods and to the street behind it. No one saw a man."

"Right."

"How's it going with the Gina Mason files?"

"I've got Logan reviewing them."

"Logan? What? He's on medical leave."

"He's a hell of a detective."

"Shouldn't he be resting and concentrating on getting better?"

Adler dug his keys from his pocket. "If you were in his spot, would you be focusing on getting better?"

She shook her head. "I'd be all over the case files."

"Exactly."

***

Adler pushed through the front door of his home and spotted the large knapsack tossed in the center of his living room. Beside it was a prosthetic leg designed for running and jumping.

He loosened his tie. "Logan."

"I'm in the kitchen."

Adler found Logan sitting in a wheelchair in front of a hot plate poised on a makeshift plywood counter. He dropped a handful of pasta into a pot of boiling water. "Hungry?"

"Always."

"Occupational therapist said cooking is a good activity to relieve stress."

"Smells good."

"It is. I had no idea you lived so well."

"Ever met a trust fund baby?" he said, smiling.

"No shit, really?"

"What can I say?"

"Damn. If I'd known you were rich, I'd have made you pick up all the dinner tabs."

Adler shrugged off his coat and draped it over the back of a chair. "How's rehab going?"

"Slow but sure. Quinn called to check in. She told me Kaitlin Roe was stabbed. How is she?" Logan asked.

"Lucky to be alive."

"Shit." Logan lifted a cup of coffee to his lips. "One of the potential witnesses in the Gina Mason case is dead, the other missing, and another stabbed."

The pattern was there. Now it was a matter of figuring out who wanted the three women dead. "What are the odds?"

"Low," Logan said.

"You had a chance to look at the file?" Adler asked.

"I read it last night. It was hard to put down. Also listened to the Jennifer interview Kaitlin conducted."

"And."

"It all doesn't add up, John."

"How so?"

"In 2004 Jennifer reported to police that she and Erika left early and her sister, Ashley, took them home. When Ashley was interviewed she said the same. She picked the girls up and took them straight home. However, on Kaitlin's interview tape, Jennifer said that her sister was arguing with someone. She wasn't sure if there was another person in the car or not. I dug into the files and found Ashley's phone records. No phone call was recorded about the time she picked up Jennifer."

"Ashley dated Derek Blackstone then. Maybe he was in the car. I'll ask Ashley."

"Might explain why Blackstone is so willing to help out his old pal."

"Maybe."

Logan stirred the sauce. "It's no wonder Jennifer didn't remember much. She tested positive for Ecstasy. No telling what her blood alcohol was when she left the river. Kaitlin's blood alcohol was point-zero-eight when it was measured at the hospital about one in the morning. And that's at least one hour after she stopped drinking, so some of the booze had already metabolized out of her system. When Gina was taken, Kaitlin was hammered. Tack on the Ecstasy and I'm stunned she could get up the hill to Jack Hudson's house."

"Adrenaline must really have kicked in that night. Were there attacks on young females similar to the one on Gina and Kaitlin?"

"There were two. Detective North spoke to them both, but there aren't a lot of details in the files."

"I'm going to try and see him this afternoon."

"Good." Logan rubbed his leg. "What about last night's attack? Does Kaitlin know who stabbed her?"

"She says she doesn't remember, but she also doesn't trust cops."

Logan continued rubbing his thigh. "Getting stabbed is a good way to deflect attention from her as a suspect."

"Quinn said the same thing, but twenty stitches. Jesus, I can't imagine cutting yourself like that," Adler said.

"Are you in Kaitlin's corner?" Logan studied him closely.

"I wouldn't put it that way. I do think it's too convenient to blame her."

"Do you want my armchair analysis of you?" Logan asked.

"Do I have a choice?"

"Not really. You both have survivor's guilt. She made it out and her cousin didn't. You made it out and I, well, not so much. You see yourself in her."

Adler's guilt and pain crowded the air from his lungs. He didn't trust his voice. "You survived."

"True. And I don't blame you for the leg," Logan said, holding up his hand. "I wanted to go into that building as much as you did. I wanted to catch that son of a bitch as much as you did. If you remember, I wanted to go in first, but you made me stay back."

"I should have expected a trap."

Annoyance flashed in Logan's gaze. "Don't give yourself so much credit."

"I made the decision to enter the building."

"If you hadn't, I would have. Let it go. I have enough on my plate without worrying about your shit."

"You're worried about me?"

"Someone has to keep your rich-boy ass out of trouble. By the way the handicap rail arrived express, and I put it up."

That coaxed a smile. "How did it go?"

"Looks great. I haven't lost the touch when it comes to carpentry."

"Good to know. I'm not going to have the time to chase the contractors coming to the house for the next few weeks. Maybe you can."

"Chase?"

"My bad." He grinned.

Logan smiled. "Just screwing with you." His expression grew serious. "I got the house covered. Already saw a few places they need to redo."

"Thanks."

"John, just make sure you don't associate yourself with Kaitlin Roe too much. For all you know, she engineered this recent attack."

"I don't believe that."

"That's not your big head doing the thinking, pal." Logan shook his head. "John, you need facts not feelings. She's a suspect until you, *the cop*, can prove otherwise."

INTERVIEW FILE #14

THE THREE AMIGOS

In the Saint Mathew's 1993 yearbook, there is a picture of Mrs. Triton's third grade class. In the back row stand three smiling boys: Randy Hayward, Brad Crowley, and Derek Blackstone. They are three fresh-faced boys, all grinning broadly as if sharing a private joke. Like the other children in the classroom, the Three Amigos, as some called them, shared a similar background. Affluent homes. Doting parents. No history of violence in the homes. Talk to the former students in their class, and they all remember the trio. Thick as thieves. Pranksters. Shouter-outers. Boys being boys.

In conversations with Mrs. Triton's former students, hints of Randy's darker traits emerge. Stolen money. Spying on girls in the restroom. The missing class gerbils. But all agreed Derek Blackstone, charming, well mannered, and attractive, was the leader and instigator of their little antics. He was always nearby when trouble began but never blamed for anything.

But remember, this was third grade, and well, boys will be boys.

CHAPTER THIRTEEN

Sunday, March 18, 2018; 3:00 p.m.

Adler had called Kaitlin's boss, Susan Saunders, and asked to meet. Ms. Saunders had agreed and requested he come to her university office.

He left Logan poring over the Gina Mason case file and drove back into the city. He parked, entered the quiet lobby in the university communications building, and rode the elevator to the third floor. As he walked down the hallways, memories of his own college days at the University of Virginia returned.

His major had been political science, but in his sophomore year he'd started picking up criminal justice courses. He was still dialed into law school, but after he'd passed the bar, he told his parents he wasn't ready for a desk job. There was plenty of time for him to be a cop and then, later, a lawyer like his old man. His father hadn't been happy but reasoned it wouldn't take long for Adler to get this "cop thing" out of his system. That was seventeen years ago.

He moved along the corridor, following the signs to the communications director's office. He found the door ajar, the light on inside. He knocked.

"Enter." The voice carried a stern edge that sounded more practiced than natural.

He pushed open the door, drawing out his badge as he entered the room. "I'm Detective Adler with the Richmond police. I spoke to you about Kaitlin Roe."

Her gray hair was arranged in a loose topknot, and dark-rimmed glasses emphasized gray eyes. She rose and extended her hand. "Yes, yes, of course. Come in. I'm Susan Saunders. We heard about Kaitlin last night. How is she?"

"On the mend. She'll be fine. I'm looking into her attack and had a few questions." And he was honest enough with himself to admit his curiosity for Kaitlin ran deeper than the case.

She gestured toward a seat in front of her desk. "How may I be of service?"

He adjusted his tie and deliberately kept his body language relaxed. "Is she a well-liked teacher?"

"Yes. And she knows PR and can teach it. She can spin a question or answer in a dozen different ways."

"You've sat in on her classes?"

"Sure, a couple of them. She is quiet outside the classroom, but when she's in front of the kids, she's very animated. She's also young and attractive, which has won her some attention from the male students."

He'd not witnessed this animated side of Kaitlin. He tried to imagine her smiling and her eyes lighting up with laughter. "Any of these students try to ask her out?"

"That's against university policy."

A horny student wouldn't have let policy get in the way of hooking up with Kaitlin. He was older, supposedly wiser than the young men in her class, and he thought about her too often.

Susan turned toward her computer. "I had a student email footage from a class project Kaitlin arranged back in early December. Remember the arsonist who burned several row houses in the city?"

"I do."

"Two of the buildings destroyed are within blocks of the school. Kaitlin took several classes over there to film and discuss their reactions." Susan turned her computer screen toward Adler and hit "Play."

The cell phone footage of the class started off shaky and out of focus. Kaitlin appeared on screen. Her head bent, she was listening to several student comments and then pointing to the burned-out wreckage of the building. He'd been to that same site several times.

The camera swung back around, capturing Kaitlin again. This time she was explaining why it was important to be a witness to moments like this.

"Can you send me that?" Adler asked.

"Sure." As he recited his email address, she typed it in and hit "Send."

"Has Kaitlin had anybody hassling her?"

"No."

"Does she date?"

"If she does, she never mentioned it."

"Anyone following her around or sending her notes?"

"No, not that I know of. Certainly none of the students have stepped out of line with her." Susan hesitated. "So you haven't caught the guy who did this?"

"Not yet."

Susan drew in a breath. "Surely what happened to her isn't linked to the Gina Mason project?"

"I don't know."

"You must have an idea, or you wouldn't be here asking about it."

"I'm gathering facts right now."

Susan arched a brow. "Should I be concerned?"

He handed her one of his cards. "No. But if you do see anything, would you call me?"

"Sure."

He made his way through the building and out to his car. He pulled up email on his phone, selected the one Susan had just sent, and opened the video attachment. He replayed the video, finding his gaze drawn to Kaitlin. It was hard to stop looking at her. Muttering an oath, he shut off the recording. Logan was right. He needed facts, not feelings.

***

While waiting in the hospital lobby for Dr. Coggin, Adler called the Oak Croft Retirement Center and learned visiting hours lasted until eight. He checked his watch and asked them to inform Joshua North he'd be by soon.

The elevator doors opened, and Dr. Coggin exited. Coggin spotted Adler, nodded, and approached. Adler extended a hand to him. The man's smooth, boyish face belied world-weary eyes.

"Thanks for meeting me, Doc," Adler said.

Dr. Coggin had been on staff the day Adler and Logan had been brought into the emergency room. The doctor had saved his partner's life.

"How's Detective Logan?" Dr. Coggin asked.

"He's making good progress," Adler said.

"That's great. I'm glad to hear it. What can I do for you?" Dr. Coggin asked.

"I'm investigating the stabbing of Kaitlin Roe," Adler said.

"Right. A nasty stab wound. She was lucky."

"How is she doing?" Fear had dogged Adler when he hurried to Kaitlin's bedside after he'd been notified about her stabbing.

"She's strong and will recover." The doctor's gaze grew quizzical, as if he were trying to figure out where this was going. "What can I do to help you?"

Adler would have to tread carefully. "Hypothetically speaking, could you determine if a wound were self-inflicted or not?"

"Theoretically?" The doctor folded his arms and leaned toward Adler a fraction. "Sometimes."

"Would the angle of the cut be important?" he pressed. Adler didn't like the line of questioning, but knew it had to be done.

"It's difficult to stab yourself with the proper force. The natural tendency is to flinch. It's also difficult to get the range of motion and momentum to drive the blade into flesh while trying not to make it a mortal wound."

"But a motivated person could stab themselves and make it appear as if they'd been attacked?" Adler said.

"Yes, it's possible," Dr. Coggin said. "But no, I don't think Ms. Roe stabbed herself. I spoke to the paramedic who treated her on scene. She was barely conscious when they arrived, but when the medic tried to cut her shirt off to evaluate her injuries, Ms. Roe started to fight as if she were still under attack. She had to be restrained so they could get an IV started."

The image of Kaitlin fighting and screaming would be hard to shake. "When do you plan to release Kaitlin?"

"Tomorrow afternoon," he said.

"Could you find a reason to keep her until Thursday? If she's here, she's safe."

"I might be able to come up with a reason or two," Dr. Coggin said. "I'll keep the extra security on her floor until she leaves."

"Thank you." Kaitlin was safe for now, and he had one less thing to worry about.

***

The drive to the retirement home took Adler to the Ginter Park area in Northside. It was a neighborhood with an array of architectural styles ranging from Tudor Revival to Spanish Colonial. The retirement home where North was living had once been an orphanage, later a school, before most recently being converted to a senior living facility.

Adler showed his badge at the front desk and was directed to the old man's room. He found the retired detective dressed in pressed pants and a crisp white shirt playing solitaire at a table.

Adler knocked. "Detective North?"

North's tired shoulders straightened at the sound of his former title. He kept his gaze on his card game. "So what can I do for you, Detective Adler?"

Adler sat in a chair across from the old man. "I have questions about Gina Mason."

The old detective looked up. "A popular case these days. About time someone started paying attention again."

The old man flipped several cards over. The game now seemed to bore him, and he set the cards down. His demeanor shifted from tired to engaged.

"That woman send you here?"

"Kaitlin Roe? No."

North grunted. "Is she going to be okay?"

"Yes."

"Good."

"How did you hear about her?" Adler asked, slightly impressed.

"We do have phones here, and believe it or not, sonny, we graduated from dial-up access to the Internet." He shrugged. "After Kaitlin's visit, I called a few buddies on the force and asked around about her. One updated me on her and Jennifer Ralston."

"Kaitlin will recover."

"Good. She might not believe it, but I like her. Takes grit to face your past. Where was she when it happened?"

"The home of Erika Travis, now Crowley. She'd received a text allegedly from Erika, who's now missing."

"Was Kaitlin set up?" North asked.

"That's what I think."

"So how can I help?"

"I'd like to pick your brain about the Gina Mason case. There's no substitute for talking to the original investigator."

"Sure."

"What was Kaitlin like?"

"She had a juvenile record in Texas. Trespassing, drugs, shoplifting. When the case landed on my desk, I figured she was culpable. I leaned on her hard, and when that didn't work, I leaked her name to the press. By the time she left Richmond, she hated all cops, but especially me. I'd do it again." His jaw pulsed, and his chin raised a fraction.

Adler knew tough calls needed to be made during homicide investigations. "Would Kaitlin be the type to fake her own attack?"

"No."

"Why?"

"She's different now. She's not the flaky kid I interviewed years ago. She's on a mission now and hell-bent on getting to the bottom of what happened to Gina."

"All right." He'd be lying if he said he wasn't happy with the older detective's characterization.

"Any leads on the Jennifer Ralston case?" The old man slowly collected the cards, but his fingers struggled to divide and shuffle the stack.

"Not yet. Remember Randy Hayward?"

"Hard to forget that piece of shit. What's he saying now?"

"Says he can lead us to Gina. Wants a plea agreement to his pending murder charge."

North sat back, his face scowling with anger and frustration. "He's admitting to killing Gina?"

"He hasn't admitted to any crime. And he expects immunity in the Mason case."

An arthritic index finger tapped on the stack. "Shit. I knew he did it. I knew it," he muttered. "He's a smart son of a bitch. His IQ tested high. He knew I couldn't make a case without a credible eyewitness or a body. Once I even pretended I had found Gina's body, but he wasn't fooled. He's scum, but don't underestimate him."

"He had an alibi for the time of Gina's attack?"

"Yes. His mother said he was at home with her, and she never wavered from that story. Usually I can crack a lie, but not hers. You'd be wise to talk to her again. I hear she's not paying his legal bills this time, and his buddy Blackstone doesn't come cheap."

"Blackstone is working pro bono."

"Maybe because Hayward's unearthing a secret too many people want left undisturbed."

"You think Blackstone is in on this?" Adler asked.

"Blackstone, Hayward, and Crowley were tight, so it's very possible." He rubbed his chin as he dropped his gaze to the cards. "Did Kaitlin tell you she dated Hayward?"

"Not initially. Kaitlin's connection to Hayward surfaced after his fencing arrest, and we placed him near Kaitlin and Gina the night of the attack. Hayward let it 'slip' he knew Kaitlin well. I confronted her, and she admitted they'd broken up over the summer."

"Did Kaitlin say he might have been involved in the crime?" Adler asked.

"We conducted a lineup of suspects. She recognized Hayward, but she said she couldn't be sure if he was our guy. Kaitlin asked each man, including Hayward, to speak a few words. She swore she didn't recognize any of them."

"Maybe she was too afraid or loyal."

"Hayward is charismatic, but he can be mean as a snake. The podcast might just be a ruse to help an old boyfriend whom she still cares about." North shrugged. "She wouldn't be the first to help out a felon."

"Do you think she was really involved?" Adler kept his tone in check.

"I know she was afraid of Hayward. After we hauled him in, she said Hayward started hanging around her aunt's house. He never threatened her, but he let her know he was watching."

"My partner is going through your old case files for me. He said there were abductions in the Richmond area similar to Gina's attack? He said the details in the Mason case files were slim."

"There were two. Both happened about two years before Gina vanished, several miles downriver. Both girls were raped, but neither could identify her attacker."

"Was the rapist wearing a mask?" Adler asked.

"Pulled panty hose over his face. This attacker made both the girls shower after the attack, so we didn't get DNA. Both also had long dark hair like Gina. I couldn't link the cases, but it might be worth your time to talk to them again."

"Any girls go missing?"

"Not a girl like Gina," North said.

White. Affluent. Easily missed. "But there are all kinds of runaways, sex workers, and undocumented all along the I-95 corridor."

"And when they go missing, few care," North said.

"If Hayward killed Gina and didn't leave a trail, it makes me think she wasn't his first. He'd had practice covering his tracks."

"The drugs have now taken their toll on him," North said. "He was sloppy with the convenience store stabbing."

"Let's hope that trend continues."

North leaned forward, holding Adler's gaze. "Do me a favor and bury him."

"I'll do my best."

The two shook hands, and Quinn's number flashed on Adler's display. Out in the hallway he answered, "Quinn."

"I spoke to Ashley Ralston. She's willing to see us now."

"Good. Could you search rapes farther downriver during the two years before Gina vanished? Detective North remembers two."

"Will do."

***

Adler drove to the station and picked up Quinn, and together they traveled across town to a new trendy apartment complex near Rocketts Landing located east of downtown Richmond. Ashley Ralston lived in a third-floor apartment overlooking the James River.

Adler knocked on the door. Seconds later footsteps preceded the click of locks, and the door opened to Ashley Ralston. She wore no makeup, and the stress of her sister's death was etched in lines around her mouth and red-rimmed eyes.

Adler and Quinn held up their badges. "Ms. Ralston."

She recognized them both, and her frown deepened. "Come on in."

She escorted them into a small living room furnished with a matching set of new furniture. A dozen moving boxes had been flattened and stacked in the corner, and several framed posters leaned against the plain antique-white walls. "I was just on the phone with the funeral home and the medical examiner's office." She ran a trembling hand over her hair. "I still can't believe she's gone. I never pictured myself having to do this."

"I'm sorry for your loss," Adler said. "Have you been able to schedule the funeral?"

"Sunday afternoon."

He had made dozens of death notices during his ten years with the homicide department. It never got easier, nor did dealing with the grieving family's desperate need for answers. "Looks like you just moved in."

She shrugged. "A few weeks ago. It was supposed to be my new life after my divorce. Jennifer and I were supposed to take a trip to Paris this summer to celebrate."

"You were close to your sister?" Adler asked.

"I haven't seen her much in the last few years. A failing marriage distracted me, but the plan was to spend more time with her."

"Did she talk about having issues with anyone?" Quinn asked.

"You mean like a stalker? Not until recently. Last week at our lunch a man kept staring at us. I found him annoying, but she freaked out and insisted we leave. Our food had just arrived, and I was annoyed to leave hungry. The waitress packed up our food, and we left."

"Did the man follow?"

"No. In the car, she told me about her stalker. I asked her if she'd spoken to the cops. She said she did."

"I remember you told me that at her home. I searched for any police reports made by your sister, but there were none," Adler said softly.

"Really? She told me she reported this guy to the cops." Tears welled in Ashley's eyes. "I guess she lied to keep me from bugging her."

"Why do you think she didn't report it?" Quinn asked.

"Embarrassed, I guess. I don't really know."

"It's unfortunate," Quinn said.

"She was wrong to be embarrassed. That's why we have cops, to take care of the wackos." Bitterness twisted around the words.

"So she never mentioned a particular individual?" Adler asked.

"No. I offered her my couch, but she insisted on staying at her own place. I should have made her stay with me."

"What about Jennifer's ex-boyfriend?" Adler asked.

"Jeremy? He's not the type. He's fairly passive. And I hear he has a new girlfriend. If anything, she still had feelings for him."

"Would there have been any reason for him to visit her a few weeks ago?"

She shrugged. "Sex. That was always great between them." She sighed. "I wish Jennifer had talked to me more, but she learned at an early age to downplay the negative."

"How so?" Adler asked.

"After Gina vanished, Jennifer was pretty freaked out. She always blamed herself. Said if she'd not gotten so drunk, she would have stuck around and been there for Gina. That night has haunted her, but my mother grew tired of hearing about it. So did I frankly, so she stopped talking about it."

"You were at the river when Gina vanished," Quinn confirmed.

"I came to pick up Jennifer and Erika. They were both too wasted to be on their own."

"Did you see Gina and Kaitlin before you left?" Adler asked.

"I did. They were waiting with Jennifer and Erika. They were all trashed."

"Why didn't you take Gina and Kaitlin home?" Adler asked.

"They said they wanted to walk. It was less than a quarter of a mile away, and I had my hands full with my sister and Erika."

"And you were alone in the car?" Adler asked.

"Yes."

"When Kaitlin interviewed your sister, Jennifer mentioned hearing you arguing with a man," Adler said.

"She must have had her timeline confused. I did argue with my boyfriend when we returned back to my mom's house. He was annoyed I'd been gone so long."

"That would be Derek Blackstone," Adler said.

"Yes."

"How long were you gone?"

"Fifteen or twenty minutes."

"What was Kaitlin's relationship with Gina like?" Quinn asked, deliberately shifting the focus.

"They fought a lot. Gina was a great kid, but Kaitlin wasn't easy. Moody. Not a hard worker. Jennifer asked Gina once why she was so nice to Kaitlin, and Gina reminded her that Kaitlin's brother had killed himself and we needed to cut her some slack."

"Was Gina dating anyone?"

"Yeah, a boy named Tom Davenport, but they broke up right before graduation."

"He's still here in Richmond and works in finance, right?"

"That's right. He can't be hard to find."

"He must have been devastated," Quinn said.

"He was. He was really angry with Jennifer, Erika, and Kaitlin. He felt like they let Gina down."

"Did Tom have any recent contact with Jennifer?"

"Not that I'm aware of. It's been fourteen years. He's grown up and matured. He knew deep down those girls were kids and would never have hurt Gina."

"What do you think, Ashley?" Quinn asked.

Ashley threaded her fingers together. "I blame all this on Kaitlin Roe. She was a troublemaker then and she's still one. Her damn interviews are reopening old wounds. I told Jennifer to stay away from her."

Adler circled back to Blackstone and Hayward. "Derek, Brad, and Randy were friends."

"Derek and Brad still are. Randy Hayward tagged along, but he was always stirring up trouble. They recognized Randy as the loser he always was."

"So you knew Randy?" Adler asked.

"We were the same age and attended the same high school, but I doubt we spoke ten words to each other." She reached for a tissue and twisted it in her hands.

"Why would Derek defend Randy now?" Adler asked.

"Loyalty. They've known each other since kindergarten. Derek is faithful to a fault when it comes to his buddies."

"You were with Derek when Jennifer called for a ride home?" Quinn asked.

"I just said that. We were at my parents' house."

"What did he do while you went to get the girls?" Adler asked.

"He hung out at my parents' house and waited for me."

"How long did it take you to pick up the girls, drop Erika off, and get back home?" Adler asked.

"Fifteen minutes," Ashley said.

Quinn looked confused. "Fifteen minutes to pick up two drunk girls, drive one home, and then put the other one to bed? That doesn't sound like enough time."

"Maybe it was thirty minutes, but it wasn't that long," Ashley said.

"But you didn't have eyes on your boyfriend for at least thirty minutes," Adler said.

"I heard the television in the family room when we came home, and I saw him seconds after I put Jennifer to bed. He was standing in the kitchen drinking water."

"How did he look?" Adler asked.

"It's been so long I don't remember."

"You remembered he was drinking water," Quinn said.

"He was annoyed." Ashley shrugged. "It was date night, and we both weren't happy about the interruption."

"Would it be fair to say you really didn't see Derek for almost an hour?" Adler said.

Ashley's face flushed. "What difference do a few minutes make?"

"They could have made a big difference," Quinn said.

"Jennifer almost lost her college acceptance offer because of all the police scrutiny. Derek was applying to law schools and couldn't be tarnished by a few missing minutes."

"Why're you still covering for him?" Quinn asked. "He broke up with you a long time ago."

"I refuse to throw him under the bus for a crime that had nothing to do with him."

"But you can confirm there was an hour when you didn't know what he was doing," Adler said.

She frowned. "Yeah, I guess. What does all this have to do with Jennifer's murder?"

"Maybe nothing," Adler said.

"Are you any closer to finding my sister's killer?"

"We're chasing every lead, Ms. Ralston," Adler said. "I'll call you as soon as I have more information."

"Thank you."

Adler and Quinn left Ashley standing in her door, staring after them. Inside the car, Quinn said, "She covered for Derek Blackstone."

"Yes, she did."

"Supposing on that road fourteen years ago Hayward hurt Gina, panicked, and called his buddy Derek, who races to help his friend. Ashley was Blackstone's girlfriend and might have known this. An hour is enough time to stash a body in a trunk or a shallow grave."

"Or Blackstone was the one who hurt Gina, and Randy raced to his aid. We know Randy was in the area at the time. Again, Ashley could have known."

"Either scenario is a reason to stop Jennifer and Erika from talking to Kaitlin."

***

"Hi, I'm Gina Mason, Saint Mathew's class of 2004! Welcome to the Rebels' soccer team—district finalists three years in a row!"

The taped voice pulled Erika toward consciousness. Her mouth was dry, and her head ached. Her legs and arms felt as if they weighed hundreds of pounds each.

Finally she found the energy to open her eyes, but was greeted by pitch blackness. She blinked, closing her eyes and opening them again. Was she really awake? Was she blind? Panic cut through her as she felt the cold cement wall and floor.

"Hi, I'm Gina Mason, Saint Mathew's class of 2004! Welcome to the Rebels' soccer team—district finalists three years in a row!"

Gina's voice echoed in the room and sent tremors of fear through her. She moistened her lips as she pressed her back to the wall behind her and slowly rose to her feet. Her legs wobbled and her head spun, forcing her to stand very still until she regained her footing.

In complete darkness, she had no frame of reference. She didn't know how high the ceiling was or if the ground around her was solid or safe.

"Hello?" she shouted. "Anyone there?"

"Hi, I'm Gina Mason, Saint Mathew's class of 2004! Welcome to the Rebels' soccer team—district finalists three years in a row!"

"Hello!" Her growing panic sharpened her tone. "Why am I here? Brad, is this you?"

She thought about the skipped yoga classes and the coffee she'd had with the reporter. Had Brad found out? He'd forbidden her to talk about Gina, but she'd been angry with him and wanted to pay him back.

"Brad, if this is you, I didn't say anything. I promise, baby."

"Hi, I'm Gina Mason, Saint Mathew's class of 2004! Welcome to the Rebels' soccer team—district finalists three years in a row!"

Gingerly she ran her fingers along the cement wall and inched her foot forward, searching for a way to escape. Her stomach churning, she skimmed carefully along the wall until she reached her first corner. Venturing onward, she moved along until her fingers touched what felt like a door.

Relieved and terrified, she pounded on the door and screamed. "Help me! Please let me out of here!"

She struck the door until her hands bled and screamed until her throat was raw.

"Hi, I'm Gina Mason, Saint Mathew's class of 2004! Welcome to the Rebels' soccer team—district finalists three years in a row!"

Exhausted and dizzy, she pressed her palms to her ears and lowered herself to the floor. "Stop it!"

She wrapped her arms around her knees as she tipped her head back against cement. She'd been walled in. It felt like a tomb.

Meanwhile, Gina's voice played over and over.

INTERVIEW FILE #15

FALSE LEADS

Five days after Gina's disappearance, the police opened a tip line. Within hours, a trickle of leads turned into a flood. At one point during the investigation, the police department had two officers dedicated to the tip line.

Some tipsters thought they'd spotted Gina alive and well living in southwest Virginia. Others swore the disturbed soil on their farm property was her shallow grave. One woman was convinced Gina was working in a convenience store in Arlington, Virginia, and had amnesia.

The cops followed up on all credible leads. Law enforcement searched vacant lots, farmers' fields, and abandoned buildings not only in the Richmond area but also throughout Virginia and into the mid-Atlantic region. In the end, none of the information panned out.

CHAPTER FOURTEEN

Monday, March 19, 2018; 10:00 a.m.

Quinn had found the names of the two girls who had been sexually assaulted two years before Gina vanished. One of the victims, Lily Jackson, had moved to California, but the other, Maureen Campbell, worked as a cop in the state police's vice unit. She discovered it was Agent Campbell's day off and arranged to meet her in her Goochland home, forty-five minutes west of Richmond.

Minutes later, Adler and Quinn were in his car driving west, and within the hour he was parking in front of a small brick house on a large wooded lot. The grass around the house was cut, and the trim around the door and windows sported a fresh coat of white paint. They made their way to the front door, and he knocked.

Footsteps in the home moved toward the door. There was a hesitation, and he sensed they were being studied through the peephole. He stepped back and rested his hands on his hips while moving his jacket back slightly so his badge was in view.

The door opened to an attractive woman with long dark hair, a fit body, and green eyes that shifted from wary to somewhat welcoming. "Detective Quinn?" she asked.

"Yes, ma'am, and this is my partner, Detective John Adler. Thanks for seeing us, Agent Campbell."

"It's Maureen." She unlatched the screened door and pushed it open. "Your timing is good. I was about to open the paint cans when you called. It's my first day off in a few weeks, and I'm determined to paint the living room."

"Sorry to disturb your plans," Adler said.

Maureen laughed. "No, any excuse to not paint is a good excuse."

In the living room, there was a couch, a couple of chairs, and a navy-blue rug covering polished wood floors. All her pictures tilted against a wall in a neat stack.

Maureen sat and motioned for them to do the same.

"Have you been here long?" Adler asked as he took one of the chairs.

"Two years, but work has kept me on the go. There's been little time to fix up the place. My unit and I infiltrated a human trafficking ring and just busted three guys controlling twenty girls."

"That's a hell of a win," Quinn said.

"It is, but it'll be a long way back for the girls." She cleared her throat. "Can I get you coffee?"

Both declined.

"We'll cut to the chase, if that works for you," Quinn said.

"Absolutely."

Quinn flipped open a notebook. "When you were sixteen a man broke into your parents' home and sexually assaulted you?"

Maureen lifted her chin a fraction. "That's correct. My parents had gone out for the evening and left me home alone. I'd fallen asleep on the couch and woke up to find a man standing over me. He had a knife pressed to my throat."

"You said that your attacker was wearing panty hose over his face," she continued.

"Yes. He kept his face covered. I later met with a police sketch artist, but the image wasn't helpful."

"Can you tell us what happened next?" Quinn asked.

Maureen shifted and then settled. "He dragged me to my room, tied me to my bed, and for approximately two hours raped me."

"Was he concerned that your parents might return?" Adler asked.

"I told him they'd be home any second, but he laughed. He said he'd been watching the house and knew Wednesday nights were their movie nights and they never returned home before eleven." She raised her fingers to the base of her throat. "Several times he put his hands around my neck and squeezed, but he seemed to grow tired."

"He underestimated how hard it is to strangle someone," Quinn said.

Maureen nodded. "Yes, I think that is exactly it. If I had to bet, I'd say I was one of his first victims."

"Any other reason to support that theory?" Adler asked.

"Even though he said he knew no one was coming to help me, he was nervous. His hands shook as he was tying mine to the headboard. And once a car passed by outside and he stopped, put his hand over my mouth, and waited until the street was silent again."

"Your attacker wore a condom, correct?" Quinn asked.

"Yes. He also made me take a shower after the attack. He stood by the shower and made me wash my hair and wash my entire body. He was smart. The forensic nurse who examined me couldn't collect any useable evidence."

"When did you learn about Gina Mason?" Adler asked.

"It was hard not to hear about her. She was in all the headlines. I was obsessed about her case. It struck very close to home for me."

"Two years after your attack, you were shown Randy Hayward's mug shot," Quinn said.

"I was. I couldn't identify him."

"Did you ever see Hayward in a lineup?" Adler asked.

"His attorney argued because I couldn't ID his mug shot and because there was no DNA in my case, a lineup wasn't warranted. A judge agreed." She sighed. "I'm older now and can see my case from a cop's perspective. The MO of my attacker was different than Gina Mason's. My attacker attacked me in my home, and he let me go. Yes, he covered his face, but many guys like that do. It's reasonable to argue we had different assailants," she said, frowning.

"Why do you think your attacker let you go?" Quinn asked.

"After he raped me, he noticed a stuffed bear on my bed. He said he'd had a bear like that when he was a kid. He asked me if I'd named my bear. I told him its name was Buddy. That seemed to amuse him. I thought we had some kind of emotional connection and he maybe finally saw me as a person. Five minutes later he left." She scanned both detectives as if they were suspects. "Why all the questions now?"

"Randy Hayward is back in custody and is willing to lead us to Gina Mason," Adler said.

Maureen stared at them both closely. "What do you want from me?"

"You know, as well as we do, that guys like Hayward evolve," Quinn said. "First stalking, then rape, and then murder. Serial offenders require more violence to get the same rush of adrenaline and sexual payoff."

Maureen drew in a breath. "When is Hayward supposed to take you to Gina?"

"End of this week," Adler said. "I don't know if we can ever link Hayward to your rape, but I hoped you might be able to tell us something we could use."

Maureen regarded him a moment. "After my rapist finished, I could tell he was worried about being captured. He climbed on top of me and put his hands around my throat again. Before he started to squeeze, I asked him if he'd named his stuffed bear. The question caught him off guard, and he released my neck and climbed off of me."

"Did he tell you the name?" Adler asked.

"Charlie. He said his bear's name was Charlie. Ask Hayward what happened to Charlie."

Adler nodded. "Will do."

"Keep me posted," Maureen said. "Whether he's my guy or not, that poor kid needs to be found."

"We will," Adler said.

They left Maureen Campbell and drove to Ruth Hayward's home, but found the house closed up, the blinds drawn, and no cars in the driveway or garage.

"Think she's left town?" Quinn asked.

"We'll find her," Adler said. "One way or another, we'll talk to her."

"She's worried. Her kid is about to spill the beans, and she's going to face a lot of questions," Quinn said.

"What's so special about Hayward? He has so many friends and family willing to protect him," Adler said.

"He was young and charming. Mama's boy. Everyone's best friend. Psychopaths can be charming manipulators," Quinn said.

"Nobody said they were stupid," Adler said.

As Adler and Quinn made their way to his car, his phone buzzed with a text from a detective in a neighboring jurisdiction. Brad Crowley had returned home and realized the police were looking for him. He was ready to be interviewed.

"We don't even know Erika is missing," Quinn pointed out as she slid on her sunglasses. "She could be on a vacation."

"You really think she's on a vacation?" Adler asked.

"No. But we don't have any evidence otherwise."

"I want to listen in on the interview," he said.

"I'd like in on it as well. I'll try not to step on toes."

A smile tugged at the edge of Adler's lips. "Don't kid yourself. You never miss a chance to stir shit up."

She laughed. "Guilty. I'm a card-carrying provocateur."

At the station, Adler and Quinn entered the room adjacent to the interview room. Through a two-way mirror, they saw Brad Crowley sitting in a plastic chair next to a scarred wooden table. Crowley wore charcoal-gray pants, a white shirt, and a yellow tie he'd loosened. His blond hair looked as if it had been slicked back but was now disheveled. His gaze downcast, he picked at a Styrofoam cup.

Detective Jeff Beck, a midsize, lean man, sported a blue suit and a full gray mustache reminiscent of the nineties. He stood outside interview room six sipping a cup of coffee.

Adler walked up to Beck and shook his hand. "Thanks for the call."

"Hey, anytime." Beck had taken a job with county police three years ago, but Adler and Beck had attended the city police academy together. Beck was one hell of a smart guy. They'd spent a few all-nighters studying for academy tests and had crossed paths during their uniformed patrol days more times than he could count. Each had attended the other's wedding, and each commiserated when those marriages fell apart under the strain of the job.

"What's his story?" Adler asked.

"He said he and his wife had an argument last week. He got angry, thought she was being unreasonable, and decided to split for a while."

"He dropped everything just like that?" Adler asked.

"I checked with his office, and his secretary did clear his schedule at the last minute. She was supposed to tell everyone that he was attending a conference. She said he had a lot of pissed-off patients. Not everyone makes logical choices when they're angry," Beck said.

"Point taken."

"Does he appear worried about his wife?" Quinn asked.

"More irritated and inconvenienced," Beck said. "He thinks this is her way of paying him back because he took off."

Adler studied Crowley through the two-way mirror. His shoulders were relaxed, and his expression oddly calm as he rolled a quarter over his fingers with practiced agility. This guy was far from stressed, or so it appeared. Even an innocent guy would be a little uncomfortable. He was trying too hard.

"I'd like to talk to him."

Beck studied him. "Sure. Why not?"

"Thanks."

"Tag team?" Quinn asked, grinning with anticipation.

Adler looked at Quinn. "Play nice."

She shrugged. "Sure, might be fun to switch it up."

Adler and Quinn entered the room. Quinn tossed a smile at Crowley and chose the seat closest to him. Crowley's glance was dismissive and defiant until he looked at Adler. Anger flashed, and he rightly identified Adler as a threat.

Crowley kept his composure. "Do you have any news about my wife?"

Where Adler sat during an interview said a lot about his goals. If he were dealing with a traumatized witness, he'd pull up his chair beside the individual as Quinn had done. Sometimes he stood. Today he sat across from Crowley to show him he wasn't his ally.

"My name is Detective Adler, and this is Detective Quinn. I understand your wife is missing."

Crowley tugged at his left cuff. "I haven't seen her since Thursday, but I wouldn't classify her as missing."

"Thursday is the last day you were home?"

"I went by my house today. I saw the police tape. And I called 911, and they told me to come here. Are you telling me my wife is injured?"

He wanted Crowley to answer as many questions as possible before he started sharing facts. "Where did you see your wife last?"

"At the house. It had been a long day for both of us, and our tempers flared. Normally, we cool off by now. I texted her several times, but she hasn't answered. That's why I went by the house looking for her."

"Is there anyone who would want to hurt your wife?"

Crowley straightened, sniffed, and cleared his throat. "Are you telling me my wife is hurt? What the hell is going on here?"

"Your wife is missing. Another woman who came to visit you was assaulted on your property by an unknown assailant."

Crowley drew in a deep breath, and he hesitated. "But Erika was not hurt, correct?"

"We have no evidence," Quinn said. "But we are concerned about her welfare."

"Why don't you know where she is? You're the damn cops, aren't you?"

"We're trying to find her," Quinn said. "There's no sign of credit card use. No one has seen her. And her cell is dead."

"Who is the woman who was hurt?" Crowley demanded.

"A friend of your wife's," Adler said.

"Who? I know all my wife's friends."

"Kaitlin Roe," Adler said.

"Roe?" Crowley shook his head. "She's not a friend of my wife's. They went to the same high school, but they haven't seen each other in years."

"Apparently, Kaitlin wanted to interview your wife for a podcast she's making on Gina Mason."

That bit of news seemed to surprise him. "Maybe Kaitlin was breaking into my house. She had a drug habit."

"No evidence of a break-in. Do you have any idea where your wife might be?"

Crowley's anger melted as the color drained from his face and the reality set in. "No. Where's her car?"

"We found it at a gas station on Route 1. We had it towed to the police impound. Right now it's with the forensic team."

"Forensic team?" He leaned forward, shaking his head. "Don't you think this is getting way out of hand? She's jerking my chain."

Adler wasn't here to answer questions but to ask them. "Are you sure you don't know where your wife might be?"

"No, damn it, I don't. Again, do you have evidence she's hurt?"

"A friend of hers was killed, and we're concerned for her safety."

"Which friend?"

"Jennifer Ralston."

"Jennifer? Jesus, what happened?"

"You didn't know about Jennifer?"

"I told you, I've been out of town. How did Jennifer die?"

"I can't discuss that now," Adler said. "What do you know about Ms. Ralston?"

"She went to high school with my wife. We saw her at a school fund-raiser last year, but haven't seen her since."

"You're sure your wife hasn't seen her?" Adler asked.

"My wife rarely leaves the house. She goes to yoga twice a week and that's about it."

"Why doesn't she leave her house?" Adler asked.

"She agoraphobic. Leaving the house creates a great deal of stress. It took a lot of therapy just to get her to yoga."

"Both your wife and Ms. Ralston were two of four girls on the river the night Gina Mason vanished."

"I know. We never talk about Gina. It upsets Erika too much, so we don't."

"Any idea where she might have gone?" Adler asked.

"Nowhere. My wife went nowhere. You're the cops, and it's your job to find her. She functions within a three-mile radius of the house."

"You sound pretty certain," Adler said.

"I'm always looking out for my wife's best interests."

"We'd like to return to your house. You can join us and tell us if any items are missing."

"Sure. Of course."

"Does now work?" Adler asked.

"Do I have a choice?" Crowley asked.

Without comment, they escorted Crowley to a car. The drive took under twenty minutes, and no one spoke. Out of the car, Crowley moved past the cops and headed up the front stairs to the door. As Crowley moved out of hearing distance, Quinn looked at Adler.

"I call bullshit," she said loud enough for only her partner to hear. "I don't think he cares about his wife."

"He appears upset, but I'm not buying it."

"If it walks like a duck and quacks like a duck," Quinn said.

Adler trailed behind Crowley up the stairs and through the front door. Crowley had flipped on the entryway lights and immediately spotted the bloodstain on the floor. He froze.

"That's not Erika's blood, correct?"

"Correct," Adler said.

"This must have been some kind of robbery gone wrong. Jesus, with all the drug addicts running around on the streets today, nice houses like ours are a soft target."

"Let's have a look around."

"How was Kaitlin Roe hurt?"

"She was stabbed," he said.

Crowley's jaw tightened. "My wife never liked Kaitlin. I can't see her allowing an interview with anyone, especially with Kaitlin."

"What did your wife tell you about the night Gina vanished?"

He moved past the bloodstain into the living room, flipping on lights as he moved through the space. "Like I said, she didn't like to talk about it."

"She must have mentioned it once or twice," Quinn said.

"She was eaten up with guilt. She felt if she'd stayed behind instead of leaving, Gina would still be alive."

"You think Gina's dead?" Adler said.

"After all this time, how could she be alive?"

"It's been known to happen," Adler said. "Where were you the night Gina vanished?"

"At my parents' house. I was waiting for Erika, but she never came." He shook his head. "The Kaitlin Roe I remember was always good at manipulating people. She convinced her aunt to take her in and pay for her tuition. If there's anyone who knows what's going on, it's Kaitlin Roe."

"Ms. Roe has no memory of the attack," Adler said.

Crowley clenched his hands. "Don't believe her," he said. "She's a fucking liar."

***

Dear Kaitlin,
You are lucky. You escaped your punishment. The plan wasn't to stab you but to take you. I have a special room for you, and nothing will make me happier than to lock you in it and then set it on fire. You are a witch. You deserve to burn and to suffer. I am coming back for you, and remember when you are drawing your dying breath, you asked for this.

The words in the note felt inadequate. They didn't begin to tap the rage he felt toward Kaitlin. Jennifer he could forgive. She'd never been strong. Even Erika would be forgiven. But Kaitlin was the one who'd had a real chance to save her friend, but literally turned her back on Gina.

He balled up the letter and threw it on the floor. He had been so careful with his planning. He'd driven Erika's car to a Route 1 gas station, bound her hands and feet with tape, and transferred her to his truck. After dumping her off at his place, he'd returned to her house to wait inside for Kaitlin. But the plan had gone to shit when Kaitlin had set off that alarm. He'd panicked and lunged with the knife, hoping only to make the noise stop.

A wave of frustration churned in his gut. Kaitlin was supposed to be here, and he wanted to snatch her now. But for the next few days, she was out of his reach. *Shit!* The agitation crawling under his skin was going to drive him mad.

He grabbed keys and unlocked the basement door, then flipped on a light and descended the rickety staircase. Another lock secured the last door.

Erika had been in the dark for forty-eight hours. No food. No water. Essentially entombed alive. It was a hell of a way to go. He wanted to leave her down here until she died of thirst and deprivation. It was another of the horrible ways he'd imagined Gina dying.

However, he no longer had the patience to kill her slowly. He had to do something to calm his nerves. Today she would be Kaitlin's proxy, and her death would ease the tightness in his chest. Give him enough relief to prepare once and for all for Kaitlin.

He slipped on a white hazmat suit and gloves before opening the door. The light streamed into the small room, illuminating walls filled with dozens of pictures of Gina. The acrid smell of urine made his nose wrinkle.

Erika struggled to sit up and raised a weak hand to shield her eyes. A person could go a long time without food, but lack of water took a much faster toll on the body.

He gave her a moment, wanting her eyes to adjust clearly enough to see the walls papered with Gina's beautiful face.

She didn't have the strength to rise. "Gina."

"That's right." Seeing Gina's smiling face always made him angry. That girl had died too young, and her death could be laid at the feet of her faithless friends who'd abandoned her. "Do you ever think about how she died?"

"What?"

Lack of water had left her lightheaded. That was unfortunate. He wanted her fully aware. "So many horrible ways she could have died. I've imagined each and every one of them."

He pulled the knife from his pocket and unfolded it. "I wanted you to die cold, abandoned, scared, and desperate." He took a step toward her and raised the knife, imagining what Kaitlin had felt.

She flinched and rolled on her belly, ready to crawl. Her fingers scraped against the stone floor. There was nowhere for her to go.

He approached her from behind and without a word cut her throat with one swipe. She flinched and then raised her filthy hands to the blood spurting from her neck. Adrenaline surged through him as he held her close. Feeling her life ebb was a release. He craved more.

Her body went limp with her last breath. He didn't move immediately, hoping the high would linger. It didn't. It evaporated almost immediately, leaving him feeling empty and angry.

He gently brushed the hair from her pale, now-angelic face. "I forgive you, Erika."

She'd gotten off easily, but Kaitlin would not.

INTERVIEW FILE #16

DESPERATION: PSYCHICS AND MEDIUMS

Monday, February 5, 2018

The pungent scent of incense clings to the red velvet drapes hanging behind a hand-carved wooden chair and matching table. Tarot cards and three lit candles are the center of attention. Crystals dangle from the ceiling, catching the morning light and flickering rainbows of color on dark indigo walls. The Old Country feel of the room stands in stark contrast to the bright-orange neon lights blinking PSYCHIC and OPEN.

Madame Solinsky wears a full-length duster with bell sleeves embroidered with stars and moons. Her hair is dyed ink black, and heavily penciled eyebrows arch in mild surprise. For a while, she was quite the media sensation after Gina vanished, even appearing on a national talk show to share her mystic visions for the lost girl.

"You said you wanted to talk about Gina Mason," Madame says.

"Yes. You worked with the police during the months after she went missing. You offered your services to the police."

"I did." She reaches for the deck of tarot cards and begins to shuffle.

"What was it that prompted you to call the police?" Madame Solinsky isn't the only psychic who called the police, but she garnered the most airtime from local television. Steven Marcus has interviewed her four times.

"I knew she was gone, and I had to tell the police."

"You had gruesome theories about her fate."

Madame lays out four cards facedown one by one in a spread resembling a cross. "In my dreams I see a man with two faces."

"Two?" The clown mask was reported to the media.

"Two."

"But the man is not important now. It's Gina who's beckoning me. She looks worried." Madame taps a ringed finger on the first card and then slowly, with the flourish of a performer, turns it over with a snap. "The Nine of Wands."

The medium wafts her hand over the card, as if conjuring the truth from the ether. "Her spirit is strong, but she needs the police to find her so that you will know peace."

"Me?"

"Yes. She's worried about you."

That churns the guilt I always carry. "How did Gina die?" I paid fifty bucks before the Madame would talk to me. I'm not expecting the smoking gun, but I want to see how far she will take this show.

"She was stabbed." Madame presses ringed fingers to the base of her neck. "She died very quickly."

"You've also said she died in a dark room and in a fire."

"I can only report what I see. Sometimes a spirit gets confused." Madame turns over the second card and studies it. "The Hanged Man. Time to reflect. Some of the knife wounds were near her throat."

She turns over the third card, which portrays a man and woman embracing. The card is upside down. "The Lovers card in reverse. Betrayal and loss."

I have to hand it to her. She puts on a good show.

Madame waves bent fingers over the three cards and then turns over a fourth. It is a castle being struck by lightning. "This is the Tower. Turmoil. You're facing a great upheaval in your life."

I close my notebook. The fifty bucks I've spent here could have gone toward a week's worth of pizzas. "Thank you for your time, Madame."

As I rise, Madame looks up, her gaze spearing me. "The killer knows what you're doing. And he doesn't like it. Beware."

CHAPTER FIFTEEN

Monday, March 19, 2018; 5:00 p.m.

Kaitlin could stand, and though she couldn't cross the room quickly, it was now possible. Her limited mobility was frustrating, but she remained focused on the progress she'd made.

Now sitting up in bed, propped on pillows, she studied the list of people she'd yet to interview. At the top of the list was Steven Marcus, the reporter who covered Gina's story. He was no longer with the paper but now operated a website and wrote freelance articles dedicated to solving cold cases. According to her research, his reporting had helped police across the country solve a dozen different crimes.

His last piece on Gina had appeared four years ago at the ten-year anniversary. Of all the reporters, he was the most prolific. Several of his articles on Gina had won literary awards.

With her laptop beside her and a pad and pencil close by, she dialed his number. He picked up on the third ring.

"Steven Marcus." His voice was deep and clear.

She sat a little straighter. "Mr. Marcus, this is Kaitlin Roe. I am—"

"I know who you are," he said. In the background a chair squeaked as if he had leaned forward. "Talk about a voice from the past. I don't know how many times I left you messages when I was writing those earlier articles on Gina. You never called back."

"I know." Maybe an apology was warranted, but she couldn't bring herself.

"And then you dropped off the radar. Where'd you go?"

"Texas, but I'm back in Richmond now."

"So why the call?" Curiosity vibrated in the tone.

"I'm making a podcast about Gina's disappearance. I'm hoping to draw attention back to her case."

"Good luck. The more time passes, the harder it gets for people to care."

"I'm hoping that'll change. I've managed to stir the pot some, and it might lead to progress in the case."

A dog barked in the background. "What kind of progress?"

"I can't say right now."

"You don't return my calls whenever I did a story on Gina, but you want background from me now."

"Yes. Shoe's on the other foot now."

Soft laughter rumbled through the phone. "You've got stones, Kaitlin."

"So I've been told."

"It's been fourteen years. I pitched a cold case article idea on her a few months ago and received no bites."

"Why're you still writing about her?" Kaitlin asked.

"Gina Mason had all the ingredients of a perfect life. Pretty. Smart. Ambitious. And then she was gone. When I first covered her, she was just another tragedy. But I never could forget her. When beautiful youth is ruined, it's gripping. James Dean. Marilyn Monroe. Princess Diana. People still talk about them. I'd hoped to elevate Gina to that higher level."

"Why?"

"I could ask you the same. Why do you suddenly care? You've been MIA for fourteen years."

She decided to be candid. "I let her down," she said. "I wasn't there for her when she needed me most."

Silence hung between them. "A lot of people would agree with you."

"I know."

"So what do you want from me?"

"I'd like to interview you. You covered her more than anyone. You know as much as the cops do."

The dog's bark blended with the laughter of children. "That's true. Perhaps more. Though I bet you've scored interviews I couldn't because of your inside track."

"The last thing I feel like is an insider."

"You were at ground zero. You saw the crime happen. Doesn't get any more inside than that."

"I'll share if you share," she said.

More silence and finally, "Sure, I'll work with you. Right now, I'm on deadline. Let's meet on Saturday?"

She felt her stitches pull as she shifted. "Sure. That actually would be perfect."

"I can reach you at this number?" Marcus asked.

"Yes."

"Looking forward to working with you, Kaitlin."

"Me, too."

She ended the call and lay back against the pillows. She felt more confident she would be able to travel with the police on Friday and see Marcus the following day. She had no choice. She might even have real news to share with Marcus.

A knock on her door had her closing her laptop. Anxious to leave the hospital, she was in no mood for a visitor, or worse a nurse poking and prodding her.

"Come in."

Susan Saunders, her boss, poked her head around the door. She carried with her a vase full of white tulips and a grin. Her thick stock of gray hair was tied back with a headband, and she wore a black blousy dress, clogs, and a mixture of thin bracelets. "Good, you're up. The nurses weren't sure if you were awake."

Kaitlin had asked Susan to pick up a few things at her apartment. She set her laptop aside. "I'm glad to see a friendly face."

Susan set the vase by the bed and sat, balancing Kaitlin's small knapsack on her lap.

Sitting up a little taller, Kaitlin studied the floral arrangement, remembering the flowers sent to Audrey Mason's hospice room and her own lecture.

"How are you feeling?" Susan asked.

Kaitlin looked away from the flowers. "Good. I'm on the mend and ready to leave."

"Do the police have any leads in your case?" She leaned in a fraction.

"The cops are on it. It'll be fine." Drawn back to the flowers, she studied the blossoms. "Where did you get these?"

"They were delivered to the office. I thought I'd bring them along because they're so lovely."

"Was there a card?"

"No, the delivery man said they were for you."

Kaitlin frowned. The flowers delivered to her aunt and to her lecture room also had no cards attached.

"What's wrong?" Susan said. "You look worried."

She smiled, but her mind didn't settle. "Nothing's wrong. I expected there would be a card."

Susan studied the flowers. "The news is reporting the woman stabbed in Church Hill might have had a stalker."

Kaitlin touched one of the soft flower petals. "That's what I heard."

"You're so careful about giving out your phone number and contact information. Even the faculty picture of you doesn't really look like you."

"I've always been a stickler for privacy. It's nothing."

Susan moved the bouquet to the windowsill. Sunlight caught the flowers, creating shadows among the delicate petals.

Susan returned to the edge of the bed. "You think the guy who stabbed you sent the flowers, don't you?" she asked.

"No," she said too quickly. This conversation dug into her worries. "Do me one more favor and give these flowers to the nurses. They're so kind. I want them to enjoy them."

"Okay." Susan looked suddenly nervous. "Don't worry about your class, I've got Lexi covering it."

"There's not much to cover. The kids should've turned in their interview films to me on Sunday, and then they're on break. I should be up and running when they get back."

"There's no rush."

Kaitlin detected an underlying meaning. "I can do my job, Susan."

Susan fiddled with a silver bracelet. "I don't want you to push yourself too hard."

"And if I say I'm fine, and I'll be back in a week?"

Susan released the bracelet and then fumbled with a loose thread on her sleeve. "Then I would say take the rest of the semester off. Give yourself a chance to heal and for the police to catch the guy who did this to you."

Embers of resentment simmered.

"They'll catch the guy who stabbed me. You have nothing to worry about." The statement was meant to convince herself as well as Susan.

"I know. I've already spoken to Detective Adler, and we discussed your case."

"Detective Adler came to see you?" She hated being discussed.

"Yes." Susan looked sheepish. "He wanted to know if there were people who wanted to hurt you. I told them I didn't know of anyone. Everyone I know thinks you're great."

Susan was killing her with kindness, but Kaitlin sensed more. "If you're firing me, have the backbone to say the words."

"I didn't say I was firing you. You need to rest, and then we will reevaluate in a few months."

"I have a signed contract for the summer session. So you better find good cause, or you're opening yourself up to a lawsuit."

Susan's lips thinned. "That's drastic."

Kaitlin tipped her head back. "Susan, you're looking out for yourself and the university. I get it. But honestly, it gets a little old when the victim gets the shaft and everyone piles on."

"That's not what I'm doing."

Kaitlin refused to have this discussion. "Don't forget the flowers."

Susan's lips pursed into a wan smile. She took the vase, holding it slightly away from her, and then left the room without looking back.

Kaitlin gripped her remote control, resisting the urge to toss it across the room. She tapped her index finger on the "On/Off" button, knowing the last thing she wanted to do was watch a stupid game show.

She closed her eyes and immediately assessed her situation. She had money in savings, which was enough for the next few months of rent but not enough for the lawsuit she'd just threatened Susan with. She had time and a place to heal. She would soon work out her next move.

Anxious to get her life back, she tossed off her covers. Drawing in a breath, she pulled her legs over the side of the bed. Fire burned in her belly. She didn't want to be here. She wanted to return to her work. Her life.

She took a step a little too quickly. She hissed in a breath as sharp pain gripped her. "This is bullshit."

Like it or not, she needed more time. For now, she was trapped.

INTERVIEW FILE #17

GINA'S BOYFRIEND, TOM DAVENPORT

Friday, February 16, 2018

"Tom Davenport." His voice is deep, crisp, and sounds annoyed over my speakerphone.

"Tom, this is Kaitlin Roe." Davenport dated Gina the spring semester of her senior year. They were king and queen of the prom and voted Most Likely to Be Amazing. Everyone thought they'd be together forever. Until Gina broke up with Tom six weeks before she vanished. She told me that their relationship didn't make sense anymore. She was going to Duke and Tom was attending Virginia Tech. Time to enjoy their new lives at college.

"Who?" Papers shuffle in the background.

"Kaitlin Roe. From Saint Mathew's High School. I was Gina Mason's cousin."

Silence settles between us. Then he mutters a curse. "What do you want?"

"I'm making a podcast. I'm trying to find Gina."

A chair squeaks in the background.

"She vanished fourteen years ago."

"But no one has found her. I'm hoping a podcast will draw attention back to her case."

He laughs, but the sound is bitter, not joyous. "That's kinda rich, don't you think?"

"Why?"

"You hated her."

Gina was everything I wasn't in high school. And admiration and resentment are a razor's edge apart. "I'm trying to make it right."

He swears again. "You can't make it right."

"I can try to find her."

"The time to fix *this* was fourteen years ago, before you abandoned Gina."

The line goes dead.

CHAPTER SIXTEEN

Monday, March 19, 2018; 7:00 p.m.

Adler returned to his desk, a large fresh coffee in hand, to find a stack of surveillance footage of the Jennifer Ralston residence. On the top was a note from Quinn. *For your viewing pleasure. Footage supplied by two homeowners near Ralston residence. I've been summoned to the forensic department on another case. Q.*

He loosened his tie and sat. Leaning back in his chair, he sipped his coffee and selected the first disc. He hit "Play," and a rear view of Ralston's residence appeared. Judging by the angle, the camera was mounted on the house across the alley.

The footage covered the nine days before Jennifer's murder. He fast-forwarded to Thursday, March 15, the day of the murder. He chose seven a.m. as a starting point.

Several cars passed down the alley, and then Jennifer Ralston appeared at 7:30 a.m. walking out her back door with a bag of trash. She was dressed in a dark skirt, a white shirt, and the pumps that still sat in her entryway. A purse dangled from her arm. Jennifer hesitated on her doorstep, glancing left and then right, before she locked her door and made her way through the yard to the alley. She tossed her trash into the dumpster and then entered her garage. A minute later the garage door opened, and she backed out. The garage door closed.

He scanned the footage covering the hours after she left for work, searching for the moment her killer arrived. At the 3:02 p.m. mark, he saw a man dressed in coveralls and a hat open her back gate. The logo on his back read COMMONWEALTH PLUMBERS, and he was carrying an oversize toolbox. He moved quickly as if he knew where he was going and disappeared inside the gate, out of camera view for several seconds. Then he stood at her back door, opened it with a key, and entered the security code before closing the door.

Adler started viewing the video frame by frame. At 3:07, a shadow passed in front of the second-floor bedroom window and then vanished.

Energy surged through him. He fast-forwarded the tape to 6:00 p.m., the approximate time of Jennifer's death. The lights in the house clicked on minutes after six, and the camera caught Jennifer through the kitchen window standing at the sink with a glass. She refilled it and then left the kitchen.

At 6:30 p.m., the back door opened. The man who had entered at 3:02 was now exiting with the same clothes and gear. He was in no rush. The killer had been in the residence for just over three hours waiting for Jennifer. He was a pro.

***

"I am coming back for you. You deserve to be punished." Kaitlin's clouded vision caught the glint of the knife's blade rising as her alarm blared.

Kaitlin's eyes popped open as an alarm went off in the hospital somewhere. She tried to sit. Pain tugged at her, but she expected it this time and gritting her teeth, pushed up into a sitting position. The blaring noise in the hallway stopped. Sweat dampened her hairline and between her shoulders and breasts. Her heart beat fast.

She eased back against the pillows. She slowly closed her eyes and breathed in and out while trying to slow her heart rate. But she couldn't stop replaying his words. *"I am coming back for you. You deserve to be punished."* Recollection danced just out of reach like a forgotten tune refusing to be remembered.

A knock on her door just after eight pulled her away from her laptop. "Come in."

It was Detective Adler. His tie was loose, and thick stubble now darkened his chin. She was glad to see him. She shouldn't have been, but there was no denying that having him close calmed her.

"What was that noise?" she asked.

"Fire alarm went off. It was a false alarm." He studied her face.

She drew in a breath. She was annoyed she'd been rocked with fear. "You look about as bad as I feel," she said.

"No rest for the wicked." He held up a bag, tossing her a boyish grin. "Brought sorbet."

Despite inner warnings to stay clear of him, she asked, "What kind?"

"Strawberry and chocolate."

She straightened. She was relieved her body didn't protest. "The nurses believe I'll heal faster if they tempt me with Jell-O and beef broth."

"Sorbet will do the trick."

She watched with unwanted excitement as he pulled up a chair and dug out the containers. She chose chocolate, and he handed it to her along with a lime-green plastic spoon.

"You're allowed to eat this, right?" he asked.

She pried off the top, savored the sight of the creamy swirls. "The doctors said soft foods. I think this qualifies."

He peeled off his container top. "How're you feeling?"

She took her first spoonful. The cool, rich chocolate was the best she'd ever eaten. "Better now."

"You're lucky."

She ate a second bite, the rich taste making her feel optimistic. "I suppose I am."

He cocked a brow. "You're listening to your doctors?"

"Generally speaking. I freaked out a nurse when I tried to walk down the hallway this morning. She wasn't happy. Made me promise to stay in bed."

He chuckled and took several bites of sorbet. He raised his gaze to her as if he were seeing her in a different light. "I didn't realize your hair was so curly."

She resisted the urge to touch a curl. She saw something in his eyes that sent nervous energy running through her body. "I call it my 'mountain woman' look. Detective, if you haven't noticed, I'm in a lockdown ward. No beauty contests here."

"I like the curls. And your natural color. Why did you dye your hair blond?"

"Other than blondes have more fun? Hiding, I think. When I returned to Texas I decided I needed to look different. Didn't want to see Gina when I looked in the mirror."

He was silent. "Keep the brown. It's you."

"Might as well. If I thought the hair color was helping me hide, I was wrong."

But she was vain enough to enjoy his compliment. She also wished she weren't dressed in a shapeless hospital gown when he looked so sharp and commanding.

Her belly tightened, so she shifted positions. Without hesitating, Adler set down his sorbet and grabbed her elbow. She felt the rough skin of his scarred palm as he steadied her while he resettled the pillow behind her. "In a week I'll be running track and jumping hurdles."

"You ever run track before?" He pulled the blanket up.

"No, but I could if I wanted to. And I just might take up running."

"That I'd like to see."

She considered telling Adler about her dream. The detective had quiet strength that calmed her anxious nerves. And right now he felt like a man she could trust.

"Forensic came back with some preliminary information," Adler said. "They did find your thumbprint on the Crowleys' front door latch. You let yourself into the house."

"Have you found Erika?"

"No. And her phone is not emitting a signal."

His blunt assessment didn't bode well for Erika. "What about her husband?"

"Brad Crowley came by the station. He says he's also searching for his wife. And he's hired a lawyer."

"Are you following him?" she asked.

"I have no cause."

"He knows more than he's saying."

"He's on my radar," Adler said. "But I don't think he knows where Erika is."

"How could he not?"

"I honestly don't think he's smart enough to have pulled it off."

She took another bite of sorbet, but suddenly found the flavor too sweet. "You went to see Susan."

His spoon hovered above his carton. "I did. I'm trying to figure you out."

"I'm very simple. I'm trying to find Gina."

"So am I."

She was doing her job. He was doing his. And as long as their priorities aligned, they'd be fine. "You know my life story, so I think you could throw me a detail or two about yours."

He dropped his gaze to his sorbet and dug out a full spoon. "Forty-one, divorced, no kids."

"Married to the job?"

"It was supposed to be a stepping stone into politics, but I discovered I liked it and am good at it. My ex had a different vision for my future."

"She wanted you to go into politics."

"She has her sights set high."

"It must have been painful when you two split."

"Not as bad as it should have been."

"How long were you married?"

"Ten years."

"I can imagine you standing before a gilded altar in a church filled with stained-glass windows and hundreds of important people." She didn't like the image.

"It was quite the society affair."

She liked John Adler a lot, and if she were going to trust someone now, it would be him. She stared at the spoon before she said, "So, I received flowers today. They were delivered to my office. No note. My boss has no idea who sent them."

He scanned the room, and his tone sharpened when he spoke, "Where are they?"

"I gave them to the nurses. Someone also sent me flowers the night of my lecture. I gave those away to a student. I don't know anyone who would send me flowers."

He was silent.

With him she was able to confess, "They gave me the creeps. Who would have thought such a pretty and perfect arrangement of white tulips would make me want to jump out of my skin."

"The other flowers were also white tulips?" he said.

"Yes. Does that mean anything?"

"I'm not sure." His expression said otherwise. He was concerned but seemed to be holding back his thoughts for her sake. "Was there a card?"

"Susan said there wasn't." She stabbed her spoon in the sorbet and set it on the table beside her. "I'm scared. I can't stop looking for Gina, but I am terrified."

Adler looked her in the eye. "You're not in this alone, Kaitlin. I've got your back."

She believed him, and that calmed some of the fears enough for her to say, "I had a dream just a few minutes ago. I woke to the alarm in the hallway. I was so terrified. I was drenched in sweat."

"Tell me about the dream."

"It was the moment I was stabbed. My attacker said, 'I am coming back for you. You deserve to be punished.'"

Adler leaned forward. His eyes were intent, but his voice was calm. "What do you remember about him?"

"I never saw his face."

"His voice? A mark on his hands? A smell?"

She drew in a breath. "The voice was muffled. A whisper. He sounded angry and frustrated, like I'd screwed up his plans." She tried to relax her clenched fists. "His hands were smooth. His breath smelled of peppermint."

"That's more than you first recalled."

"My head is finally clearing."

"Did anything about this man's voice remind you of the man that took Gina?"

A swell of emotion tightened her voice. "No. I know it's been fourteen years, but nothing about this guy made me think of Gina's kidnapper. I know this guy wasn't on the road that night."

"Who would care about this case as much as you now?"

"Gina and I don't have any family left to speak of, but her face was in the news so much fourteen years ago. Even last year a reporter did a story about her unsolved case."

"Someone might see themselves as Gina's champion."

"And he's come back for all the girls on the road with her that last night. Jennifer is dead. Erika's missing. And I'm stabbed." She felt vulnerable and fought a rush of tears.

"He's not going to hurt you," Adler said.

"I've survived years of self-destructive behavior. Now I'm faced with a real threat, and I'm afraid of dying. How's that for a turnaround?"

"It's healthy. And I'm going to keep you safe."

"How can you be sure?"

"I'm very good at what I do."

She searched his face for any sign that he was playing her. "I'm going to have to believe you, Detective Adler. You're all I've got right now."

A grin tugged at the edge of his lips as he set his sorbet on the side table next to hers. "I met with Ashley Ralston."

She sensed he didn't share his thoughts easily either. "I remember her. She's four years older than me."

"What do you remember about her?"

"When I saw her at a July Fourth party, she had a bruise on her cheek. I can't remember the reason she gave then, but I didn't question it."

"You think Derek hit her?"

"I can't say for sure. But they were dating at the time."

"What about Hayward? Was he around?"

"He was at that party and several others. He was around a lot that summer."

"How tight were you with Hayward?" he asked.

"There was a time when I thought he was the answer to all the pain I carried after my brother's death. For a brief time I forgot about all the guilt and suffering and had fun." She plucked at a thread on her blanket. "But his smiles hid a lot of darkness."

"When did you two stop dating?"

"Right after that July Fourth party in 2004."

"Why'd you break it off?"

"He lost his temper, and he hit me."

Adler didn't comment, but a muscle pulsed in his jaw. "Did he hurt any other girls?"

"I'm sure he did. He showed no remorse when he struck me."

Fury smoldered in his eyes. "He will spend the rest of his life behind bars."

"What about his deal?"

"I'll find a loophole. When do you get discharged?"

"Thursday morning."

"You have a ride and a brush?"

She smiled, reminding herself that relying on him too much was a slippery slope. "Got them both covered," she lied.

INTERVIEW FILE #18

MORE FRIENDS—NADINE SPENCER

Friday, March 2, 2018; 2:00 p.m.

Nadine Spencer touches the microphone that's clipped to her lapel and glances nervously toward me. "This seems weird."

I sit in the chair across from the tall, big-boned woman. Her cheeks are a little too pink and her eyelids too blue for her pale skin. She is dressed in an expensive white silk blouse and slacks that tug at her pudgy frame in all the wrong places. Hair dyed-blond hair skims her shoulders, and though the color is flattering, an overabundance of spray leaves her coif stiff and unnatural.

"Thank you for seeing me."

"Why wouldn't I? God, after that night. The senior class is bonded forever." She shakes her head. "I was supposed be there with you, but I had a date with Randy Hayward."

"Randy? I didn't realize you two were close."

"Not exactly close. And honestly, I was relieved when the date ended. He was weird that night."

"How so?"

"Wired. Angry. Physical." She rubs her hand over her arm as if soothing an old wound. "Now that I know he was a drug addict, it makes sense."

"Did he ever talk about Gina?"

"Sure. He asked me if she still had her *v*-card." Nadine sits silent for a moment. "That was odd, even for Randy."

"Knowing Gina, what do you think happened to her?"

Nadine folds a small sticky note and creases the edges until the paper frays. "I think Gina's temper is what got her."

"Why do you say that?"

"I believe whoever took her thought he had a sweet, gentle girl. But she was a strong athlete who was a soccer goalie. I bet she landed a good kick or two and she hurt the guy. That set him off, and he killed her." She shakes her head. "Breaks my heart to think about all the damage done by one sick person. My daddy used to say fear and self-pity don't mend broken hearts. He said anger does because it motivates us to do the impossible."

CHAPTER SEVENTEEN

Tuesday, March 20, 2018; 9:00 a.m.

A cold front had blown into Richmond, chasing away any hint of spring they'd enjoyed a few days ago. It was thirty degrees when Adler arrived at the Main Street Station office complex.

Turning up the collar of his overcoat, he pushed into the marble lobby. A check of the directory told him Davenport was on the third floor. He rode the elevator and followed the signs to an open doorway at the end of the hall. There was no one at the receptionist desk, and the door behind it was closed. This gave him a moment to study the room's rich Oriental carpet, the three overstuffed waiting chairs, and a stack of sleek magazines catering to the wealthy. He rapped his knuckles on the desk. "Hello."

"Yes, I'm here." The door opened to a man wearing dark pleated pants, a white collared shirt, and blue tie. He was in his midthirties, had sandy-brown hair, and looked like a former jock carrying an extra thirty pounds. After he took a good look at Adler, he reached for a suit jacket and pulled it on.

"I'm Tom Davenport." He smiled and extended his hand.

Adler shook it and then reached for his badge. "I'm Detective John Adler."

"Detective." The smile waned. "What can I do for you?"

"Is there somewhere private we could talk?"

"Sure. The conference room."

Adler followed Davenport, and when he closed the door, Adler said, "I'm working a murder case. Jennifer Ralston."

"I heard about that. We went to high school together, but I haven't seen her for several years. May I ask why you're here?"

"Gina Mason's name has come up several times during this investigation. You dated Gina, didn't you?"

Davenport slid a hand into his pocket. "I did."

"She broke up with you?"

"That's right. And yes, I was pissed at the time, but looking back I can see she was right. A clean break made the best sense."

"Looking back as you say, it had to hurt like hell."

"Sure. But as I told the cops fourteen years ago, I wasn't angry enough to hurt her. I loved her and was devastated when she vanished." He rattled change in his pocket. "Did Kaitlin Roe send you? She wanted to interview me for some project, but I hung up on her."

"No, but why hang up?"

"I don't need any more of her manipulative bullshit."

"How so?"

"She was trouble. Gina and I were doing great, and then Kaitlin moved in with the Masons. She brought so much chaos with her. Gina felt obligated to spend more time with her cousin. I even tried to help where I could, but I got pushed out."

"How is that Kaitlin's fault?"

"Gina and I were fine before her." He shook his head. "I wouldn't have left Gina that night when she needed help. And now Kaitlin has some fleeting idea she's going to fix all this, now?"

"It sounds like you're still mad."

"Not at Gina. But sure, I didn't and still don't trust Kaitlin Roe." He shook his head as he dropped his gaze to the floor. "I wish she'd been the one taken, not Gina."

Davenport had known Jennifer, Erika, and Kaitlin, but Kaitlin had been certain she didn't recognize her attacker's voice. She'd spoken to Davenport recently, so she should have been able to identify him. "Did you know someone stabbed Kaitlin?"

His eyes widened with shock. "She's dead?"

"No, she'll recover."

Davenport drew in what felt like a calculated breath.

"Where were you on Saturday afternoon?" Adler asked.

"With my wife and son."

"And she can confirm this?"

"Yes, but why should she have to?" Davenport was growing angry.

"I'm just covering all the bases."

"It sounds more like you think I'm a suspect. But then why shouldn't you? Cops go for the low-hanging fruit, don't they?" He sounded outraged, insulted, and afraid.

The original investigation had nearly cost him his future, and now he sounded scared this one would as well. "Should you be, Mr. Davenport?"

A bitter smile twisted his lips. "You cops raked me over the coals fourteen years ago. If you have any more questions, submit them to my lawyer."

***

Adler had read nothing overtly threatening in the notes written to Jennifer. Now at the state forensic department, Adler would have the opportunity to discuss the handwriting with the technician in charge of the case.

Adler rode the elevator to the fifth floor and made his way down the hall. The glass walls offered a peek into the scientists' workstations, which were equipped with high-powered microscopes designed to analyze everything from bullet striations to automobile paint chips. Other work zones were outfitted with powerful computers built to analyze drug toxicity, DNA, and any other evidence left at the scene of a crime.

Down the hallway at a lone door, he pressed the intercom button and identified himself. The door latch opened with a click, and he pushed through the secured entrance to find Dana Tipton sitting at her desk peering into a microscope. A white lab coat covered her short frame, and her curly hair was twisted into a tight knot, accentuating large dark-rimmed glasses and sharp green eyes. She rose to shake his hand. "Detective Adler."

"Dana, thanks for seeing me. I understand you had a chance to look at the notes from the Ralston homicide."

"I did. I went through them late yesterday." She carried a file to a light table. She spread out the five notes and clicked on the light. "I checked all for fingerprints. I was able to pull a partial print from the fifth note. It's a right thumb. But there aren't enough indicators to make a definitive identification."

"How many?" Fingerprints had dozens of characteristics, but to make a conclusive identification, the technician needed to match at least six traits.

"I identified four indicators within the print. But I did submit the partial to AFIS. We'll see what pops." The Automated Fingerprint Identification System was administered by state police throughout the country and contained millions of criminal and civilian prints. If the owner of this fingerprint had a record or ever worked for the government, it was in the system.

"Okay. Anything else you can tell me?"

She adjusted her glasses. "I do have some ideas about the author."

Handwriting analysis wasn't an exact science, but it still could help. "Let's have it."

"Every letter begins with 'My Girl.' 'My Girl, you're still a beautiful woman. My Girl, would you like a ride to work?' At first glance, the words could be considered an endearment, but 'My Girl' is written in bolder letters than the others. The author pressed down much harder when he wrote those words."

"He's angry."

"He's certainly making a point when he calls her 'My Girl.'"

"He considers her a child? Lesser than himself, perhaps?"

"Maybe. Or she's a possession." She adjusted her glasses again. "The text suggests their connection goes way back. 'My Girl, remember that last summer by the river?'"

"He's known her a long time, or he's stalked her for a long time. What're the chances it's a woman?"

She shrugged. "Given the shapes of the letters and the nature of the crime? Slim to none."

"What else?"

"The handwriting is deliberate and written with care. Note how well formed and neat the letters are."

"Remind you of an engineer?"

"A drafter's style exhibits a more specific block style, which I don't see here. These letters also slant to the right, suggesting he's left-handed."

"Could all this have been written deliberately?"

"Sure." She pointed. "The last note is different than the others. 'My Girl, what is your biggest regret?' It appears to have been written quickly, and the letter formations are slightly different than those in the first four. Basically, he's showing more of himself here whether he realizes it or not."

"Any indication of when it was written?"

"Unfortunately, no. But if you find this guy, and you can get a handwriting sample, I can match it, Detective."

Forensic analysis was great at supporting an arrest in court, but when it came to finding a killer, old-fashioned detective work ran circles around the science. In the first few critical days after a murder, every hour counted. "There's a heart drawn at the bottom of each page."

She nodded. "It's not symmetrical, but it also doesn't feel casually drawn to me. And because it appears in each note, it has meaning to him. I understand the flowers under the victim's bed were arranged in the shape of a heart."

"Correct. Anything else?"

"The author chose a nice paper stock. White vellum. Not cheap. Makes me think it's the second page of more formal stationary."

"A brand used by one of a million offices?"

"I would say professional offices."

"What else can you tell me about the author?"

"I'm no profiler, Detective. And some in law enforcement see graphology as one step above witchcraft."

"Understood. Just looking for general impressions that will help narrow down the author."

She paused over the third note. "The overall shape of the letters is smaller in scale. People who write smaller tend to be shy and more introverted. The spacing between the words is large, suggesting he likes his space. The edges are sharp, meaning he's aggressive and assertive."

"Anything else?"

"That's all I've got for now."

"Have the techs had a chance to examine Erika Crowley's car?"

"We are pulling prints, and I know multiple dark-hair samples have been found. Mrs. Crowley had blond hair, so we know they don't belong to her. We did find samples of blond hair in the trunk as well as urine."

"He put her in the trunk."

"That's my guess. I can tell you the GPS in her car tracked the vehicle path. It went directly from the yoga studio to the gas station on Route 1. A forensic technician did take several tire casts beside the vehicle."

"He switched cars."

"Most likely."

"Thanks, Dana."

As he left the offices his phone rang. It was Quinn.

"I just received a call from a local vet. A woman found a Siamese stray and dropped it off at the vet. He checked for a chip."

"It's Jennifer Ralston's cat?"

"Yes, it is."

"Where was the cat found?"

"Chesterfield County near Hull Street and Courthouse Road."

"That's twenty miles from Church Hill."

"The vet had no other information. He did say his client is keeping the cat unless someone claims it. I have her name and number if you want to talk to her."

"Okay."

"I also received several more security videos of Erika's house. I've been watching them for the last couple of hours. Brad Crowley last appeared on tape five days ago."

"Five days. Erika vanished on Saturday. Did any of the neighbors make a comment about seeing him?"

"A few did. He came and went from the home several times a day, even during a normal workweek. Apparently, he liked to have lunch at home."

"And Erika?"

"She doesn't leave the house much. Just as her husband said, she travels to her yoga studio two mornings a week and that's about it. Groceries and most clothing are delivered. She tells everyone she's an artist and is working in her home studio."

"So either she's agoraphobic or she was a virtual prisoner in her home."

***

The sun had set when he looked through the cab window to the tarp wrapped around Erika's body in the bed of his truck. It was hidden under random debris so it wasn't visible, though soon it would smell. He'd killed her in a spontaneous moment that he now regretted. He should have left her in her cell to rot.

He could have buried Erika. There were plenty of places he could put her where she'd never be found. But he didn't want her death to be a waste. He wanted her found. Displayed. Erika would help send a message to Kaitlin. *You're next.*

He started the engine and drove toward the city. The truck bed rattled, but Erika's body was nice and snug.

As he drove toward the heart of Richmond on the expressway, police lights flashed in his rearview mirror and he tensed, gripping the wheel until his knuckles whitened. He was driving the speed limit. He'd used a turn signal when crossing lanes. What the hell?

The cop car hit his siren, a sure sign he had to pull over. Tension crept up his spine. His breathing grew shallow as he glanced in the mirror again and then back at the road.

He could stomp on the gas and make a run for it. But that wouldn't end well. Better to stay calm and play along. He could fool anybody.

"I can do this," he said to himself. "I can do this." He repeated the words like a mantra until the stress eased.

He turned on his blinker and pulled off on the shoulder of the road. He reached for his driver's license and registration. He rolled down his window and placed his hands on the steering wheel.

The cop got out of his car and moved toward the truck. He touched the tailgate to leave fingerprints, proof he had made contact if it all went sour, and then he walked up slowly along the truck.

"Good evening," the officer said.

"Yes, sir. Good evening. Was I speeding?"

"No, sir, but your back taillight is out."

"Really? I had no idea." He handed the officer his driver's license and registration. "Figured you need these."

"I'll be right back."

He glanced in the rearview mirror and watched the cop return to his vehicle and type his plates into his computer. The cop would search his record for warrants and other traffic violations, and he'd find only a fourteen-year-old speeding ticket. He was the good boy. Just play it cool.

For a brief moment he imagined the plastic tarp moved in the breeze. He blinked and watched closely in the rearview mirror, his heart beating faster, as he waited for the wind to calm.

The cop came back to the car. "Looks like you have a pretty clean driving record."

He smiled. "I do try."

"I'm going to have to give you a ticket. But if you get pulled over again in the next forty-eight hours, show them this. You need to get the light fixed for your own safety."

"I was working on the damn thing last week. There must be a short in the wires. I'll take it to a garage first thing."

The officer stared at him an extra beat and then handed him the ticket. He signed it and handed it back.

The officer ripped off his portion of the ticket. "Have a nice evening."

"Will do. Thank you, Officer."

He sat still, not moving for a moment. Jesus, that cop was less than a foot from the body. He'd come so close to capture.

But he hadn't been caught. He was getting better at this, and if he were real careful, he'd never be caught.

Drawing in a breath, he waited for the all clear and pulled into traffic. Time to dump the body.

He drove to the Shockoe Bottom section of Richmond and located the alley he had already searched for surveillance cameras. It was one block from Kaitlin's apartment.

Moving quickly, he backed into the alley and cut the lights. Tugging a ball cap over his eyes, he opened the back tailgate, reached under the tarp, and grabbed Erika's ankles. Her skin was cold to the touch, but the rigor mortis had left her limbs, and she was again pliable.

He pulled her forward and carried her limp body to the end of the alley. Quickly he leaned her against the dumpster. He brushed the hair back from her eyes and smoothed it over her shoulders. He spread her legs and placed each hand on an inner thigh.

Pulling a red marker from his pocket, he drew a heart on her chest. "This is for you, Gina," he whispered.

***

It was after visitor's hours when there was a knock on Kaitlin's door. She was surfing the television channels to pass the time. "Time for another lab sample?" She resigned herself to another procedure.

Instead of the young nurse with glasses and brown hair, Adler appeared. His tie was loose, and the stubble on his jaw was thick. "Sorry, no nurse."

"Too bad." Stupid, but she was glad to see him. "It's always a treat to have a nurse jab a needle in my arm. What are you doing here?"

He held up a bag.

"Sorbet, again?" Beware of cops bearing gifts.

"Doughnuts. Cops know where to get the best ones in the city."

"Is it true?" She grinned.

"It is." The half smile was charming, and if Adler wasn't a cop, she might have been charmed.

"As it so happens, I'm now on some solid foods."

"Then you're in luck."

He pulled up his chair and handed her a napkin. He glanced in the bag. "Chocolate glazed or plain?"

"Plain. Let's keep it simple."

With a napkin he plucked out a plain one and handed it to her. Its aroma made her mouth water. She bit into it. Adler was batting two for two with her so far.

She took another bite before she asked, "So what're you really here for? Feeding me isn't a priority. You look like a man with questions."

He tossed her a sideways glance meant to disarm. "Am I that obvious?"

She chuckled and felt charmed nonetheless. "You use that look with suspects?"

"I do." He bit into the doughnut with no air of repentance or worry about calories. "I met with a forensic investigator who is analyzing several notes Jennifer received."

She pulled off a piece. "And?"

"Without getting into too much detail, I can tell you he signed each one with a heart. Does that mean anything to you?"

Kaitlin set her doughnut down as a memory rushed out from the past. If the killer had left a heart, he'd definitely been involved in the search for Gina. She reached for a pad and pen on her nightstand and drew a particular heart she'd seen many times. "When Gina was first missing, the volunteer groups developed a kind of logo. It was Gina's name with a heart drawn over top of it."

"Who came up with the logo?"

She handed him the paper. "It was my idea to add it to the flyer, because she loved hearts. She had several necklaces that were heart shaped."

"It was your idea?"

"Yeah."

"The heart symbol was well known?"

"Yes. All the volunteer posters and flyers had it, and several news organizations came up with graphics that incorporated it. It would have been hard to miss."

"A colleague of mine is reading the file, but our focus has been on the abduction and not the search. How many volunteers were on the search teams?"

"Hundreds. There was an organized system, and in that group there were teams of ten. Volunteers stood side by side and walked open fields and brush for hours searching for clues. There were also people who weren't sanctioned as official searchers, and they ventured out on their own."

"Have you spoken to any of those volunteers?"

"George Dunkin. He's on a canine tracking team who volunteered over a hundred hours on the search."

"You gave me Jennifer's tape, but I need all of them, Kaitlin."

"Sure. I'll send them all."

"Can you do it now?"

"Hand me my laptop."

He dusted off his crumbs, tossing the half-eaten doughnut in the trash. He retrieved the laptop from the side table and gently set it on her lap. She opened it, pushed a few buttons, and hit "Send."

"On their way."

"Thank you."

"I'm not sure how my interviews will help."

"Jennifer's stalking, her murder, Erika's disappearance, and your stabbing all started when you began your research." He wasn't smiling now, and his tone had sharpened just a little.

There was a time she'd have felt backed into a corner by his harsh tone. But she was coming to recognize this was how he sounded when he was working a case. She drew in a breath. She needed and wanted to believe he wasn't going to throw her under the bus if the case got too hot to handle.

He held her gaze. "Are you sharing everything with me?"

"You know all that I know now, Detective."

"And you will keep me in the loop if you learn anything new?"

"Yes. Will you do the same?"

"I can't promise that right now. I wish that I could, but I can't. The case has to come first."

She didn't like hearing that, but she sensed he was being honest.

"How did you choose your interview subjects?" If Adler realized he'd upset her, he didn't seem to care.

"I went through all the media reports I could find and made a list of everyone mentioned and went from there. I interviewed whoever would talk to me."

"Any idea who killed Jennifer?"

She ran a trembling hand through her hair. She felt like a raw nerve. "I want to help and to remember. I've been through hypnotherapy before, but I could do it again."

Adler arched a brow. "If it comes to that, we'll talk about it. What does your gut say about this killer?"

She drew in a breath, dialing down her anger. "I'm trying to set up an appointment with Steven Marcus, the reporter who covered Gina's disappearance extensively and who knows the case better than anyone. I'm hoping he has more ideas."

"I haven't talked to Marcus."

"Excluding North, he's your best expert on Gina's case."

Adler wrote down the name. "Do you have a number?"

She reached for her phone and rattled it off. "He's on deadline and won't be available until Saturday."

"Maybe you can include me in your meeting."

"Sure. I'll let you know when we make contact."

His phone buzzed, and he looked down. A heavy sigh hissed over clenched teeth. "Erika Crowley has been found."

"Is she all right?"

Mary Burton

"I'll catch up with you tomorrow."

She tried to swing her legs over the side of the bed, forgetting for a split second why she was here. A shot of white-hot pain reminded her. "So you're just going to leave me hanging like this? You aren't going to tell me what's going on?"

"For now, no."

INTERVIEW FILE #19

The Search and Rescue Team

Saturday, March 3, 2018; 2:00 p.m.

The three barking bloodhounds move around me with a playful energy, but they sniff my outstretched hands with a keen intensity. Larry, Moe, and Curley range in age from one to six years old, and they belong to search and rescue expert George Dunkin. They are his pride and joy. Dunkin is the brainchild behind K-9 Find, a nonprofit group that has logged thousands of search hours and recovered over a dozen missing people.

"Basically, a dog's brain can evaluate smells forty times better than a human's. We walk into a room and smell the beef stew cooking. They smell all the beef, potatoes, carrots, peas, garlic, onions, and whatever other ingredients are in that stew."

George and his K-9 Lucy spent hundreds of hours in the woods searching for Gina. With Lucy at his side, Dunkin was interviewed four times on the evening news as well as the morning shows.

"Why did you and Lucy spend so many hours on this particular search?"

His brown eyes grow wistful at the mention of Lucy's name. He sorely misses that dog. "She was the best dog I've ever had. The best." Absently he rubs Moe's head. "We were at home watching the news when Gina Mason's face appeared on the screen. There was something about her smile that touched my heart. I couldn't sit by and do nothing, so Lucy and I got to work." He's silent for a moment. "I still have one of Gina's T-shirts that we used to search for her."

"You saved her shirt?"

"I couldn't let it go."

CHAPTER EIGHTEEN

Tuesday, March 20, 2018; 10:00 p.m.

Erika Crowley's body was found in a cobblestone alley near Eighteenth Street in the Shockoe Bottom district of the city. The anonymous call had come in at nine p.m., and the caller sounded drunk on the 911 tape when he reported he'd gone behind the dumpster to urinate and spotted the body. He'd called from an untraceable cell phone.

The police cruisers were nosed in the alley's entrance, and their lights flashed bright blue onto a fading cigarette ad painted a half century ago on a brick warehouse.

Adler pulled on latex gloves as Quinn came around the side of her car to meet him. "Anyone spoken to Brad Crowley?"

"No. We've kept a tight lid on this," Quinn said.

They crossed the cobblestone street to the alley's entrance. Each nodded to the uniformed officer and then ducked under the crime scene tape. The camera lights of a forensic technician flashed behind the dumpster.

The tech, Dana Tipton, rose up, and spotting Adler and Quinn, she backed up several steps so they could see the body.

Erika's body lay propped against the dumpster. Her thick blond hair swooped around her neck and draped over her chest, but she was posed as Jennifer had been. Her clothes were intact, but her legs were spread and each hand rested on the inner thigh. Though Jennifer hadn't been sexually assaulted, he couldn't yet rule it out in this case. Some attackers made their victims redress, or they did it themselves postmortem. Again, the medical examiner would have to make the call.

Her manicured hands were scraped, torn, and bruised. Her yoga clothes were soaked in sweat and urine, and her white V-neck pullover was coated in grime, dirt, and blood. Her left slip-on shoe was missing.

Painted on her chest in red marker was a heart that resembled the one found in Jennifer's shower.

Adler squatted, and using the tip of a pen, pushed back the top fold of Erika's pullover. One deep knife cut slashed across her jugular.

"Wound is consistent with Jennifer Ralston's," Quinn said.

"But there's no blood around her. Her clothes are soaked, but no blood. And the urine smell and the trauma to her hands suggest she was held somewhere before she was killed. If it's the same guy, he's changed tactics."

"Why hold her for several days, kill her, and bring her here?" Quinn asked.

"I don't know." Adler studied the victim's pale-blue lips. "And unless Kaitlin healed magically and escaped the hospital, she couldn't have done this."

"No, she couldn't," Quinn conceded.

"You sound disappointed," Adler said.

"John, I don't trust her."

Erika's engagement ring was still on her finger. "Our anonymous caller didn't take her rings," Adler said.

"Maybe he was spooked," Quinn said.

"Very possible. But down here, a ring like that doesn't last long. When did the 911 call come in?" Adler asked.

"At 9:02 p.m. A uniform was on scene by 9:07 p.m."

"Did the officer see anyone loitering around?"

"No." She studied the large diamond catching the forensic technician's light. "You think the killer called it in?"

"Whoever killed her wasn't motivated by her diamonds."

Her wrists were red and dotted with a sticky substance, suggesting she had been restrained with tape of some kind. The same material dotted her pale and drawn lips. "Where the hell has she been the last few days?" he said, more to himself.

"She wasn't killed here," Dana said. "The lack of blood, as well as the lividity on her backside, proves that." Dana tilted the body forward and lifted the shirt to reveal the black-and-blue markings. When the heart stopped pumping, the blood settled at the lowest point. "In her case, it was her entire back and buttocks, suggesting after she died she was laid on her back. As you can see she's been propped up here."

Adler stared around the dark alley. It was a half block off Eighteenth Street, wedged between two buildings, and neither wall facing the alley had windows or a camera. They were less than five blocks from Jennifer's house and less than a block from Kaitlin's apartment. It occurred to him it would have been easy enough for the killer to pose her body and leave in a matter of minutes.

"How long do you think she's been dead?" Adler asked.

"Rough guess?" Dana asked. "Twenty-four hours give or take. Rigor mortis has come and gone."

"Did cold weather conditions prolong it?" Adler asked.

"I don't think so. I'm assuming the body was kept in a warm place," Dana said.

"That puts time of death around two or three p.m. yesterday," Adler said.

"She bled out quickly," Dana added. "The knife wound was on target."

"She's murdered, he lays her out for twenty-plus hours, and then brings her here. Why the delay?"

"The million dollar question," Quinn said.

He rose and stepped back. "Dana, is that heart painted in blood?"

"It's marker," she said.

"Thanks, Dana," he said. "Let me know if you find anything else."

"It's going to take us a few hours to process this scene."

"All right. Keep me posted."

As he and Quinn walked to the end of the alley, he thought about his conversation with Kaitlin. "Jennifer's and Erika's deaths are tied to Gina. Now I need to prove it."

***

Adler and Quinn spent most of the night talking to business owners near the alley, hoping someone had seen something. One bartender thought he'd spotted a truck vanish into the alley but had no details to give.

Through the course of the night, Adler placed three calls and left messages on Brad Crowley's cell before the return call came after sunrise. Adler and Quinn were going through a drive-through and he'd just made twin orders of an egg biscuit, hash browns, and coffee when his phone rang.

He answered, "Mr. Crowley. Thank you for calling me back." He nodded to the cashier, accepted his credit card, and pulled ahead into a parking spot.

"Have you found my wife?" Crowley sounded annoyed, almost put out. In the background, the downbeat of rock music pulsed.

Adler stared ahead. "I'd like to meet you in person."

"Can't you answer my question?" Crowley demanded.

"Not over the phone."

"Why not? Tell me!"

Crowley sounded more the bully than a man worried about his wife. Quinn heard Crowley's outburst, and she bit her lip to keep from saying something.

Adler reached for his coffee. "I'll meet you in person."

Crowley said in a softer tone, "I'm sorry to sound annoyed. I've not slept much in the last couple of weeks."

"Where can we meet?" Adler said.

"I've been staying at my hotel since I saw you last."

"We'll meet you there," Adler said.

"That's not the place to meet. Can't you just tell me?"

"No."

Finally Crowley said, "My attorney's office is the best place." He rattled off the address. "I can be there in a half hour."

So they were playing hardball. Fine. "See you then." He hung up. "Crowley wants to meet at his attorney's office, who just happens to be Derek Blackstone."

"Really?" Quinn said as he handed her an egg-and-bacon biscuit. "This should be fun."

As he snatched a hash brown from his bag, she took a large bite of her biscuit. It was their first meal in twelve hours. The food was good and satisfying, to a point, but they ate every bite. After tossing their trash, he and Quinn covered the drive to the lawyer's office in fifteen minutes.

Blackstone's office was located in a hundred-year-old Colonial Revival building on the Boulevard. It wasn't glitzy, but every detail was meticulous, from the grounds and trimmed boxwoods to the painted trim around the arched windows and the brick herringbone driveway.

Out of the car, he matched Quinn's quick, determined strides as she moved toward the front entrance. She pulled off her glasses, taking a moment to clean the lens with the hem of her shirt. "Can I be the bearer of bad news? Normally, I don't enjoy this kind of thing, but I don't like Mr. Crowley."

"He's all yours."

She tucked the glasses in her coat pocket. "You're too good to me."

They walked inside and showed their badges to a young receptionist with dark hair that swept over her shoulders. She didn't look surprised by their badges as she picked up the phone and announced them. "I can show you to the conference room."

"Thank you," Adler said.

They traveled down a short hallway and into a conference room with a large window that faced the front parking lot. There was no sign of Crowley or his attorney.

The receptionist offered coffee. They both declined. Adler opted to sit. Quinn paced. They waited almost five minutes before the door opened to Crowley. His hair was neatly combed, and he was wearing khakis, a dark V-neck sweater, and polished loafers.

Blackstone stood behind Crowley. He wore a charcoal-gray suit, white shirt, and blue tie. A gold Rolex on Blackstone's wrist caught the sunlight leaking in through the shades.

"Mr. Blackstone, good to see you again," Adler said.

Blackstone's welcoming look held steady. "Why don't we have a seat?"

When they were all seated, Adler looked to Quinn. "Detective?"

"Mr. Crowley, we found your wife," Quinn said. "She's dead."

"What?" Crowley sat back in his chair. His face paled, and he began to tap an index finger on the arm of the chair. After a moment of silence, Crowley said, "How did she die?"

"We can't say right now," Quinn said. She was waiting, or in her case, hoping for him to slip up and reveal more than he should.

"Why can't you say? She's my wife." Crowley looked to his attorney. "Blackstone, I want to know."

"It's not an unreasonable question," Blackstone said to Quinn. The attorney's mannerisms and tone were smooth and controlled, but his eyes burned with keen interest.

Quinn shook her head. She wasn't answering any questions until hers had been satisfied. "When is the last time you saw your wife?"

Crowley looked to his lawyer. The widower might be an ass, but he was smart, and he knew when the sharks were circling. "We already had this conversation at the station when I came to you looking for my wife."

"My memory is sometimes faulty. Refresh it." Quinn's memory was a steel trap. A fact went in, and it never escaped.

"I told you, about five days ago," Crowley said.

"Can you be more specific?" she asked. "What time of day was it?"

"Morning."

"And where did you see her?" she pressed.

"At our house." He shook his head. "I know how this goes. The cops are always looking to blame the spouse. I didn't kill my wife."

"Where have you been the last couple of days?" Adler asked.

"In my hotel room." His grief appeared to dissolve.

"Can you prove it?"

Now he looked outraged, concerned about himself, and slightly annoyed. "I shouldn't have to, but yes, I can."

"What kind of relationship did you have with your wife?" Adler said.

"What do you mean?" Crowley demanded.

"What kind of marriage? Happy, contentious, ambivalent, or what?"

Worry deepened the lines framing his mouth. "We loved each other. We've known each other since high school."

"That doesn't sound very convincing," Quinn said.

"What does convincing sound like?" Blackstone asked.

She smiled. "Not like that."

"Does this have anything to do with Kaitlin's stabbing?" Crowley asked. "If it does, ask her what's going on, because clearly she knows more than my wife or I."

"I did my research on Kaitlin," Blackstone said. "With her past, she must be a suspect."

Adler ignored the comment, keeping his gaze trained on Crowley. "I've listened to Ms. Roe's interview with your wife." He let the statement hang.

Crowley fidgeted with his wedding band. "Whatever Erika thought she remembered from that night is corrupted. She was drunk."

"She recalled the details pretty well," Adler said.

Blackstone injected, "What does Ms. Roe's interview have to do with Mrs. Crowley's death?"

Adler ignored the comment. "Mr. Crowley, was your wife involved in any kind of lifestyle that might be considered risky?"

"Like an affair?" Crowley asked.

"Boyfriend, swinger, drug use? I don't know. You tell me. People who live in perfect houses don't always lead perfect lives. Her yoga teacher said she often parked in the back of the studio, but skipped the class. Did she meet a friend or go somewhere more intimate?"

Crowley's confusion was enough of an answer. "Erika was a good woman. She was not into any secret kinky shit, and if you spread anything like that about her, I will have Mr. Blackstone sue you and your department."

"We're simply asking questions here. No one is passing judgment."

"I don't like your tone," Crowley said.

Adler had touched on a nerve. "Are you engaged in any kind of extracurricular activities that we need to know about?"

"I am not."

"If I trace your credit card receipts and phone records, I won't find anything?" Adler asked.

Crowley shifted and looked to his attorney.

Blackstone held up his hand. "Officers, stop with the cat and mouse. You have just shared some very upsetting news with my client. There's no way he can be completely rational right now. We're going to have to suspend this interview for another day." He rose and bade his client to do the same. "You can show yourselves out."

Adler wasn't surprised by Blackstone's request, but he was still frustrated. He'd dealt with too many men like Blackstone who shadowed the truth in words and legal maneuvers. He and Quinn rose but made no move toward the door.

"How well did you know Gina Mason?" Adler asked.

Crowley's frown deepened with anger, and then as if he couldn't resist, he broke from his attorney and stepped toward them. "She was a friend of my wife's. I didn't know her."

Blackstone raised his hand. "This ends now."

"I did not kill my wife." Crowley punctuated each word with the poke of a finger.

"Good. Whoever killed her was a monster." Adler wanted to get a rise out of Crowley. "No one deserves to die the way she did."

"Are you trying to make me feel worse?" Crowley asked. His attorney placed a hand on his arm, but Crowley jerked it away. "I didn't kill her."

"Enough, Detectives," Blackstone said.

"We'll be revisiting this conversation again, Mr. Crowley," Adler said. "Are you staying in the same hotel?"

"The Richmond Inn on Broad Street."

It was an expensive boutique hotel that catered to tourists and business travelers. "And there's someone who can vouch for you there?"

"Talk to the manager. He knows me well."

"Anyone else?"

Crowley's chin lifted and he looked to Blackstone, who nodded. "There's a woman."

"Her name?" Adler asked.

"Barbara Austin. She'll vouch for me."

Adler scribbled down the name and the phone number Crowley provided. "She's your girlfriend?"

"Not that formal. But we were intimate."

"Adultery doesn't translate into murder," Blackstone said.

"Your client wasn't forthcoming about Ms. Austin. What else is he holding back?"

"That's it," Crowley said. "I was afraid how it would look."

Blackstone all but shoved Crowley out of the conference room, leaving Quinn and Adler to saunter out behind them. They pushed through the front door into the bright sunshine.

"On a scale of one to ten, how guilty do you think he is?" Quinn asked.

Adler knew Crowley was hiding something and Blackstone was helping him do it. But was their secret murder? That he couldn't say right now. "He's no choir boy."

"A mistress could be motive for murder."

"Sure. But what's the motive for killing Jennifer Ralston?" The two women knew each other and had seen each other occasionally at Saint Mathew's events, but he believed more than ever that their deaths were linked to Kaitlin's stabbing and whatever happened to Gina. He didn't have all the answers yet, but he was getting closer. "The motive goes beyond a girlfriend and a bad marriage."

"Back to Gina?"

"Yep," he said.

INTERVIEW FILE #20

HIDDEN MESSAGES

After the police released my name to the media, I started to get letters. A few weren't bad. There were people praying for me. Others wanted to shame me. Most were menacing.

> *You don't deserve to live.*
> *God will punish you.*
> *Judgment Day is coming.*

Some were sent via US Mail with no return address, and some were left at my aunt's house. Those letters, coupled with continued media scrutiny, were what finally drove me out of Virginia. I moved back to Dallas, changed my name, and dyed my hair blond. The letters and media calls finally stopped, and I had an opportunity to start over. I threw myself into school and later my career. And in the rare off hours, I partied hard like there was no tomorrow.

Over the years, there were times when I could almost believe losing Gina wasn't my fault, and I didn't deserve to be punished.

CHAPTER NINETEEN

Wednesday, March 21, 2018; 9:00 a.m.

Randy Hayward watched Steven Marcus lift the jailhouse phone as he stared through the thick glass separating them. The reporter's build was still slight, and he couldn't be much older than Randy, but he looked like the boy next door. A place like this would eat him alive.

Hayward raised the phone to his ear and grinned. "I didn't think you'd come. I figured you were done with me after our meeting in January."

"I wasn't interested in playing games."

They'd met after Randy's release from prison in early January. Marcus asked for an interview, and Randy had agreed in exchanged for cash. But when the time came to meet, Randy had had better things to do and had blown off their appointment. "You won't be sorry you came."

Marcus didn't look convinced. "Why am I here?"

"I'm in a bad way. I need a friend," Randy said.

"If you want a friend, then tell me where Gina is. You know I want to find her."

Randy looked to the guard standing nearby and leaned forward. "I can't tell you right now."

"Then we aren't friends." The reporter's eyes flashed with unexpected anger as he rose and looked ready to leave.

Randy had a knack for knowing how far to push his luck, and with Marcus he was reaching his limit. "Hey now, don't be so harsh. I can give you what you want, just not right this minute."

Marcus released a breath and stared through the glass at him. "What do you want?"

"I need the public to know I'm not a monster."

"I'd say you fit the bill. I know you killed Gina, and the cops have you on security footage stabbing the woman in the convenience store you robbed."

Randy shook his head, but his grin turned sly. "The attorneys have worked out a deal. I'm gonna be taking the cops to Gina real soon."

Marcus sat back. "You made a deal?"

"A real sweet one."

"What happened to Gina?"

Randy rubbed the side of his head, his handcuffs jostling on his wrists. "I can't tell you before the cops."

"Why did you kill her?"

"I'll tell you that after Friday."

"Friday?"

"That's when I talk to the cops about her. I'd do it today, but Kaitlin's the one holding up the show. Cops say she can't come with us until Friday, and I've got to have my sweet Kaitlin at the big reveal."

"She was stabbed. She's out of the hospital tomorrow."

Randy couldn't say he was sorry. He should have done the same to her years ago. "Ouch. Stabbed. Well, if there ever was a bitch who deserved it, it was her."

"I thought you were tight with Kaitlin Roe? She was your girlfriend. From what people told me, she would have done anything for you at one point."

"Not anymore. She's a viper." He'd been real nice to her when they'd been dating, and then at the Fourth of July party, he'd gotten a little too drunk. Yeah, he'd hit her, but looking back, he knew both she and Gina got what they deserved.

"When's the last time you saw her?" Marcus asked.

"Last week." He made a sucking sound as he ran his tongue over his teeth. "She'd been trying to talk to me for months, visiting and hoping I'd open up to her. She's like you. She wants your precious little Gina found."

Marcus shook his head. "Gina was never mine. I never knew her."

"But you did all kinds of research on her, and you fell for her just like any other guy who spent any time with her. Shit, even dead, Gina could win a man's heart."

"If you're talking to the cops, why am I here?"

"Like I said, I need my story told. I'm going to be on trial, and public opinion matters. You can tell my story best because you understand the effect Gina had on men."

Marcus shifted, as if uncomfortable with the idea that he'd have anything in common with this piece of garbage.

Randy smiled. "You're gonna have to put your own shit aside and suck it up if you want the whole story. You look like the kind of man who'd deal with the devil for a good story."

Marcus tapped a finger on the phone. "What do you want?"

"Money in my cantina account is a nice start. And if you write about me favorably during my trial, I can tell you things that readers will eat up."

"Consider it done."

"And give a message to Kaitlin for me."

"What's that?"

"Tell her the next time, I hope whoever hates her as much as me finishes the job."

***

248

Kaitlin pulled off the earphones and hit "Mute" on her computer, silencing Jennifer Ralston's voice. Hearing the dead woman left her unsettled and more worried than ever about Erika. Adler had not returned last night, and she was anxious to see him not only for news but because, like it or not, she felt better when he was around. She'd left him one message, but he'd not called her back. Damn. If she could just get out of this hospital room, she wouldn't feel so cut off.

She ran a hand through the tangle of her hair. More than ever, she wanted to see this podcast to the end.

The four walls of her hospital room seemed to close in around her. She now knew every inch of this room, and it was driving her stir-crazy. She'd watched more television in the last few days than she had in the last five years, and if one more nurse prodded her, she'd go nuts.

The nurses had said no more walking today. She'd pushed herself too hard already. But unable to sit any longer, she swung her legs over the side of the bed, grimacing as her stitches pulled a little. Drawing in a breath, she placed her feet on the floor, stood, and rolled her IV forward a few inches. The discomfort was manageable. She started a slow and steady walk toward the door and the hallway.

Moving more easily, she felt stronger, less vulnerable. She welcomed the buzz of activity at the nurse's station as family and friends visited loved ones, but the strangers made her uneasy, and she had to remind herself she was safe here. Though tomorrow she'd be back in the real world.

When she made the turn around the corner, the ward doors whooshed open behind her. She turned to see Detective Adler. Relief flooded her, and she had to struggle not to smile.

His tie was neatly tied and his hair combed, but there were dark circles under his eyes. As he approached, his jacket flapped open, revealing his badge and weapon. As soon as their gazes locked, she saw his annoyance and anger. Whatever he had to tell her wouldn't be good.

"You saw Erika?" she asked.

"I did." He placed his hand under her elbow and started walking her back toward her room.

Calloused fingers rubbed against her skin, sending energy racing through her body. "Where did you find her?"

"In the city." His jaw was clenched, and he seemed very aware that there were several people in the hallway watching them. The nurses knew he'd been here shortly after she'd been brought in and he'd sat by her bed for several hours until she had awakened. A few thought they were dating.

"Can you be more specific?" she asked.

"Not here."

She wondered if he'd heard the nurses' gossip about them. Either way, he didn't look pleased by anything right now.

In her room, he closed the door behind them and walked her to the bed. She sat, and he gently helped her into it and then pulled the blanket up to her waist.

"Where is Erika?" Kaitlin asked again.

His expression softened. "She's dead."

The air whooshed from her lungs, and her head grew light. "How did she die?"

He pulled up a chair and sat beside her. "I can't talk about that now."

"Why not?" Frustration chewed at her. "Jennifer and Erika are dead, and I was stabbed. And you can't tell me!"

"I would if I could, Kaitlin." He sounded so damn calm. "But right now I've got to put the investigation first."

Reason cut through her temper and reminded her that he couldn't keep her in the loop and do his job. "I know. You're right. Have you spoken to Brad?" she asked.

"I have. But that's all I can say now."

Being shut out was frustrating. "When is Hayward taking you to Gina?"

"Friday. Are you up for it?"

"I am." The statement was more for her benefit than his. "I will be fine."

He studied her a moment, and she sensed he wanted to say something, but whatever it was, it got shoved to a back burner. Not spoken. But not gone. "Okay."

***

When Adler walked through the front door of his home, it was late afternoon. He'd stopped by only to shower, change, and eat a quick meal. However, his gaze was immediately drawn to the light in the dining room. Two sawhorses were balancing a large piece of plywood. The makeshift table was covered with papers and files.

As he shrugged off his jacket, the downstairs toilet flushed, and the sink turned on and off. Logan's steady, almost rhythmic steps echoed down the hallway. When he rounded the corner, Logan's hand was on the grip of his 9mm Sig Sauer.

Logan looked at Adler and clicked the safety back on. "Paranoia is my new friend."

"Really? I thought he was my friend. Fickle bastard." Adler moved into the kitchen and said a prayer of thanks when he saw the two pizza boxes on top of his newly delivered six-burner stove. "When did the stove arrive?"

"This morning. Countertops come tomorrow."

He snapped up a piece of cold pepperoni pizza and savoring the flavor, took a bite. He hadn't realized how hungry he was.

"I ordered pepperoni last night knowing it's your favorite. Wasn't sure when you were going to get your ass in the house, but figured I'd leave some out for you. You remind me of my pet dog when I was a kid. He would run off for days at a time, too."

Adler chuckled and moved to the coffee maker that had gurgled out a fresh pot. "I needed a little time to clear my head." He sipped the brew, remembering that Logan always liked it strong and bitter. "How's it going with the case?"

"So far, she's not telling me too much. Trying to get her to whisper her secrets, but she won't."

"You listen to the interviews Kaitlin Roe made?" Adler asked.

"Most of them. She's got twenty hours of conversation. I can tell you not everyone was glad to hear from her. But no matter what they hurled at her, she stayed on task. She's like a dog with a bone."

"What're your impressions of her during the recent interviews with Detective North?" Adler asked.

"There's a calm steadiness about her. Her voice trembled a little during the initial questions, but after a few minutes she sounded steady."

Adler ran his hand over his head. "She's smart and determined. Times when I think she should be a cop."

"John, you sound like you want her to really trust you."

"Don't all detectives want total trust?"

"Sure. But you and I were partners for over a year. I've seen more emotion aimed at Kaitlin than at your ex-wife."

Adler agreed. There was something about Kaitlin. She'd gotten under his skin the moment he'd first met her. And the more he was around her, the more he wanted to be with her.

Logan sipped his coffee and changed gears. "Has Hayward's attorney called you?"

"He has. The deal is simple. He tells us what happened to Gina Mason and no charges will be filed on her case, and he gets reduced charges on the one pending."

Adler shifted his thoughts back to the case and the files Logan had been studying almost nonstop. "What do you think went down on that road with Kaitlin, Gina, and the masked man?"

"Hayward killed her."

"Did he plan out the abduction and murder, or was it a crime of opportunity?"

"I'd have said opportunity if not for the drugs spiking the booze the girls were drinking. I think Randy had a grudge against Kaitlin and he got Brad to put his girlfriend up to spiking it. All Randy had to do was wait by the river. But he got bored and decided to steal some silver from his mother because he was always cash strapped. He grabbed the silver and waited for the girls. He'd had an obsession with Gina and wanted to hurt Kaitlin, and in one act of violence got everything he wanted."

"What did he do with Gina?"

"His mother had a garden shed that 'burned' to the ground just days after Gina vanished. No one thought much of it at the time, but I think that's where he stashed her until he could take her wherever he took her. Once she was taken care of, all he had to do was sit back and watch Kaitlin suffer."

"Shit." Kaitlin had been a lost, confused kid when she crossed Hayward's path, and she'd spent the last fourteen years paying for her association with him.

"So, is the DA going to take the deal?"

"Yes, with my blessings as well as the police commissioner's. It'll be null and void if Hayward doesn't show us Gina's body."

Logan balled his fingers into a tight fist. "Jesus, that sucks. That piece of shit is getting away with Gina's murder as well as the convenience store killing."

"Yes, he is."

"When does this go down?" Logan asked.

"Friday morning." He ate another slice of pizza. "Whoever killed Jennifer and Erika was invested in Gina's case. There was a heart painted at both the Ralston and Crowley murder scenes. One was in blood and the other in red marker. Kaitlin said it reminded her of the logo used for Gina's search updates."

Logan crossed to his papers on the sawhorse table and flipped through the case file until he found a copy of a handout. "This flyer and others like it were posted all over Richmond after Gina went missing."

"Kaitlin said the heart was her idea."

"Interesting. It's lopsided and off balance."

"Like the girl she was."

Logan held up the flyer. "This particular search was organized by Gina's church. Dozens of search teams walked along the river and surrounding areas for weeks."

"Kaitlin said there were also lots of unauthorized searchers."

"She's correct. There was a tremendous outpouring of search volunteers. And I'd bet money Jennifer's and Erika's killer was on one of the teams."

"Are there any records of the team members?"

"There are names of the sponsoring organizations but not individual members."

"So why after all this time did Jennifer's and Erika's killer decide to act?"

"You know how it goes. The fuse never really goes out on the crazy ones," Logan said.

"A trigger could have been a job loss, an angry wife or girlfriend, or what I think happened, Kaitlin returned to Richmond and reawakened all his old demons."

"What about Steven Marcus? He might have information we're not seeing."

"I'm meeting with Kaitlin and him on Saturday. Join us."

"I'm not technically on the homicide unit."

Adler shrugged. "We've bent a few rules before. Come with us. You have good instincts."

"Am I gonna make Quinn jealous?"

Adler laughed. "She'll survive."

INTERVIEW FILE #21

The Deal

Friday, June 1, 2018

Trey Ricker of the Commonwealth Attorney's office is a tall, lean man with a face too weathered for someone in his late thirties. He frowns when I ask him about the deal with Hayward. The arrangement between the Commonwealth and Hayward remains under bitter media scrutiny, and many of Ricker's critics are calling foul.

"No one wants to deal with the devil." Ricker's voice is rough and deep. "And I was prepared to take the heat for it if it went sideways."

"Would you do it again?"

"In a heartbeat."

CHAPTER TWENTY

Thursday, March 22, 2018; 10:00 a.m.

With discharge papers and instructions in hand, Kaitlin could not wait to be sprung. Freshly showered, she'd gingerly slid on a loose T-shirt, sweats, and canvas slip-on shoes. Certainly not the most attractive look, but it was progress. A knock on the door had her turning. "Come in."

A nurse appeared with a wheelchair. "Ready to go home?"

"More than you know," she said, smiling. She bundled up the plastic bag of her belongings with her backpack and lowered into the wheelchair.

"Do you have someone to drive you home?" the nurse asked.

She fished her cell from her backpack. "Taxi."

The nursed hesitated. "You don't have anyone?"

"Friends offered, but it's simpler this way. It's not a big deal. A short car ride home, and then I'll go straight to the couch and put my feet up."

The nurse unlocked the brakes. "Who's going to take care of you at home?"

"I'll be fine. I'll order a few pizzas and just chill. Honestly, it's going to be a vacation." She kept her smile fixed as if she were pitching to a big client. "Any more flower deliveries?"

"No, just the one. Such a pretty arrangement. Someone thinks a lot of you."

That's what she was afraid of. "Yes, he certainly does."

The nurse turned the chair around, pushed it out the door and toward the elevator. When the doors opened, Detective Adler stepped off. He wore jeans, a white shirt with sleeves rolled up above thick wrists to muscled forearms dusted with hair, and no tie today.

"Good, I caught you," he said, holding the door open with his arm.

"What're you doing here?"

"Taking you home," Adler said.

"I have a taxi."

"You did. I sent the taxi on his way."

Aware the nurse was watching, she kept her tone even. "I had it worked out."

He shrugged. "The best-laid plans."

The nurse pushed Kaitlin past him onto the elevator. "I was worried she'd be on her own. I'm glad she has you."

Kaitlin didn't *have* John Adler. He wasn't here for her. He was here to monitor her because she was a key component of Hayward's deal.

The challenge in his gaze dared her to get into an argument in front of the nurse. She swallowed her pride as well as a few choice words for Adler until she was actually free of the hospital.

She tossed another winning smile at the nurse. The nurse gave her a thumbs-up.

The three rode the elevator down in silence. When the doors opened, the nurse wheeled her through the automatic doors toward a black SUV. Adler moved past them and opened the passenger door. He took her backpack and bag and set them inside. As she rose, he supported her weight with his hand. She didn't fight it. When she'd set-tled into the seat and snapped the seat belt, he closed the door, moved around the front of the car, and slid behind the wheel.

"I appreciate the lift," she said.

"Sure." He slipped on dark sunglasses.

Absently she glanced in the rearview mirror to make sure no one was following. It was a habit that she'd finally broken until recently.

"How're you feeling?"

"Like a million bucks. Ready to get back to work."

He frowned. "Your plan is to rest, correct?"

"Yeah, yeah, I get it. Feet up. Lift nothing heavier than a book for two weeks."

"And you're going to do that?"

"Sure. Don't worry about me."

She'd been going it alone for a long time, but it was nice to have someone in her corner even if it was just for a little while. "What else have you learned about Erika?" she asked.

"Not much. Her autopsy is today." He was silent for a moment, tightening and releasing his hands on the steering wheel.

Neither spoke as they crossed the river and hooked a left down a side street that led them to an industrial building converted into apart-ments. A patch of asphalt dotted with cracks and potholes surrounded the brick exterior. The front entryway was made of metal. There was a security pad to the right.

He parked by the front entrance and came around to her side of the car as she opened the door. He pulled it open the rest of the way and held out his hand for her. It was another moment of pride versus practicality. Like it or not, pride was a luxury she could not afford. She laid her hand in his and allowed him to support her as she gingerly stood. "Thanks."

"I'll see you up." He collected her backpack and bag of personal belongings.

"Not necessary. It's a few steps inside and then a short elevator ride. I'll take it from here." She looked toward her parking spot and spotted her SUV.

She walked slowly toward the front entrance. Adler followed behind and appeared content to move at her pace, as if he had all the time in the world. She punched four numbers into the keypad. The lock on the door clicked open. He reached around her, his arm brushing her shoulder, and opened the door. He waited for her to pass.

She walked down the hallway toward a lobby mirror that tossed back their reflections. She was shocked how pale and thin she'd become. Haggard was a better description, especially compared to Adler's olive complexion and toned body.

They rode the elevator to the fifth floor and walked the long corridor to her apartment. Fumbling with her keys, she had trouble supporting the backpack's weight and her hand began to shake very slightly. She let her pack slide down her arm to the floor and finally jammed the key in her door.

Without the strength to lean over and pick up the discarded pack, she nudged it over the threshold like it were a football goal line score.

"Please, let me pick it up," he said.

"It's inside. That's all that counts." She held out her hand for her plastic bag. "I've got it from here."

He scooped up the backpack and moved past her. He set her belongings on a large worktable filled with her case notes on Gina. When she'd been in public relations and responsible for multiple projects, she'd been organized to the point of OCD. Now everything was in such a jumble, only she could make sense of it.

The apartment with its high ceilings was large, and noise traveled easily through it. There was a tall bank of windows that faced the river and the city skyline. The walls were brick, and the black ceiling ductwork was exposed. Hints of family money showed in a four-poster bed, a dining set, and a twelve-piece set of china, silver, and crystal that had all been inherited from her aunt. However, her couch was a secondhand purchase, as were the coffee table made from shipping pallets and rustic desk holding audio equipment and computers.

She could almost hear his mind clicking: *Who the hell was this woman?*

She faced him. "I felt like myself when I left the hospital, but now, I'm beat."

Less than a foot separated them, and she could feel energy radiating from him.

"What're your plans for today, Kaitlin?"

"Other than crawling into bed?"

"Good. Tomorrow is going to be a big day." He studied her as if he wanted to say something else, but only said, "Watch your six."

"Always." She walked him to the door.

He inspected the line of locks.

"A girl can't be too careful," she said.

"You're doing everything but being careful."

"Those allow me to sleep at night, so I'm bright eyed and bushy tailed in the morning."

"You checked the rearview mirror five or six times while we drove here from the hospital. You also cupped your hand over the keypad when you punched in the code. Each move was automatic. Well practiced."

"Trouble seems to find me."

He stood at the door. "I'll be here early tomorrow. About seven."

She raised her hand. "Ready with bells on."

Again he paused and studied her, and she could almost read his thoughts in his frown. "I know," she said. "I'm a puzzle with too many missing pieces."

"You sure as hell are."

He strode down the hallway while she stood for just a moment watching him. She closed the door and fastened all the locks. The apartment had never felt empty until this moment.

She moved across the open space to the antique bed behind a silk screen. Relief leaked over her lips in one breath as she sat down and eased back against the pillows. She adjusted her body once or twice until the incision in her abdomen didn't pull.

She opened the bedside table drawer and removed a small box. From it, she pulled one of Gina's heart necklaces left to her by her aunt. She touched the gold and then, taking a deep breath, fastened it around her neck. She lay back on the bed and touched the cool, delicate metal as she watched the reflection of light on the wooden ceiling beams.

***

He'd been watching the hospital parking lot and the cab, expecting Kaitlin to emerge alone. He had another opportunity to take her, and he'd been so tempted to do just that. But the black SUV pulled up, and Detective John Adler stepped out and sent the cab away. He disappeared through the double doors.

Twenty minutes of waiting and the cop reappeared. This time he was escorting Kaitlin, who sat in a wheelchair pushed by a nurse. The detective was almost solicitous as he opened the passenger door and helped Kaitlin into her seat. Anyone else watching might think the detective was concerned about her.

Adler would be a fool to care for her. She was a chameleon. She wasn't the poor victim. And though she was making a lot of noise about finding Gina, there was no fixing her betrayal.

He was careful to stay back several car lengths as he followed them, and he sped by as Kaitlin got out of the car. Her SUV was still in the lot, and Kaitlin was now locked inside her apartment and alone. But she couldn't stay inside forever. Sooner or later, she would have to venture out.

A resident hustled up the stairs to the front door and punched in the security code on the keypad. Propping the door with a rock, the young woman hurried back to her car and grabbed what looked like a large framed picture. She set the picture inside and then removed the rock. The door closed.

It would be easy to slip past a resident with overloaded arms, but that would leave a witness. Better to wait until he could get Kaitlin alone.

INTERVIEW FILE #22

PERSONS OF INTEREST—DEREK BLACKSTONE AND BRAD CROWLEY

The former hell-raisers, Derek Blackstone and Brad Crowley, maintained a close friendship. They liked the clubs, the cigar rooms, and the ladies. As it so happened, they both had solid alibis the nights of Jennifer's and Erika's murders. And despite intensified focus, the cops could find no forensic or eyewitness evidence to link either man to the murders. But Detective John Adler would soon unearth their role in the Gina Mason case.

CHAPTER
TWENTY-ONE

Thursday, March 22, 2018; 4:00 p.m.

Kaitlin slept the entire afternoon, and when she awoke the sunlight had dimmed across her apartment. Rolling on her side, she rose up on her right arm. Her head had cleared, and her gut didn't ache as badly. She eased her bare feet to the floor and stood. She actually felt human.

Crossing the cold floor toward the kitchen, she opened the freezer, grabbed a frozen pizza, peeled off the packaging, and tossed it in the oven, which she turned on.

While the oven heated, she dug her phone out of her backpack, irritated to discover the battery was dead. Plugging it in, she waited as the device charged.

She removed her recorder and notepad on the Gina Mason case. She turned on her computer and began to dig through her emails.

She spent the next twenty minutes reading her students' messages.

The smell of cheese, tomato, and garlic drew her attention from the screen. She grabbed a large plate, opened the oven door, and slid the pizza onto the dish. She sliced it into wedges and returned to the sofa.

After living on hospital food for several days, the pizza tasted wonderful. She picked up her phone and read through texts until she reached Steven Marcus's name. She agreed to meet him on Saturday evening with Adler at a coffee shop near her apartment.

Scrolling through the phone, she found Erika's last text. I'm ready to be interviewed, but it has to be today. Come to my house. Now before I lose my nerve.

Sitting back in her chair, she closed her eyes and imagined herself leaving her classroom and driving to Erika's house.

She stepped into Erika's home. The situation didn't feel right. And then the rush of footsteps, the crack of pain to her head, and the softly spoken words.

"I am coming back for you. You deserve to be punished."

She'd thought she'd dreamed the words, but realized her mind had been replaying a memory.

"I am coming back for you. You deserve to be punished."

***

Adler and Logan pulled up in front of the small brick rancher set on an acre of land on the city's south side a few minutes after four in the afternoon.

Logan rubbed his hand over his leg. "It feels good to be back in this car. Still smells like cheeseburgers and your damn aftershave, but it's nice. Never thought I'd get anywhere close to a cop car again."

"You'll be back soon enough."

Logan shook his head. "I could use a break. Today the hits keep coming." Hands at his sides, he wiggled his fingers before fisting and unfisting them. "Suzanne called this morning. She's filing for divorce."

"Shit. I'm sorry."

"As much as I want to blame it on the injury, it's been coming for some time. Being a cop's wife is not what she bargained for."

"Your ex and my ex could start their own club."

A mirthless grin tugged at Logan's lips. "I don't even want to guess what they'd call it."

Adler shook his head, knowing losing even a bad marriage was a punch in the gut. "Let's focus on Steven Marcus. He's not expecting us until Saturday. He told Kaitlin something about a deadline, but I don't think it would hurt for us to talk to him for a few minutes now. I'm going to let you ask the questions. You know the Mason case better than me at this point."

"I'm not an official cop."

"You're a homicide detective. You just happen to be on leave. Besides, we aren't arresting Marcus. We're just looking for background information."

Logan shifted his gaze to the house and, grabbing his cane, opened the door. "Let's do this."

Adler came around the side of the car. Another cop might have hesitated to help Logan stand, but he had no reservations. They were a team, and he knew Logan would have done the same for him if the situation were reversed. He grabbed Logan by the arm and helped him to his feet.

"Thanks." Logan righted himself and gripped his cane.

Adler let Logan go first up the sidewalk, and he slowed his pace. Logan leaned heavily on a wrought iron railing and climbed the three steps.

"Not bad," Adler said.

"Give me a week and I'll be doing backflips." He rang the bell. "I called ahead, and he seemed happy to meet with us."

"Good."

The front door opened to a lean, midsize man with short-cropped hair. He sported glasses and wore a blue collared shirt and jeans. "Detective Logan?"

Logan shifted and tightened his grip on his cane. "That's right. Thanks for seeing us."

Adler leaned in, his hand extended. "I'm Detective Adler. I understand you're the expert on the Gina Mason case."

Marcus grinned. "I don't know about that, but I spent a good deal of time on it. A case gets under your skin, and it's hard to let go. You two must understand that."

Logan's shoulders relaxed a fraction. "I hear you. Sorry to bother you. You must be pretty busy."

"Nothing I can't handle. Please, come in. I'm afraid the house is a bit of a mess. My wife is out of town, and I'm letting the place go to hell. Figured I'd do something about the mess right before she comes home."

A half-dozen different newspapers were spread across a long worn couch set up in front of a wide-screen television that played a muted twenty-four-hour news station.

"I'm a bit of a news junkie," Marcus said. "I can't help but follow everything." He scooped the newspapers off the couch and carried them into a nearby kitchen. "Can I get you two coffee?"

"No, thanks," Logan said, leaning on his cane. "We don't want to hold you up too long."

Over a small fireplace were ten different awards Marcus had won a decade ago. "You left your job with the newspaper," Adler said.

"Cutbacks," Marcus said, returning to the room. "I wasn't crazy about losing the steady paycheck, but I'm excited to do my own thing. I've already started a new website." He motioned for them to both sit. Each took one of the easy chairs that faced the couch.

"I looked it up online," Logan said. "Your site is dedicated to finding lost people."

"Like I said, Gina got under my skin. I want to carry on the work."

"Did you interview any of the girls who were with Gina the night she vanished?"

"I talked to Jennifer Ralston about six months after it all went down. She was just back from college. She said her first semester of college had been a nightmare and as long as she lived she'd never forget Gina. She was too upset to talk to me."

"What about Erika Crowley?" Logan asked.

"As a matter of fact, I reconnected with her over the winter. I ran into her in a coffee shop. She still looks the same, so I introduced myself. She was open to talking, and we started meeting on a weekly basis. I think talking was like therapy to her."

"What did she say?" Adler asked.

"She started off admitting she'd been afraid to leave her house the last few years, but she was trying to get better. We just chatted that first time. The next visit, she was annoyed with her husband. She said he was having an affair with a woman in his office. She was trying to figure out what a divorce would cost her."

"What about Kaitlin?" Adler asked.

"We spoke on the phone and set up a meeting for Saturday. She's interested in some kind of collaboration down the road. We both want the same thing, so it makes sense." He shook his head. "I feel for all these women. They were young girls who were having fun, got a little drunk, and then Kaitlin and Gina happened onto trouble."

"You must have theories about who did this," Logan said.

"It's pretty obvious. It was Hayward." He shifted and leaned forward a fraction. "A lot of what he did before Gina vanished was kept off the record by his parents, but I'm not afraid to bend a few rules, and I found out a few things."

"Such as?"

"When he was fifteen and a camp counselor at a coed camp, he had sex with a fourteen-year-old girl. She told the camp director, and his parents were contacted. They paid off the girl and her family, so it went away. A year later it was almost the same scenario at an out-of-state computer camp. After that there were no more complaints, but I think he just got more careful. Say what you want, but he is smart as hell. But no amount of smarts changed the fact he was a time bomb ready to go off."

"You've heard about Jennifer Ralston and Erika Crowley?" Logan asked.

"I still can't get over that they're dead. And it's not lost on me that they were with Gina that last night."

Logan adjusted his grip on his cane and shifted his prosthetic leg. "Any theories?"

"Derek Blackstone. He looked after Hayward like he was his kid brother. It's why he defended him in the robbery case four years ago and why he stepped up to defend him in that recent stabbing. I caught up to Blackstone fourteen years ago when the spotlight turned on Hayward. He said he, Crowley, and Hayward had sworn an oath of loyalty and they'd never turn their backs on each other." Marcus shrugged. "Say what you want about them, but they stuck to their word on that promise, and nothing you say or do will change it."

***

"The surveillance footage at the Crowleys' shows Kaitlin pulling up at 2:05 p.m." Quinn was sitting in the front passenger seat, flipping the pages of her small notebook. "She hesitates at the base of the stairs and checks her phone before she moves toward the front door and opens it. She steps inside, out of camera range."

"Any sign of her attacker?" Adler said as they drove west on I-64. Using Erika Crowley's calendar notations, Adler had located Diane Wallace, an employee of Margie's Maids, who regularly cleaned the couple's home. They were headed toward her house in a working-class neighborhood off Derbyshire Road.

"There's a figure that passes in front of the window about a half hour before Kaitlin arrives," Quinn said. "The figure appears to be male."

"Someone was waiting for her just like Jennifer's killer."

"It appears so. I checked all the available security cameras nearby. One catches the intruder coming from the woods behind the Crowleys' house."

"What do those woods back up to?" Adler asked.

"A cul-de-sac in a middle-class neighborhood. No one on the cul-de-sac has cameras, but I had an officer knock on a few doors. Several people reported seeing a black or dark-blue American-made pickup truck parked in the cul-de-sac early that afternoon. One woman thought maybe it had to do with an electrical contractor. No one recalls the license plate."

"Several of Jennifer's neighbors said there was a dark truck with a plumbing sign on the side," Adler said.

"Magnetic signs are easy enough to change," Quinn added.

"A tradesman doesn't set off alarm bells right away. And we know Kaitlin didn't stab herself," Adler said more to himself.

"Assuming she wasn't working with someone."

"Kaitlin with a partner? All I've learned about her suggests she's a loner."

Quinn shrugged. "Okay, maybe you're right on that one."

"Don't sound so disappointed, Quinn."

"I don't like citizens like Kaitlin playing detective. They end up getting in our way or injured. She's managed to do both in short order."

It was dusk when he parked in front of Diane Wallace's small brick house. The lawn was large, a throwback to the dairy farm that had occupied the land for a half century. In the last few years, the area around these small homes had filled in with increasingly larger homes on smaller lots.

There were several bikes in the front yard. In the driveway, an old Toyota truck sporting a magnetic sign that read MARGIE'S MAIDS was parked.

The detectives crossed the concrete sidewalk and climbed the front steps to a green door.

Adler rang the bell. "I called ahead and told Mrs. Wallace we were coming."

"Right."

Footsteps clattered inside the house seconds before the door opened to a pale woman with red hair streaked with gray. She wore a large oversize T-shirt that bloused over full breasts and faded jeans. She appeared to be in her midforties.

"Mrs. Wallace?" Adler said, holding up his badge as Quinn did the same. He introduced them.

She studied the badges and frowned before pushing the door open. "I'm not sure what I can tell you."

They stepped inside to a small living room. A worn beige couch, flanked by two burgundy recliners, faced a sixty-five-inch television now playing a muted cooking show.

After taking a seat, Adler asked, "Mrs. Wallace, can you tell us about the most recent day you cleaned the Crowleys' house?"

"When I got there, Mrs. Crowley wasn't home. But the last few months she's been at yoga on Saturdays, so I didn't expect her until about nine."

"What time did you leave the house?"

"About nine thirty. It takes me almost two hours to clean it. I'm in the house six days a week."

"Six days?" Quinn said.

"The Crowleys don't like anything out of place."

"Were you worried when Mrs. Crowley didn't come home?" Adler asked.

"I thought it was unusual. She doesn't leave the house much."

"Why is that?" Quinn asked.

Mrs. Wallace rubbed her hands over her jeans. "I think she's afraid to leave her house alone. She never discussed her fears with me, but I could see she was afraid. It was a big step for her when she started the yoga classes late last year." She hesitated and then said, "She'd been seeing a doctor. I think he was helping."

"So, Mrs. Crowley didn't come home," Adler said, doubling back. "What did you do?"

"I waited an extra fifteen minutes. She likes to review the work I've done. But finally I had to leave. I had another job."

"You locked up the house."

"I did," Mrs. Wallace said. "I am sure of that."

"Who has keys to the house?"

"The Crowleys, of course. Me. I think there's a neighbor who does."

"We checked. None of them had a key."

She shifted, looking uncomfortable. "I know I locked that door."

"I'm not accusing you of anything. It's just that there were no signs of forced entry." Adler smiled. "Did Mrs. Crowley have any friends?"

"None. For the longest time she kept to herself. She told everyone she was an artist, but she never painted. Her art studio was as pristine as the day she set it up. The canvases were all blank."

"There's a woman in town named Kaitlin Roe who's interviewing people related to a cold case. Do you know if she ever met with Mrs. Crowley?"

"I heard Mrs. Crowley talking to a reporter on the phone once. But I think that reporter was a man."

"You're sure?" Adler asked.

"Yes. She was speaking on her cell, and his voice carried."

"Any other visitors or callers?" Quinn asked. "You work in this house every morning. You hear and see things."

"No. It was a good job and it paid well, but every day I was glad to get out of that house." She shook her head. "And now she's dead."

"Did you ever hear the name Jennifer Ralston?" Adler asked.

"Yes, she was a friend of Mrs. Crowley's. She visited the house sometimes. I cleaned for her once a few months ago."

Adler tensed. "You had a key to Jennifer Ralston's house."

"Yes."

"Did you hear what happened to Ms. Ralston?" he asked.

"No."

"She was murdered in her home."

Mrs. Wallace sat back, and her face tightened with tension. "I don't have time for much television. I didn't know."

"What did you do with the key to Ms. Ralston's house?" Adler asked.

"When I receive my work assignments from the central office, they give me a key. I turn it in at the end of the day with my time sheet."

"You do that even for regulars like the Crowleys?"

"Yes. The company is very security conscious."

"Did you ever bring any keys home?" he asked.

"No, never. I'd get fired for that."

"Who else lives in this house with you?" Quinn asked.

"It's me. Sometimes my grandson comes over to play."

"Who's your boss?" Adler asked.

"Am I in trouble?"

"No, ma'am, you're not in trouble. You're actually a big help."

"My boss is Kelly Dixon." She supplied her number.

"Thank you," he said.

The detectives thanked Mrs. Wallace, and once in the car, Adler called Kelly Dixon at Margie's Maids. His call went to voicemail, and he left his name and number.

He drove directly to Café Express, a funky shop with purple walls, modern art, and beads hanging over the front window. It looked as if it belonged in the city near the university and not in the suburban West End.

Out of the car, they crossed the lot and stepped inside. The scents of coffee and cinnamon greeted them. The shop had a collection of round tables and wooden chairs all painted vibrant colors. The place was empty.

Quinn glanced at her watch. "It's almost closing time."

A young woman holding two clean pitchers came out from the back. She glanced up and smiled. "Can I help you?"

Adler showed his badge and introduced them. "We're trying to retrace the last few days of a murder victim."

Her smile fading, she set down the pitchers and dried her hands on her green apron. "I'm Dot Lawrence, and I own the shop. I'm here a good bit of each day."

Adler pulled up Erika's picture on his phone. "Have you seen her?"

Dot studied the picture, nodding almost immediately. "Sure. That's Erika. Are you saying Erika is dead?"

Adler accepted his phone back and tucked it in his breast pocket. "She is. When was Erika here last?"

"My God, that's awful." Dot brushed a loose strand away from her flushed face with the back of her hand. "Last Wednesday. She missed Saturday."

"When she was here, did she meet with anyone?" Adler asked.

"Yeah. A guy. Had a young face, nicely dressed. He seemed very into her when she spoke. He was always taking notes during each of their meetings." She shrugged. "Erika looked nervous."

"Do you know his name?"

"No, sorry. He always paid in cash. I do remember his order: black coffee, heavy cream, and a couple of sugars. I don't suppose that helps you too much."

"You have security cameras?"

"Can't afford one. But there are shops around here that do. I can tell you Erika was always here at 8:15 a.m. on Wednesdays and at 6:00 a.m. on Saturdays. He came in right after."

"Did she meet with anyone else?" Quinn asked.

"No, just that guy."

"Ever overhear them?"

"He was after something," Dot said.

"Why do you say that?" Adler asked.

"A feeling. You stand behind this counter long enough and you learn to read people."

Adler nodded. "We'll check into the cameras, but if we can't find one that monitors this store, would you be willing to sit down with a sketch artist?"

"Absolutely. I'll do whatever I can to help."

INTERVIEW FILE #23

NOTHING TO LOSE

Monday, May 21, 2018

When Gina, Jennifer, Erika, and I crossed paths with Randy, he was a twenty-one-year-old man already showing signs of substance abuse. He had dropped out of college with no plans to return, and his relationship with his parents was already strained.

"The plan started simple," Randy tells me later from his jail cell months after the police closed the case. "I just wanted to have some fun with the girls."

"What was the plan?"

"Erika would do anything for Brad, and when Brad asked her to spike the bottle of lemonade with Ecstasy, she did. Later, when the shit hit the fan, Brad warned her not to tell, because if she did, she'd go down as an accessory. So she kept quiet."

"What did you plan to do once we were drugged?"

"Nothing terrible. I didn't want to hurt anyone."

"But you were high, too, that day, right?"

"It was supposed to be fun, and no one was going to get hurt."

CHAPTER
TWENTY-TWO

Friday, March 23, 2018; 6:00 a.m.

Margie's Maids was located on Midlothian Turnpike and housed in a small industrial-style building. Parked out front was a collection of cars and trucks, each bearing a magnetic sign with the company's name on the side.

Adler strode toward the front door, opened it, and paused as two women dressed in pink Margie's Maids shirts hurried past him. He crossed the room to the front desk, where a stocky redheaded woman wearing one of the company's pink shirts checked off what looked like the morning's assignments.

Adler pulled out his badge. "I'd like to speak to the owner," he said.

The woman peered up over pink reading glasses. "That's me. I'm Margie Smith."

"Ms. Smith, your company cleans for the Crowleys, and you did a job for Jennifer Ralston a few weeks ago."

"That's right." She pulled off her glasses. "I heard about Ms. Ralston. She was a nice lady, and I was sorry to hear about it."

Adler pulled a notebook from his breast pocket. "You have keys and security system codes for all your clients, correct?"

She frowned. "We do. But we're very careful with alarm codes and keys around here. I insist that my cleaning professionals log out and log in all keys each day. I check them in myself."

He flipped a page in his book. "I ran a check on your business in our police database. Did you report a break-in four weeks ago?"

"Yes, my assistant manager opened that day, and she thought we'd been robbed. She called the cops before I could stop her."

"Why stop her?"

"Like I told the officer, nothing was taken."

"Are you certain?"

"I accounted for all the cash in the safe, and every client key was on its hook. Nothing was missing."

"Was anything disturbed?"

"Only thing my manager noticed was her mug."

"Her mug?"

"She always keeps it on the right side of her desk, and she found it on the left. In my book, that wasn't worth calling the cops."

"Did you alert your clients?"

Her shoulders stiffened. "No. I didn't see cause. We service over one hundred homes. That's a lot of locks to be rekeyed and security codes changed."

"A key can be made using a molding compound. Where do you keep the security codes?"

She drew in a breath. "In my assistant manager's desk."

"And she noticed her desk had been disturbed."

"Just a mug," the woman said. "It was just a mug."

"What kind of security do you have here?"

"Locks. A security system."

"Your alarm didn't go off during the night of the alleged breaking and entering?"

"We had a power outage that night, so no, it didn't go off."

"I want a list of all your clients. And I suggest you alert each one about the break-in."

***

When the apartment doorbell buzzed, Kaitlin rose off the couch, moving with careful precision toward the call box. She pressed the red button. "Yes."

"It's Detective Adler."

She glanced toward the security camera screen now projecting his tall, wide shoulders and short dark hair. She admired his strong jaw and angled features before she caught herself and pressed the door release button.

She collected a plate of leftover pizza and an empty coffee cup from last night and took them to the kitchen. She quickly rinsed off both and placed them in the drying rack as the doorbell rang.

Anxious and nervous, she dried her hands and then ran fingers through her hair. She opened the door. "Good morning, Detective."

Sharp eyes studied her. "Have you been resting, Kaitlin?"

"I feel great. I've turned a corner." *Well, maybe not a full corner, but close enough to get through this day.*

"Ready?"

"Yes. Let me just grab my backpack."

He stepped into the foyer and scanned her apartment as he must have when he'd dropped her off.

"I could lie and say the place isn't normally this messy, but it is," she said.

"It's eclectic. That bed is an antique. Queen Anne, right?"

"I suppose. My aunt left it to me. It's been in our family for three generations."

His gaze dropped to the heart pendant around her neck. "Did your aunt also leave you that?"

Automatically her fingertips brushed over it. "Yes, this was Gina's."

"It's nice."

Kaitlin hefted her backpack without too much of a wince or pull. "Ready."

"You look a little stiff."

"I worked too hard yesterday grading my students' projects. I figured with all that was going on, I better get the grades in now."

"Are you sure you're really up to the trip today?"

"Yes."

He studied her closely. "There's going to be no filming or recording today. This is an open murder investigation."

"Understood."

He opened her front door and waited as she passed. It locked automatically, but he checked to make sure it was secure before the two made their way to his waiting SUV. She clicked on her seat belt and settled into the seat as he slid behind the wheel.

He backed out of the spot in one swift, smooth move. "I was able to get the video footage from several Crowley neighbors."

"What did you find?"

"You approached the front door, just as you said, hesitated a beat or two, and then entered the residence. The camera caught a shadow moving through the house just before you arrived."

"It was a trap."

"Yes." Adler tightened his fingers on the wheel.

"Where are we going?" she asked.

"There's a farm about twenty miles outside of the city. That's where Hayward and the uniforms are meeting us." He flashed his police lights, and slower-moving vehicles parted, allowing him to glide past.

He took a westbound exit, drove past a mile's worth of strip malls, and headed toward open country. They drove for ten minutes before he slowed. Automatically she unzipped her backpack and pulled out her phone.

"No recordings."

"Just a description of the area for later."

"Until the case is closed, no recordings." When she readied a rebuttal he said, "Do you always press the boundaries?"

She shrugged and put her phone back in her backpack. "Every chance I get."

"Not here. Especially not today."

She would play nice because she needed to see this to the end. "Fine. No recording."

His gaze traveled over her. "What're your plans after you finish this podcast?" he asked.

"Good question. I have lots of contacts in Dallas, so I can return and find work fairly easily."

"Is that what you want? To go back?"

"I don't think so. I have about six months' worth of savings, and if I'm careful, I won't have to rush the decision." She looked out the window toward the rolling land. "I've been here before."

"When?"

"About a month before Gina vanished. There was a party here."

The road grew bumpier, and he slowed down the car so the ruts weren't as jarring. "Who owns the property?"

"I don't know. I didn't ask a lot of questions back then."

Looking out of the car, she stared at the yellow crime scene tape rippling in the wind. The sky above was dark, and the plump clouds were heavy with rain. The wind skimmed over the top of the sprouting new green grass, and her skin tingled with unease. She wrapped her arms around her midsection. She edged closer to Adler.

"Gina loved her country parties," Kaitlin said. "My aunt wasn't crazy about us going."

"She had cause to worry. Out here if something went wrong, no one could get in or out quickly."

"I only came once on the Fourth of July. Randy and Derek shot off fireworks. There were a dozen kegs and fifty kids here."

"Where was Gina?"

"She and her ex-boyfriend spent most of the night together. They looked like they were having intense conversations."

"Were they fighting?"

"No. They still had feelings for each other, and breaking up was harder than Gina imagined."

"Were Erika and Jennifer here?"

"They were. Jennifer had a date with Larry Jenkins."

"I didn't realize they were romantic."

"It was just the one date." Being here and talking about the past released a flood of emotions. "We might be on the verge of finding Gina, and I'm terrified."

"That's natural."

"I've made so many mistakes," she said, more to herself.

"When I visited with Hayward, he talked about the night Gina vanished," Adler said.

"Did he admit he took Gina?"

"No."

"Did he say if someone else was on the road that night?" she asked.

"No."

She breathed in deeply. "He had to have had help that night."

"He's not giving us any details beyond Gina's location."

"I wish I could have saved her."

"You were intoxicated and a confused, scared kid. You were no match for this guy." He stopped and leaned in. "You could have stayed hiding in Dallas. Instead, you sobered up and came back here. We wouldn't be this close to finding Gina now if not for you."

"Was it worth the cost if Jennifer and Erika had their lives taken?"

He touched her arm. "You're not to blame. You were the only one who gave a shit to reopen this case."

A gust of wind cut through the tree branches heavy with spring buds. They followed a narrow path through the woods into a clearing. There were a dozen cop cars from city, county, and state, the medical examiner's state forensics vans, and a shiny black Lexus.

"Everyone's here," Adler said, parking.

She scanned the crowd for Hayward. "I don't see him."

Adler came around the car and joined her. "He's in the police car. Blackstone is standing by Hayward's city police car."

Blackstone wore a charcoal-gray suit, a dark fitted overcoat, and a stoic expression. The age difference between him and Gina had kept him on the periphery of her crowd, but he'd been at that Fourth of July party. Several times that night she'd caught him staring at her. His expression had left her unsettled.

Another well-dressed man got out of an unmarked state car and strode toward Blackstone. They shook hands, but it was clear that tension simmered between the two.

"Who's that?" Kaitlin asked.

"Trey Ricker. He's with the Commonwealth Attorney's office," Adler said. "He negotiated the plea agreement."

Adler kept their pace slow as they moved through the grass toward the line of cops. Several officers and sheriff's deputies shook his hand, welcoming him back to the job. The line finally parted and allowed them access to Hayward's car.

When they reached the patrol car, Quinn got out and tossed a look of disgust toward the backseat.

"How long have you been here?" Adler said.

"About twenty minutes," Quinn asked.

"Did Hayward have any trouble finding the place?"

"Nope. He knew exactly where he was going. But he said he wouldn't say a word about Gina until Kaitlin arrived." Quinn eyed Adler. "Randy and I did have a chance to chat a bit in the car."

"That so?" Adler said.

"Of course, we didn't talk about the Mason case. But I let it slip I had a dog once when I was a kid. You remember me talking about Charlie, right, Adler?"

Adler nodded. "I do."

"Turns out Randy had a teddy bear named Charlie," Quinn said.

"Did he?" Adler said.

Quinn shrugged. "Small world."

Blackstone regarded Quinn closely, then shifted his attention to Kaitlin. "Now that Ms. Roe is here, let's get this started."

When Kaitlin was younger, she hadn't known what to make of Blackstone's intense looks. Now, she recognized him for the dangerous predator he was.

"I'm ready when you are," she said.

"Ms. Roe," Blackstone said. "I wasn't sure you'd be able to make it after your mishap."

"Nothing would keep me away," she said.

"You don't look well," Blackstone said.

She smiled and locked on his gaze. "Don't worry yourself about me."

Ricker extended his hand to her. "We owe this moment to you."

"Let's hope we find Gina," she said.

Ricker's frown deepened. "Let's get started."

"Remember," Blackstone said. "My client has complete immunity regarding any and all of the Gina Mason abduction and/or death."

"Understood," Ricker said.

Quinn opened the back door of the squad car and hauled out Hayward, who drew in a deep breath, tipping his face toward the cloudy sky.

"Too bad the sun isn't shining," Quinn quipped.

Hayward winked. "Baby, it's always shining when you're around."

Quinn gripped his arm even tighter and smiled.

Hayward shifted his attention to Kaitlin and slowly looked her over. "You smell good. And your skin looks so soft. Maybe when this is over we could meet again, and I can give you another interview."

She didn't draw back. "Let's see how today goes."

"I loved to come out here. I'd sit in my tree stand over there and just enjoy the view." He looked toward a stand of trees and then back at Kaitlin. "Remember when we all used to come out here?" Hayward teased.

Blackstone shook his head. "No chitchat, Mr. Hayward. This isn't a social call."

Kaitlin couldn't help but prod him. "The Fourth of July bonfire."

He winked. "Remember the barn? We had a good time in there."

The barn. That, she did remember. She couldn't even blame booze for the stupid choices of that night. She'd made them all stone-cold sober. "I'm also remembering now that Brad, Derek, and you got into a fight. Brad looked like he wanted to take your head off. What did you say to him that made him so mad?"

"Don't answer that," Blackstone said.

Hayward chuckled. "You know how it goes—boys will be boys."

"Looked pretty intense," she pressed.

Blackstone stepped between them. "Show us what you promised to show us."

"We just got here," Hayward said. "I'm trying to catch up with my girl."

Ricker's face darkened. "We're waiting."

"Kaitlin's coming, right? I want her to see this. This could have been her," Hayward teased.

She tipped her chin up a notch. "Let's do this."

"Can I have a cigarette?" Hayward asked. "I think better when I smoke."

Quinn mimicked a pout. "Sorry, fresh out."

"Come on," Hayward coaxed. "There's got to be a cop here who's got smokes."

Blackstone shook his head. "I don't smoke."

Ricker shrugged, held up empty hands.

Adler strode back to the cops and after a quick survey returned with a crumpled pack of Marlboros. He fished out a cigarette and a lighter from the pack and lit the tip. Hayward's cuffs rattled as he accepted it. When he raised it to his lips, his hands trembled slightly.

"Nervous?" Kaitlin asked.

He took another pull. "Being around you always makes me weak in the knees, girl." He took two more drags and then threw it down and ground his foot into it. "You've got more in that packet, Detective?" Hayward asked.

Adler tucked the packet in his pocket. "I do."

Hayward seemed to understand he'd danced up to the line. Another minute and Adler would transport him back to jail. "Sure. Why not?"

"Where to?" Adler snapped.

Hayward nodded toward the graveled road ahead. "About a quarter mile up that way on the other side of the barn."

"Let's go." Adler took him by the arm and hauled him forward.

Hayward started walking. "Showtime!"

Even with the cool breeze, Kaitlin quickly started sweating as she struggled to keep pace. If Adler had slowed up for her before, he didn't this time. And she was glad. She didn't want to slow him down. The priority was finding Gina.

"How you doing, girl?" Hayward glanced back over his shoulder at her.

"What's taking you so long?" Kaitlin refused to show Hayward any weakness.

Hayward laughed. "Don't pass out on me."

The dirt road doglegged to the right, but Hayward turned left down a well-worn dirt path made by hunters, farmers, and most likely, moonshiners.

"When's the last time you were here, Hayward?" Adler asked.

"I've been here a few times in between stints in prison. Last time was in mid-January."

"Why return?" Adler asked.

"To see if Gina was still here. I always liked her. That hasn't changed. No one else knew where she was, but I did. And that made it special between us."

Kaitlin sympathized with the officers' feelings of anger and frustration. This was a joke to Hayward. A parlor game.

Hayward ducked under a branch and pushed through the thicket of trees. "Good thing it's early in the year. The bugs will eat you alive in the summer. One time I was here I got a terrible case of chiggers."

Kaitlin pressed her hand to her side, keeping a sharp eye on the ground. As "fast" as she moved, Adler, Quinn, Ricker, Blackstone, and Hayward were putting distance between them. She wasn't sure how much farther she could walk when Hayward pushed through to a small clearing.

In the center was the barn. Once it had been painted red, but in the last decade, sun, wind, and rain had stripped most of its color.

Hayward's smile turned electric. He counted off fifty paces from the north corner and stopped at a patch of ground under a collection of young oak trees.

The untrained eye wouldn't notice the sparse patch of vegetation or the slight dip in the land. A small part of her had hoped Gina had somehow survived, but Adler's and Quinn's deepening frowns telegraphed what she'd known in her heart for fourteen years.

Gina was really dead. And they were looking at a shallow grave.

INTERVIEW FILE #24

RETIRED FORENSIC INVESTIGATOR

Sunday, March 4, 2018

Sam Weston has been retired from the Richmond City Police for three years. He lives in the country now, and his small ranch-style house looks out over a pond. He's feeding his two dozen chickens as we talk.

"The problem with that Mason scene was the weather. Right after the 911 call came in, there was a hell of a rainstorm. It was a real gully washer. The river rose, and part of the street flooded. The entire riverbank was immersed with rising water and debris."

"Were you able to collect anything of use at the abduction site?"

"Not at first. Everything looked like it had been through a car wash. But we stayed out there for several days. Finally, one of the investigators found part of a green dress a quarter of a mile down the road. It was stuck on a tree branch. We bagged it and took it back to the lab. Gina's mother said the fabric looked like the dress her daughter had been wearing. We did DNA testing on the fabric, and some of it matched Gina and some did not."

"There were two blood samples on the cloth?"

"Yes."

"Did you ever identify who the second sample belonged to?"

"We thought it might be Hayward, but it wasn't a match. We compared it to several other known sex offenders in the area, but in the end, we never came up with a match."

"Someone else was on that road?"

"That's my best guess."

CHAPTER
TWENTY-THREE

Friday, March 23, 2018; 10:00 a.m.

Adler had the excavation crew on standby, and as soon as he gave the go-ahead, a technician equipped with ground-penetrating radar (GPR) moved into position. The technician began his search several feet away from the target area now designated with orange flags. Working slowly in a grid pattern, the technician swept the device in straight lines.

The machine transmitted a gray image to a computer screen. During the first few passes, the picture produced was smooth with no signs of any discovery. But as the passes grew closer to the orange flag, small ripples appeared. No telling what was in the ground, but there was something there. Closer to the flags, the waves grew in size and frequency. The technician marked the spot where excavation could begin.

Hayward's expression grew somber as two technicians approached with shovels. "I'm going to miss her."

"Get him out of here," Adler said to a uniformed officer.

"I want to stay," Hayward countered. "I want to see Kaitlin's face when she sees Gina again."

Adler motioned to the officer, and he escorted Hayward back to the cruiser. Adler continued, "Blackstone, you can leave, too."

"I'm staying. I have to look out for my client's best interest."

"Your client is leaving, and so are you," Adler ordered. "I will have you arrested."

Blackstone studied Adler's face and seemed to sense now was not the time to push. "I want notification the instant you identify what's in the ground."

"I'll let Ricker decide what he wants you to know."

Blackstone looked as if he'd say more but turned and left.

Kaitlin moved toward Adler. She had been silent and kept her distance from Hayward. Her skin was pale and her lips drawn into a thin line. He reminded himself she was only six days out from a brutal attack. "How are you holding up?"

"I'm doing fine. Did the GPR tell them what's in the ground?"

"We won't know until they clear some dirt."

"How long will it take?" she asked.

"Not long. The technicians estimate they need to dig down about two feet."

"Okay." She stood rigid with her arms crossed, and her gaze rarely wavered from the dig. She was upset and nervous, and this time didn't care who saw it.

"Did Hayward ever talk about this place?" Adler asked.

"He talked about how much he enjoyed hunting in the country. I assume now this was the place. He used to talk about sitting in his tree stand hunting deer and enjoying the view."

"He mentioned that stand. Where is it exactly?"

She scanned the tree line and pointed. "Over there. I remember because he wanted me to climb the ladder, but I got spooked and wouldn't do it."

Dr. McGowan, who'd arrived with the medical examiner's team two hours ago, watched as the technicians dug. Suddenly she asked them to stop. She knelt and brushed away the top layer of soil with her gloved hand. Finally she leaned back on her heels and rubbed the back of her wrist under her chin. She rose and approached Adler.

"Is it human bones?" he asked.

"I think so," Dr. McGowan said. She turned to Kaitlin. "What was Gina Mason wearing when you last saw her?"

"A green sundress," Kaitlin said.

"You're sure?" Dr. McGowan asked.

"I've had fourteen years to replay that night. Yes, I'm sure."

A grim acceptance swept over the doctor. "Okay."

"Does this mean you found her?" Kaitlin asked.

Dr. McGowan shook her head. "It means I have to talk to the detectives first."

"You can't just shut me out," Kaitlin said. "Can you at least tell me what you found?"

Ricker approached. "I can shut you out." His tone wasn't cruel, but it was firm. "I don't want anything or anyone compromising this case."

"I don't see how my being here impacts the case."

Adler's tone was softer. "I know you want to be here, but this is not the place for you, Kaitlin. This is what we do best, and you need to let us do our jobs."

Kaitlin usually came out swinging with him, but this time her shoulders slumped slightly. "Sure. Of course," she said. "Thank you, Detectives, Dr. McGowan."

As Dr. McGowan returned to the gravesite, Adler motioned for a city police officer, and when he approached Adler instructed him to take Kaitlin home. Kaitlin's gaze was still full of questions and emotions, but she left without a word.

When the officer and Kaitlin drove off, Dr. McGowan said, "It's going to take some time to excavate the bones. I can tell you we unearthed remnants of green cloth."

Anger mingled with relief. Finding Gina would be considered a win, but there was no victory in bringing home a kid in a body bag.

"Do you know if the body is male or female?" Ricker asked.

"A young female," she said. "I'll report back to you both when I know more."

As the doctor moved toward the back of the excavation site, Adler turned toward the tree stand. Instinct and restless energy had him moving through the grass toward the stand.

"Where are you going?" Ricker asked, following.

"It's a hunch."

"What's that mean?" he asked.

"Kaitlin said Hayward liked sitting in his tree stand."

Adler strode toward the wooden platform mounted between two sturdy, naked branches. A makeshift ladder made of scrap wood ran up the tree in twelve-inch intervals. It looked sturdy enough to support his weight.

"What are you doing?" Ricker said as he approached.

"I want to see what Hayward saw." He shrugged off his suit jacket and handed it to Ricker. Fifteen feet up he reached the small platform and sat.

This high he could see everything surrounding the excavation. If Hayward needed a place to sit and remember what he'd done to Gina, this would be the spot. It wasn't uncommon for a killer to return to a victim's burial site and relive the crime.

"What do you see?" Ricker asked.

A cold wind chilled his skin. "A bird's-eye view of Gina's final resting place."

Ricker cursed, understanding the implication. "Hayward is a sick bastard."

As Adler was turning to descend, his gaze skimmed the grassy rolling landscape. At first glance, he almost missed it, but then something about the indented patch of grass caught his attention. For several beats he said nothing, simply staring.

"What is it?" Ricker asked.

"I'll be damned."

***

Kaitlin changed into sweats and downed three over-the-counter pain-killers, opting to skip the prescription meds because the sooner she was off the stuff, the better. She owed it to Gina to stay awake until Adler called. She should have rested and put her feet up. God knows she was exhausted, but the four walls of her apartment seemed to creep inward with each passing moment.

She'd already texted Adler twice but not heard back from him. He was doing his job. He would call her when he could, but the waiting was agonizing.

Finally, too restless to sit, she grabbed her phone and wallet. There was a small bar down the block. It wasn't too far. There she could get a soda, maybe something to eat, and listen to the buzz of conversation.

Down the elevator, she pushed aside the tingle of warning and headed down the brick sidewalk. The streets weren't too crowded yet, but after five the area offices would let out. The city found a second life after the sun set.

She pushed through the front door of the Irish pub, found a booth in the back, and ordered a soda and a bowl of chili. As she waited, her phone buzzed with a call. She didn't recognize the number and normally didn't answer unknown numbers, but with so much pending, she accepted the call. "This is Kaitlin Roe."

"This is Ashley Ralston. Jennifer's sister."

"Ashley." They'd not spoken in almost fourteen years. "How did you get my number?"

"I can be persuasive."

"With whom?"

"Your apartment manager."

She gripped her phone. She'd deal with him later.

"Look, I'm not trying to freak you out. I just want to talk about Jennifer, Erika, and Gina. Are you doing anything right now?"

"I'm at an Irish pub grabbing a bite to eat. If you want to see me, it'll have to be here."

"Sure. Give me the address."

She read the street number off the menu as the waitress set down her food and soda.

"Great, I'll see you in twenty minutes," Ashley said.

Kaitlin took a bite, not expecting to be so hungry, but the chili tasted good and this was her first real meal since last night's pizza. The soda was cold and refreshing.

A couple across from her leaned in for a kiss. They were smiling and enjoying themselves. She envied their connection. She'd never really had anything like that before.

The pub was starting to fill, and she missed Ashley's entrance until she was right on top of her. Kaitlin lowered the soda from her lips and slowly, gingerly rose.

Ashley regarded her with a mixture of curiosity, anger, and pity. Neither leaned in for a hug, so Kaitlin extended her hand to the opposite side of the booth.

Kaitlin settled in. "I'm so sorry about Jennifer."

Ashley sat and tapped her index finger on the table. A waitress appeared, took her order of vodka soda, double. "The medical examiner's office released her body yesterday."

"This must be terrible for you."

"It was. I never thought I'd ever go through something like this. After Gina vanished, it was bad enough, but this is almost unbearable."

"I'm sorry."

Her drink arrived, and she took a sip. "The funeral home cleaned my sister up and let me see her. I could tell they were proud of her. 'So lifelike,' the attendant said. I didn't think she looked anywhere close to a living person. It was still and plastic, nothing like my Jennifer."

"When is the funeral?"

"The viewing is tomorrow, and the service is on Sunday afternoon."

A clawing sadness scraped the inside of her throat. She struggled for words that would make all this better but knew there was nothing she could say.

Ashley reached for a paper napkin and folded it in half and then in quarters. "She told me about your interview. She was actually relieved after you two spoke. That night had been bottled up inside her and was preventing her from being happy." Ice clinked in the glass. She took another big swallow.

"I'm glad it helped." Kaitlin took a sip of her soda. "I remember your car pulling up, but I didn't see you."

"So, is it my turn to be interviewed?"

"I just want to understand what happened that night."

Ashley shrugged. "Jennifer didn't want Mom knowing she was wasted, so she called me. Big sis to the rescue." She shook her head. "I was pissed, but I came right away to pick her up."

"You told the police she passed out in the backseat."

"She did, the second she climbed in. She and Erika both were pretty wasted."

"You dropped Erika off first?"

"That's right. And then I drove home with Jennifer."

"How'd you get her inside the house?"

"It was hard. She could barely stand."

Kaitlin traced her finger through the condensation on the glass. "Jennifer remembered hearing you argue with a man."

Ashley stilled. "She was mistaken. I got her to bed and then joined Derek in the family den. About one a.m., we left for a party."

"Derek was never alone with her?"

"No. I saw to that."

"Did you have to protect her from Derek?"

She traced the rim of her glass. "No. Stop making him sound like a monster."

"You're still loyal to him, aren't you?"

She lifted her chin. "I can't betray someone I loved so much. He's not perfect, but he's always there for me."

"Randy and Derek were good buddies." Kaitlin thought about the country, the barn, and the grim faces of the medical examiner as she'd asked her what Gina had been wearing. "Remember the parties they used to have at the barn?"

"Sure." Ashley sat back as if the memory bothered her.

"Did Derek ever talk about Gina?"

Ashley studied her a long moment. "Randy talked about her. Randy, *not* Derek, was obsessed with Gina."

"Did you tell the cops about Randy's obsession?"

"Derek asked me not to. He said the guy was a fuck-up but no killer."

How many half truths and omissions had saved Randy from a murder-one charge? "It might have made a difference."

"Come on, this is Randy we're talking about. He isn't a killer."

"A security camera filmed him stabbing a woman in mid-February."

"That was an accident. He was on drugs. It's not like he planned to do it." She shook her head. "If having a thing for Gina was a crime, half the guys at Saint Mathew's would have been suspects. Besides, he's been back in jail since late February. He couldn't have killed Erika or Jennifer."

"What about Derek? Would he have killed them to protect a secret for an old friend?"

Ashley reached for her glass and downed the last of the vodka. "No."

Kaitlin watched as Ashley's gaze dropped to her glass. It didn't take a body-language expert to recognize possible signs of deceptive behavior. "Was Derek in the car that night?"

Absently Ashley nodded, indicating a yes even as she said, "I already told you he wasn't."

Kaitlin took a chance, figuring she had nothing to lose by provoking Ashley. "I think you're lying."

Ashley looked up as if she'd been struck. Her eyes sparked with challenge. "Fuck you."

Kaitlin leaned in, knowing she'd struck a nerve. "The cops have all my interview tapes now. They know Jennifer brought the booze and Erika put the Ecstasy in it."

Ashley pushed out of the booth. "The cops have long forgotten about who was where that night."

"Don't bet on it."

Ashley stood. "I hope you're right." Gripping her purse, she turned away from Kaitlin and cut through the crowd and out the front door.

Kaitlin sat in the booth, tracing her finger through the condensation on the side of her glass. She took no joy in hurting people or making them remember such a painful time. But if she didn't keep pushing, the truth might still get swallowed up by time.

Her phone rang, startling her from her thoughts. The screen displayed Steven Marcus's name.

She cleared her throat and pushed her hand through her hair before answering. "Mr. Marcus."

"I hear you've been busy today."

"What's that mean?"

"I still have friends in the police department. They said a forensic team was headed for Hanover County and that Randy Hayward was along for the ride. They also said the cops think they've found Gina."

"If you've got friends in the department, then you know more about it than I do."

"I know you were up there."

"Really, how?"

"Randy Hayward called me, and I went by to see him. He wants me to write his side of the story."

She gripped the phone. "He craves attention. And he's also looking to hurt me."

"Why?"

"Because I rejected him. Sure he didn't have any nasty parting shots for me?"

He was silent for a moment. "Nothing earth shattering."

She wasn't sure if she believed him but didn't have the energy to press it now. "Just don't be fooled by him."

"Don't worry. I'm not that naive. I do want to get your take on the guy. It will make for a more balanced piece."

"Sure. I'll share what I know about him."

Silence echoed through the line. Then, "Tomorrow evening. By then you should have something to comment on."

INTERVIEW FILE #25

A Story That Wouldn't Let Go

Friday, August 15, 2014

"This is Steven Marcus, and I first learned about Gina Mason the day after she vanished. The instant I saw her picture, I knew I would do anything I could to find her. I covered her story several times over those first few months, speaking to the cops, the search crews, and her mother. The story was so raw in those days, and I was new to reporting. I was certain no one would forget about her. But as weeks turned into months and then years, people did move on with their lives. I always cover the story the anniversary of Gina's disappearance. I refuse to let this story disappear like Gina."

CHAPTER TWENTY-FOUR

Friday, March 23, 2018; 5:00 p.m.

As Ricker stood by him, Adler knelt by the path of scraggly grass he'd spotted from the tree stand. He scooped up a handful of soil and slowly let it trickle from his fingers.

"Detective Adler. If you don't need us anymore, we'll take off." The question came from one of the members of the GPR crew.

Adler wiped his hands and rose. "Before you pack up, would you scan this area?"

"Sure. I'll get the crew right now."

"Give me a shout if you find something," Adler said.

"Will do, Detective," he said.

Ricker studied the patch of ground. "Do you think it's another one?"

"God, I hope not," Adler said.

Dr. McGowan motioned them over. A humming generator powered the lights at the excavation site as Adler and Ricker strode across undergrowth toward the forensic van she stood beside.

"Detective, Mr. Ricker, I have news," she said.

Quinn approached the doctor and handed her a hot cup of coffee. "Not the best cup, but it'll warm you up."

Dr. McGowan took a sip. "Thanks."

Quinn shrugged. "Sure."

"As I said earlier, I found green cloth. I really only have fragments that are clinging to a metal snap." She handed a plastic evidence bag to Quinn.

The detective held up the bag. "There's not much of it left, but looks like the remnants of a green dress."

Adler searched his phone for the picture Jennifer had saved of the four girls by the river. He handed it to Dr. McGowan. "Gina is wearing the green sundress."

The doctor studied the image. "I see design similarities between this and what I found."

Adler tucked the phone back in his pocket. "What else have you found?"

"I have unearthed the top portion of the skull. Based on a thin brow line, I can say the victim is a young female."

"How do you know her age?" Quinn handed the evidence bag to Ricker.

"The sagittal suture." Dr. McGowan drew her gloved finger over the top of her head. "When we're born there's a soft spot in the center of our head. The bones need to be flexible so the brain can grow. But from the day we're born, the left and right sides of our skull begin to close and create the sagittal suture, which is basically a line down the center of our skull. It continues to harden and close until we're in our midthirties. Based on this victim's skull, I believe she was less than twenty years old."

"Do you know how she died?" Adler asked.

"Too early to say. I don't see any trauma on the skull, but I have a lot more bones to excavate. I did find the hyoid bone, and it appears intact." This horseshoe-shaped bone was located in the neck and would snap when a victim was strangled.

"Is she Gina Mason?" Ricker asked.

"My office has requested dental records, so we'll make a comparison at the lab once I unearth the mandible. I understand Gina had several fillings on her two back molars, so it shouldn't be too hard."

"Did you find anything with the bones?" Adler asked.

"Nothing yet, but we'll be sifting all the dirt as we go."

Adler remembered Gina's smiling picture at Kaitlin's lecture. "How long will it take?" he asked.

"Several hours. There's no point in you remaining here. I'll contact you when I'm finished."

"Thanks, Doc," Ricker said.

Dr. McGowan left the trio and returned to her crew.

"She's meticulous and won't miss a thing." Quinn rolled her shoulders, then turned her head from side to side.

"Did you bring your yoga mat, Quinn?" Adler asked.

She laughed. "I would have if there weren't so many cops here."

The GPR technician called out to Adler and Quinn, "Detectives. A word?"

"I don't like that look," Ricker muttered.

"Me neither," Adler said.

The detectives and Ricker moved toward the technician. The gray image on the radar screen showed a series of waves.

"A body?" Adler asked.

"Looks like it."

"Jesus, another one?" Quinn whispered.

Adler studied the waves that rolled through the center of the gray image. He turned toward Dr. McGowan and called her over. She slowly rose and crossed the field.

"Have a look at this."

It took her just a split second. "I'll get a shovel."

Without raising his gaze from the screen, Adler said to the technician, "You're going to need a bigger scanner."

INTERVIEW FILE #26
WHO KILLED JENNIFER AND ERIKA?

The discovery of Gina's bones directly implicated Randy Hayward in Gina's death. He had motive and opportunity, and most of all, he had taken the cops to her body. However, finding Gina didn't answer the question of who killed Jennifer and Erika. Who stabbed me? Derek Blackstone and Brad Crowley had been friends of Randy Hayward's in high school and college. They were a triple threat. They had vowed to always stick together and protect each other. And neither had ever had their DNA tested to see if their blood matched the blood on the fragment of dress found by the original crime scene.

CHAPTER
TWENTY-FIVE

Saturday, March 24, 2018; 8:00 a.m.

With her body healing and her mind clearing, Kaitlin could shift her attention to Derek Blackstone, who she was certain knew far more about Gina's fate than he was letting on. She'd spent most of the night reading up on Derek, scraping together all the details she could find about him. His credentials were impressive. There was nothing that set off alarm bells.

So, when the clock struck eight, Kaitlin decided to shake the trees a little harder and see if anything new fell out. Drawing in a breath, she dialed Derek's home number. A cleaning lady answered.

"Mr. Blackstone's residence."

"This is Kathryn Sommers." She wasn't police and therefore not bound by honesty. Lying wasn't against the law. "I'm calling from Mr. Blackstone's office building. Is he there?"

"No, he left a half hour ago. He should be arriving there now."

"Oh, right. I think I see him. Thank you."

Her next call was to his office, wondering if she'd get anyone to answer on Saturday. As the phone rang, she sat straighter when she heard a woman's crisp voice say, "Hawthorn, Blackstone, and Myers."

"I'm calling for Derek Blackstone. I'm a neighbor of his." She'd thought up a dozen scenarios to get him on the phone, but in the end opted to keep it simple. "I think his house is on fire."

A leaden silence filled the next few seconds before the woman said, "He's out of the office today."

"He is? I just saw him, and he said he was going to the office."

"Not today."

"Oh, wow. I called the fire department." If he were in the office, this would get him to the phone. "Are you sure he's not there?"

Phones rang in the background. "Look, I can take your name and number and track him down."

She decided to go aggressive. "What's your name?"

"I'm sorry?"

"What is your name? And do you have a supervisor?"

"Who is this?" the woman insisted.

She gripped the phone. This ruse wasn't going to work. "Tell him Gina Mason called. He can call me back at this number."

She dialed Adler's number. It rang twice and went to voicemail. A now-familiar graveled tone hummed over her nerves. "Adler, this is Kaitlin. I'm calling about Derek Blackstone. I think his link to this case goes way deeper than attorney-client relationship."

***

Adler's phone buzzed in his pocket, but he let it go to voicemail. He was standing in the medical examiner's autopsy suite with Quinn and Dr. McGowan. On the two stainless-steel tables were separate sets of bones. Neither set had yet been arranged in anatomical order.

Dr. McGowan clicked on an overhead light. Gingerly she lifted the first skull. "We've already taken X-rays and cross-referenced dental records. This is Gina Mason. She's finally come home."

He studied the skull cradled in the doctor's hands. Images of the young woman's smiling face stoked his anger. This kid had not deserved such a violent fate. "And the other one?"

Dr. McGowan had set the first skull down and picked up the second. "Female. Under the age of twenty, I think." She turned the skull to the side and traced her finger down a fracture. "Someone hit her hard on the back of her head. The blow was enough to knock her out and maybe kill her. I also noticed that her pelvic bone is broken, suggesting there was more trauma. I can't tell you if that occurred ante- or postmortem. The pelvis is very vascular, and if she were alive, this would have caused tremendous bleeding and pain."

He hoped to hell it was postmortem. "Can you determine the cause of death?"

She gently set the skull down and lifted one of the victim's ribs. "There are distinct markings here." She ran her finger along an angled indention. "It was caused by a large knife. If you look carefully you'll see the edges are slightly serrated. Maybe it was a hunting knife. If you found the knife I'm confident I could match it."

"How long has she been dead?" Adler asked.

"I'd say a couple of years longer than Miss Mason."

"And Miss Mason was also stabbed?" Quinn asked.

"Yes. There are knife marks on at least two of her left ribs. If you look closely at the marks, you'll notice the blade is serrated and matches the other rib we just examined."

Quinn shook her head with contempt. "Two women murdered within a couple of years. Hayward goes to prison on drug and burglary charges, and within four weeks of being out, he knifes a woman to death."

"The knife recovered from the convenience store murder was a hunting knife," Adler said. "That victim was stabbed in the ribs."

"You just took the words right out of my mouth," Dr. McGowan said. "I pulled the complete set of records from that autopsy. The knife that killed that victim was also serrated."

"Hayward said he went up to the barn after he was released from prison," Adler said. "He finds the murder weapon he stashed fourteen years ago, thinks enough time has gone by, and the stupid shit pockets it."

"He saved the knife as some kind of trophy?"

"That's my guess," Adler said.

"Do you really think Hayward would be so stupid to take us to Gina's body knowing Jane Doe is one hundred yards away?" Quinn asked.

"I think he's that arrogant and also that desperate. Gina was his one shot to save himself."

"So he assumes our attention would be exclusively on unearthing Gina's body and bets we won't look anywhere else," Quinn said incredulously.

"Have the GPR technicians found any other bodies near these two?" Dr. McGowan asked.

"No. Not yet," Adler said.

"You think Blackstone knew about the second body?" Quinn asked.

"I don't know," Adler said.

Quinn's grin was sly. "The immunity deal with Hayward covers the Gina Mason and convenience store murders only, correct?"

He smiled. "Correct. It does not cover Jane Doe."

"So if we can tie Hayward to Jane Doe's murder, we can charge him with murder."

"That's the goal."

They spent several more minutes discussing the cases before Adler could step away and check his voicemail. He played back Kaitlin's message.

He didn't like the idea of her chasing Blackstone. If Blackstone had been covering for Hayward all these years, he had a lot to lose. And that made him very dangerous.

Adler dialed Logan's number. He answered on the second ring, his voice thick and heavy with sleep.

"Did I wake you up, Logan?"

"Up until four a.m."

"I didn't sleep all night."

"Aren't you a badass?" Logan coughed. "What do you need other than to hear my manly voice?"

The sarcasm was a good sign. Soon Logan would be back to his old smartass self. "Randy Hayward dropped out of college during his sophomore year. We all assumed he left because of the drugs. But I looked up his school record. He was making the dean's list right up until he left, so if he was using, it wasn't interfering with his schoolwork."

He told Logan about the second set of remains. "Check to see if any girl went missing about that time in that area."

"Will do."

***

Adler and Quinn arrived at the city jail. They didn't have to wait long before Hayward arrived cuffed and wearing a shit-eating grin.

Hayward's chest puffed with the bravado of a card player holding a royal flush. He sat and sniffed. "You don't look like you slept so well, Detective."

Adler shook his head. "It was a long night."

"I slept like a baby," Hayward said and winked at Quinn.

Adler allowed Hayward to bask in the glow of immunity. "The medical examiner identified the remains. They belong to Gina."

"I told you. I don't lie when it comes to important shit like that."

"Your deal with Ricker is ironclad," Adler said. "Blackstone made sure of it."

"Gotta love that buddy of mine."

Adler sat back while Quinn leaned forward with the next question. Anger burned in his belly, but a good hunter was always patient when stalking his prey.

"Can you tell me what happened with Gina? It won't make a difference to anyone now."

"It will to Kaitlin. Sweet Kaitlin will want to know all the terrible details."

"Yes, she'll want to know," Adler admitted.

"Tell us what happened on the road that night," Quinn said.

Hayward scratched his head. "Nothing complicated. I liked Gina. I'd been watching her for years. So perfect, so sweet."

"Did you get Erika to drug their booze?" Adler asked.

"No, that was all Erika."

"Erika said it was Brad's idea to drug the girls."

"She's a liar. I heard her telling Brad she was going do it. She and Jennifer wanted to really fuck with Kaitlin's sobriety. Like the booze wasn't bad enough. All I had to do was sit and wait."

With Erika dead, there was no way to prove if she'd lied or not. "So Jennifer and Erika leave. How did you get to the river?"

"I drove upriver a quarter of a mile and parked the farm truck." Hayward hesitated. He'd been in and out of the system long enough to know deals could sour. "Why do you want all the gritty details?" His voice now took on a more serious tone.

The slow burn of anger in Adler's gut grew hotter. "For posterity. This case will be talked about for years to come. Besides, I can't touch you."

Hayward shrugged with false modesty. "When I saw Gina come stumbling down the road, I grabbed her. Kaitlin ran up and tried to save her cousin. I sliced off Gina's ear, and little Kaitlin ran wee-wee-wee all the way home."

"What did you do with Gina?"

"I taped up her hands, feet, and mouth, tossed her in the bed of the farm truck, and covered her with a tarp. I took her to the barn."

"Who owns that land?"

"It used to be owned by the Blackstone family, but they sold it twenty years ago. But Derek has permission from the new owners to hunt."

"And if Derek had access, so did you."

He tapped the end of his nose. "Bingo."

"The farm truck was from that land."

"It was."

"What happened next?"

His eyes brightened. "When I untied her, I told her I didn't want to hurt her. I just wanted to have fun."

"She must have been bleeding badly at that point," Adler said.

"When I taped up her mouth, I also taped the ear. It wasn't so bad by then."

"So you were having fun?"

"I thought so until I untied her and she elbowed me in the nuts. That really pissed me off. Hurt my feelings. I was trying to be nice." He shrugged. "I lost it and stabbed her right then. She started bleeding real bad. She begged me for help, but I knew she would never like me, so I stabbed her again and watched her bleed out."

Neither detective spoke for a moment. Adler's anger intensified, but he fought to remain tame. "So you buried her on the farm."

"That's right."

Adler's voice was as calm as a Sunday school teacher's. "The knife left marks on her rib."

"Okay."

"I'm guessing the first strike hit bone, which called for the second strike hitting meat." Quinn shifted and tugged the edge of her blazer forward. "That about right, Randy?"

Hayward's cuffs clinked when he rubbed his nose. "I just told you I stabbed her. Why do I care if her ribs got marks?"

"Why did you take her to the country?" Adler asked. "What was it about that place?"

"I liked it there. I figured we'd have all the privacy we needed." Hayward folded his arms over his chest and leaned back.

"You buried her there because you were familiar with the land?" Adler asked. "Funny how we're all creatures of habit."

"Derek Blackstone. You've known him a long time, right, Randy?" Quinn asked.

"You know I have. Why do you care?" Hayward flashed a grin and glanced up toward the security camera he knew was taping this conversation. "You're fishing for something, Detectives."

Adler held up his hand in surrender. Every primal instinct in him demanded he reach across the table and beat the hell out of this animal. But this wasn't about him. And anger wasn't going to get the justice he craved. "What can I say, they pay me the big bucks to catch the big fish."

"I'm a big fish, but you didn't catch me," he gloated.

"Randy, you're the biggest fish in the state right now."

He grinned. "And here my mother told me I wouldn't amount to much."

"Why would she say that? You're intelligent. I know you attended UVA."

"I did."

"Why did you leave?"

"I got bored. Didn't like the rules. I hated conforming."

"But you were tearing it up academically. Dean's list."

"I have an IQ of one fifty-two."

Adler glanced at the scar on the back of his hand. "Damn. I had to work for every grade I earned."

"Not me. I knew more than the teachers."

Adler's phone dinged with a text. It was from Logan. Maria Thomas, migrant worker, missing April 2002.

Adler shook his head. "You and I do have a deal. No charges will be brought for Gina's death, and the other murder still receives a reduced sentence. You've lived up to your end of the deal, and the state will, too."

"Damn right," he smirked.

Adler leaned back, watching Hayward's face carefully. "Who's Maria Thomas?"

Hayward's grin faded. "I don't know."

"She was a migrant worker who went missing in Charlottesville right before you dropped out of college."

Hayward stilled. "I want my attorney."

"I'll be sure to call him right away," Adler said. "But I wanted you to know we found a second girl up on the property. You figured we'd be so anxious to find Gina that we would just pack up afterward, thankful to close the case." He leaned forward. "But I climbed up into your tree stand, and I looked around just like you said you did. That's when I saw it." He raised his brow in mock surprise. "When a body decomposes, it shrinks and the soil around it dips and cracks. The grass also doesn't grow so well on that spot. It's the kind of thing that's easy to miss unless you're looking for it. And with your help, I was."

"You're bullshitting me," Hayward said. "There's no other girl. There's no Maria *Whoever*."

"But there is, Randy."

Hayward rubbed his eyes. "I don't believe you."

"You don't have to. Ask Derek. If he'll still take your calls." He grinned. "I can't wait to tell my friend, Trey Ricker."

"There're no other bitches!" Hayward shouted. "You're bluffing."

Adler laughed. "So clever and so fucking dumb, Hayward."

Quinn grinned. "Randy, you're really cute when you're wound up."

Adler and Quinn rose, and he banged on the door. The guard opened it. In a low voice Hayward couldn't hear, Adler said, "If Mr. Hayward needs to make a few extra calls today, let 'im. I want recordings of all those calls."

"Consider it done."

***

Kaitlin had spent most of the day trying to find out more about Derek but hit a brick wall. When she heard the buzz from the call button, she checked the monitor and saw Adler. Without a word of greeting she buzzed him up. She opened the door, tense, anxious, and glad he was the one answering the question that had stalked her for fourteen years.

When he rounded the corridor, she asked, "Was it Gina?"

"Yes."

The relief she'd sought for so many years was nonexistent. Instead, defeat filled her voice. On the heels of sweet victory came bitterness. She stepped aside, allowing him into her apartment. "Thank you." She could barely get out the words.

He studied her face a long moment. "I'm sorry."

"Deep down, I never held out hope we'd find her alive. She's gone, but at least we know the truth."

"Kaitlin, there's more."

"What do you mean?"

"We found another body buried near the first discovery. This victim is female and young. We think she's been there a couple of years longer than Gina."

"Oh God." The news slashed through her as she thought of another family enduring the same agony. She lowered slowly to a seat. "Who is she?"

"We don't know for sure. We've requested medical records on a missing person's case from Charlottesville. This girl Maria vanished in the spring of '02."

"How did Gina and the other girl die?"

He studied her a beat. "They were both stabbed."

Her knife wound had been so painful. "Did Randy kill that Maria girl, too?"

"I think he did it. It might also explain why he dropped out of college so suddenly his sophomore year."

"What about Blackstone and Crowley. Did they help him?"

"I have no evidence yet. But every instinct in me says that they must have. I'm having Gina's clothes retested. There was foreign blood found on them. If it matches Blackstone or Crowley, we'll have them, but if not I'd need Hayward to turn on them."

She sighed. "If Randy is good at anything, it is self-preservation."

He rubbed his eyes. "I'm counting on it."

The first time she'd seen him in the police station, he'd been annoyed and rushed, and he'd fed into her image of the uncaring cop. But she'd come to see him differently. He cared very much about the victims, and he fought like hell to find them justice.

Now it was her turn to take care of him. "You look exhausted. Let me make you some coffee."

A half smile tipped the edge of his lips. "Sounds good."

Kaitlin moved into the kitchen and set up a pot. Here alone with him, she could admit to herself that she found him attractive. And she'd seen the way he looked at her when he didn't think she could see. He liked what he saw.

She raised her gaze to Adler. The overhead light cut across his face. There'd been so much death and loss in her life, and for right now she was tired of thinking about it. Later, she'd think about it again, and again feel the pull to make injustice right, but right now she just wanted to feel good, hopeful even.

She'd kept to herself for the last couple of years, reasoning the solitude would help her get back on more solid footing emotionally. But as she stood here, the weight of loneliness settled on her shoulders. Adler was definitely a shot to the loins, he was a good man, and if there was any man she'd bother to figure out again, she wanted it to be him.

Nerves bunched in her stomach, and she felt as giddy as she had when she was a teenager. She would have wished for better timing, but the perfect time might not ever come. She came around the breakfast bar and moved toward him.

He didn't flinch, but the way he regarded her turned careful and focused. Inches separated them. She reached out and took his hand in hers. She rubbed her fingers against the rough texture of the scars on his palm.

Challenge sparked in his eyes. "I wasn't expecting this."

"You've never thought about it?"

"Oh, I've thought about it. Too many times."

In a few unguarded moments she'd allowed herself to imagine his arms around her. "I like you," she said. "I shouldn't. But I do."

His eyes looked more blue than gray now. "Why shouldn't you like me?"

"You're a cop. You'd turn the tables on me in a heartbeat to solve a case."

He didn't respond. "I'd like to think I'd do my job no matter what."

"Honest. And refreshing."

He shook his head slowly. "But I'm not sure if I could do my job when it comes to you."

"Really?"

"I like you. Very much." His voice sounded rusted and a little unsure.

But no lies. No promises. And that was okay. She rose up on her toes and kissed him. He didn't touch her. Didn't move.

"Am I your weakness?" she asked.

No answer. But he didn't draw away, and those blue eyes sharpened. Good. She'd take that as a yes.

She kissed him again, this time cupping his shoulder as she pressed her lips against his. His hand came up to her waist.

The rough edges of his touch sent electricity shooting through her body as he moved his fingertips back and forth along her shoulder.

His fingertips moved to her jaw, tracing the sharp line. Her heartbeat kicked up, and breathing evenly became a challenge. When he ran his fingers over her lips, she parted them and gently bit his finger as she teased the tip with her tongue.

He cupped her face, and she leaned into the touch, absorbing his energy. He leaned forward, and tilting his head, pressed his lips to hers. The kiss was tentative, as if he were handling crystal. His lips hovered over hers.

"I won't break," she murmured against his lips. To prove it, she wrapped her arms around his neck and pulled him into a deeper kiss. His hand went to her waist, and his fingertips slid just below the waistband of her jeans. She opened her mouth, allowing him to slide his tongue inside. She leaned into the kiss, pressing her breasts against his chest. Her body pulsed.

His other hand cupped her breast, and his fingertips captured her nipple, pinching gently. When he drew his head up, his eyes were as black as coal. A muscle pulsed in his jaw.

Urgency swept over her. She needed to feel his touch, to feel him moving inside of her.

He dropped his head to her breast and lightly kissed. His other hand slid lower over her moist mound. The twin sensations took her breath away. She was hungry for more.

He sucked the top of her breast and then moved to her nipple. He circled his tongue around the stiff peak. She arched against him.

"Please," she whispered.

"Please what?" he said.

She ran her hand over the firm, flat muscles of his belly, her fingers inching toward his belt buckle. He captured her hand and held it close to his heart as he kissed her hard. She pulled free, pushed his jacket off his shoulders, and laid it on the sofa. He loosened his tie and pulled it free.

Slowly she unbuttoned his shirt. He took it off and tossed it on the jacket. She gripped the edges of his T-shirt and tugged. He flinched, seemed to hesitate, and then allowed her to lift the shirt up. He watched her face closely as she pulled off the shirt.

She dropped her gaze to the scars that marred his shoulders. She gently traced them with her fingers. He flinched but didn't pull away as she explored. Instead of being repulsed, she saw a man who had sacrificed to save his friend.

"Do they hurt?" she asked.

"No. Not anymore."

She felt a pulse of emotion as she leaned forward and kissed the scars. For a moment he didn't move. Then he ran his fingers through her hair, fisting a handful.

She wanted him. Never before had she wanted anyone like this.

He reached for the hem of her shirt. In a smooth, swift move he tugged it over her head, leaving her naked from the waist up. He looked down at the bandage on her side and skimmed his fingertips over it.

"I barely notice it anymore," she said.

A smile tipped the edges of his lips as he reached for the snap on her jeans. With the flick of a finger, the snap came loose. He slid the zipper down slowly. "I've been wanting to do this since the first night I saw you."

He slid the pants down over her slim hips until they fell to the floor. Cool air brushed her legs. She stood before him in white cotton panties. He smoothed his hand over her flat belly. Heat smoldered in his gaze. He took her by the hand and led her to the bed.

When she sat and stared up at him, he unzipped his own pants and pushed them to the floor. His erection pulsed, and the look in his gaze sent a tremor of excitement through her body. He turned and reached for his pants. He fished a condom from his wallet.

He tossed the condom on the bed, and she crawled backward until she was settled in the middle. He straddled her and pressed the tip of his erection against the cotton panties, rubbing against her. She grew wet. Slick. And she ached for him to be inside her. He pressed his hand to her center, smiling when he felt her moisture.

He reached for the condom, tore off the package, and slid it over his shaft. Then he reached for the waistband of her panties, and as she raised her hips, he slid them down her legs.

"So nice," he whispered.

"You're so hot," she said.

His gaze darkened, and he spread her legs with his hands. He pushed his finger between the folds and inside her, moving in and out and making her so wet and horny she could barely think. Her blood raced, and her heart slammed against her ribs. She could feel the tempo building inside her, but ached to release.

He sensed her desire and pulled out his finger. "Not yet."

She reached for his erection and slid her fingers around it. Slowly she moved her hands up and down the shaft as he pressed it into her hand. He leaned down for a kiss and cupped the back of her head, bringing her face up to his.

When he broke away, they were both breathless. She pulled her fingers down over his scarred back. He didn't flinch this time.

She opened her legs, and he pressed the tip of his erection into her folds. He pushed in a fraction and pulled back. He pressed in again, pulled back. The exquisite torture made her dizzy with wanting. His hands slid down her belly to her engorged flesh and touched the sensitive spot that cried out for release.

He captured her hand in his, kissed the slick fingertips, and then roughly pushed inside her. She arched back, accepting all of him. A moan escaped her lips as he moved back and forth inside her and suckled her fingers. He released her hand and moved back and forth. She matched his rhythm, lifting her hips to all of his thrusts.

The tension built inside her, and she could feel he was coming. She cupped her breast and moaned. A muscle in his neck flexed like a tight cord, and his thrusts came faster with greater urgency.

When the wave washed toward her, she embraced it and gave herself over to the sensations that tore through her body. He groaned, and with one last thrust, his body tensed. For one blinding moment the two were bound by the most overwhelming sensation.

He collapsed on top of her and dropped his face in the crook of her neck. Her heart hammered, her muscles reduced to jelly. Finally she opened her eyes and focused on the ceiling.

"What was that?" she breathed.

He rolled off her, and they lay side by side, their naked bodies still touching. "I thought it was fairly obvious."

That coaxed a smile. "My way of saying it was nice."

"Nice?"

"Great."

She couldn't bring herself to believe it wasn't anything more than great sex. She'd felt a connection. And it was that link that worried her. She didn't want to have feelings for a guy, knowing whatever they shared was likely fleeting.

"I can hear your wheels turning," he said, his eyes still closed.

"It's what I do. I think."

"You didn't seem to be thinking a minute ago."

"No, I certainly wasn't."

He rose up on his elbow and rested his head on his hand. He traced his other hand over her bandage and over her breast. This time he touched her with a familiarity that was as gentle as it was unnerving. "I might need a few minutes, but I'm always ready not to think again."

"That sounds very appealing."

His phone buzzed. He rose and fished it from his coat pocket. He glanced at the display and shoved out a sigh. "I need to take this."

"Of course."

He grabbed her arm and kissed her. "We're going to do this again."

She kissed him on the lips. She didn't make promises.

INTERVIEW FILE #27

THE OTHER LOST GIRL

Her name was Maria Thomas, the oldest daughter of an immigrant family who lived fifty miles north of Charlottesville. There'd been no money in Maria's family for college, so she took a job near the university working at an all-night convenience store, hoping one day she would attend the school.

Her parents reported her missing immediately, but police were hesitant to get involved because Maria liked to stay out late with her friends and often missed her curfew. By the next evening when cops started asking questions, Maria was already seventy miles east, dead and buried in a shallow grave near Richmond. It would take DNA to identify her remains.

CHAPTER
TWENTY-SIX

Saturday, March 24, 2018; 4:00 p.m.

Kaitlin didn't want Adler to leave, but as she stood with him at her front door, she understood he had to see this investigation through. He pulled her toward him and kissed her.

"Be careful," he said.

"Always."

He shook his head. "I mean it, Kaitlin. Whoever stabbed you is still out there, and he's made it clear he's coming back for you."

"I won't take any unnecessary risks."

"Take absolutely no risks until I can catch this guy."

She shrugged. "I'll be fine."

"If you see anyone who looks suspicious, call me."

"I will."

"See you later for our date with Marcus."

"Yes." She rode the elevator down with him and walked him to the front door. He glanced back, a smile flickered, but the investigation's weight was already pulling him away. She tossed him a final wave and disappeared back into the building. Up the elevator, she pushed through the front door of her apartment. While a strong cup of coffee brewed, she checked the time for Jennifer's memorial service.

The viewing was from three to five. If she hurried, she could make the tail end of it. Ashley would be there and wouldn't be happy to see Kaitlin, but she had to pay her respects.

She slid her phone on the charger as she showered and then changed the bandage on her side. She found a slim black dress in her closet and slid it on. She'd lost weight since the stabbing, and the dress hung loosely around her midsection. She dug in the bottom of her closet for her lone pair of heeled ankle boots. She slid on her leather jacket and quickly dabbed on rouge, mascara, and lipstick.

Out the lobby door, she paused, making sure there was no one lurking in the parking lot. She hurried to her car.

The drive west took almost twenty minutes, and when she pulled into the funeral home, a man greeted her with a smile as bland as his worn suit.

"I'm here to pay respects to Jennifer Ralston," she said.

"Second door on the right."

Tensing, she moved down the carpeted hallway toward the open door. As she grew closer she tugged her phone from her pocket and turned on the recorder. Holding it in her hand, she moved toward the murmur of soft voices. Pausing, she straightened her shoulders and stepped into the room.

Two older women looked at her, frowning. No doubt they couldn't place her and wondered why she was there. Kaitlin ignored them as she scanned the room for Ashley.

She found Jennifer's sister by a casket covered in a large arrangement of red roses. Ashley saw her, too, and her smile evaporated. She whispered something to the women around her and moved toward Kaitlin.

"What're you doing here?" Ashley said.

"Paying my respects."

Ashley shook her head. "Now you have. So please leave."

"I'm sorry," Kaitlin said. She wanted to tell her Gina had been found, but now wasn't the time or place. "She didn't deserve this."

"No, she didn't."

Kaitlin left the room. The heavy weight of guilt pressed on her. She looked up and saw Steven Marcus leaving. What was he doing here? Had he come to pay his respects or gather more details for his story?

Her phone pinged with a text from Adler.

Are you resting?

It wasn't like her to feel accountable to anyone, but she also didn't want to be stupid. Adler was watching her back for now, and she was glad.

She texted back. Attending Jennifer's viewing. Steven Marcus is here. Guess our meeting got moved up. Afterward, I'll go straight home. ☺

She dropped her phone in her pocket as Marcus approached her.

"Kaitlin Roe," Marcus said, smiling. "I thought you might be here." He was dressed in khakis, a white shirt, and a blue sports jacket.

"I shouldn't be surprised to see you here."

"I feel like I knew Jennifer, Erika, and you. I covered the story for so long. I had to stop by and pay my respects."

"Did her sister appreciate your being here?"

He shook his head with a wry smile. "She wasn't happy."

"Me, too. But I can't blame her."

"Neither can I," he said. "It's a hell of a thing to lose someone you love."

"Yeah."

He nodded toward the exit. "Why don't we get that coffee now?"

"Okay." She followed him out of the building. "I can follow you."

"Sure, if you want, or you can let me drive. You look pretty exhausted."

"Saying I look rough?" she said with a grin.

He laughed. "Not at all. Just saying you look tired."

For a moment the fatigue slid through her body, reminding her that she'd been pushing her limits. "It's been a long week."

"How about I drive us to a coffee shop, and then I'll bring you back here?" He grinned, leaning in. "I couldn't forgive myself if something happened to you."

"Okay, thank you." Kaitlin was glad to have the company as they crossed the lot to his blue four door. He clicked open the locks, and she slid into the front passenger seat and twisted toward him. "How about I ask you a few questions first?"

He grinned as he started the engine. "You can ask. But no promises."

She laughed. "Fair enough."

"The café is less than a mile from here. I'll have you back in an hour. If you have a sweet tooth, you'll love this café. The best. I write there when I'm on deadline."

She grabbed ahold of the buckle, twisted back, and clicked it in place. She looked over at Marcus as he fumbled with something under his seat. "Tell me more about your visit with Randy."

His face was grim, determined. "He said he hoped 'whoever hates her as much as me finishes the job.'"

She looked into his blackened eyes, and alarm bells sounded in her head. Despite his expression, his tone carried notes of glee and purpose, as if this was *his* job to finish.

She scrambled for her seat belt and then to open the door. She was seconds away from being out of this car. The belt clicked open, and she was free as she turned back toward the door and clawed at the handle.

Before she could open the door, she felt the sting of a needle go into her arm. She tried to swat it away, but Marcus was already pulling away an empty syringe.

"What the hell?" She kept working at the door handle, but found her motor skills growing clumsier. She looked out the window for anyone who could help her, but as her head spun faster and faster the scream died in her throat. "You're the one. You killed them."

His expression was void of emotion. "Just relax into it. Don't fight it."

"Why?"

"Shh. We'll have plenty of time to talk about that later."

She screamed, but the sound was strangled and muted by an overwhelming wave of fatigue. Her eyes drooped shut, and she was able to pry them back open with a force of will. But they were so heavy. And she was so tired. Her vision blurred. And this time when her lids fell shut, she couldn't summon the strength to open them again.

She thought about Adler. Hoping he'd find her even as a darker fear told her she'd never see him again.

"Now, we can spend some real quality time together, Kaitlin," Marcus said. "And this time I won't be in such a rush. We have all the time in the world."

***

"Adler, you may now call me a genius." Logan limped forward, leaning heavily on a cane, and dumped a file on his desk.

Adler studied Logan's triumphant grin. "What am I looking at?"

"I won't bore you with the hoops I jumped through to get this information. And I admit, I did play the pity card."

"You've got me on pins and needles."

Logan lowered into a seat. "I dug into Maria Thomas's life."

"The girl who went missing about the time Hayward left college."

"That's correct."

"She worked near Hayward's college in a convenience store, and on the night she vanished she was working alone and in charge of closing the store. Normally, the company required two employees for the night shift, but her coworker left early saying she was sick. She told police Maria insisted she leave and that she would be fine."

Some killers stalk their victims, but others act when the opportunity presents itself. A woman alone at night was a tempting target.

Adler sat back in his chair, remembering the skull in the medical examiner's office and the ribs nicked by a knife. "Hayward was still around about that time."

"He was. Police reviewed the store's security footage, but he never showed up on it."

"Okay."

"So I asked the cop on the case to send me the surveillance footage."

"And?"

"It captured the partial plate on a Toyota Highlander that matched several vehicles. One of those vehicles was registered to Derek Blackstone."

"He was in college up in the northeast."

"A day after Maria vanished, he reported his car stolen. It was never found."

"A car that could have been Derek's was placed at the scene, but he was not?"

"Correct. He had a solid alibi for that night. Several witnesses placed him five hundred miles away."

"Was there a record of Hayward visiting Derek?"

"Hayward was never a suspect in the case, so no one checked."

"What about Crowley?"

"That I don't know. But we know Hayward, Blackstone, and Crowley stick together. Maybe now that Hayward's back in the crosshairs, he'll talk."

Adler tapped his index finger on his desk. He would see to it that Hayward's life in prison was miserable if he didn't talk. "Great work, Logan. Great work."

"Do you think Blackstone or Crowley killed Jennifer and Erika?"

"Maybe both might have been worried about loose ends when Kaitlin started asking questions about Gina."

"And then Hayward offers up Gina when he's facing the death penalty," Logan said.

It was a plausible theory, but all the pieces didn't fit. "Why draw the hearts at the murder scenes? Those hearts link directly back to the *search* for Gina Mason," Adler said.

"Maybe they thought they were being clever. Thought they'd throw the cops off their trail."

"Blackstone certainly calculates every move. The body's positioning suggests the killer didn't just want to silence Jennifer and Erika, he wanted to humiliate them. He was angry with them," Adler said.

"There were a lot of people who loved Gina," Logan said.

"And one of those loving people hated Erika, Jennifer, and Kaitlin enough to kill two of the three." And whoever carried this grudge was still out there and, he feared, ready to make another attempt on Kaitlin's life. He dialed her number. It rang five times and went to voicemail. He listened to her voice, unease growing in his gut. When the tone beeped, his voice was terse when he said, "Kaitlin, call me."

"You're worried about her."

"Someone tried to kill her. And we still don't know who the hell that someone is." He reread his last text from her. "She's having coffee with Steven Marcus now."

"The reporter?"

"The one that covered the Gina Mason murder extensively. They'll have a lot to talk about now that Gina's been found." He accessed his computer and searched Steven Marcus in the DMV records. Marcus's name and picture popped up. "There are no priors, but there's a ticket for a broken taillight on Tuesday. The night Erika's body was found in the city."

"Where was the ticket issued?"

"On the expressway headed into Richmond." Adler checked the time. "I need to try and catch the tail end of Ms. Ralston's viewing."

"Think the killer will show up?"

"I can only hope." He clapped Logan on the shoulder. "Solid work."

"Thanks."

***

"Hi, I'm Gina Mason."

The familiar voice echoed over a loudspeaker as a bright light glared in Kaitlin's eyes. Her brain was mired in a drugged haze that made it hard for her to focus. Drawing in a breath, she blinked until her vision finally cleared. She pushed herself up into a sitting position and pressed her back against a hard surface. Where the hell was she?

"Hi, I'm Gina Mason."

The room was windowless, and the concrete walls were papered in hundreds of pictures of Gina Mason. As she pushed herself to her feet, her heart beat faster. She fought a wave of nausea. She pressed the back of her hand to her mouth and took several deep breaths until her stomach settled.

"Hi, I'm Gina Mason."

Something deep inside her prodded her and told her she'd been a damn fool and was now going to die because of her own stupidity. She'd recognized fear because she'd faced it so often and for many years allowed it to run her life. But this time, she pushed it away and refused to listen to the horrible things it wanted to whisper.

She had to find a way to reach Marcus. They'd both wanted the same thing—to find Gina—for fourteen years.

Drawing in a breath she said, "Stop playing the games, Marcus. You've been wanting to face me for a long time, so show yourself so we can talk." Her voice was hoarse and her throat dry. "We have more in common than you realize."

Silence.

She pushed back a rising sense of panic. "We have a lot to talk about. I have information about Gina. I know who killed her."

"Hi, I'm Gina Mason."

***

Adler found Quinn, and as the two drove across town to Ashley's viewing, he briefed her on what Logan had told him. At the funeral home, he spotted Kaitlin's SUV. He crossed to the vehicle and put his hand on the hood. It was cold.

"She said she's with Marcus," Quinn said.

Adler called Kaitlin again. It went to voicemail. "This is not good."

They strode inside and followed the directional signs to the Ralston room. There were still a handful of people gathered around the closed casket. Ashley was dressed in black and dabbing a tissue to her red-rimmed eyes.

Ashley spotted Adler and, breaking away from the group, moved toward them. "Detectives."

"We came to pay our respects."

"Thank you."

"I'm sorry for your loss," Quinn said softly.

"I spotted Kaitlin Roe's car outside," Adler said.

Ashley's lips flattened into a grim line. "She left here about an hour ago. The woman has nerve. She said she was paying her respects, but I half expected her to pull out her recorder to capture a sound bite for that damn podcast of hers. What the hell is it with the media? Do they have any shame?"

"Them? Who else from the media was here?" Quinn asked.

"Steven Marcus. Another liar who's working on his book."

"He spoke to you?"

"He dropped off flowers, but when I saw him approach, I turned my back to him."

"Where are the flowers he brought?" Quinn asked.

"Over there by the others. White tulips, I think."

Quinn met Adler's gaze and crossed the room to the arrangement.

"Did you notice the type of car he was driving?" Adler asked.

Ashley laughed. "No. I kind of had my hands full here."

Quinn returned from the arrangement. "There's no card."

Adler's gaze swept the room. "Thank you, Ms. Ralston."

As the detectives left, Adler double-checked his phone. There was a text from Kaitlin.

John, I'm at Marcus's house. Help me.

"What the hell is she doing at his house?" Adler opened the computer in his vehicle and typed in Marcus's residence. As the directions appeared, he dialed Logan and thought about the text. She'd called him John. She'd never called him John, not even when they were making love.

When Logan picked up, Adler said, "I need everything you can find out about Steven Marcus. Anything I can use. And I need it now."

"I'm on it."

INTERVIEW FILE #28

Is a Psychopath Made or Born?

Some of the most successful people are psychopaths. Many are leaders in the business world, politics, journalism, and organized crime. Their underlying trait is selfishness. They know what they want and will do whatever it takes to get it. They have no remorse.

The reality is very few psychopaths commit murder. Why they do cross that line is anyone's guess. Is it predisposed in their DNA? Is there a trigger that sets them off? The truth is, no one really knows.

CHAPTER
TWENTY-SEVEN

Saturday, March 24, 2018; 8:00 p.m.

"Hi, I'm Gina Mason."

The tape was on a loop, and it repeated over and over so often she'd lost count of how many times. "Is the plan to drive me insane, Marcus?" she shouted. "If you think hearing her voice over and over again is going to drive me mad, you're a little late. Her voice is all I've heard for the last fourteen years. Why don't you turn up the volume? Maybe put a soundtrack on it."

"Hi, I'm Gina Mason."

Footsteps sounded outside the room, and a switch clicked on, leaking light through the edges of the door. She was relieved. At least she had his attention.

"That's right, Marcus, come and talk to me. We are the last two people on this planet who still give a shit about Gina." No answer. "I know you must care a lot about her. All the guys loved her. She was too hard to resist."

"Hi, I'm Gina Mason."

Shifting feet cast shadows in front of the door. He was at least listening to her. "Steven, if you open the door I'll tell you exactly what happened on that road the night Randy took her."

She waited a beat, expecting to hear the recording again, but it was silent. A small victory.

The rattle of metal against metal had her sitting straighter. She winced as she pulled harder on the tape. Her skin was raw, bleeding now on her right hand, but the ropes had a little more slack in them.

The door opened, and Marcus stepped inside holding a water bottle. His boyish face was a study in anger and curiosity. He twisted off the top of the bottle and approached her. He pulled a long knife from a sheath on his belt. As he brought the knife to the tape binding her hands, she tensed. He sliced the tape and handed her the water bottle.

He stepped away from her and sat, his back to the wall.

"What did he do to her?"

He might hate her, but he needed answers as much as she did. The trick now was to feed him information slowly and hope she bought enough time to find a way out. "He cut off her ear. He told me he'd cut off the other one if I didn't run."

He closed his eyes and tipped his head back against the wall. For a moment, he said nothing. "I'd hoped she didn't suffer. I'd prayed her death was at least quick."

She didn't know, but she would bluff. Keep him talking. Buy time. Maybe even forge some kind of connection with him. "The cops know someone was working with him. They found part of her dress. There was someone else's blood on it."

He raised his hand to his neck, rubbing it as if he felt a rope constricting around it. "Are you sure?"

"Adler is certain."

A moan that sounded more like a wounded animal rumbled through his chest. "It had to be Blackstone or Crowley. Those three stick together."

The longer he stayed focused on the men who'd helped Hayward, the better. "It must have been awful for her. I bet she was alive, and when she saw the others she thought help had arrived, but it hadn't," Kaitlin said. "I can't imagine how painful it was to die knowing Derek and Brad wouldn't help."

Marcus studied her. "Why would the police tell you all this?"

"Detective Adler and I have gotten close."

He stared at her with such hate and loathing it was all she could do not to tremble and weep.

"You're good at landing on your feet. You know how to use people. I heard that time and time again about you."

She needed Marcus to believe they were very close. "Adler is very special to me." And that was the truth. The idea that she might not see him again nearly broke her. "I told him I was with you."

"I know. I saw the text you exchanged with him on your phone, and I texted him again and told him we were here."

A cold chill slid down her spine, and whatever control she thought she'd mastered over her fear slipped. "Why would you text him? What are you doing?"

Marcus paused and let her question hang. He liked seeing her worried and scared. "He can't stop what I'm going to do next."

Instinct demanded she press him for answers. She wanted to know what he'd planned. But if she showed him her weakness, he'd use it against her. Pulling in a slow breath, she turned the tables, hoping she could use his own demons against him. "When did you fall in love with Gina?"

That caught him by surprise. "I'm a reporter. I don't get involved in my stories."

"You did this time. I understand. Gina was hard to resist. She was perfect. When did you know you loved her?"

He swallowed. His guard dropped, and for an instant she saw the longing in his eyes that suddenly glistened with tears. "Almost from the beginning. How could I not? Like you said, she was perfect."

"All the pictures of her in this room and all the work you did to find her shows your love. No one else did this for her, but you did. You're the one person who struggled to keep her memory alive."

"There were times when no one cared. No one wanted to remember. But I couldn't let her go, and the deeper I looked into her life, the more my love for her grew and the more I needed to do something to avenge her death. When I read about Hayward killing that woman in the convenience store, I felt so helpless. She shouldn't have died. It was wrong."

"She didn't deserve it."

"I could have written about the story, but suddenly it wasn't enough to write about her. I knew I'd never get to Hayward in jail, but when I saw you at Audrey Mason's funeral, I knew I had to act."

Her return had been the trigger. More guilt threatened to cloud her thoughts, but she pushed it away. "That's why you came after Jennifer, Erika, and me?"

"That's right." Hate and anger sharpened his brown eyes. "You three little bitches left her on that road. You all abandoned her. If you hadn't, she'd be alive today."

Guilt and fear hammered in her chest. He was right, but her dying now wouldn't do Gina or the others any good. She'd run once before, but she'd stand her ground this time. She wouldn't plead or cower. She'd come too far in the last year to die a coward.

"I want to interview you," she said.

Laughter rumbled. "Me. Why do you care what I have to say?"

"It's important. You're not insignificant. Everyone forgot her but you."

Silence.

She moistened dry lips. If he were going to reject the idea outright, he'd have done it immediately. "You were one of the first reporters to cover the case. And you covered it nineteen times."

"You read my articles?"

"You were my number-one source, because the cops wouldn't speak to me."

"No. They were very tight lipped about their details with me."

Good, he was talking. And talking might build a connection with him and humanize her. And at the very least it would buy more time.

"Why did my return matter so much to you?"

"Because Gina was *your* family. Your responsibility. Hayward told you to run, and you did. Gina was always there for you, and you repaid her how? By leaving her to die alone."

Tears she'd held back for so long filled her eyes. "You're right. I don't deserve her forgiveness, or yours."

He shook his head, seemingly unmoved by her tears. "And you could have nailed Hayward fourteen years ago, but you chickened out. Do you have any backbone?"

"I wasn't sure it was him."

"It didn't matter! You blew it! Everyone knew it was him." He shook his head again. "He's escaped punishment for fourteen years while Gina rotted in the cold ground."

"You have to understand I wasn't covering for him."

"That was Jennifer's and Erika's fault, wasn't it? They supplied the booze and drugs."

"How did you know that?"

"Erika and I got to be good friends. She was so lonely in her big house and so tired of hiding behind walls. I approached her when she came out of yoga one day and asked to speak to her. I told her I was writing a book. She didn't want to at first, so I made sure she found out about her husband's affair. When I came back the next week, she agreed, and our meetings became regular. She was so ready to unburden herself and stick it to her husband."

"What about Blackstone and Crowley? They're Hayward's friends. They covered for him all these years."

"So did Hayward's mother. She lied for him, too."

"Are you going after them as well? How many people are you going to kill?"

"You're the last."

"Who else have you killed?"

"Just know I have punished the guilty."

Sharing anything with Marcus now was a calculated risk. But she had to prove her worth to him to stay alive and buy time. "Adler told me something you don't know."

He looked amused.

"When they found Gina, they found another girl. She was buried in a grave near Gina."

Marcus shook his head. "You're lying."

"I'm not. Adler spotted the shallow grave from a tree stand. They excavated it and found another girl about Gina's age."

Marcus shook his head. "Hayward killed another girl?"

"That's what the cops think."

He curled his fingers into a fist and pressed it to his temple. "Does his deal with the Commonwealth Attorney cover that murder?"

"No."

"So he's going to be punished?" He sounded hopeful and happy.

"Yes." She leaned forward. "Neither Gina nor the other girl would have been found if I hadn't come back."

"It wasn't your return that led to Gina's discovery. It was my work. Killing Jennifer and Erika reopened Gina's case, not your bullshit podcast project."

She smiled. "It still makes us a team."

"We're not a team."

She knew she was pressing, and he could turn on her in an instant. "Yes, we are. We've both wanted the same thing for fourteen years. We're the only two people who did something about finding her."

Anger flared in his eyes, and he crossed the room and hit her hard across the face. Pain rocketed through her head, and she could taste blood.

He'd raised his hand to strike her again when a phone rang. He pulled her phone from his pocket. "Detective Adler is calling you again. Should I text him back and tell him not to worry? Maybe I should say our interview is going long?"

"He will find you."

"Maybe. I'm ready for that."

When he dropped his gaze to send the text, she stepped toward him. "We can work together," she said. "You can interview me. I can tell you all about that night. I can tell you about Gina's hopes and fears."

"I don't need anyone's help."

"There's no one else alive who can confirm your findings. Why would you want to burn your ultimate source?"

A loud pounding echoed through the house. It sounded like someone was beating on the front door. Oh God, it had to be Adler. Marcus had told him where to find her.

"It's Adler." She moistened her lips. "Send him away so we can talk. It's been fourteen years, and I haven't told my story."

Again, he studied her. He touched the blood on her lip and gently brushed it away. "In the right light you look like her."

She raised her chin. "Thank you. She was so pretty."

He rubbed her blood between his thumb and index finger. "You aren't her."

"I know."

The pounding upstairs grew louder.

"Get rid of them," she said. "We need more time."

He wiped the blood on his pant leg. "No, that's the thing, Kaitlin. I've been expecting them." He crossed the room, opened the door, and closed it behind him.

***

Marcus's black truck was parked at the beginning of the long driveway that led to a one-story ranch home situated in the center of a large lot surrounded by a ribbon of woods. The lawn nearer the house was neat and the hedges trimmed, but all the shades in the house were drawn.

Adler called Kaitlin's number, but it went to voicemail. He pounded on the door as Quinn stood to the side, her hand on her weapon. "He's here," he said. "The truck is in the driveway. And Kaitlin sent the text. She wouldn't ignore my calls now."

"That's assuming she sent the text," Quinn said. "Kaitlin was lured into a trap with a text. You really think he brought her to his home?"

He drew his weapon. "Why not? The closest house is a hundred yards away. There are woods around the lot. He has privacy."

"We're assuming she's still alive," Quinn said carefully.

That thought had also occurred to him, but he'd chased it away. "I'm betting on Kaitlin. She's resourceful, and she's found a reason for him to keep her alive."

"He already tried to kill her once. Why bother with bringing her here and then telling you what he's doing?"

"I don't know. Keep pounding on the door. I'm going around back."

The flashing lights of four police cars pulled into the driveway and raced toward them.

Adler's phone rang. It was Logan. "What do you have?"

"Marcus's wife left him seven months ago. She packed up their kid and moved back to her mother's in Maryland."

"That's the trigger," Adler said.

341

"It's enough to send a sane man over the edge," Logan said. "The guy's written hundreds of articles, not only about cold cases, but he seemed particularly obsessed with how the victims died."

"Roger that," Adler said.

"Jesus, man, be careful."

"Right." He ended the call. "I'm not waiting," Adler said.

"What are you going to do?"

"I'm going around the back to see if there's another entrance. You and the uniforms break the front door down."

As Quinn pounded on the door, he ran around the side of the house to a back door leading onto a screened porch. To the right was a set of freshly painted cellar doors.

He looked up and saw Marcus standing by the kitchen window. The man's expression was calm, too calm. He wasn't the least bit surprised to see Adler or the growing number of cops in his yard. This felt like a trap, just like the one the arsonist set.

Adler leveled his weapon, but Marcus laughed as he regarded him. He looked confident, almost triumphant as he watched the cop cars arriving. And then he raised a gun to his own head. In one second Adler tensed, shouted for him to put the gun down. And in the next instant, Marcus fired. His head snapped as the bullet cut through it, and blood sprayed the wall. His body went limp, and he dropped out of sight.

Adler's gut clenched. None of this felt right. Why take Kaitlin, text him, and then just kill himself? Again, he smelled a trap.

He called Quinn. "Marcus shot himself."

"I heard the gunshot. Are you sure?"

"I saw him drop. The suspect is down. I repeat he is down."

"We're going in the front door."

He heard the front doorframe crack and then slam open. "I'm going through the cellar doors."

Adler threw back the doors and immediately was hit with the thick scent of gasoline. Weapon drawn and the phone still connected in his hand, he moved down the side cellar staircase. Instantly he spotted the drums and the wires that led into them. On top of them was a digital clock ticking down. Thirty seconds remained. Marcus had wired the house to explode. Adler realized this was Marcus's last stand.

Kaitlin pushed through a door and looked up at him. He saw the fear etched in her features as he ran toward her and grabbed her arm.

Time stopped, and each second played out agonizingly slow.

He holstered his weapon and shouted into his phone. "The house is rigged, Quinn. Clear everyone."

Twenty seconds.

Adler and Kaitlin raced up the cellar steps. She tripped on the top step, and he gripped her hand tighter and steadied her as she caught herself. The land behind the house was open. He ran faster, pulling her with him. His heart pumped. Her breathing was fast and labored.

Ten seconds. They'd put forty feet between them and the house. He heard the shouts of the other cops yelling to retreat. He could only hope the house had been cleared.

Five seconds. He threw Kaitlin to the ground and covered her body with his. *Three seconds. Two seconds.* "Don't breathe."

The house exploded.

Time slowed as the blaze licked over their bodies, singeing his hair and exposed skin. It roared around them, like a destructive monster. He remembered the last fire that had almost killed him and Logan's scream and his own flesh feeling as if it were being peeled away. But he kept his body tightly pressed against hers. She tensed and buried her face in the cool ground.

The heat engulfed them, making it unbreathable. Seconds ticked by. And then as quickly as the flames rushed out, they receded. But for several seconds he didn't move, fearing another explosion. The fire had singed the grass around them, but the air began to cool. Finally he rose, dragging Kaitlin with him and away from the structure. "Are you okay?"

She coughed and nodded. "Yes, I'm fine."

The house was engulfed in fire and heat. The basement and single story had been consumed.

A uniformed officer approached, and Adler shoved Kaitlin toward him as he ran around the side of the house to the front entrance. There were four patrol cars there now, and in the distance he could hear the fire trucks' sirens.

He searched the crowd for his partner, but there was no sign of Quinn. Another explosion detonated in the house, and everyone dropped to the ground.

Adler was assailed with memories of Logan screaming in pain as the lapping flames scorched his own skin. He'd been close enough to save Logan, but he hadn't been there for Quinn.

"Quinn, where the fuck are you?" Adler said.

The heat was so intense the exterior siding was peeling away.

"Quinn!"

The sirens grew louder, and more marked cars arrived on scene.

"Quinn!"

"Over here," Quinn said.

A fresh rush of adrenaline clawed through his body as he turned. He spotted his partner as she rose up from behind an old oak tree. She was covered in dirt and soot, there were ashes in her hair, and her jacket was torn. She still gripped her weapon.

"Jesus," he said, rushing toward her. Relief and gratitude nearly brought him to his knees. "I thought you'd gone inside."

She holstered her weapon. Her hand trembled slightly as she looked back toward the house consumed in flames. "We all scattered when you sounded the alarm. Hell, I thought you were caught up in the explosion. Where's Kaitlin?"

He'd been blessed with a lifetime of luck today. Whether he deserved it or not wasn't for him to say, but he was taking all he could get. "She made it out. She's fine."

The blare of fire engine sirens grew deafening. Lights flashed on the trees, the house, and the drawn faces of the cops. Adler rubbed his hand over the back of his neck.

Kaitlin came up behind Adler. She slid up next to him. He wrapped his arm around her shoulder and pulled her close. She relaxed into him.

"Is Marcus inside?" she asked.

"He shot himself in the kitchen," Adler said.

"He planned all this, didn't he?" Quinn asked. "He wanted to kill you and as many other cops as he could manage."

"He felt like everyone let Gina down," Kaitlin said.

Quinn's lips curled with disgust. "I won't be satisfied until I see his body and know for certain he rots in hell," she said.

She moved away from them to check on an officer who had been struck in the arm by flying debris.

Adler again hugged Kaitlin to him, holding her tight. He could feel her trembling and heard her short, agitated breaths. "You should never have gone with him. You scared the shit out of me."

"I should have seen through it. I knew he was obsessed with Gina."

"We all missed the signs until it was almost too late." He kissed her on the temple and kept his face close to hers. "I don't want to lose you."

Her laugh sounded nervous and relieved when she turned and looked up at him. "Wait until you get to know me," she teased.

Adler let out a breath. "I'm looking forward to doing just that."

INTERVIEW FILE #29

OBSESSIONS OF A KILLER

Steven Marcus's house was destroyed, but he'd left his laptop in his truck, which had been parked farther down the driveway. No one was sure if he expected to escape the fire. But I seriously doubt it. The recorded files on the laptop offered some insight into the man obsessed with justice for Gina Mason at any cost.

"This is Steven Marcus, and the first time I learned about Gina was the day after she vanished. When I saw a picture of her, I was stunned by her beauty and bright smile. I knew I had to find her. The harder I searched for her and the answers behind her disappearance, the more obsessed I became with her. She invaded my thoughts, my dreams, and finally my everyday life. My wife saw it. She tried to understand at first, but as the years passed and I became more obsessed with knowing Gina's fate, she started to pull away. When she left me, I was certain if I could just try a little harder and discover the truth, the obsession would loosen its hold and I could get back to a normal life. All I wanted was the truth. And when I couldn't find that, my thoughts turned to revenge."

EPILOGUE

Tuesday, May 8, 2018; 6:00 a.m.

Kaitlin shut off the audiotape. She'd listened to it three more times and knew if she kept reviewing it she'd start making changes. Adler still owed her a few updates, but all in all, she was pleased with the final project and grateful it was a few sound bites away from finished.

The morning sun rose up over the east end of the city and streamed through her bedroom window. A knock on the front door had her rising and setting aside her computer. She stretched before she padded down the hallway barefoot, still wearing flannel plaid pajama pants and a worn police academy T-shirt. The time had come to shower, dress in something nice, and get out into the world.

She glanced in the peephole and smiled when she saw Adler's stern profile. Heat rose through her body as she imagined having him in her bed and spending the morning making love to him. She flipped open the three locks.

"You're here bright and early," she said.

"Wrapped up a case last night." His gaze trailed over her, lingering on her breasts before he met her stare. "Thought I'd take you to breakfast."

Breakfast sounded good . . . in a bit. "My favorite meal of the day."

Adler leaned forward and kissed her, cupping the back of her head. She slid her hand up his flat belly and wrapped her arm around his waist. She pressed those breasts he'd just been admiring against his chest.

"Are you sure you want breakfast first?"

His hand slid to her butt, and he squeezed gently. "I'm flexible."

"Good, I like a man who can adapt."

He entered the apartment and saw the setup of her computers, stacks of legal pads with notes, and sticky notes stuck randomly on the large table by her bed. "You've been working, too."

"I've almost wrapped up the podcast and was just listening to what I have."

"How does it sound?"

This had been an emotional journey and one of the hardest things she'd ever done. There were still missing pieces from that night on the road. How had Gina's blood gotten on her shirt? She still didn't remember, but Adler theorized she had resisted Randy and tried to save Gina. She clung to that explanation when Gina's loss troubled her in the middle of the night as it likely always would. "It's pretty good, if I do say so myself."

He picked up a purple sticky note that read *Randy Hayward*. As he flicked the edge with his finger, his eyes hardened. "Ricker is now seeking the death penalty in the Maria Thomas murder case."

This was a new development since she'd seen Adler two days ago. "Does Randy's mother know?"

"I don't know. She's still not accepting her son's calls and has only spoken to me once. Her attorney was very careful about the questions he'd let her answer."

"She had to have known what Randy did. She deliberately withheld information, and she had her shed torn down. She must have been covering for her son."

"I think you're right. But I'm not sure we will be able to prove that."

"Do you think Mrs. Hayward knew about what Randy did to Maria Thomas?"

"She must have sensed a pattern with her son and women. We can't link the sexual assaults that occurred near him in college, but thanks to our conversation with Maureen, there's a chance there might be some closure in that case, too."

A pattern of cover-ups in the Hayward family had contributed to so much suffering. "I interviewed the Thomas family about their daughter, Maria. They were devastated to learn she's dead," she said.

He captured a strand of her hair and gently rubbed it between this thumb and forefinger. "There is no happy ending for the Thomas family, but at least they know what happened to their daughter."

"Knowing is better than all the terrible scenarios that dog you, but it still hurts."

"Maybe now they have a chance to move on with their lives."

"Like me."

He kissed her on the forehead. "Yes, like you."

She wanted to lean into him and forget all about this case, but there were still details she needed to clarify. "I know Ricker got his court order for Blackstone's and Crowley's DNA. Have the results come back? Was there a match?"

"There was, and the results match Logan's theory."

"The blood on Gina's dress was Blackstone's," she said.

"Yes."

"I never remembered Blackstone."

"You couldn't have. By the time Blackstone appeared on the scene, you had already run for help. Logan and I believe that Gina fought harder than Randy had expected, so after you left, he called the friend who had always helped him."

She felt a bitter satisfaction knowing Gina had ultimately helped catch her killers. "Gina fought so hard it took two men to subdue her."

"And she hurt Blackstone in some way, which explained his blood on her dress. Randy and Blackstone took Gina to the shed on the Hayward property and stashed her body there until they could bury her in the country."

All the pieces tumbled together, forming a gruesome picture that the world would finally see. "Blackstone is going to fight you."

"Oh, I know. He's already hired his own forensic expert to explain the blood, but the test results are ironclad."

"What about Ashley?"

"I pressed her for more details. When I threw accessory-to-murder charges at her, she admitted Blackstone had been wearing shorts and had a large cut on his thigh above his knee that night. She said it looked like he'd been hit with a rock."

Again, Kaitlin imagined Gina's last desperate fight to stay alive and had to pause until she could speak without her voice breaking.

"Does Randy know this?"

"Quinn spoke to him yesterday. He said he'd tell us more about Gina if Ricker took the death penalty off the table in the Thomas case. Ricker refused. But Randy isn't as cocky as he once was, and I'm betting it won't be long before he tells us what happened and how Blackstone fit into the equation."

"I remember Randy and Derek fighting at that last Fourth of July party. When Randy approached me, he was very frustrated, angry, and drunk. I wasn't sure what set him off because he and Derek never fought. Something must have come up that day about Maria." She shook her head. "I should never have been with Randy."

He laid his hand on her shoulder. "But you walked away from him."

"I did. But that set him on a collision course with Gina." She shook off a jab of guilt and focused on what she'd done. "I've been digging into Marcus's past. The deeper I go the more I realize how troubled he was."

"Logan discovered that Marcus's wife left him last year and took their son. When Logan interviewed Mrs. Marcus, she said her husband's obsession with finding Gina finally drove her away."

"And when he couldn't find Gina, he shifted his focus to Jennifer, Erika, and me."

"According to a journal found in his car, he said he could die in peace knowing Gina was waiting for him on the other side. He'd known all along that day that I would come after you and he'd kill us all in the fire."

She still had nightmares about the explosion. Several times she'd awakened in the middle of the night drenched in sweat. Most of those nights, Adler was with her, and he'd pulled her into his embrace until she stopped shaking. "It's all heartbreaking."

Adler traced her jaw with his finger and then kissed her. "It's all out in the open now because of you."

And that did give her comfort. "On the bright side, I did get a corporate sponsor, Shield Security. I won't be getting rich, but it's enough to cover my bills, promote the project, and buy time until the next project."

He cocked his head. "The next project?"

She laughed as she snuggled close to him. When she was in his arms, the world simply felt right. "There's always going to be a next project."

He tipped her chin up so he could look into her eyes, and he kissed her on the lips. "As long as you keep me involved with your next endeavor."

He'd been a rock for her, and she didn't want to imagine him not being in her life. She kissed him back. "Endeavor? That's such a professional word." Her hand slid to his belt buckle. "Is that what we have?" She unfastened the buckle, already anxious to have him inside her. "A strictly professional relationship?"

He slid his hand down her spine and under the waistband of her pajama pants. He cupped her buttocks and pushed her pelvis toward him as she unfastened the belt. "No, not just professional. I love the personal, and you, far too much to settle for just that."

She stilled. "You love me?"

He nodded, smiling. "I love you."

Tears welled in her eyes. "And I love you right back."

INTERVIEW FILE #30

WHAT'S NEXT?

Gina was laid to rest beside her parents on a warm April day. It had been so cold, but for whatever reason, the air warmed to the low seventies and the clouds cleared. I was glad the Mason family was united again. I was glad Gina had been found. But I was also glad that this time, when Gina needed me again, I'd stayed by her side, I'd fought, and I hadn't run.

ABOUT THE AUTHOR

Photo © 2015 Studio FBJ

New York Times and *USA Today* bestselling novelist Mary Burton is the popular author of thirty-three romance and suspense novels, as well as five novellas. She currently lives in Virginia with her husband and three miniature dachshunds. Visit her at www.maryburton.com.